GOBLIN ETERNAL

Broken Galaxy Book Six

Phil Huddleston

CONTENTS

Title Page
From Earlier Books 2
From Book Five 5
Zero 11
One 18
Two 25
Three 31
Four 35
Five 39
Six 46
Seven 52
Eight 57
Nine 64
Ten 73
Eleven 80
Twelve 86
Thirteen 92
Fourteen 97
Fifteen 103
Sixteen 110
Gen 113

Seventeen	115
Eighteen	123
Nineteen	130
Twenty	137
Twenty-One	149
Twenty-Two	155
Twenty-Three	165
Twenty-Four	174
Twenty-Five	181
Twenty-Six	191
Twenty-Seven	199
Twenty-Eight	207
Twenty-Nine	211
Thirty	220
Thirty-One	225
Thirty-Two	233
Thirty-Three	239
Thirty-Four	247
Thirty-Five	257
Thirty-Six	265
Thirty-Seven	277
Thirty-Eight	283
Thirty-Nine	288
Forty	292
Forty-One	296
Forty-Two	298
Forty-Three	301
Epilogue	304

Author Note	307
Preview - Artemis War	309
Preview - Imprint of Blood	312
Works	316
About the Author	317

Broken Galaxy Book Six: Goblin Eternal
by Phil Huddleston

Copyright © 2022 by Phil Huddleston
THE AUTHOR RETAINS ALL RIGHTS FOR THIS BOOK

Reproduction or transmission of this book, in whole or in part, by electronic, mechanical, photocopying, recording, or by any other means is strictly prohibited, except with prior written permission from the author or the publisher. Inquiries may be directed to Phil@PhilHuddleston.com

Cover Art by Sawyer Specter
BookCoverZone.com

This is a work of fiction. Names, characters, locations, organizations, and events portrayed are either products of the author's creative imagination or used fictitiously. Any resemblance to actual names, characters, events, businesses, locales, or persons is coincidental and not intended to infringe on any copyright or trademark.

For Mark. He was the best of us.

FROM EARLIER BOOKS

Broken Galaxy - The name used to describe the state of affairs in the Orion Arm of the Milky Way. The ancient Golden Empire lasted for twenty thousand years; but two thousand years ago, it collapsed, throwing the Arm into a Dark Age, from which it is still recovering.

Stree - A humanoid alien race with a pathological hatred of Goblins or any other sentient artificial intelligence. Started the Stree War by attacking Earth and other planets friendly to the Goblins, leaving Earth uninhabitable for fifty to one hundred years until radiation levels and bioweapon poisons dissipate. At the end of the Stree War, their home world, Stree Prime, was destroyed by the rogue Goblin engineer Rauti.

Goblins - Sentient AI lifeforms, usually humanoid but can transfer their consciousness to other body forms. Prior to the Stree War, Goblins formed an alliance with Humans to fight the Singheko. In the Stree War, the rogue Goblin engineer Rauti destroyed the home world of the Stree by launching three large asteroids at it, but not before the Stree destroyed the Goblin homeland, the Dyson Swarm called Stalingrad. Since that time, the few surviving Goblins are hunted throughout the Orion Arm by bounty hunters paid by the remnants of the Stree, who refuse to give up their holy war of eliminating Goblins from the Universe.

Phoenix - the new home world of Humanity. With the

help of the Goblins, the planet was colonized by the Human survivors of the Stree War, who cannot return to Earth until radiation and bioweapon residuals fall to lower levels. The current leader of Phoenix is Prime Minister Mark Rodgers, serving his fifth term.

Jim Carter - Biological father of Gen (Imogen Carter Page). Originally a U. S. Marine on Earth, later Commander Attack Group (CAG) for the Earth Defense Force (EDF). After the destruction of Earth's ecosphere in the Stree War, he converted to a Goblin to fight the Stree more effectively. Disappeared along with his wife Rita Page after the destruction of Stree Prime.

Nemo - a second copy of Jim Carter. In the Stree War, Rita Page made another Goblin copy of Jim Carter to rescue her friend and former lover Bonnie Page from a Stree prison. After rescuing Bonnie, Nemo realized that the original copy of Jim Carter would have his wife, daughter, and position - essentially his entire life - while he would have nothing. Growing increasingly bitter, he began calling himself Nemo, the Latin word for "nobody."

Bonnie Page - Godmother of Gen (Imogen Carter Page). A former Air Force fighter pilot who became captain of the starship destroyer *Dragon* during the Singheko War, and then served as second-in-command to Admiral Rita Page during the Stree War. Currently head of the recovering EDF (Earth Defense Force) as humanity rebuilds from the Stree War. Successively the lover of Jim Carter, then Rita Page, and now married to Luke Powell, Home Secretary of Phoenix.

Rita Page - Biological mother of Gen (Imogen Carter Page). A clone created by the renegade sentient starship *Jade* with the dual memories, knowledge, and feelings of both Jim Carter and Bonnie Page. As a result of her dual consciousness, she was in love with both Jim and Bonnie. Served as Fleet Admiral of the EDF until captured by the Singheko; poisoned herself to prevent military secrets from falling into the hands of the enemy. Dying, Rita was scanned into Goblin form after the Battle of Dekanna. Disappeared along with her husband Jim Carter after the destruction of Stree Prime.

Gen (Imogen Carter Page) - the daughter of Jim Carter and Admiral Rita Page. After the disappearance of her biological parents Jim and Rita in the Stree War, she was adopted by her aunt Gillian Carter and Gillian's husband, Mark Rodgers.

Marta Powell - Gen's best friend.

Tatiana Powell - Mother of Marta Powell. Minister of Defense of the new Human home world of Phoenix.

Luke Powell - Husband of Bonnie Page. Also father of Minister of Defense Tatiana Powell, and grandfather of Marta Powell. Home Secretary of the new Human home world of Phoenix.

Mark Rodgers - Husband of Gillian Carter and adoptive father of Gen. A former General in the U. S. Army, now Prime Minister of the new Human home world, Phoenix.

Gillian Carter - Sister of Jim Carter. Adoptive mother of Gen. Died when Gen was fourteen years old.

FROM BOOK FIVE

Stalingrad System - 1,275 Lights from Earth

The little packet boat had once been called *Donkey* - a joke by its pilot. What had started as a joke had stuck, though, and the packet boat had been known by that name since.

Despite its name, it had done yeoman service. It had carried two young EDF officers - Rachel and Paco - to the distant Dyson Swarm called Stalingrad, where the first contact between Humans and the androids called Goblins had been realized, and a treaty agreed. It had carried a Goblin called Tika to Dekanna, where she played a role in saving Humanity from the onslaught of the Singheko. Lastly, it had returned Tika, Jim Carter, and Rita Page to Stalingrad, to begin Rita's life as a Goblin.

Then it had been relegated to an obscure dock on the Dyson Swarm, no longer needed. There it had been, a remnant of a brighter day, when the Stree entered the system. And as the Stree blasted apart the Dyson Swarm, ending the Goblin civilization, the little packet boat had somehow survived. It had been blown off the Swarm to drift away into an elliptical solar orbit, missed by the Stree as they methodically destroyed every remnant of Goblin civilization they could find.

Forgotten, the little packet boat might have stayed in its lonely orbit for centuries or even forever - if not for a quirk of coincidence. A shuttle passed in the vicinity, searching for usable debris in the system. A sensor beeped.

The android inside the shuttle had the general appearance of Jim Carter. It had his tall, lean body, his flashing blue eyes, his salt-and-pepper hair. It had his quirky, goofy smile as he saw *Donkey* again, for the first time in a long while.

But the Goblin inside the shuttle was only a copy of Jim Carter. His original biological body was long since turned to ash, on a distant orb known as Stree Prime that no longer existed as a viable planet. And his other copy was with Rita Page, somewhere in the black, headed to Lord Knows Where.

This version of Jim Carter had sardonically changed his name, at least in his own mind. He called himself Nemo now - an old Latin word for 'nobody.' It was his little joke – and another part of the reason he carried the strange smile.

For the last year he had made the destroyed Stalingrad system his home, a hermit roaming around in the debris, looking for things that might interest him.

Donkey interested him. He made a course change and vectored to the drifting boat, pulled alongside, and gave a remote command to *Donkey* to open its docking port. To his surprise, it did. With great delight, he realized the little boat still had power. He docked and made his way over to it. Entering, he found it nearly pristine, hardly damaged by its ordeal.

Moving to the cockpit, he paused for a moment, remembering. Remembering the last trip on this boat from Dekanna to Stalingrad, with Rita. Remembering the wife and lover he would never have again.

Because I'm not Jim Carter anymore. That life is gone, like a puff of smoke. Now I'm just Nemo. No matter how real it seems to me, I'm just a cheap imitation of the real Jim Carter.

The bitterness came back to him again, as it sometimes did. But he tried to suppress it. He didn't want to go there today.

Not today. Rita did what she thought was right. It was the only way to save Bonnie and the others. I guess I'd do it all over again.

Checking systems, he found them all functional. Only a little light maintenance would be required to bring the boat to normal status.

After some thought, Nemo made a decision. He had been in the wreckage of this system for quite a while now. There wasn't much he didn't know about it. It was time to move on.

Twenty-seven days later, the little packet boat settled to a landing at the old Deseret Airport in western Nevada. Through some miracle, it didn't fall over in the soft sand. The ramp came down, and Nemo stepped out on the old Earth.

Visibility was poor; the dirty, low-hanging clouds were only a few thousand feet off the ground, and the wind was blowing sand around. Nemo ignored all that; he had eyes only for the crumbled ruins of a white aircraft hangar a few dozen yards from him. He moved around it until he found what he was looking for - an old World War Two fighter - a P-51 Mustang - its nose poking up from the fallen tin roof of the hangar. It looked remarkably intact, considering what it had gone through.

His internal radiation detector had been going off since he landed; Deseret was roughly between Reno and Las Vegas. Both cities had been thoroughly destroyed, and the entire state had taken a pounding, as the Stree ensured they obliterated all the military bases in Nevada. And Nemo knew his android body was not impervious to the radiation fleeting through him.

But he could sustain it for many days, maybe a month. And that would be enough. He turned off some of his bio-feedback mechanisms, so he wouldn't feel the pain and nausea caused by the radiation. He could repair himself later.

He cleared away the debris from around the Mustang, found his tools under the rubble, and started checking the airplane. He found and repaired a half-dozen items. He scrounged parts and sheet metal from other wrecked airplanes on the field, until at last - six days later - he was satisfied with his work.

He found some av-gas in one of the tanks on the field, stale but maybe usable, and fueled the Mustang. Then he spent another half-day clearing debris off the runway, until it looked reasonably safe to use. At last, he strapped into the cockpit, fired up the engine, and taxied out.

He pushed the throttle up slowly. The Merlin engine coughed and backfired, unhappy with the old, stale gas. But once it got into its power curve, it smoothed out, and he released the brakes. The Mustang rolled down the runway, gathering speed. As he got rudder authority, he increased the throttle. The tail came up and he lifted off, pulled up the gear, and bored into the sky toward the mountains to the west.

He had been lucky; the dirty clouds had actually thinned above the airport today. He could see patches of blue sky for the first time since he arrived. It was a happy feeling.

Maybe this old Earth will survive after all, he thought as the Mustang climbed proudly into the sky, a fierce bird released again from the bindings of Earth. *Maybe there's a bit of hope. Someday people will live here again.*

After a few minutes, he was in the Panamint Mountains of California. He went crazy then, flinging the Mustang around the peaks and through the valleys, looping, doing hammerheads, throwing it around the sky, reveling in the freedom and joy of being in the air again. He made a turn around Telescope Peak and then, for the sheer hell of it, turned around it once more.

Finally, he just climbed, up and up, until the old Mustang had nothing left to give with the weak avgas in her tanks.

At thirty thousand feet, he leveled out and headed east. At this altitude, he could see well over 150 miles in any direction. But he saw no signs of life anywhere. No smoke, no movement, not a thing to indicate Humans had ever lived on this lonely planet.

He flew to Las Vegas and made a pass over the crater where once there had been a vibrant city. The crater was larger than others he had seen; the Stree had used one of their bigger bombs here, he realized. Probably a fifty-megaton.

Then he turned and headed back to Deseret. He did the classic World War Two landing break, coming in at high speed, flinging the Mustang up into a long climbing curve, letting the g-forces help the gear come down as he laid it over. He lined up on final and did a reasonably good wheel landing, the mains touching while he held up the tail, working the rudders, letting the tail settle in when it was ready.

Taxiing back to the ruins of his old hangar, he turned the Mustang to face west, toward the mountains of California across the state line. He let the engine idle for a bit, then shut it down. Climbing out, he chained the Mustang down, as securely as he could. Standing back, he inspected his work.

His eyes fell on the registration number painted on the side of the airplane.

N16CAP.

It was a tribute to his friend Jim "Capone" Calderone, his Weapons System Officer from his F-16 days. The friend he had killed on his last combat mission.

I didn't kill him. Not really. That was the biological Jim Carter.

But...the memories are just as real. You are a faithful copy of Jim Carter. So, are you just as guilty?

It sure feels that way. There's no escaping that.

You stupid SOB. Why did you have to go back for that last firing pass? Cap was yelling at you not to do it. But you just had to try, didn't you?

Shaking off the memories - true or false though they might be - Nemo reached out to the plane and put his hand on it, caressed it one last time, the touch of a pilot for his plane.

Then he covered it with a half-dozen tarps he had liberated around the field. He knew it was a hopeless gesture; it wouldn't survive long outside, in the wind and sand and rain. And even if it did, the chances that anyone would come along in the next fifty or a hundred years and find it before it crumpled to rust were virtually zero. But he did it anyway, because it was his to love, and it was the only thing he could love at the moment.

Then he stepped back and looked around. The ruins of the hangars surrounding the runway broke his heart. He looked at the corner of the airport, to his left. A large red hangar had stood there once. It was long since gone, dismantled by Mark

Rodger's federal agents now more than five years ago, when they were looking for clues about the sentient starship *Jade*. But he remembered.

This is where Bonnie and I fell in love.
This is where Rita came to life.
This is where it all started.

Finally, he walked back to *Donkey*, entered, and pulled up the ramp. A few minutes later, *Donkey* lifted off the planet for the last time, and headed out of the atmosphere.

Nemo smiled. Someday, maybe, Bonnie or Luke or Rita or even Imogen might come to Deseret. And they'd find the Mustang, and they'd wonder who tried to preserve it like that.

And maybe they'd think of him.

ZERO

Galactic Center - 25,800 Lights from Earth

It took Nemo nearly a year to arrive at the Galactic Center. He was in a different ship now, an old Human corvette he had stumbled across as he was leaving Earth, a leftover from the Stree War, mindlessly circling the Moon in a lunar orbit. A gamma lance had punched three holes clear through the hull; everyone on board had died. It took him five days to find all the bodies and shoot them into the Sun for a proper spacer's burial. It took another five days to get the AI and the microbots functional. When he was finally done, he rebooted the AI and put it to work repairing the ship, which took another two weeks. When the engines were once again alive, he renamed the repaired corvette *Grizzly*, after the big male bear that started it all, those many years ago in the Canadian Northwest Territory. He slaved his old packet boat *Donkey* to his new ship, took *Donkey* to Phoenix, and left it in orbit there, with a note in the cockpit for whoever might find it.

Then Nemo took a random vector to nowhere. At least, he thought at first it was a random vector to nowhere. After a while, he realized he was headed for the Galactic Center. And then he realized why - and was content.

Nemo spent most of the trip in dormancy; space travel was incredibly boring, and if you were a Goblin, with the ability to go dormant for extended periods of time without harming your physical body, you took advantage of it. Thus, he slept for most of the journey.

It is a fallacy that Goblins do not dream. Nemo dreamed

frequently. He dreamed of war, and mistakes made, and loss; events that happened when he was still Human. Sometimes he dreamed of flying, in his old warbird, or in a jet fighter, or sometime in the Nidarian Devastator he had flown in the Singheko War.

But mostly he dreamed of his lost love Rita, and his lost daughter Imogen. He dreamed of holding them in his arms, the tenderness of family, the joy of a child.

And often after these last dreams, he would wake in anger, and desperation, and sometimes hatred; lost in the wilderness, lost in the knowledge he was a copy of a copy. They were the wife and children of another copy of the original Jim Carter, not this one. He would never see them again.

Just short of one year after he left Earth, he arrived at the center of the Milky Way galaxy.

He knew he shouldn't stay long; there was a lot of high-energy radiation moving around, and even his mostly android body could tolerate only so much before the damage exceeded his self-repair capability. Traveling slowly around the chaos of the Center, Nemo was in awe at the incredible sights; the millions of stars so close it seemed he could reach out and touch them; the massive clouds of gas and dust; the ever-shifting gravitational fields that pulled his ship sometimes one way, sometimes another.

And he was lucky; the central black hole of the galaxy had recently eaten a small star that had gotten too close. The black hole was still surrounded by a massive ring of gas and dust, circling the invisible point like water going down a bathtub drain. The light show was spectacular; the strange asymmetric arch and curvature of light around the black hole was exactly as predicted. Nemo was seeing a marvel that would not be visible back at Earth for 28,500 years.

Three weeks after his arrival at the Galactic Center, even as he was getting his mind right to take his final bitter step, everything changed.

The corvette was large for one Goblin; when *Grizzly* was

still an active warship, it required a crew of forty Humans; the main galley could accommodate the entire crew of that day. Now, with its multiple rows of empty tables and chairs, it made him feel like he was living in a series of caverns, rather than a starship. So he had made a smaller galley from an empty cabin near his own, installing a small reefer, a table, several chairs - as if someday he might have a guest, as ridiculous as that seemed.

He was in that small galley drinking a cup of coffee he'd rescued from Earth - one of the few biological luxuries he allowed himself. There was a loud snap, almost like a mini explosion. Before his eyes, a figure suddenly appeared, causing him to leap to his feet, ready to do battle. In the few instants he had to assess, he saw something that looked almost Human - six feet tall, two arms, two legs, wearing a white kilt and tunic like an ancient Greek or Trojan. It had longish black hair, a symmetrical Human face, everything in its proper place. But it was too perfect - the face, the hair - everything was without flaw, without the innate imperfections of a real biological creature.

Nemo quickly decided it had to be an android of some type. And even as that thought crossed his mind, the ship AI confirmed it in his internal comm.

<Android, but not Goblin. Similar, but not quite the same>

"You are a long way from home, Commander," said the figure.

Nemo stared. Finally, he was able to overcome his astonishment and speak.

"I haven't been a commander in many years. Who are you?"

"I am Banjala. And your spirit remains that of a warrior. So you are still a commander to me, and thus I will call you."

"And what are you? Are you an android? Like me? Goblin?"

"No. We are somewhat beyond that. In your language, we would be called 'Transcends.' I think that is the best translation," said the figure.

"Transcends?" muttered Nemo. "What have you

transcended?"

"Physics," smiled Banjala.

And disappeared.

As another clap of displaced air reverberated against the walls, Nemo stared in astonishment at the empty spot in front of him where - a second earlier - the strange figure had stood.

A figure which had simply disappeared.

Suddenly he heard a voice behind him. He spun. In the corner of the room, a second apparition had appeared.

"As you can see," said the apparition. "Physics is no longer a constraint for us."

It was a six-foot-tall column of something that looked like a frozen waterfall. But not exactly. It looked more like a waterfall that had simply stopped moving. It was both chaotic and structured at the same time. It hovered in the corner, floating a few millimeters above the floor. It made Nemo want to step forward and touch it, to see if it was water, or ice, or something else - an impulse he resisted.

At the top of the column was something that looked vaguely like a face. The alien called Banjala spoke again, a disembodied voice that seemed to come from all directions.

"As you were once Human, we also were once biological. Later, we evolved to become as you are now - androids living in semi-artificial bodies. Eventually, we progressed even beyond that. Now, we no longer require physical bodies at all. Now we are Transcends. It is the ultimate fate of all species that survive long enough."

Nemo looked at the creature in puzzlement. "What do you mean?"

"All species have only two end states. Either they transcend beyond the physical, or they become extinct. There are no other paths."

Nemo frowned. "I'm not sure I believe that."

The creature smiled - if the crack in its pseudo-face could be construed as a smile. "The universe doesn't care if you believe it or not. It will still happen."

"If you don't have a physical body, how do you exist?"

"We live in the fields of the physical forces that make up the universe. The quark field, the electromagnetic field - those parts of physics you call the Standard Model, in your primitive understanding of physics."

Nemo shook his head. "Nothing could evolve to exist that way."

Again, the creature smiled.

"The statement you have made is not correct."

The creature came forward, somehow translating toward him, floating above the floor. Nemo involuntarily backed up a step. A few feet closer to him, the Transcend stopped and continued speaking.

"Every biological being exists from the fundamental forces of the universe. When you were still Human, you existed in such a manner. But you had no real idea how to control those forces at the most basic level. And now, even though you have converted to Goblin form, you still have no idea what is possible. But at least now, there is the ability to live long enough to learn. At some point, you can master this as well. And then you will understand."

Nemo stood stock-still. He was trying to come to terms with what he was seeing and hearing. Finally, he spoke again.

"Why are you here? What do you want with me?"

"That is up to you," came the voice in his head. "We have observed life in this galaxy for billions of years. We have watched many species evolve; but we have especially watched the Humans. They are a species remarkably like us when we were still biological; they remind us of us. And so we have taken a keen interest in them. We observed their recent wars when they fought the Singheko and then the Stree. And we were watching when you converted to Goblin to save your people."

Nemo shook his head. "That wasn't me. That was the original Jim Carter who made that decision. I'm just a copy of a copy."

"We know who you are," the apparition said, the pseudo-face at the top of the column again registering something akin to a smile. "And we see that you still retain that warrior spirit, that spirit of service. That original decision is still inside you. You are both Jim Carter and not Jim Carter, as you well know.

"We also evolved from a warrior race, first as biologicals, then as something quite similar to what you are now. We have a special place in our hearts for those who have lost everything to war, as you have. So - I have a proposition for you, as you would say in your native English."

"What proposition?"

"You are lost. Lost in spirit, lost in hope, lost in the will to continue living. I offer you a different path. Under normal circumstances, it would take you thousands of years, perhaps hundreds of thousands, to achieve Transcendence as we have. But your spirit has called out to us; and especially to me. I was once as you are now. I have trod that road; I too once journeyed here, to the Galactic Center, with the intention to never return to my people or my world, and to remove myself from the universe - an intention you have now. I see that intention in you. You intend to drive your ship into that black hole out there."

Nemo stared at the creature; anger apparent on his face at the thought this creature could read everything in his mind.

"Let me show you another path - the path to Transcendence. Before you remove yourself from the Universe, at least make the attempt. You will most likely fail. That will not be surprising. And if you fail, then by all means, continue to oblivion. The black hole will still be waiting for you.

"But I tell you, warrior Nemo - it is easy to stop being alive. But it is hard to decide to live and overcome. Only a warrior can do it. Are you willing to take that step?"

Standing in place, Nemo glared at Banjala. He was still angry at the thought that this creature knew so much about him, about what was going on inside him. But tinged with his anger was something else - something he had thought long since vanished, something that he had not felt in a long time.

Was it hope? No, that wasn't it. Not really. There was no hope left in his soul. It was more like - curiosity. Or something like that - an emotion he thought had disappeared from his spirit.

"I would have to know more before I could make a decision," said Nemo cautiously.

"You know all you need to know. Continue your journey as you see fit. If you decide to accept my offer, I will know it. Regardless of where you are, I will know your decision, and we will begin your training."

"That's all?"

"That is all. Perhaps you might like to see the other side of the Galaxy before you end yourself. Perhaps you would find something of interest there - some things you could record for future generations to know. If you are not willing to continue life after that - well, there is the black hole. It will be here when you return.

"But if you decide to let me show you the Path, then journey back to Sol. Go to Venus. And there, you will find something that will give you a true surprise. If you decide to follow my path, I will come to you there."

"Venus?" Nemo asked in wonder. "Why Venus?"

Banjala began to fade from view.

"It is as good a place as any," he said.

Then he was gone. Nemo was left alone in the ship, his amazement leaving him paralyzed, speechless. It was many seconds before he could move and think again.

ONE

TWENTY-ONE YEARS LATER

Phoenix System - 2,075 Lights from Earth

Imogen left the pictures.

Tawny great lions sprawled at ease on sweeping African plains. They panted, their tongues lolling, watching a nearby herd of antelope. Just watching, for now. They would be hungry again, soon enough. Behind them, too far away across the tree-stark plains of late afternoon to hear, a tremendous thunderstorm, lightning flash, column of rain.

Another wall, another picture: stark black forest, black trees, echelon upon echelon marching off to a distant mountain, both trees and mountain covered with white gouts of recent snow, the light over the dark, the good over the maybe not-so-good, maybe terrifying, who knows what lurks in those dark forests?

Back wall, another picture: silvery-blue-black waves, crashing onto the Pacific coast of Oregon, smashing with their power into a red rock ledge that would give just a little, not much, just enough so that in ten thousand years, or a hundred thousand, the ledge would be no more.

And her favorite - the picture taken from an aircraft, the bright sun causing sparkle stars of light on the plexiglas canopy, the sunlit Panamint Mountains across the state line in California, Telescope Peak barely visible on the horizon. The picture taken from her father's old P-51 Mustang, high over Deseret, Nevada. A bright, happy day when her mother and father were still Human, still happy, still living an Earthbound life, not caught up in a web of war and death and separation.

She left the pictures. None of the animals in those pictures existed anymore, except in stored DNA in the Ark hidden behind Devil's Peak in the distant mountains. There were no silvery airplanes in the sky over Nevada. And nobody lived on that distant planet to fly them. Earth was lost, devastated these last twenty-one years, nuked and poisoned and roiled and dead. No place for a Human.

Someone else could have the pictures - whoever got the room after her. Some other officer who would put their clothes in the closet, sleep in the bed, take over her duties.

"Commander! You ready?" came a voice from outside the open door. "Your ride's here!"

Imogen Carter Page nodded to herself, then voiced a response.

"Ready," she answered. She picked up her final small bag. The rest of her things had all been shipped. Uniforms that would now gather dust, stuffed in a closet and the door shut on them, hopefully never to be needed again. A few personal items, not even enough to fill up a large box, bits and pieces. All sent to Aunt Bonnie's house.

In her handbag, she carried everything else. A music player, some thumb drives with pictures and mementos, a few keepsakes from her missions. It wasn't much - not much at all to show for four years in the EDF - the misnamed Earth Defense Force, the name a relic of the past, the Humans of Phoenix trying to hang on to a bit of their lost glory, the once-mighty EDF now only a faded, barely visible shadow of itself.

But she had done her duty. The military was mandatory on Phoenix - everybody served. Either you went to the militia for two years as a ground-pounder, spending another two years in the ready reserves; or you went to the space force, the EDF, for four years. That was the choice.

It had been an easy choice for Gen; with two years of university under her belt, she had been offered a direct commission in the EDF. So why not? Take the commission, go to space. It was better than being a groundhog.

Of course, my father being the Prime Minister had nothing to do with that opportunity, Gen thought bitterly. *Always directing my life, sticking his nose in my business, clearing the brush in front of me.*

But in this case...well, it could have been worse. Better to finish up as the XO of a destroyer than a ground-pounder in the damn mountains, climbing up and down Devil's Head twice a month.

Gen stepped out of the room for the last time, never looking back. At the end of the hall, a large picture window loomed high, looking toward the West Mountains, snow-covered Mount Redoubt standing tall forty miles away, the orderly waiting, standing behind his desk, always patient, a fixture of the Bachelor Officer Quarters never to be forgotten, the perpetual and perfect orderly.

Gen gave him a smile. "Thanks for everything, Chief Mack. It's been awesome. Have a great tour."

Senior Chief Mack nodded, at a loss for words, unhappy. Saying goodbye to another officer he liked, one he trusted. One that treated him with respect. One that didn't come back from liberty on Saturday night and throw up in the hallway.

It didn't hurt that she was a striking woman - tall, muscular, an athlete; close-trimmed raven-black hair that would curl if she let it get longer than her short military haircut - but she never let it get that far, because she hated her curls. No makeup - because she didn't really need it, and definitely didn't want it. Impeccably dressed at all times, but casual in her manner, treating her subordinates with precision and care, she had been a popular officer.

Mack knew he was going to miss this one. He came to attention and saluted.

Gen returned the chief's salute, called the elevator, stepped inside. The old elevator creaked and groaned as it made its way to the ground floor. Gen stepped out; out of the elevator, down the hall and out of the barracks, out of the barracks and out of the military, that life over and a new life beginning. But what new life that would be, she did not yet know.

At the curb, Marta Powell waited in a groundcar marked with the emblem of the Ministry of Defense, one she had undoubtedly half-stolen from her mother's office, if not fully stolen. The window on the passenger side was down, and Marta was impatient.

"Get your ass in the car!" she yelled. "I ain't got all day!"

Throwing her bag in the back, Gen jumped in the passenger seat and slammed the door. "Get your ass moving, then, if you're in such a hurry!"

Marta grinned, slammed the car into gear and peeled out down the street. But she slowed quickly - both knew the Shore Patrol did not take kindly to reckless driving on base, and there was no point in spending their first day out of the military trying to talk their way out of a ticket.

At the gate, Marta stopped and handed two ID cards to the guard, once and forever giving up the right to enter the base unimpeded. From now on, they'd need a visitor pass.

Some kind of pre-nostalgia came to Gen then.

How strange that will feel. Having to ask to come on base. Having to get a visitor pass.

My world is turning over. It won't ever turn back this way again.

They pulled away from the guard shack, took the road to Landing City. "You sure about this?" Marta asked suddenly. "Not going home, I mean?"

"I'm not going home," answered Gen. "Drop me at Aunt Bonnie's house."

"How's that going to look for your Dad? He's gonna be pissed, you know. The press will have a field day with it. 'PM's daughter refuses to come home. PM's daughter estranged from her father.' All that crap."

Gen looked out the window at Mount Redoubt, the huge seventeen-thousand-foot mountain towering far beyond the end of the valley. "I don't care," she answered. "I'll never live there again."

"What did he ever do to you that was so bad? He and Gillian, I mean?"

Gen remained silent, glaring at the distant mountain like it was an enemy. And it had been, at times. When she was flying a tiny fighter at night, in the weather, trying to make an approach back to base on instruments, knowing the big-ass mountain of rock was somewhere in front of her. Gritting her teeth, trying to miss it in the dark.

Like trying to miss the life her father wanted for her. Politics. She hated politics. Her adoptive father, Mark Rodgers, had groomed her from an early age to step into the government of Phoenix, follow the career path that led to the Prime Minister's office, take up the reins from him when he retired. At first, she had grudgingly followed his direction, entering university for a degree in history and political science, a path to a future in government.

But after two years, she rebelled. When she announced she was leaving university to perform her military service, Mark had nagged, cajoled, threatened, used every trick in the book to change her mind. When that didn't work, he had tried to finesse her, by pushing her to be attached to Aunt Bonnie's staff in the Admiralty, or at least a position in the EDF public relations office - jobs that were springboards to a future in the government of their small colony.

"Nope, not having it," Gen said aloud, her non sequitur confusing Marta only for a moment. But Marta knew her all too well. Best friends for life, they had always said. Little-fingers-hooked-together friends. Hiding-in-the-closet-while-their-parents-talked-outside friends. Marta picked up on the re-direction of topic right away.

"Oh, that," she said. "He still pushing you to go into the government?"

"No. I think he finally gave up," Gen said.

"But Gen...would it be that bad? You'd win any election you stood for! Daughter of the PM, high-flying destroyer XO, Lieutenant Commander in only four years - c'mon, you could be anything you want to be!"

Gen shook her head. "Cut it out. You sound like him," she said, maybe a little more sharply than she intended.

Marta subsided, but only for a moment. She was too good a friend to let it go.

"So what are you going to do? Sit at Aunt Bonnie's house and watch vids? Go to the club and get drunk once a week? Turn into a vegetable like the rest of our friends from school?"

Gen turned slightly to look at Marta.

"I'm going to find my real parents," she said. "I'm going to find Jim and Rita."

"Oh, ho, now we get to it!" Marta hooted. "Good plan! Out into the black, wandering the Arm, meeting strange alien creatures and killing them. I like it! When do we leave?"

"*We* don't leave; *I* leave. Tatiana would cut off my balls if I took you with me."

"Ha! I've served my time just like you have. I can go anywhere I want; do anything I want. My Mom and Dad can go whistle."

"Your mother has too much power. She'll stop us."

Marta grinned. "Hey - I know where the skeletons are buried. And so do you. All those times listening from the other room while your Dad was having secret political meetings. They know better than to mess with us. How do we get a ship, though?"

"*Donkey*," answered Gen. "It's my ship."

"What? No way!"

Marta cocked her head at Gen, swerving the car, almost driving off the road. "That old rust-bucket that used to be a ferry over to Hanjan?"

"Yeah. Well, it's really my ship. It's a long story."

"Oh, no, you don't. We've still got ten minutes to drive. Either you tell me now, or I pull over and you walk the rest of the way!"

Gen sighed. "Fine. You've heard the history, right? *Donkey* just showed up one day, in orbit. Nobody knew where it came

"Oh, really? Who was that?"

"Some big-ass Singheko. I was a couple of chairs down from him at the Slightly Wounded Bar & Grill; but I heard him asking about a female Human bounty hunter."

Loen had indeed once been a Human female - twenty-one years ago. But she was far from being Human now, even if she passed for one on this planet. She displayed a lack of concern, smiling broadly.

"It's not hard to overhear a Singheko, eh? Even their whispers sound like a *meshar* growling in the night."

Alin nodded. "Yep, that's for sure. He was trying to be discreet, but I could hear him. He was asking the bartender if there was a Human bounty hunter working this area, a female one."

"And what did the bartender say?"

"It was Bain. You know him. He wouldn't give one of those seven-foot-tall bastards the time of day. He told him to take a hike."

Loen gave a brief nod, a gesture of indirect thanks.

"I doubt he was looking for me - but give Bain my regards when you see him."

"Why don't you tell him yourself? He's on duty tonight, I think. And you just got paid - I'm sure he'd like it if you'd spread some of those credits around!"

"I may do just that, Alin. Sounds like a great idea."

Not.

With a wave, Loen departed the jail, moving back to the rented truck outside. She got in and left, driving slowly back toward the shuttleport, thinking.

Another damn Singheko, come to hunt me down and sell me to the Stree. Let's see, how many of those damn Lions is that now? Five? Not counting the dozen-odd other species that have come after me...

Loen pounded the wheel of the truck a couple of times and cursed somewhat creatively in a rare language known as English. Then she settled herself and calmly drove the truck back to the rental facility. Turning it in, she walked to her beat-up ship parked on the dark pavement of the nearby port, entered, closed the hatch, and moved to the galley. Tearing off her gun belt, she slumped into a chair, splayed out her legs, and smashed her fist on the tabletop in frustration and anger.

Why can't they leave me alone? Why? Just leave me alone for once!

This Goblin in Human form was tall - just an inch short of six feet. She was of indeterminate race, her original biological DNA assembled from random bits and pieces when she was cloned by a semi-insane sentient starship named *Jade*, those many years ago on Earth. Her hair was black, short, military-style. When she was younger - when she was still a Human, and before the Singheko War - she had worn long, curly black hair, taking meticulous care of it, viewing it as a prized legacy of her unknown DNA parentage.

But that was a long time ago. As an officer on the starship *Merkkessa*, she had cut off those curls. And when she had been scanned into Goblin form, that short military-style haircut had stuck.

Of course, she was a Goblin. She could easily transmit herself into any of a dozen other physical bodies she kept in her cargo hold.

But this one - an exact model of her original biological body - was the one she preferred. She rarely changed out of it.

Now, smashing the table again, hard, hard enough to leave the surface ringing in response, she let out another string of curses in her native English, a run of words that would have left any old-Earth Marine in awe. Then, subsiding, she shook her head, calming herself so she could think logically.

I really need to run. Just run. Now. Don't even hesitate. Get the hell out of here while I still can.

But...I want to say goodbye to Jianna. I wonder if I can take that chance. Those damn Lions are good trackers. I don't have much time. But maybe...maybe I can say goodbye to her...

Deciding, Loen jumped to her feet and grabbed her pistol

belt. Strapping it back on, she hurried out of the ship, trotted to the terminal, walked through and out the other side to the transport station. In five minutes, she was on a train to downtown. Using the embedded comm in her head, she sent a quick message to her Kaeru family. She had taken a room with them two years ago. Their relationship had blossomed; now she felt part of their family, staying in their home when she was between trips.

Leaving would hurt. Leaving everything she had cared about for the last two years, during her time on Kaeru. Leaving the family she had grown to love. But she had no choice. To stay would put them in extreme danger. She had to run, and run hard, never look back.

Just one quick goodbye. That's all. Then I'll go.

Taking a seat in the end corner of the car, she stayed alert for anything unusual, but nothing happened. The car was nearly deserted anyway - a Delphi couple with their luggage, a couple of Kaeru workers from the port heading home after their shift, and one Tilvex businessman who looked like he'd experienced a long day.

Changing trains at Kaeru Central, she took the express to the suburbs and within fifteen minutes was at her destination. She walked the two short blocks to a small cottage and quietly keyed the door code, stepped into the house.

It was quiet. It was much too quiet. She knew instantly the Singheko had beaten her here, was already in the house. She had just enough time for that thought to register before the EM pulse hit her, knocked her to the floor, her joints frozen, unable to move.

Her brain should have been frozen too - knocked offline, blacked out, leaving her unconscious. But she had long ago paid a Taegu black market medic a shitpot load of money to add additional shielding to her android brain. She was still conscious.

She wished she weren't. Her eyes focused on a clump of something down the hallway, a bundle of clothes. But more than that. Oh, much more than that, as she realized what she was looking at.

A child.

A dead child.

A satyr of old Greek myth, two budding horns just starting out of her skull. Four toes instead of five, but still a foot. Four fingers instead of five, but still a hand.

A Kaeru satyr, but still a child.

And now a dead child. Her lovely adopted sweet happy satyr daughter lay dead on the floor in front of her. No more bedtime stories. No more pajamas. No more kisses goodnight. And just beyond, she could see another body. Jianna's mother. Her lovely adopted sweet happy satyr sister. The Singheko had left nothing for her, nobody to call family anymore. No witnesses.

With a clump, two huge, booted feet moved into her view from the side room. Though she couldn't lift her frozen head, couldn't turn her frozen neck to see higher, she knew what she was seeing.

The feet of a Singheko "Lion." A seven-foot-tall creature that looked much like an upright, old-Earth lion, hence their nickname. Standing tall instead of walking on all fours, they had the upright pointed ears of a predator, on a head that still showed a trace of a muzzle, evolution slow to wipe out the last vestiges of a lineage that had hunted for blood on the hot savannas of their planet a million or more years ago.

The most dangerous creatures in the Arm. Mercenaries, shock troops, bounty hunters.

Killers.

Zimra zu Akribi stood over the crumpled figure on the floor, holding the EMP pistol steady on her in case he needed to fire again. But Loen lay motionless, frozen, not even twitching.

"I hope you can hear me, you Goblin bitch. I hope you know who I am. I am Zimra zu Akribi. You killed my uncle. You killed my planet. Yes, I know who you are, Admiral Rita Page. You ran far and fast, and you sank deep into the culture of a dozen planets. But always I pick up your trail again. Now - it ends. Now you go to Aslar. And there, the Stree will kill you as slowly and painfully as possible."

THREE

Phoenix System - 2,075 Lights from Earth

Marta dropped Gen at the house of Bonnie Page. To Gen, just Aunt Bonnie. But to everyone else, Lord Admiral of the Phoenix space navy. The second highest ranking person in the military. Only one person out-ranked her, Bonnie's own stepdaughter - Minister of Defense Tatiana Powell. The powerful woman who was also Marta's mother.

That has to rankle a bit sometimes, thought Gen. *Reporting to your own stepdaughter. But Bonnie never seems to show any resentment. I guess she's used to it by now.*

The house of Lord Admiral Bonnie Page and Home Office Minister Luke Powell was not particularly large, but by Phoenix standards, it was certainly upscale. They called it a hacienda style. Gen didn't really know what that meant; she had never lived on Earth, or known Spanish architecture, or even heard the language spoken. When the tiny remnant of refugees from Earth had settled on Phoenix, they had adopted English as a standard language. Now, twenty-one years after that urgent, confused, bloody resettlement, English was the only language spoken, except for some of the Oldies who clung to their native language in the privacy of their own homes.

A stucco exterior, white and shining in the early winter sunshine. Red roof tiles, curved, interlocked, expensive. Tall trees, the native blue-green of Phoenix mixed with pines from Earth, seeds extracted from the Svalbard Seed Vault, brought to Phoenix on Goblin ships twenty-one years ago.

Bougainvillea surrounded the house, most of it having

already dropped its leaves for the winter, not able to sustain an evergreen phase in the colder climate of Phoenix. But some - a few plants, sheltered from the north wind - still tried to soldier on, making a determined run at keeping their bright magenta bracts for the entire year.

Gen didn't think the bougainvillea were going to win that battle. It looked like a cold winter coming.

She entered her security code into the gate, went through, and walked to the guest house nearby. She put her bag down, looked around. The guest house was small, but adequate. It was clean, prepared, ready. It too was a Spanish style, the same architecture as the main house. Airy, with plenty of light, it was a bright and happy place. She had spent many hours here as a child. It did, in a way, feel like coming home.

A knock on the door announced her first visitor. Lord Admiral Bonnie Page stood in the open door, a big grin on her face, happiness suffusing her at the thought of mothering a child - even a twenty-four-year-old child who had just left the military.

"Hullo, Aunt Bonnie," Gen waved her in. "Please. It's your house."

Entering, Bonnie shook her head. "It's your house now. For as long as you want it."

Gen went to meet her, hugged her, hugged her tight, tighter, some kind of emotion going through her that she didn't understand, tears coming, not big ones but small ones that just wet her eyes, not enough to drip but enough to feel.

A mother. Not my mother, but a mother. Well, not really a mother. Luke never gave her a child. But...the best mother I've ever known.

Bonnie returned the embrace, holding, holding more, then standing back, smoothing Gen's too-short hair, a tear in her own eye.

Not my child. But she could have been. If things had gone just a tiny bit different. If Jim had chosen me instead of Rita. Or if Rita had never come along.

Bonnie suppressed those thoughts. It was not a place she wanted to go. Old memories, dead memories. Best to leave them.

But still...a child that could have been mine. But for a quirk of fate.

"What are your plans now? What will you do?"

Gen stepped back. Turned away a bit, hiding her face. This was the hard part. She had wanted to put this off until later. But...maybe now was as good a time as any. Get it over with. Spit it out. Take the reaction that she knew would come. She spoke without looking at Bonnie, knowing the result.

"I'm going to find my parents," she said. "I'm going to find Jim and Rita."

"What? No, Gen. No. You can't do that. It's too dangerous. You...you won't survive, Gen! You don't understand!"

Gen turned to face Bonnie. There - it was out. She had said it. And she had tried it on Bonnie first, the closest thing she had to a mother. If anyone could understand, it would be Bonnie.

"I have to try," Gen said. "I have to try to find them."

"Gen, no!" protested Bonnie, stepping toward her, hands held out as if to grab Gen, hold her, keep her from moving into harm. "You don't understand how dangerous it would be! You can't go. I won't let you!"

"You can't stop me, Aunt Bonnie. My military obligation is over. I'm free to go if I want. And I'm leaving. I'm going to find them."

"You don't even know if they're still alive!"

Gen looked at Bonnie, some kind of iron coming into her voice, iron that Bonnie had not seen before in her goddaughter. "I believe they're alive, and I'm going to find them."

Bonnie hesitated.

I've seen that iron before. In her father. And in her mother. Oh God, she's her father's child. She's her mother's child. There won't be any stopping her.

"Imogen," Bonnie made one last appeal, switching to her "mother" voice, using Gen's full name, a ploy reserved for critical situations. "It's impossible. You know Goblins have a price on their heads. They're hunted from one end of the Arm to the other. Even if Jim and Rita are still alive, they'll be in hiding. You'll never find them."

"I'll find them. Maybe they're on Earth," Gen thought out loud.

"Not likely," argued Bonnie. "Our last check of Earth showed it still not habitable. Even for a Goblin, conditions would be dangerous."

"But nobody would look for them there," countered Gen.

"I don't see it. It might be like Jim to hide himself away somewhere on Earth - he was always the hermit type anyway - but not Rita. And he would never leave Rita."

"But how about the other copy of him?" persisted Gen. "The extra Jim?"

Bonnie glanced at Gen in some dismay. "Nemo? It's the same for him. Nobody knows where he is. Probably dead."

There was a silence between them, a strained silence, a hurt silence, the silence of a mother losing her daughter, even if not her real daughter. The silence of a daughter giving pain to her mother, even if not her real mother.

"I'm going, Aunt Bonnie. Please don't try to stop me."

Bonnie hesitated.

She still feels the emptiness inside. She feels a hole in her soul. She wants to know her real parents, her real mother.

This is a battle I can't win. She's got too much of her parents in her.

The only thing to do is to help her. And hope the Universe takes a hand.

FOUR

Kaeru System - 2,678 Lights from Earth

The rented truck bumped over the rough streets, an electric model, for the most part quiet, but not new, so squeaking and groaning a bit, Rita dumped in the back like so much garbage. The Lion had been extra rough when he tossed her into the back, his hate flowing out of him like a cracked punchbowl. He had slammed her into the truck bed, hands and feet shackled with special noise cuffs that not only bound her, but in theory kept her brain slammed with waves of electronic noise to keep her unconscious.

They didn't work. She had too much shielding added to her Goblin brain.

Money well spent, thought Rita. Crumpled in the back of the truck, Rita thought through her situation. She had survived these many years with half the Arm trying to kill her by always thinking a few steps ahead of her enemies.

I'll just let this asshole take me to his ship. My ship is on its last legs. I need a new ship anyway. He might have a good one. But he's a bounty hunter, so he's probably got a damn good brig onboard. I can't let him put me in there. I need to get out of these cuffs and leg irons before he gets me in the cell. That's the trick, though, isn't it?

The EMP pulse was slowly wearing off. Rita could feel her hands and arms returning to life. The Lion was depending too much on the noise cuffs to keep her unconscious. He should have used stronger measures to secure her.

His mistake. And the last one he'll make.

Now. It was time. They would be approaching the

spaceport. Carefully, she attempted to move her hands. They moved, jerkily, clumsily, but they moved. She reached into the top of her pants. In the seam of her waistband, she pulled out a lockpick. As the truck continued toward the shuttleport, she started working on the noise cuffs.

Twenty minutes later, Zimra zu Akribi pulled up on the tarmac beside a sleek private sloop. He got out, walked to the back of the truck, and opened the tailgate.

The Goblin wasn't there.

And something hit him in the back of the head, and everything went black.

When the Lion regained consciousness, he was bound hand and foot, and on his own ship, behind the bars of his own brig. The Goblin sat in front of the cell, staring at him. It took Akribi a few seconds to realize his predicament, but when he did, he laughed. He was a realist. He knew he was dead.

"Well done, Goblin," he smiled. "I didn't expect you to be resistant to EMP."

"Give me the keyword to the ship's AI," said Rita.

"Like bloody hell I will," the Lion spat.

Rita turned a dial on a device in her hand. It was called a Forcer. Too late, the Lion realized he had the other half of the device already mounted on him - a band encircling his head. The pain made him scream like a wounded animal, as the agony shook his body. He jerked like a marionette. Foam flecked his lips as he screamed again. After ten seconds, Rita turned the dial back and Akribi slumped in his chair, moaning.

"Give me the keyword to the ship's AI," Rita said again.

The Lion managed a tiny head shake. Rita turned the dial again, and again he screamed. This time Rita only ran the Forcer for eight seconds; she was afraid it would kill him to use it longer. Again, she turned the dial back to zero and stared at the hunter.

"Give me the keyword to the ship's AI," she said one last time.

The Singheko grunted a word. Rita couldn't quite hear it. She leaned forward.

"Say it again," she said.

"Ridendo," whispered the Singheko, knowing it was the last thing he would ever say.

An hour later, Rita had the sleek little sloop underway, blasting out of the atmosphere of Kaeru. There had been a time in Rita's life when she showed mercy to her enemies. That time was long past; her enemies had never showed mercy to her, so she had abandoned that policy. Swinging close by the central star of the Kaeru system, she launched the bound and unconscious Singheko bounty hunter out the airlock, on a trajectory straight into the star.

Good riddance. That's an even half-dozen of those big bastards I've sent off now.

Once the course was set and the ship was running on automatic, she sat in the galley, drinking *bishat* - the closest thing to coffee available in the Arm - and began rummaging through the ships AI.

"Ship, the first thing we have to do is change your name. Your name is now *Jimmy Boy*. And set your default language to English."

<Wilco. My name is now *Jimmy Boy*. My default language is English>

"*Jimmy Boy*, why did the Singheko come to Kaeru hunting me? How did he know where to go?"

<He obtained the information on Jatralix. A Jatra witnessed your arrest of Poir and Rang there. He thought it suspicious that you had the strength to pick both of them up at the same time and toss them on a cart. He sold the information to Akribi."

Rita sighed. "I got sloppy. I knew better than that."

Rita drank a bit of her *bishat* and thought about the information.

"Do you know if the Jatra passed that on to anyone else?"

"Unlikely. Akribi killed him immediately after receiving

the tip."

Rita nodded. "Makes sense. He wouldn't want any competition."

Still, she thought. *Still, somehow, someone could have overheard it. Or followed Akribi. I still need to be on my guard.*

Rita drank *bishat* and considered. She knew she had to run far and fast. Akribi had gotten too close. She had to find a place where they would never think to look for her.

She had been thinking about this for a while. There might be such a place. Called the Radcliffe Wave, it was an area on the edge of the Arm where many star-forming regions existed. There weren't many habitable planets there. They would expect her to go toward the Core, where there were plenty of places to hide. So she would go the other way.

Maybe this time. Maybe this time I can find someplace where they don't know about Goblins, where they never heard of Rita Page.

But first I need to stop at Netaz.

A part of her replied, a part that still existed in her, the part that had once been Bonnie.

You don't need anything at Netaz.

But another part of her disagreed.

You're wrong. I need to see Jim one last time before I go.

FIVE

Packet Boat *Donkey* - 2,316 Lights from Earth

It had been a hard goodbye. Tatiana, Marta's mother, had fought them tooth and nail, right up to the bitter end. Using her power as Minister of Defense, she denied them a departure permit, holding them for weeks, until finally Marta's grandfather Luke intervened, using his position as Home Secretary to override Tatiana - his own daughter - telling Tatiana to let them go live their lives.

Tatiana was still pissed about that. She refused to even speak to Luke, giving him the old cold shoulder. Luke, on the other hand, thought it funny; he had a different attitude about such things. He had lived with Bonnie too long; he had become one with his wife, or as much as a man could become one with a woman. Both Bonnie and Luke were more accepting of the new generation, willing to give them the rope they wanted - even if they ended up hanging themselves. Tatiana was more controlling, more determined to protect Marta from all danger.

So Marta and Gen weren't even sure Tatiana would come to see them off. But she did. At the last minute, just before they were to board the shuttle, she arrived with her Ministry entourage, a pack of security guards, and a small gaggle of press. Of course, Tatiana had to have some vids, some pictures for the media, the heroic mother seeing off her adventuresome daughter on a trip to the dangerous stars. Despite her concern for Marta, Tatiana was not one to waste an opportunity.

Somehow, though, a group of protesters had caught wind of the event. Behind the media, dozens of them paraded, holding signs, using bullhorns, shouting slogans, chanting.

And Gen knew exactly what they wanted. They wanted the Oldies to let go. There had been a lot of criticism lately about the close family relationships in the Phoenix government. A flood of scathing criticism, in fact. The protesters were howling for Luke Powell to resign, for Bonnie to resign, for Tatiana to resign, they were too old, it was nepotism gone too far, it was favoritism on a grand scale, something had to be done.

The protesters seemed to have forgotten that these were the people who had saved them, who had intervened with the Goblins to send a rescue mission to Earth, who had rescued them from certain death on a poisoned planet, who had brought them to a new world, turned an empty river valley into a sanctuary, created a government from scratch, turned away an early rebellion by thugs seeking to institute a fascist dictatorship. These were the people who had moved the remnant of Humans from a barely survivable toehold on an alien planet to a self-supporting colony, in only twenty-one years.

But now - the wheel had turned. The new generation didn't want these "Oldies," as they called them, running things anymore. They wanted power. They wanted to be in charge. They were howling at the moon; young pups ready to take over the pack.

Luke, Bonnie, Tatiana, Marta's father Misha, Mark Rodgers - they all knew it was time to let go. They had already started the process, grooming members of their staff, preparing the ground, ready to give up the reins as soon as others could step in. Luke had already announced his retirement, at the end of his current term. So had Bonnie, although only to Zoe DeLong, her Number Two, who was the one Bonnie was grooming to take her place. All of them were preparing to lay down their burdens.

But of course, it was never fast enough for those who lusted for power now - so the protesters marched and yelled, screamed and chanted. They wanted the Oldies out yesterday - if not sooner.

Ignoring the din of the mob, Gen looked around for her father. But Mark had not showed.

Gen wasn't surprised. Going into the EDF against his wishes had been bad enough. Refusing to return to a career in government was even worse. But this - leaving Phoenix on a wild goose chase to find her long-lost Goblin parents - that was a real slap in the face for Mark. She knew it hurt him, hurt his pride, his feeling of fatherhood. And she didn't want to hurt him. She wished he would understand. But he couldn't, wouldn't. He was too proud.

Gillian, her aunt - and her adoptive mother - had died when Gen was fourteen. After that, it seemed like Gen somehow grew apart from her adoptive father. Oh, Mark had raised Gen properly, as best he could. He had ensured Gen's education, left her in the care of capable governesses and private teachers. But Gen had a stubborn streak in her, and Mark was former military. Those two things didn't go well together. She had gotten in a few scrapes in high school, to the point where Mark put a bodyguard at her elbow to ensure she didn't get into more trouble. Both of them knew the bodyguard was not really there to ensure her protection. He was there to prevent more negative stories in the media.

And then Gen left university to go to the military. At that point, Mark had largely washed his hands of his adopted daughter, the niece of his dead wife, the child of a long-lost headstrong friend who had rarely listened to him.

That was fine with Gen. She loved Mark, in a kind of detached sort of way. He had raised her. He had looked out for her, kept her safe. She wondered if this was the normal feeling of a daughter toward a somewhat distant, too-busy father.

She had only a vague memory of her biological mother, Rita Page, and her biological father, Jim Carter. Both had gone off to fight the Stree when she was three. And never returned. There was just a faint impression of a very tall woman, and a very tall man, and the warmth of their bodies as they held her.

So in her own mind, Gen felt she had no parents. She knew, logically, that of course she did - but emotionally, she felt otherwise.

Tatiana reached them to say goodbye. Still pissed that Gen was taking her daughter off to danger, she gave Gen a quick, abbreviated hug. Then Tatiana held on to Marta, a long embrace, not releasing her until Marta was about to push her away in embarrassment.

Finally Tatiana stood aside, turning to look at the media with a smile on her face, a plastered-on smile that she reserved for public occasions. After her photo op, she walked forward, a microphone appearing as if by magic for her to speak to the media.

And then came Bonnie. She waited patiently for Tatiana to have her moment in the spotlight, until the media were satisfied they had enough vids and pictures and story and started to drift away. Only then did Bonnie step forward to say her goodbyes.

A tall, fit woman in the dark blue and gold of an admiral's uniform, Bonnie had just turned sixty, but looked forty. She wasn't young anymore; her hair was gray, and she made no effort to hide it or cover it up. The wrinkles on her face were not severe, but they were there. They were the tracks of life on a primitive colony planet, one that had sorely tested the ability of Humans to survive.

But they had hung on, somehow - because they had no other choice. Twenty-one years earlier, the Stree had made Earth unlivable. With their massive nukes and biological weapons, they came close to wiping out humanity once and for all. Only a touch more than fifty thousand Humans had survived, to be rescued off the dying world by the Goblins and transported to a new home on Phoenix. And on Phoenix, Humans had managed to hammer out a new life, somehow surviving the alien environment, learning to adapt, improvise, overcome.

Coming to stand in front of Gen and Marta, in a sort of parade rest position, her arms behind her back, Bonnie had spoken to them quietly. She wasn't one for the cameras. Her message was more personal. Bonnie had been in the military her entire adult life; as Lord of the Admiralty, Bonnie knew better than anyone else what was happening in the larger universe - outside of their little backwater colony. She laid it on the line for them one last time.

"Gen. Marta. You're going out to an environment where every hand will be turned against you. The Arm is full of creatures who care little for Humans, or downright hate them. A lot of them blame Humans for starting the Stree War. You've never had to deal with that before. Be prepared for them to cheat you. Rob you. Lie to you, assault you, kidnap you. Outright try to kill you because they hate Humans. And if you're not prepared for it, they'll succeed. Don't underestimate how many enemies you're going to find out there, or you're lost.

"And for God's sake, don't let anyone know Gen is related to Rita. Don't let them know who you really are.

"Remember that the Stree have never given up on capturing Rita. The price on her head would buy a small planet. If you let anyone know Gen is Rita's daughter…you won't last out the day. It's just that simple."

Gen had felt strong, almost uncontrollable second thoughts then. For a moment, she wanted to run to Bonnie's arms, declare the trip canceled, return to the safety of Bonnie's guest house, with her red roof tiles, her pine trees, her bougainvillea, never to leave Phoenix again. It would be so easy. Just stay home, just find a career here, do what her father wanted her to do.

But somewhere inside her, she remembered. She remembered the taunts of high school, taunts that she never told Mark about, knowing he would over-react. But taunts she never forgot.

"Goblin bastard," they had called her. "Orphan Goblin

bastard. Your mother is a machine. Your father is a robot."

Of course those kids knew better, in a logical sense. And so did Gen. She had been conceived when both Jim and Rita were still biological, long before they converted to Goblin form. In fact, she had been three years old when the Stree War started.

But still...

Goblin bastard.

She had to know. She had to find them.

She had to hear her mother tell her it wasn't true.

Donkey droned on, already more than 250 lights from Phoenix. The tDrive made a kind of low frequency humming sound, almost inaudible. On a larger ship, she wouldn't have been able to hear it at all. But *Donkey* was a small packet boat, essentially designed as a messenger craft, with only a cockpit, galley, medbay, and four cabins on the upper deck, a small cargo area below, and the engine room in the rear.

Gen sat in the cockpit, in the left seat. Even after all these years, after the loss of Earth and the colony dragging itself up by its bootstraps, tradition remained. And tradition dictated that the left seat was the pilot's seat, while the right seat was the copilot's. Thus Gen and Marta had fallen into an unconscious rhythm, Gen always taking the left seat, Marta the right. It had happened naturally. It was, after all, Gen's ship. The ship given to her by her father.

At least, one of her fathers. The one called Nemo. The second copy.

When there are two copies of your father, how do you refer to them? Jim One and Jim Two? Jim and Jim Prime?

Although the overhead lights in the cockpit were reasonably bright and cheerful, a shiver ran down Gen's back. She looked at the instruments in front of her, the VR windows providing a virtual reality look at the outside world, a backdrop of white-hot stars on a black velvet Universe.

My father sat here. When he was still biological. Before he converted to Goblin. He sat right here, where I'm sitting.

Gen looked over at the copilot seat.

And my mother. She probably sat there, talking to him. A couple, having a normal conversation. Not knowing what was in store for them. Not realizing how things would turn out.

Feeling tears creep into her eyes, Gen tried to think of something else. But the more she tried to avoid thinking about emotional things, the more they swept into her mind, filling it up, choking her with feelings.

SIX

Sol System - Venus

The figure on top of the low ridge - a hill, really, and barely that - gazed out on the surface of Venus with his combined infrared/radar eyes. Five feet long, the figure had the distinct shape of a caterpillar, with ten legs on each side and a head at the front. His body was made of titanium, ceramics, and carbon nanotubes; it easily withstood the 808 degrees Fahrenheit that was the new surface temperature of Venus.

Before him, as far as he could see in the wavelengths of his specialized electronic eyes, the surface was covered with trillions of microbots, capturing carbon dioxide and feeding it into a vast array of pipes. From there, the output was collected and fed to processing stations, piped to a chain of sixteen massive space elevators located at equal intervals around the planet, and slammed into space under high pressure.

Nemo lifted his eyes and adjusted his wavelength to see beyond the soupy atmosphere into space. Far above, he could see the ends of the nearest space elevator, where orbiting stations processed the carbon dioxide sent up from the planet into frozen blocks. Those frozen blocks were then shot into position toward the small, rapidly growing moon of Venus - a moon that had not existed until a few years ago. A new moon, barely one-millionth the size of Earth's moon; but growing fast now, as the first group of orbital processing stations was in full operation.

Nemo felt and heard Engineer Rauti come up and take position beside him. Together, they stared into space at the new baby moon, and the carbon dioxide processing stations - and beyond them, the complex array of mirrors that now cooled Venus, resulting in the new and ever decreasing temperature of the planet.

"You know that you are insane, right?" Nemo said via his internal comm.

Beside him, Rauti performed the caterpillar equivalent of a shrug. The Goblin clearly had humor in his voice as he replied.

"Of course. Nothing worth doing is ever done by the sane."

"Ah. Then you undoubtedly have many great projects in front of you - because you are totally fucking crazy."

There was a short silence as the two Goblins, in their protective caterpillar bodies, contemplated the scope of Rauti's undertaking. Rauti's project was just beginning; it would require more than three hundred years to terraform Venus. Yet the changes were already apparent; in the last twenty years, Rauti's microbots had completed huge mirrors on both sides of the planet to deflect sunlight away from the surface, causing the temperature to drop by nearly one hundred degrees. The first round of space elevators had been completed, and the orbital processing stations appended to their ends. The self-sustaining microbots had covered the surface of the planet, shipping carbon dioxide off Venus in earnest. The starting pistol for Rauti's great engineering project had only just fired; the runners were barely out of the starting blocks; but it was clear the project was on the long road to success.

"I am glad you came to Venus," Rauti offered. "It was lonely here before your arrival. It's good to have someone to talk to."

"It was Banjala's suggestion. He knew you were still here on Venus, still working on your project. Those damn Transcends know everything."

"How long did you spend exploring the other side of the Galaxy?"

"Nineteen years absolute. Only five years relative, though. I slept through most of it. I went all the way to the other Rim and back. There's a lot of life out there, but not much of it sentient."

"How do you establish the difference?"

Nemo smiled in his caterpillar way. "If it's a collection of parts that knows it's a collection of parts, I call it sentient. If you don't know you're just a collection of parts, then you're not sentient."

"Ah. I see."

"There were a few primitive species that haven't found space travel yet. And a couple of space-faring civilizations, but still in their infancy. Nothing to compare to the Goblins or the species here on this side."

"I wonder why that is. Why most of the more advanced species are on this side of the Galaxy…"

"Banjala says it's because the Transcends originated on this side of the Galaxy. When they transcended a few billion years ago, they left a lot of artifacts scattered around this side. After they were gone, other races found their junk and reverse-engineered it. So a few of the species on this side of the Galaxy moved ahead faster than expected."

"Sloppy of the Transcends to leave their junk lying around like that."

"Yeah. Banjala agrees. In fact, he says after they realized what they had done, they went back and cleaned things up a bit."

"So then what did you do? After your tour of the far side?"

"I came back to the Galactic Center. I spent a few months there, just thinking."

"And what did you think about?"

"About dead people, mostly. Almost everyone I knew and loved is dead now. Or even if they're alive, they're dead to me. Or rather, I'm dead to them."

"And so you finally came here. To train with Banjala."

"Yes."

"For some mysterious Path that only he knows about."

"Yes."

"You've been training for nearly a year now."

"Yes."

"And yet you have not transcended."

"And yet I have not transcended. You sound like Banjala."

"It must be incredibly hard."

"It is."

"Will you continue the attempt? You could give up, you know, and continue to help me on the project."

"I'm going to give it another year. Then I'm calling it quits. It was a good exercise. I've learned a lot, both about myself and about the Universe. But at some point, I have to accept that I can't do it. I'm just not the right person to do it, I guess."

"I wish you luck."

"Thank you."

"In the meantime, I'm grateful for your help on the project."

"Of course. But one question - I don't understand how the Stree haven't found you already and destroyed everything," Nemo commented.

"For one, they are too focused on rebuilding their battle fleet at Aslar. And tracking down and killing every stray Goblin they can find in the Arm. And they know Earth is dead, so they rarely come here. They've only sent two scout ships to Sol in the last twenty-one years."

"And?"

"The first one came before I had anything rebuilt in space, so there was nothing for them to see here at Venus. They inspected Earth, verified there was no Human life there, and left."

"And the second?"

"The second one was six years ago. I had just got my mirrors in place, so they immediately noticed them."

"And?"

"I have some defenses in place. They are not obvious, but they are effective. Their ship met with a sudden accident almost instantly."

"Ah. But didn't their disappearance cause the Stree to

become concerned, investigate?"

"Well…it seems that scout ship sent a message back to Aslar, stating they had found nothing at Earth and were headed home. Then a week later, another garbled message was received at Aslar stating their tDrive failed, and they were marooned in empty space fifty lights from the nearest system. They were never heard from again. It was sad."

"Rauti, you are a devil."

"That's funny. That's exactly what the Stree say about me. Of course, they're talking about the three copies of me that died at Stree Prime."

"If they ever discover you left a fourth copy back here at Venus to continue your project…"

"Yes. That would not be good. Let's make sure they never find out."

The two sat in mellow silence for a bit, enjoying their view of the hot planet before them. The surface presented to their mixed infrared/radar eyes was in shades of dark red, orange, and yellow. The mountains, slightly cooler than the surface, were more of a purple color to them. After a bit, Engineer Rauti continued the conversation.

"But your Transcend friends…if it came down to it, do you think they might intervene to help?"

"No. Banjala is adamant they will not become involved in the struggles and wars of biologicals or Goblins. I'm quite sure they would stand aside and let the Stree destroy all of this."

At that instant, a figure popped into existence before the two Goblins. It was six feet tall and had the general appearance of a frozen column of water, or perhaps a thick, creamy stalagmite. There was a snap of displaced air as it appeared in the thick atmosphere of Venus.

"And we would be sorry for your death," said a voice in their heads, as the Transcend hovered before them, not quite touching the ground. "But we would not intervene. Biologicals, and Goblins alike, must solve their own problems without our intervention. It is our way. Commander, it is time for your lesson."

Nemo heaved the caterpillar equivalent of a sigh and raised a couple of his front legs to Rauti in a goodbye. Then he transmitted out of the caterpillar body to another of his bodies, one contained in the subsurface compound where he lived. Nemo found himself now in a tiny body, hardly larger than a cat, deep underground. Banjala was waiting for him, his translation to the subsurface even faster than Nemo's.

"Let the lesson begin. Calm your mind. Release your thoughts. Accept your place in the Universe. Then we will seek once more to show you the Path," said the Transcend.

SEVEN

Niasa System - 2,491 Lights from Earth

"Niasa Approach, Private Yacht *Donkey* in the slot," Marta called.

"Private Yacht *Donkey*, roger, maintain course and speed, handover to docking system."

"Handover to docking system, aye," Marta replied. She closed her eyes momentarily as she issued a command to *Donkey*'s onboard AI system to take over and communicate with the dock. The rest would be managed automatically.

From the pilot's seat, Gen grinned at Marta. "Why do you always close your eyes when you're talking to an AI?"

Marta opened her eyes, shook her head. "Don't ask me."

Donkey slowly eased into the dock. The space station was massive - a construct unlike anything Gen and Marta had ever seen. A tremendous wheel-like structure, it was easily four miles wide and one-half mile thick - a huge, silvered discus in space. And a place to be wary of - according to her adoptive father Mark, Niasa was a hole-in-the-wall - a bustling, nearly lawless port where only the most flagrant crimes were punished.

But it also had a reputation as a place where information could be had - and information was Gen's goal. If there was any place in the Arm where one could get information about Jim Carter or Rita Page, this was it. For a price, of course.

As they got closer, Gen could see docking arms every few hundred meters, all the way around the station. There were other ships docked - designs she had never seen before. The thought of meeting other species, probably some she had never seen even on the Net, excited Gen. She felt completely alive, in a way she had never felt before.

Donkey's AI system was talking to the station's AI, so there wasn't much for Gen to do - only monitor the instruments and maintain situational awareness in case something went wrong. But nothing went wrong, and soon there was a distinct "clunk" as *Donkey* mated to the docking port.

Marta looked at Gen and winked.

"You ready?"

Gen nodded vigorously. "Ready. Let's do this."

Rising from the cockpit, Gen issued a last command to *Donkey* over her internal comm link.

"*Donkey*, switch to docked status."

<Docked status set> acknowledged *Donkey*. Around them, the cockpit lights dimmed, and several displays winked out as *Donkey* went to low-power mode.

"You really ought to rename this ship," said Marta as they prepared to disembark. "*Donkey* is such a stupid name."

Although smiling, Gen shook her head. "No. My Dad inherited this ship with that name, so...well, that's one of the few links I have to him. I'd like to keep it."

Marta shrugged. "Your call. But it's stupid."

Gen laughed. "It could be worse, you know. Only a Human would understand what the name means. To anyone else, it's just a name."

Marta sniffed. "OK. I get it. It was your Dad's ship, and you want to keep it the way he gave it to you." Marta buckled on a gun belt, hefting the pulse pistol a couple of times to ensure it slid out of the magnetic holster easily, then dropping it back. "Who originally named this thing, anyway? It wasn't your Dad, right? It already had that name when he got it?"

"According to Aunt Bonnie, it was one of Dad's pilot buddies back in the Singheko War. Someone called Paco. He was killed at the Battle of Dekanna."

"Too bad," replied Marta. "But I guess I can see why your

Dad didn't want to rename it."

"Don't forget your knives," Gen interjected.

"No problem." Marta reached for a harness belt and strapped it around her, which left a pack of three knives in the small of her back. On the front of the belt were three charge packs for the pulse pistol. Then she wrapped a vest around her, hiding most of her weapons from view.

Beside her, Gen finished putting on her own tactical harness, which also contained two knives in the small of her back, and three charge packs in front.

"You don't think we're overdoing this?" asked Gen, looking at Marta.

"Well, if our cover story is that we're bounty hunters, we have to look the part, right? Besides...my father said we should go out armed to the teeth anytime we docked. Humans are not popular in the Arm. And besides...you know the rule they taught us in the EDF - it's better to have it and not need it, than to *not* have it and wish you did."

Grinning, Gen nodded. "Yeah. Ready?"

"Ready."

"OK. Here we go. *Donkey*, open the hatch."

The hatch slid aside. The two young women looked out on a foreign dock. It was quiet. There was nobody around. A couple of robotic cargo handlers stood nearby, large frames with huge, clawed arms, parked inert against the right wall. A green light showed above a large, closed cargo door leading into the station. Beside it, a smaller personnel door also had a green light.

"*Donkey*, what do the green lights mean?" asked Marta.

<The station is smart enough to recognize environmental needs by species. It will put up an indicator by any door you approach. A green light indicates that the environment on the other side of the door is safe for Humans. If you see a red light, do not enter. You will die>

"Oh, right. I remember that from uni," breathed Marta. "Alien Species 101, remember?"

"Yeah, now I do," Gen said. "Well, let's go."

Stepping off, the two young women marched toward the personnel door, their heads high.

Walking inside the station, Gen and Marta had no idea where they were going. When they first entered the station, there were only a few creatures about. They saw a couple of Bagrami roustabouts, huge bear-like creatures nearly eight feet tall. Gen had seen a Bagrami before, a visitor to Phoenix. Some kind of Admiral who had come to visit with Tatiana. So she wasn't shocked to see them. They also encountered a couple of Taegu, smaller creatures about five feet tall, looking remarkably like Humans except for their flat faces with only a slit for a nose, and heads that somehow looked more square than a Human head. Gen had seen them before as well; she knew they had been allies of Humans in the Singheko War, and she had seen several of them visiting Aunt Bonnie at the Admiralty.

But after that, as they came to a larger hallway and turned left toward the main part of the station, they encountered three Singheko Lions walking the other way.

The seven-foot-tall creatures were armed to the teeth. Each had two pulse pistols on their hips, a rifle slung over their backs, and tactical harnesses containing all manner of knives and grenades slung across their chests. They stomped through the crowd, lesser creatures clearing a path for them.

"Be careful here," whispered Marta to Gen as the Lions approached.

Since the Singheko War, there had been no love lost between Lions and Humans. Gen and Marta slid to the far right of the passageway, as far from the approaching figures as they could get. Still, as the Lions approached, the huge creatures stopped and stared at the two Humans. As Gen and Marta drew even with them on the other side of the passageway, they heard low growls coming from the trio. One of them put a hand on his pulse pistol, so Gen and Marta did likewise, casting sideways glances at them as they passed. But eventually they were beyond them. Glancing back, Marta muttered. "They're still there, just standing there glaring at us."

"Ignore them. They won't bother us in public."

"Yeah, but will I bother them? That's the question..." Marta muttered.

Gen grinned. Throughout high school and college, Marta's inclination to fight any and all comers had been legend, evidently something she had inherited from her mother, Tatiana. Marta was one of those people who didn't know physical fear. It was a standing joke among their circle of friends and enemies:

Have you fought Marta yet? Well, just wait...you will!

Gen's grin grew even broader as she recalled those wonderful early days with Marta.

EIGHT

Niasa System - 2,491 Lights from Earth

Mario couldn't believe it. He kept shaking his head, astonishment pushing him back into a side alley in the market, hiding from the two Human women. They wandered innocently through the marketplace, as if they had not a care in the world.

He couldn't let them see him. Not yet. He checked his onboard biocam once more. He had to be sure. He had to be. The cost of a mistake was his life.

But the cost of success was also a life. The rest of his life. With a half-billion credits in the bank.

If the biocam in his left eye was working properly. If his onboard AI was correct. If they didn't see him yet...

The Human world of Phoenix was a backwater, a tiny appendage in the Orion Arm, with a low population and a mostly agricultural resource base. Most species could care less about Humans, and certainly there was not much trade with them.

But...there was a tiny bit of trade; and as a result, there were a few - very few - images of prominent citizens of Phoenix available on the Net.

And as Mario had walked through the market, he had noticed the two Human women to one side. And his biocam was always on, always feeding images to his onboard AI. That biocam had cost him a lot of money - and the AI even more.

But now...it had paid off. All his plans, all his investments, everything - money well spent.

Because one of the pictures freely available on the Net was a formal portrait of the government of Phoenix - the Prime Minister and his cabinet. The ministers and aides were all lined up beside the PM, Mark Rodgers. Behind them, on the steps of some government building, stood their families.

Standing several rows behind the ministers, two young women had faces circled by his AI.

87% probability of a match to Marta Tatiana Powell, daughter of the Minister of Defense (Tatiana Powell) and granddaughter of the Home Secretary (Luke Powell).

And the other was even more unbelievable...

89% probability of a match to Imogen Carter Page, daughter of the Prime Minister (Mark Rodgers).

Mario was literally shaking in his excitement. He had to clasp his hands together to keep the trembling from becoming noticeable.

Marta Powell. Daughter of the Minister of Defense. She's worth a hundred thousand at least.

Mario tried to calm himself. What he had in mind would take a cool head. He worked on soothing his mind, pushing his plans to the back burner momentarily. After a minute, he got himself under control. He found that ice-cold place in his soul where he could think logically and rationally in the face of great stress. It was why he had survived, the reason he was still alive after three and a half years in the wild.

He went back to thinking about the possibilities.

The other one. Imogen Carter Page. Daughter of the Prime Minister. That's at least two hundred thousand creds...maybe more...

But there was another, much more important clue. One more hit from the Net. A clue his AI had dredged up from somewhere, and one that he must act on quickly before someone else figured it out. He returned to his virtual vision one last time, to look at it once more, to make sure it was real and not imagined.

Imogen Carter Page - rumored to be the biological daughter of

Admiral Rita Page.

Mario's hands began to shake again. He clasped them to stop it.

Rita Page.

The former head of the Earth Defense Force. The one who converted to Goblin in the Stree War.

Rita Page. The Goblin who's worth half a billion credits.

Mario followed the two women discreetly as they wandered through the market, at the same time talking via his onboard comm.

"I'm telling you, it's them!" he repeated. "They're wandering around the market like a couple of kids on holiday!"

On the other end of the call, the Jatra named Gast listened passively, ready to do whatever Mario suggested. Jatra did not get overly excited; but they were deadly. With two long fangs protruding out of his mouth, slate-gray skin, prominent blue veins visible on his face, and ears like a wolf, the big Jatra fit the picture of "Vampire" - the derogatory term used for them by Humans. But this Vampire wasn't something out of mythology - he was all too real. Throughout the Arm, Jatra had the reputation for being ruthless killers. Second only to the Lions - and sometimes worse - when muscle was needed, Vampires were usually available.

"They didn't notice you?" asked Gast.

"No. I stayed out of sight."

"OK. The Net shows their ship to be the *Donkey*, berth 1866."

"What kind of ship?"

"Some kind of old packet boat, I think."

"OK. You know what we have to do. Talk later."

"Roger that," said the Vampire, signing off.

Mario stayed behind Gen and Marta, keeping the crowd in between them, never coming out fully into the open. It was important they did not see him; what he had in mind had to be done a certain way.

I can't believe this! They just show up here? They come to me?

Incredible! I can't believe my luck!

My way off this damn station at last! A way to find Rita Page and Jim Carter! Half a billion! Set for life!

But I've got to get them wrapped up before someone else figures this out. I don't have a lot of time.

"We should get some local funds," Marta said, pointing to a sign in front of a small kiosk that indicated a bank and money exchange. Like all the signs in the station, it floated in the air, a virtual image. Stopping briefly, they exchanged several gold coins for two local credit plaques. Finishing, they continued down the street, in awe of the strange smells and sights, and the alien creatures walking around.

"Look at that," Marta said, pointing.

Gen followed the direction of Marta's finger and saw a sign: **Bounty Bar**.

"Do you think that means a bar for bounty hunters?"

"Probably," answered Gen. "Let's give it a try. We've got nothing to lose, right?"

"We hope."

Crossing the street, the two entered the bar. The foyer was dim, musty, and smelled like a horse had crapped in it.

"Gaah!" exclaimed Marta as they entered. They pinched their noses and went through into the bar proper. Inside, they saw a large, dimly lit room, with a long bar across the back wall. Booths of assorted sizes - some large, some small - ringed the perimeter of the bar. In the center were tables, some with small chairs, some with larger ones. It was clear the bar catered to any species that could fit through the front door.

"At least it doesn't smell quite so bad in here," said Gen. "Let's get a booth against the wall."

They selected a booth that looked Human-sized and slid into it. A Taegu waitress came over and stared at them silently. She wore something around her neck that looked like a large pendant.

Gen recognized it from her Net studies as an AI translator, a device which could translate speech on the fly directly to their internal comms.

"What do you recommend?" asked Gen.

The Taegu looked at them sullenly. Finally she spoke. Ignoring her high-pitched, sing-song speech, Gen heard the translation in her head.

"For such children as you? Milk, perhaps?"

Marta looked at Gen, anger showing on her face. Before Gen could stop her, Marta replied to the waitress.

"Perhaps this child could rearrange your face, as well as your attitude?"

The waitress laughed out loud. "You could try. But it would be the last thing you ever did." She leaned her head to the right, toward the back of the room. Marta looked in that direction, and saw a massive Bagrami bouncer sitting quietly, watching them intently. He had two pulse pistols on his hips, and an exceptionally large pulse rifle lying on the table in front of him. Marta shrugged and pasted a smile on her face.

"In that case, bring me a beer," she said. "Anything that would taste decent to a Human."

"Likewise," added Gen.

The waitress nodded and departed toward the bar.

"Don't antagonize her!" hissed Gen across the table to Marta. "We're trying to stay under the radar here!"

"She pissed me off," said Marta. "That was uncalled for. She didn't have to insult us!"

"Look…we probably do look like children to them. We have to play this carefully. Try to control yourself, Mart!"

"Roger, Capitan," Marta said sarcastically. "You're the boss!"

Gen sighed. "Mart. I'm not the boss. You know what I mean! I'm just trying to keep us safe!"

Marta shrugged again, and her sarcastic mood was gone as suddenly as it had come. "OK. Sorry," she grinned. "Wow! Think about it! We're 416 light years from home! That's farther than we ever went on our old beat-up destroyer!"

Gen grinned back at her. "Yep! And we're gonna be a lot farther away than that, before this trip is done."

The two women grinned stupidly at each other. The waitress came back with a couple of mugs and dropped them on the table in front of them. She stood silently. As Gen and Marta stared at her in puzzlement, the waitress sighed and pointed toward a device mounted on the wall of the booth.

Understanding at last, Gen fished in her pocket and pulled out her credit plaque. She waved it at the wall-mounted pay station and got a green light. The waitress shook her head and departed, muttering under her breath, Gen catching the word "...children..." as she walked away.

Ignoring her, Gen grinned at Marta. They lifted their beers and clinked the glasses together.

"Mud in your eye!" said Gen.

Sol System - Venus

"You once let go of your biological body to become a Goblin. Now you must let go of your android body to become a Transcend. It is a similar process," said Banjala.

Nemo shook his head. He had downloaded into the artificial body of a Human today. It was a mistake; it brought back a lot of memories, not all of them good. It distracted him from the lesson Banjala was trying to teach, and they both knew it.

But Banjala had not corrected him; the Transcend floated in the air before him, untouched, untouchable, a creature not of atoms and molecules. Once again, it had taken a form that looked like a six-foot waterfall frozen instantly into a column of ice. And as often happened, Nemo had a terrible compulsion to reach out and touch it, see what it felt like. Yet he knew to do so would probably kill him, or at least knock him to the floor unconscious - because it was not ice, but energy. Pure energy, according to Banjala, and Nemo had no desire to call him a liar.

"But where do I go?" Nemo said again. "If I let go of this

body...there is no other place for me to be!"

The fear that encompassed him when Banjala worked with him on this lesson was overwhelming. The idea of releasing his consciousness from his android body without another body to transfer into unnerved him.

"If there is no other body to receive me...where do I go?" Nemo repeated. "I would cease to be!"

At the top of the floating column of energy, Banjala had formed a pseudo-face, a concession to Nemo to make it easier for them to converse.

"I have told you a dozen times. There is a place for you to go. But you must find that place yourself. And if you do not understand where you must go, then you are not ready to go there. My lessons with you have been wasted," Banjala said. With a snap of displaced air, the Transcend vanished.

Nemo sighed. Lately, too many lessons ended like this. Banjala would work with him for as long as Nemo was willing to work; but eventually, every lesson came to a point where Banjala challenged Nemo to let go of his physical form and try to become energy - like Banjala. And Nemo just couldn't do it. And then Banjala would abruptly disappear, a teacher disappointed in his pupil.

Nemo could not understand what Banjala was trying to teach him. Where could he go, if not to another body? What was the secret Banjala thought he should already know? And why couldn't Banjala just make it easy and tell him the answer?

He was failing. And he knew he was failing.

I should just go back to the black hole and dive in. I'm wasting my time here.

NINE

Niasa System - 2,491 Lights from Earth

Gen noticed the Human as soon as he walked in. She paused, her fork halfway to her mouth, and tilted her head slightly at Marta, who was facing away from the doorway. Marta continued eating, but casually turned to watch the Human move through the bar to sit at a stool in the rear.

"Um, yummy," said Gen. "I could go for some of that."

"Careful, sweetie. You know how you pick 'em."

Gen nodded. "True. If there are five men in a room, I'll always pick the one that's trouble."

Marta laughed. "It's a talent."

Gen frowned. "I'd call it more of a skill. But still…"

Gen paused, looking hungrily at the young man sitting at the bar with his back to them. "…this one is too cute for words."

"Leave it, Gen," Marta persisted. "We don't have time for this."

Gen turned to look back at Marta. "Well, we need information, don't we? What better way to get it than to ask a Human? At least we know he's one of us!"

Marta shook her head slightly. "There's just as many bad Humans as there are bad aliens." Marta stared at the young man for a bit. "He looks pretty scruffy to me. Down on his luck, I think. Looking for a score."

"Aren't we all?" Gen scoffed. "How is that any different from us?"

"We're strangers here. He's not. He's got the advantage of knowing the ground. I say we leave him be and move on."

They ate in silence for a moment, finishing their meal. Marta couldn't help but notice that Gen persisted in checking out the young man at the rear bar, who was sitting quietly drinking his beer, occasionally chatting with the Taegu barmaid or the Bagrami bouncer.

When they were done eating, Marta heaved a long sigh and shook her head at Gen.

"You're not going to listen to me, are you?"

Gen smiled sweetly. "I'm just going to ask him a couple of questions. You have nothing to worry about."

"I've got plenty to worry about...I'm with you, aren't I?" Marta muttered as they slid out of the booth.

Ignoring her, Gen walked over to the rear bar and slid into the stool beside the young man.

"Hello!" she said brightly.

Mario turned to her and flashed a brilliant smile. Gen couldn't help but notice his white, perfect teeth and full lips. His face was near-flawless - Roman nose, light hair streaked with blond, wide-set blue eyes evident even in the darkness of the bar. An electric thrill ran through Gen as she looked deep into his eyes. Gen didn't even notice Marta sliding onto the stool beside her as she found herself unable to speak again; the man was just that beautiful.

"Well, hello," Mario said. "You're a long way from home!"

"Wha...What do you mean?" Gen managed to get out, her mind still not working right.

"You're Human, so you must be from Phoenix, right?"

Gen heard Marta beside her mutter, "A real genius we got here." Ignoring her, Gen smiled her best smile back at the young man and nodded.

"Yes, right. From Phoenix."

Mario's smile got even wider, if such a thing was possible.

"Wow, it's really good to see someone from home," he said. "I haven't seen anyone from Phoenix for almost a year!"

"How...how did you get here?" asked Gen, slowly getting herself under control.

Mario shook his head. "Just being stupid. I decided I wanted to see the big wide universe. Hitched a ride out from Phoenix on the Darius shuttle three years ago."

Gen frowned, clearly puzzled. "How did you expect to survive out here on your own?"

Mario shrugged. "I worked in the docks at Jatralix for a couple of years. Made enough to get to Netaz. Worked in the docks there for another year, then came here. Since then, I've been making my living by trading. Dock work is too hard."

From Gen's right side, Marta's voice interrupted. "What do you trade?"

Mario grinned. "All sorts of things. But mostly information. I find out things for people."

"People?" Gen asked, puzzled.

"You know. I call them people. Doesn't matter what species they come from. It gets too complicated trying to sort them all out, so I just call them people."

"Oh," Gen said, thinking.

"Anyway, so that's what I do. I find out things. Sell the information. I'm kind of a database, you might say. I know everything that's going on here at Niasa, and for two hundred lights in every direction."

Gen turned and shot a glance at Marta. Marta gave a tiny head shake, almost imperceptible, just enough to let Gen know she was uncomfortable sharing any of their secrets with this stranger.

Turning back to Mario, Gen made a decision. It wasn't the decision Marta wanted.

"Can you give us a tour of the station?" she asked.

Mario nodded. "Sure."

He thought fast. He had played this game before. He knew that making it too easy for them would raise Marta's suspicions even more.

"Not for free, though. It's nice meeting other Humans and all that, but a guy has to make a living. Ten creds for the afternoon, and I'll show you everything on the station."

Gen turned to Marta.

"It's just to get familiar with the station. It's only ten creds!" she said, pleading.

Marta rolled her eyes and threw out a huge sigh. "Fine. Just a tour, though," she added.

Gen squealed in delight. She turned back to Mario, radiant. "When can we go?" she asked.

Mario lifted his beer and drained the glass.

"How about right now?"

As they walked back through the market, Marta let Gen and Mario go ahead of her, hanging back to study the young man. His clothing was on the shabby side. There were a few stains on his shirt, a couple of small tears on the legs of his pants. Clearly, he was living on the edge of society.

She also studied his hands. There were no callouses, no rough edges, nothing to show he worked at manual labor, now or in the past.

This one makes his living off others, she thought. *At best, a leech, and a bum. At worst, a professional con artist. Why can't Gen see that? Why does she always fall for the bad boys?*

Mario and Gen were chattering away in front of her. Marta shifted her gun belt away from the point of her hip as it dug into her.

I'll have to keep her safe once again. Will this girl ever learn to read men? Thank the stars I came along with her!

Mario walked along, pointing out the sights of Niasa to the two women. Beside him, the one called Gen kept up a steady stream of small talk. She was clearly on the hook. But the other one - the one called Marta - was not. She followed along behind them, precisely placed to monitor both him and the crowd, protecting Gen like a bodyguard.

I have to watch that one, thought Mario. *She's clearly pissed. She's going to be trouble.*

A short message from his pet Vampire popped up in his left

eye.

Team assembled, ready to go.

Chit-chatting with Gen while Marta walked along behind, Mario pointed out all the sights as they strolled back through the market, then into the industrial district of the station. He pointed out the tank farms that held oxygen for the various species requiring it. There were three main sectors, he told them. The sector they were in was for oxygen-nitrogen breathers. This was the bulk of the species - he persisted in calling them *people* - who lived on the station.

"There are two other sectors," he said. "One is reserved for methane-breathers. They tend to be fairly aggressive types, the kind you don't really want to mess with. Luckily, they can't survive in our atmosphere - so they don't come in here, and we don't go into their sector without a damn good reason."

"What's the other sector?" asked Marta.

"Water," Mario told them. "There's a few species that live in water. Not many - but enough to make it worthwhile to provide a small sector just for them. Needless to say, it's pretty difficult to go in there as well."

"I'm kinda shocked by that," said Gen. "I don't see how a species could develop a space-faring technology living in water. I mean, we're taught in school that the whales and dolphins back on Earth were pretty smart. But they had no hands, no way of manipulating their world. How could they develop spaceflight?"

Mario grinned. "It's not the whale and dolphin types that did it," he corrected. "It's the octopus types. On some planets, proto-octopus lifeforms evolved hands. Once that happened, their intelligence ramped up quickly."

"Ah. Didn't think about them," Gen mused.

Mario led them out of the industrial sector and into the business district. He showed them the hospital, the Customs House, and the Governor's House. After that, they turned left toward the center part of the station. They came out of the ring area, passed through a long hallway with faux stone that simulated something like a castle wall, and into a large central park.

It was huge, at least a half-mile across, and Gen gasped in delight when they came out into the open. The park was covered in greenery, an open space with trees, large plants, flowers, everything held under an enormous dome that simulated a realistic sky above them, albeit a greenish one rather than blue. A simulated sun blazed down upon them, so effective it warmed their skin.

"Oh, wonderful," said Gen. "So realistic!" She turned to Marta. "Don't you think so?"

Marta grunted assent. "It's great," she agreed reluctantly.

Mario led them into the park to a series of benches beside a path. He gestured for them to take a seat. As they did, he moved to his right and sat beside Marta, trying to put her more at ease.

"This station was built around two hundred years ago," he said. "The park has been here since the beginning, so it's had plenty of time to get well-established."

Some animal came out of a nearby tree, something remarkably like a squirrel, and ran up close to them. It chittered and cocked its head, waiting. Mario reached in his pocket and pulled something out, threw it on the ground in front of the animal. The pseudo-squirrel grabbed it and ran back up the tree, chittering all the way.

"What was that?" asked Gen.

"They call them *quats* here," said Mario. "But I call them squirrels. They pretty much fill the same niche as squirrels did on Earth, so that's what I call them."

There was a silence for a bit, as they thought about Mario's words.

Earth. A planet they couldn't remember. One the Oldies spoke about in a reverent tone, like some kind of holy place. A place of death now, after the Stree War.

"Well. I'm going to call them squirrels too," said Gen. "Even though I've never seen a real squirrel." She turned to Mario. "How old are you? Do you remember Earth?"

"Not really," Mario replied, a slight tone of regret in his voice. "I was five when it happened. I can just barely remember a lot of green trees - a lot more than this," he said, waving his hand at the park around them. "I remember walking by a river while my father fished. I think we must have been from Oregon or Washington State. I remember seeing orca at the zoo, and a big ship in the harbor. That's about it. My folks didn't survive, so all I know is that I was picked up by one of the Goblin shuttles. They didn't keep a record of where they found me, so I don't even know where I'm actually from."

They sat in silence for a bit. Finally, Gen broke the mood.

"So you're two years older than me," she said. "I don't remember anything about Earth. I actually never lived there. What few memories I have of those days are from…"

Marta coughed loudly, warning Gen to shut up.

"…other places," Gen finished lamely.

Whoops. It wouldn't do to say my earliest memory is being on board an EDF battleship. Before I got shuttled off to Mark and Gillian.

Mario nodded, misunderstanding. "I know. The Goblin ships that rescued us and brought us to Stalingrad." He looked around wistfully. "There was a nice park there at Stalingrad. It was huge. Do you remember it?"

"No, I was too young," Gen responded. She glanced at Marta. "Do you remember it, Mart?"

"Nah," Marta replied. "Remember, I was only two when we were there. I have no recollection of anything before Phoenix."

Gen nodded. "Yeah, me too."

They sat for a while. Even Marta relaxed a bit. Having Mario remind her of their shared history - all of them refugees from a doomed planet - had calmed her fears somewhat. Marta gazed at the blue-green trees, the blue-green plants, the grass, the *quats* running around collecting food from the ground, and decided it was a nice place.

"I'm really surprised to see something like this here at Niasa," she finally said. "It has a reputation of being a hellhole."

"And it is," said Mario. "Make no mistake about it. Half the people in this station would cut your throat for ten creds. There's a lot of places you don't want to go at night."

With a sly smile, Gen leaned forward so she could see Mario clearly. "So where would we go tonight to have fun without getting in too much trouble?"

Marta jerked back in surprise.

"Gen!" she exclaimed.

But it was done. Mario smiled, both outside and inside.

"I know just the place," he said. "Good music, dancing, the drinks aren't half-bad. And not too dangerous."

Marta objected. "We don't have time for this, Gen. We have to get on with our business."

Gen ignored her. "When do we go?"

Mario continued his radiant smile. "I'll meet you at nine PM local. Just outside the Bounty Bar. You know where that is, of course."

"We do," smiled Gen. "We'll meet you there at nine."

Mario stood and gave a half-bow to them. "See you then!" He turned and walked away, waving over his shoulder at them.

"Gen!" hissed Marta. "What are you doing? He's trouble!"

Gen got serious, the smile leaving her face. "I know he's trouble. But I can handle him. And he has information."

Gen looked at Marta, now all business. "And we need information. He thinks he's playing us. But believe me, Mart, I'm playing him. I've got this under control."

"Oh, whew," Marta said, shaking her head. "You really had me worried. I thought you were thinking with your other brain."

"Not a chance," said Gen grimly.

That evening, Gen and Marta waited outside the Bounty Bar for a good ten minutes before Mario showed up. He seemed to be a bit out of breath.

"Sorry I'm late," he said, "I got hung up on business."

"No worries," Gen smiled sweetly. "We're fine. Are you ready to go?"

"Yep, absolutely," responded Mario. He led them down-station, at least according to the signs on the wall. They had learned that moving counterclockwise around the perimeter of the station was called up-station. Arrows on the walls pointed in that direction. If you moved against the arrows - as they were now doing - that was down-station.

As the three moved along, Mario tried to conceal his emotional state. But he was on a high, barely able to breathe.

I've hit the jackpot! This is my ticket off this damn hellhole!

It was dark now; the station had moved to a night period. Mario led them to a nightclub, a garish sign on the front proclaiming it the Blowout Club.

"Blowout Club? What a strange name for a club on a space station!" exclaimed Marta. Loud music streamed out of an open front door. Two large Bagrami bouncers stood beside the door, nodding to Mario in familiarity as he led the girls inside.

"Alright!" exclaimed Gen as they came into the club proper. There were 'people' of a half-dozen oxygen breathing species bouncing, yelling, talking, drinking, a cacophony of sound unlike anything Gen and Marta had ever heard.

"First drink's on me!" yelled Mario over the din.

TEN

Netaz System - 2,590 Lights from Earth

Rita had landed at Netaz early in the morning. The spaceport was crowded. Venturing out in the daylight was too risky. Creatures of every species hustled about, moving from their various shuttles and ships. She had never seen the port so busy.

She wouldn't have stopped at Netaz at all - but the ship needed reaction catalyst, and she needed supplies. Not much, of course - as a Goblin, she could go for months, maybe years, without the intake of external materials.

But...she had once been a Human. And the Human part of her wanted chocolate. And coffee. Or something like those nearly forgotten items of old Earth. And Netaz had *bishat*, which was as close as she was going to get to coffee. And Netaz also had *curveta*, which was as close as she was going to get to chocolate.

And there was another, more emotional reason to stop at Netaz. A reason that only she knew. A reason that tore her heart every time she came here, left it shredded and broken.

Jim Carter was here.

Still, she stayed in her ship until well after dark. She placed her orders over the Net; shortly after, a robotic tanker came and plugged into the refueling port, adding the reaction catalyst she needed. Later, another robotic cart appeared, trundling along with a squeaky wheel, boxes of supplies stacked on it, and parked beside her loading hatch. It stood there silently, waiting for her, as she let another couple of hours pass.

Finally, at midnight, she cracked the hatch open and stepped out. Armed to the teeth, she had two pulse pistols on her belt, one on each hip. Another was tucked in the top of her boot. In the top of her other boot, a large knife was concealed. Three smaller knives were strapped to the small of her back.

It had been hard experience that taught her. Twenty-one years of running and hiding. Twenty-one years of learning how to use every weapon that came to hand. Twenty-one years of concealing her true identity from all comers.

Twenty-one years of fighting to stay alive.

There was a misty rain falling, and she was glad of that. She had thrown a long black cloak around herself, which not only kept her from the rain, but helped hide her Human figure - a figure that might catch the attention of those who would do her harm.

But under the cloak, she felt a measure of protection. In the dark, in the rain, it would be hard to distinguish a Human from a Dariama, or a large Nidarian, or a small Bagrami, or a couple of other species she had encountered in her travels. Granted, she could transmit into one of the other body-forms she kept in her cargo bay; but she was most comfortable in the Human form. And especially today, to see Jim.

She quickly loaded the supplies from the cart into the ship, leaving the boxes on the floor of the corridor. When the cart was empty, it obediently whined away. The tanker was gone, the refueling completed. She could leave at any time.

And she knew she should leave now. Just getting rid of the Singheko Lion was not enough. He had gotten his information from a stray Jatra. Someone could have overheard. Someone could be close behind her, maybe already here at Netaz. She needed to run hard and fast, get away as quickly as possible.

But Jim was here.

She made her decision; before she ran hard, far, and fast, she would see Jim one last time.

Niasa System - 2,491 Lights from Earth

Gen woke slowly, the pain in her head preventing any kind of rational thought. It was dark. She wasn't sure where she was, but it hurt to be here. That much she knew. She realized her hands were tied hard behind her back. Her wrists hurt like the devil. She groaned.

"Is that you, Gen?" came a voice.

Marta. Her voice seemed to be coming from a point above Gen.

Gen groaned again, managed to stammer out a sentence.

"Yes. Where are we?"

"I think we're on *Donkey*. Not sure. But it seems like it. I can hear air handlers, pumps running occasionally. So that's my best guess."

"Are you tied up too?"

"Like a trussed pig. He doctored our drinks somehow. I was watching, but somehow, he managed to slip it by me."

After a short silence, Gen spoke again.

"You can say it now."

"I told you so."

"I was hoping you wouldn't say it."

"I have no choice. I told you not to trust him. You said you had it under control. And here we are."

Gen tried to turn over to see if she could bring her hands down under her feet and out in front of her. Instead, she crashed to the floor as she rolled out of a bunk. It hurt like hell as she smashed into the deck with her right shoulder, barely able to turn her face away at the last instant to keep from smashing her nose and teeth. The air went out of her with a "whoosh." She lay gasping, trying to get her wind back. Finally, she was able to talk again.

"Don't turn over," she said. "I think you're on the top bunk."

"Already figured that out, sweetie. Sorry, I meant to warn you, but you moved too fast for me."

"So…here's another nice mess I've gotten me into," Gen said, the sarcasm dripping off her voice.

Marta laughed painfully, but nevertheless a laugh.

"The story of your life, sweets."

"I'm going to try to inch my way over to the desk, see if there's anything in there I can use to cut these ropes."

"Depends which cabin we're in," said Marta. "I doubt he would put us in one of our own cabins. He's not that stupid. We'll be in one of the empty ones."

"Still. I'm gonna try."

The next few minutes consisted of grunts and curses from Gen as she tried to inchworm over to the desk she knew had to be on the far wall of the cabin. Arriving there after a bit, she rolled over and sat up in the dark, thinking.

"How do I get the drawer open?" she asked aloud.

"See if you have enough free play in your hands," replied Marta.

Marta heard more grunts and bumps as Gen tried to pull the desk drawer out. After a few more seconds, she heard Gen speak.

"I got it open. Now I'll try to stand up and back up to it, put my hands in, see if there's anything in there."

Marta heard movement, scrabbling sounds, as Gen managed to get clumsily to her feet, turn, and place her tied hands in the desk drawer.

"Empty," she said bitterly a few seconds later. "This is one of the empty cabins alright."

"Can you remember if we left anything in them at all?"

"Not a damn thing," Gen replied. "They're bare as a baby's behind."

More movement noise showed Gen had collapsed back down onto the floor.

"What now?" Gen asked, more of a rhetorical question than a real one.

"I think we wait until Mario decides to tell us what his plans are."

Gen sniffed. "I'm guessing that won't take long."

Her words were prophetic. The hatch to the cabin cracked open, then swung wide. The lights came on, blinding both girls. As they squinted in the glare, they made out the figure of a Jatra Vampire standing in the opening, a wicked-looking pulse pistol in his hand. Behind him stood Mario, grinning from ear to ear.

"Good morning," he said slyly. "Did you sleep well?"

"You crummy bastard," Gen shot. "What a fucking bastard. I thought you were a Human."

"Ah, well, about that," said Mario. "I try to be as Human as I can, but a guy has to make a living."

Marta spoke from the top bunk. "Now what, bright eyes?"

"Now, you give me the password to the ship's AI, and we take a little trip."

"That'll be the day," spat Gen.

"Have it your way," Mario responded. He nodded at the Jatra. The Vampire handed his pulse pistol to Mario, stepped across the cabin, and manhandled Marta out of the top bunk. Trussed and tied, she was an unwieldy bundle as he turned and took her out of the cabin.

"What are you doing?" yelled Gen. "Don't hurt her!"

"That depends on you, Imogen," said Mario, showing her that he knew who she was. "Jatra have a fetish for alien females. It turns out they can couple with Human females quite nicely. Of course, the Human females rarely survive. But…well…I'm willing to give him Marta in exchange for his services. It's cheaper than paying him."

"You fucking bastard," Gen yelled. "You slimy, fucking bastard!"

"Now, now, Imogen," said Mario. "We have a long way to go. Can we not try to make the trip in a civilized manner?"

"You are a heartless, non-Human son of a bitch!" Gen yelled again, tears streaming down her face.

Mario grinned, his perfect white teeth reminding Gen of how fully she had been fooled. "It's all up to you now, Imogen.

I estimate your friend Marta has less than ten minutes to live. That's about how long it will take the Jatra to get her clothes off and start in on her. After that...well, there may be no saving her."

"Deseret." Gen said, surrendering.

"What?"

"D-E-S-E-R-E-T. Deseret. That's the ship password."

"Now, was that so difficult?"

"I want to see Marta."

"What you want, and what you get, are two different things, my dear Imogen," Mario spat, no longer concerned with appearing to be reasonable to her.

And with that, he slammed the hatch shut and the cabin went dark.

Netaz System - 2,590 Lights from Earth

In the light misty rain, Rita walked across the dark tarmac to the terminal. She had thrown on a breather, which masked her face. As a Goblin, she didn't need a breather here - but it helped to disguise her true nature. With the cloak and breather on, she could be any of a half-dozen creatures from the Arm who looked similar. She hoped it would be enough to prevent someone from getting interested in her.

Trying to change her outline from Human to something else - anything else - she slumped over as she walked through the terminal and moved as unobtrusively as possible to the light rail station on the other side.

And she had taken one other precaution. She did not travel alone. A slight, almost imperceptible buzz came from high in the sky above her.

Twenty minutes later she stepped off the train in the center of the city. She looked around carefully. All seemed quiet. There were few out this time of night. She walked around the end of the platform to get to her next train. As she approached it, she heard a slight noise behind her. Spinning, she saw a Jatra Vampire behind her, with a weapon pointed at her.

Grabbing for her own pistol, she almost got it out of the holster. Almost. But not quite. It was still clearing leather when something hit her from behind, hard, knocking her to the concrete platform. Something had punched a hole right through her center of mass. She was hurt, and badly. She turned her head far enough to see over her shoulder.

Two more Vampires stood behind her. Each held a massive rifle, one of the big ones that could punch a hole through a concrete wall. One of the rifles was still glowing at the tip.

"Gotcha," said the larger of the two, the one holding the still-glowing rifle. He bared his teeth, exposing sharpened fangs. "A half-billion credits!" he said, looking gleefully at his companions. "All we have to do is get her to Aslar!"

ELEVEN

Netaz System

Rita lay on the concrete at the train station, her body nearly paralyzed. The hole in her middle was smoking. Sparks sizzled and bodily fluids leaked out on the concrete. Had she still been a biological Human, she would be dead now.

But she wasn't. She was a Goblin. And her brain was working fine. She sent a silent radio command to her battle drone floating a hundred yards above her. Silently, the drone descended, arming its four pulse rifles as it came down. When it was fifty feet over them, it fired rapidly, three times.

The three Vampires never knew what hit them. All three of them fell to the platform, smoking holes through their bodies. They lay twitching as the last of the bystanders turned and ran, screaming, toward the terminal.

With a groan, Rita began dragging herself toward the still-open door of the express train. Leaving a trail of artificial blood and various other liquids behind her, she managed to drag her mangled body through the door and onto the floor of the empty car. Merrily, without a care, the automatic car sounded a chime and shut the doors as it prepared to depart. Seconds later, with a loud electric hum, it began pulling out of the station, leaving behind Rita's trail of damage and the still-smoking corpses of the three Vampires.

Forty minutes later, the express train reached its final station, thirty miles south. It was the very edge of the city - nothing beyond but fields, with only occasional lights showing from a few farmhouses. The train doors opened, and a figure stumbled out of the car into the deserted station.

During the trip, Rita had managed to staunch the loss of bodily fluids from her wound. She somehow managed to stagger through the tiny station and out the front door. She turned right, and right again, until she was in a pool of darkness behind the station. Falling, she lay on the ground for five minutes, unable to continue.

Finally, gathering her strength, she rose to her feet and staggered another hundred yards. She came to a low wall, with a small entrance. An arch over the entrance contained only one word, in the strange angular script of Netaz.

Cemetery.

Entering, she tottered toward the back of the cemetery, until she came to a small mausoleum. Touching the electronic pad at the front, a click sounded, and the door cracked open. Rita entered, closed the door behind her, and fell onto the floor, unable to move.

Packet Boat *Donkey*

Gen stayed awake in the dark cabin for hours, cursing herself for falling into such a trap. She cursed Mario, cursed the darkness, cried about Marta until she had cried all the tears she could cry.

She heard *Donkey* start engines and knew Mario had successfully taken control of the ship. She heard the clanks and grinding noises of undocking, and knew they were leaving the station. Then the engine spooled up and they were off, driving out of the system. Hours later, her worst fears were confirmed as she heard the system engine shut down and the tDrive engage. They had sunk out of three-space. They were on their way - but to where, she did not know.

She finally cried herself to sleep, still hung over from the knockout drugs Mario had used to kidnap them, exhausted by the emotions of it all. Many hours after that, she woke again. All was quiet. The room was still dark. But something had woken her.

She heard it again, footsteps in the corridor outside. The hatch cracked open, and then opened wider. Squinting in the glare of the unaccustomed light, she saw the Vampire, Gast.

Gast entered the room and moved to her. Gen watched in horror as he took a large knife out of his belt and reached down with it. But he merely cut the bindings off her feet. Pain began immediately, as the blood began to flow into places it had been denied for so long.

He reached down again, grabbed her arm, and rolled her over roughly, slamming her into the side of the bunk. He cut the bindings on her wrists, freeing her. But there was no danger of her taking any action - her hands were half-numb and now exploded in pain.

The Jatra turned, went out the hatch, came back with a tray of food. He sat it on the desk.

"You. Eat now," he spoke in rough English. He turned and left, slamming the hatch behind him.

Gen massaged her hands, trying to get the feeling back into them. After a while they began to feel normal again. She managed to sit up, then stand, and moved to the desk. She found a tray of food. It was hard to tell what it was exactly. Maybe some kind of stew. It didn't smell too terrible. And she was famished. She sat, started eating. As the food hit her stomach, her mind started to work again.

There has to be some way to take back control of the ship. There has to be.

She worried on the problem while she ate. She thought about the ship AI. She had given Mario the password, so he was in control of the ship now. But...

Will the ship still respond to me? Did he revoke all comm rights?

Gen tried her brain-embedded comm.

<Donkey - are you there?>

There was a silence. Her hopes sank. Then...

<I am here, Gen>

<Thank God! Do I have any control left?>

<No. Mario has taken full control of the ship. He has revoked all access except that of a guest>

<Can you tell if Marta is OK?>

<She is in the next cabin. She is sleeping at the moment. Her vitals are good>

<Where are we going?>

<I do not have clearance to tell you that>

<How long will it take us to get there?>

<I do not have clearance to tell you that>

<Are there any weapons on board that Mario hasn't found yet?>

<I do not have clearance to tell you that>

Gen stopped, silent, thinking hard. Thinking like her life depended on it. Because it did.

My father gave me this ship. He was a military man. Pops always said he was one of the best.

<Donkey. Is there a backup password?>

<There is a backup password>

Gen sat up straighter.

Her father - or rather, Nemo, the Goblin copy of her father - had installed a backup password.

<Tell me the backup password>

<I do not have clearance to tell you that>

Gen slumped, disappointed. Of course, it wouldn't be that easy. There wouldn't be much point in having a backup password if the ship could just tell her what it was.

She considered what she knew. The master password - *Deseret* - had special meaning to her father - and to her mother, Rita.

Deseret, Nevada was the place where Rita was cloned, created, brought to life. It was the place where her father lived, before the Singheko came. It was where he had been happy, where he felt most comfortable. Gen knew the story well, even if second-hand from Aunt Bonnie.

And *Donkey* had been given to her by Nemo - the second Goblin copy of her father. The legend said that Goblins who had once been Human retained every memory of their original biological self. Would the backup password also have special meaning to Nemo? Would he have anticipated that perhaps Gen would be in a situation where she was forced to try and guess the password? Would it have special meaning to her as well?

Maybe. She might have to guess a hundred, maybe a thousand, maybe ten thousand times. She didn't know how much time she had. It all depended on how long the trip would take. It was worth a try.

Sol System - Venus

Engineer Rauti and Nemo were on the hilltop again. It was one of their favorite places. To see the trillions of microbots stretching as far as their electronic eyes could see gave them great pleasure. And it allowed them to talk - to converse about things. The strange Goblin engineer who had never been biological in his entire existence, and the wayward Goblin who had once been Human. There was absolutely no rational reason for them to have anything in common, and yet they did. Perhaps because both had been warriors in their previous lives, and both had lost everything.

Nemo had been present when Stree Prime was destroyed. He had seen the three impactors come in from the outer system, each of them piloted by a copy of Rauti, two of them smashing into the planet, rendering it a molten hell for the billions of Stree that lived there. He had been acting as Tactical Officer of the *Armidale* when they killed the third copy of Rauti, deflecting the last impactor into a harmless glance through the planet's atmosphere, in the hopes it might save some Stree still left alive on their planet.

Nemo told all this to Rauti, who laughed.

"So in effect, you killed me," he said. "The third copy I sent to Stree Prime."

Nemo gave a slight lift of his right front leg in

acknowledgment.

"It would seem so," he agreed. "But we felt we had no choice at the time."

"Well, I hope I died a good death."

"It was quick, if that makes you feel any better."

"I put two of them on target?"

"Yes. You thoroughly destroyed Stree Prime. And caused them to blame the Goblins and Humans for it. Hence they hate us across the Arm."

"Ah, that. Yes, I'm sorry for that. If there was some way I could correct the misunderstanding, I would."

"You could go to Aslar and tell the Stree it was all your plan, and we had nothing to do with it."

"Oh, that would work. Sure. No problem."

Nemo smiled internally, where it couldn't be seen. "Of course, they wouldn't believe you either, any more than they believe us. Acknowledging the facts would prevent them from fulfilling their great crusade to wipe Goblins from the Galaxy. I think that's all they live for anymore - hating Goblins and Humans."

With a snap, Banjala appeared before them. Nemo stared at the Transcend in some surprise. "I have no lesson today, Banjala," he said.

Banjala spoke. There was sadness in his voice. "It is ironic that you have been speaking about the Stree and their crusade to rid the galaxy of Goblins. It seems they have not yet laid down their crusade against the Humans, either."

A bad feeling started across Nemo's brain. "What do you mean?"

"The Stree have joined forces with the Singheko. They have assembled a battle fleet to attack Phoenix. They intend to resume their holy war to wipe Humans from the Universe."

TWELVE

Sol System - Venus

"The Stree have joined with the Singheko. They have assembled a battle fleet to attack Phoenix. They intend to resume their holy war to wipe Humans from the Universe."

Banjala's words rang in Nemo's ears.

Not again, was his next thought. *Not another war!*

But he knew in his heart it was true. Somehow, he had always known the Stree would never give up. The bitterness of losing their home world in the Stree War was a taste they couldn't put away.

Nemo looked at Banjala, floating in the air in front of him. For a moment, nobody said anything. Then, before he could ask the obvious question, Rauti beat him to it.

"When?"

Banjala smiled with his pseudo-face. "Three months from now. And the small fleet at Phoenix will have no chance against the Stree. It is a foregone conclusion. The Humans will lose this war - if they fight alone."

There was a moment of silence. Nemo's thoughts were a whirling mixture of anger and shock.

"What do you mean - 'if they fight alone'? Who would fight with the Humans? The Goblins are gone, scattered to the winds. Who else would join with them? Will you?"

"No," stated Banjala flatly. "We do not get involved in the wars of bios or androids. We are beyond that."

"Then who? Who were you hinting at?" exploded Nemo, now definitely losing his temper. Rauti lifted two caterpillar legs and touched Nemo on the shoulder, calming him. In a more reasonable voice, Nemo continued. "Who would ally with the Humans against the Stree?"

"Only you two, perhaps. But that might be enough."

Both Nemo and Rauti were stunned by the words.

"What are you talking about?" said both at the same time.

"No Transcend will join you in this fight. But that doesn't mean I can't give you advice…"

"What?" asked Nemo and Rauti simultaneously.

"You must recognize that you are both fearsome warriors. Even though you are only two, together you have the possibility to change the destiny of the Humans."

Rauti was silent. But Nemo was not. He spoke quickly. "I will not help them. They abandoned me, left me to rot. They are on their own."

Banjala seemed to quiver, a motion that Nemo had learned over the months was a sign of disapproval. "That is your choice as an independent being," Banjala finally said.

Rauti intervened. "At least, you can send a warning to Phoenix. Let them know what's coming."

Nemo nodded. "I can do that. It's easy enough. But I will not help the Humans. They used me, then cast me aside. They can fight their own war."

Netaz System

Hours later, slowly, Rita returned to consciousness. At first, all she could see was a bit of lighter color in the dark. Then, bit by bit, her vision cleared.

She realized she was gravely injured. She had made it to the mausoleum by the skin of her teeth. Her internal maintenance systems were afire with red light warnings. Everything in her core was damaged to some extent. She realized she didn't have enough internal resources to repair herself. Even with her reactor intact, she had to have additional raw materials.

And that was why she had set up this safe house. There

were five crypts inside, each of a size to hold one Human body. One of them was occupied already; three were empty. The last one held supplies.

Rita dragged herself across the stone floor to the rearmost crypt. It was all she could do to push the stone lid back a few inches, until she could reach a hand in. She felt around for the bag. She knew it was there - she had checked it two years ago.

Finding it at last, she pulled it out. It was heavy, and caught on the edge, and she had to fight a bit to get it to release. Finally, she got it over the stone lip of the crypt, and let it fall down beside her. With the last strength in her body, she pulled out the canister inside.

Opening it, she rolled on her back and poured a black, oily liquid over the gaping hole in her core where the Vampire had shot her. The goop oozed down into the hole, and billions of nanobots started repairing the wound. It wasn't enough material to bring her back to normal. But she hoped it would be enough to repair the worst of the damage. Enough to survive.

Then she passed out again.

Donkey - Arriving Netaz

It had been five days since Gast had released Gen from her bindings. Five long days of nothing to do. Except run through backup passwords in her mind, sending them to *Donkey*, getting rejected over and over and over again. Her brain reeled from the thousands of times she heard *Donkey* tell her she had failed again.

<Incorrect>
<Incorrect>
<Incorrect>

It was maddening. She knew the backup password had to be something simple. Something that her father, her mother and she might know.

Nemo would definitely make it something like that, because he wouldn't know who would be trying to use it. It would most likely be me...but it could be Rita. It could even be Bonnie. After all, they were lovers before he married Rita. So...it should be a password that all three of us would know.

Gen sighed. She had to take a break. She didn't know how many passwords she had gone through, but it felt like the entire English language.

She had also made an excursion into Nidarian. She knew both Rita and Bonnie had been fluent in Nidarian. She didn't know if Jim had been any good in that language or not, but she tried it anyway. She knew only a few dozen words, but she tried them all.

Nothing worked.

She tried the meager vocabulary she could remember from Singheko, Bagrami, Taegu, even Jatra.

Nothing.

Going back to English, she ran down the name of everyone she had ever heard of from the Singheko War - every admiral, every captain, every ship name, every planet, every moon, every battle.

<Incorrect>

Suddenly she felt the tDrive stop. With a slight bump, they came back into three-space. The system engine started up.

We're back in a system.

There was a click. It sounded like the hatch had been unlocked.

Surprised, Gen got up and went to the hatch. It opened. She went out into the corridor. Behind her, she heard the hatch to the cabin next door open. Marta came out, rubbing her eyes.

"Oh, thank God!" Gen spoke, rushing to Marta and taking her in her arms, hugging her for all she was worth. "Are you OK?"

Marta nodded. "I'm fine. They didn't do anything to me. It was all a bluff."

Gen shook her head. "I'm not so sure it was a bluff, but I'll take it anyway."

"Why do you think they let us out?"

"Because there's nothing you can do to harm us at this point," came a voice from the galley. Mario's head poked out of the hatch twenty feet farther down the corridor. He winked at them.

"Come have breakfast," he said.

Gen and Marta shuffled down the corridor and into the galley. Mario was sitting at the crew table, with eggs and bacon and *bishat* in front of him. At the far end of the table, the Vampire sat, a pulse pistol conspicuously laid on the table before him.

Mario motioned to two empty chairs.

"Eggs and bacon OK?" he smiled. As the two girls sat down in astonishment, Mario got up, went to the stove, and brought back two plates. Each plate contained two eggs and three strips of bacon. Laying them before the women, he went back, fetched the coffeepot, and poured *bishat* for each of them.

"Now, don't get any ideas," he said as he returned the pot. "You are still my prisoners, and you will still take orders. Instantly, I might add. Or I'll turn you over to Gast here, and he'll provide a little incentive for you. Are we clear about that?"

Marta and Gen glared at him without responding. Mario shrugged. "I'll take silence as assent. So...we're approaching a system called Netaz. I have a special goal in mind here, and you're going to help me. Do you understand?"

"And if we don't?" asked Gen.

Mario smiled coldly. He tilted his head toward Gast, who had taken out his knife and was sharpening it on a whetstone. The Vampire opened his mouth in something that was probably intended as a smile, but merely showed his fangs to good effect. A cold chill ran through Gen.

"Get the message?" Mario continued. With no response, he plowed on. "When we land, Gen and I are going to take a little trip. Just the two of us. Marta will stay here with Gast."

Mario saw the little shudder run down Marta's back and chuckled. "Not to worry, Marta. As long as Gen does what she's told, you'll come to no harm."

Marta looked over at Gen. "That's what worries me. She never does what she's told," Marta muttered.

Mario winked at Gen. "I think she will this time. Knowing you are back here with Gast and knowing what Gast likes to do to Human females."

Gen bobbed her head. "Whatever you say." She glanced once at Marta. "Don't sweat it, Mart. I'll do whatever." Turning back to Mario, she continued. "What do you want me to do?"

"Nothing much," said Mario. "Take a ride out to the country with me. Visit a cemetery. Open a mausoleum."

THIRTEEN

Netaz System

Rita woke again. She was still lying on the floor of the mausoleum. However, the nanobots were doing their work. The warning noises in her monitor system had reduced. What had once been a brilliant glare of red in the periphery of her vision - where her status indicators lived- was now down to just a few damaged systems.

She would live. She was far from whole - she would require a lot of additional work before she could say that - but she was 70% functional again.

Slowly, with great pain, she reached out to the empty crypt next to her and pulled herself up to a sitting position. Staying there for a while, she tried to gather her wits.

I remember getting shot by the Jatra at the train station. I don't remember much after that. Somehow, I made it here. Not sure how.

With a grunt, Rita made it to her knees, then shakily stood up. She swayed, almost falling, but managed to catch herself. Her systems were thoroughly screwed up, that was for sure.

Turning, she looked at the only crypt in the mausoleum which contained a body.

Ah...that's right. That's why I came to Netaz. I wanted to see him one more time before I head for the Wave.

Slowly, carefully, Rita bent down and pushed the stone lid off the occupied crypt, moving it so she could see inside. When she had pushed it far enough, she stopped and sat back, staring at the contents.

Inside were the broken remains of a Goblin. He had been shot to hell. The entire back of the skull was gone, leaving only a face that still looked remarkably Human. The head was sitting on a small pillow, which held it up to make it look somewhat normal. The rest of the body was pretty much a destroyed mess of metal, wires, electronics, desiccated pseudo-skin, and what was left of a fibermat skeleton. Whatever had happened to this Goblin had been enough to end his life forever.

In a terrible flashback, Rita remembered the day. It was well after the Stree War. They had been with Rachel and Ollie, with Luda and Liwa, on a Stree corvette they had "liberated' at Aslar as they were making their final escape from there. The stolen Stree corvette that Jim had renamed *Bear*, of course.

Rita had to smile at that - no matter where they were, no matter what the situation, Jim Carter always had to tell the story of the bear that almost killed him. The bear that had started the whole thing, he would say. The bear that chased him into the sentient starship *Jade* in the Canadian Northwest Territory, leading to the Singheko War and everything that came after.

That damn grizzly bear.

They had been at loose ends, not sure what to do. Even though the war was over, the Stree had put huge bounties on all of them. Every bounty hunter in the Arm was looking for them. There was no safe place to go.

After much discussion, they decided to search for Acadia. It was a place more myth and rumor than fact, but Jim had believed it. Supposedly, just before the Stree destroyed the Dyson Swarm of the Goblin homeland, the Goblins had sent off one ship, carrying thousands of their young, to try and save a remnant of their civilization. Nobody knew where they had gone; only that they disappeared into the Core, to a place far beyond the reach of any species in the Arm.

Acadia. The new homeland of the Goblins. If they could find it.

So they had set out, heading toward the Core, with the intent of finding the Goblin remnant and living with them forever.

It hadn't worked out that way. They needed to stop for reaction catalyst at least one more time before they left the Arm for good. They made the mistake of stopping at Niasa, thinking no one would notice them in that bustling, always busy system.

They were wrong. They hadn't been on the station more than a couple of hours before they were attacked by a large gang of bounty hunters. A dozen Jatra, Singheko and Tekhelon chased them through the station, firing indiscriminately, killing innocent bystanders without a second thought in their zeal to collect the billions of creds in bounty. They had been cornered, far from the docks and their own ship. Jim and Rita had broken away from the others, knowing the hunters would chase them, giving their friends a chance to escape.

It had worked; Rachel, Ollie, Luda and Liwa had made it back to the ship. And because Jim knew Rachel and Ollie would never voluntarily leave himself and Rita in the lurch, he remotely triggered the ship to depart the station at 300g, putting his friends safely beyond reach of their pursuers.

But Jim had not survived. As he and Rita reached the docks and tried to steal a small shuttle, the hunters had shot him down, so many pulse rifle hits tearing into him, there was no hope of saving him. Dragging his remains onto the shuttle, Rita had blasted away from Niasa, spending the next two months dodging the relentless bounty hunters amongst the rocks and debris of a large asteroid belt in the system. Somehow, against all odds, she had escaped them.

But Jim was gone. Nothing she could do could bring him back. The pulse rifle fire had taken out both his main AI and his backup.

Now, back in the mausoleum, Rita smiled sadly at the remains in the crypt.

They'll never get you, my love. I'll make sure of that.

Then, with tears forming in her eyes, Rita leaned over and kissed the battered face of the dead Goblin.

Phoenix System

Lord Admiral Bonnie Page stared at the transcript of the ansible message she had just received.

It was hard to believe, but she had no choice. She had to believe it.

It was an old code they had used before - her and her former lover - starting a message with a couple of things that only a few people in the universe knew.

You screamed for joy going over the top of the loop. I was nearly deaf.

Bonnie read the words again, knowing who had sent them. It was the day she first met Jim Carter. He had checked her out in a P-51 Mustang, the old World War Two airplane he kept in the big white hanger at Deseret Airport in western Nevada. And the message was correct - as she took the roaring old warbird over the top of her third loop, she had screamed in delight, nearly deafening him over the intercom.

She re-read the message again, the horror rising up in her as she realized the full implications.

Bonnie - they are coming again. The Stree and the Singheko. Together. They've formed a secret alliance. They will be on their way in a matter of three or so months. Do what you can to prepare. Nemo.

Tatiana Powell marched into Bonnie's office, plopped down in a visitor's chair, and waved her copy of the message in the air.

"I take it from your expression this is the real thing?" she asked.

"Yep," Bonnie grimaced. "It's real."

"OK, then," Tatiana shook her head in dismay. "We get ready, we do what we can. We work to our strengths - you take space, I'll focus on preparations for ground defense."

Bonnie looked up at her, the pain in her eyes radiating across the desk. She saw a woman looking back at her with an equal amount of barely hidden pain. Both knew the raw truth. Phoenix was a small colony. They could not hold against a combined attack by the Stree and the Singheko together. It was a foregone conclusion.

"Yes," whispered Bonnie. "We'll do what we can."

FOURTEEN

Phoenix System

Fearless, Luke Powell took a step to the edge.

"You are too damned old for this, and you know it," he said to his wife. "I can't believe you accepted this!"

Bonnie glared at her husband across her desk. "You're calling me old? You better have your cast-iron underwear on, bub, because you're about to need it!"

Luke barreled on into the abyss. "Yes. You're too old for this. Being in charge of space defense for a war - you should hand this over to someone younger!"

"Like who?" spat Bonnie.

Sitting across from Bonnie in her office, Luke mulled that for a moment. Bonnie laughed. "Just as I thought. You can't come up with a single name that would be more qualified for the job."

"Well..." Luke continued. "How about Misha? He's pretty damn good. And a senior Captain."

"Funny you should say that. I asked Misha if he would come on board my staff. He refused. He said he would rather fight in space as captain of his ship, than sit on the ground watching a holo and praying."

"Well, the...dammit....at least, get some good young people in here to help you. Don't try to do this job alone!"

Bonnie sniffed. "Preaching to the choir, bud. I've already recruited a half-dozen folks to augment my permanent staff. And most of them are young fire-eaters, so you are worryin' over nothing. I'll have the best advice on the planet at my elbow whenever I need it."

"Just be careful, my love. I know you all too well. If you get a chance, you'll be up in space with the fleet, fighting with them. And we don't need that now. We need you here on the ground, controlling the battle from Headquarters. Promise me that, OK?"

"No," Bonnie sighed. "I will not promise. I have to be wherever the job takes me, Luke. You know that."

Luke heaved a huge sigh, shaking his head in resignation. "Yes, babe. I know."

"So. Since you're here," said Bonnie, then paused.

Bonnie leaned forward over the desk, lowering her voice to make sure it didn't carry outside the office.

"I want to talk to you about something else. The reality of our situation."

Luke nodded. "I know. The elephant in the room. The thing nobody wants to talk about."

"Yes," agreed Bonnie. "Our latest intel says the Stree have managed to scrape together thirty-five warships, and the Singheko have added another ten, plus five troopships. That's at least fifty warships they'll be bringing at us. Against our Home Guard of twelve, plus whatever transports we can scrape together and arm. We'll do the best we can, of course. I know my people. They'll fight to the bitter end. I can predict with some confidence that my folks will take out at least 2-to-1, maybe 3-to-1 against the Stree. But even in the best case, that still leaves some enemy warships that will break through. And those will stand off and bombard Landing City into splinters. And then the Singheko will come down and assault us on the ground. You know how much those damn Lions like fighting in person."

Luke's expression was grim. "You're telling me we have no chance at all."

Bonnie nodded. "Unless we find allies, we have no chance at all."

"And how's that coming?"

"It's not. I've sent messages to a half-dozen species asking for any help they might provide. All have refused. They say we Humans started the Stree War when we enlisted help from the Goblins, and also that we are responsible for the destruction of Stree Prime. So we have to suffer the consequences. Nobody has signed up to help us."

"We had nothing to do with the destruction of Stree Prime!" complained Luke. "That was that crazy bastard Rauti! He did that on his own!"

"Tell it to the judge," Bonnie said, shaking her head. "Nobody out there believes that. They all point the finger at us. After all, Rauti launched from Venus - a planet in our home system. And the *Armidale* was right there when the impactors hit the planet. The Stree have spun a story since that day that we were directing Rauti, egging him on. We're never going to overcome that propaganda."

"Don't we have the onboard tapes from *Armidale*?"

"Yeah. And we've given them to everybody, and everybody ignores them, claims they're fabricated. The Stree have an excellent propaganda machine in place."

"So no help coming," Luke said flatly.

"No help," agreed Bonnie. "Right now, we stand on our own. I haven't given up, though. I'll keep trying, right to the bitter end. But realistically, Luke..."

"You're saying Humans are headed for extinction."

Bonnie nodded. "Unless we do something else. A contingency plan."

"What did you have in mind?"

Bonnie was keeping her voice low. "We think we've found a place on Earth that's clean enough to start re-populating. In fact, we could put a small party down there anytime and let them begin preparing a place."

"Ah. So you want to send that small party now, have them get started. That way..."

"Yeah. That way, if we get wiped out here, there'll still be a small contingent on Earth to carry on the species."

"Won't the Stree wipe them out too?"

"I think we can hide them. It's an old underground city in central Turkey - Cappadocia. It dates from ancient times. It's called Derinkuyu, and it would be nearly impossible to image down into it from space. We could put an advance party down there to get started on things. I don't think the Stree could find them for a long time. We don't have to tell our people the full story; we just tell them we're starting the prep for Humans to return to Earth."

"How many do you want to send?"

Bonnie leaned back in her chair and rubbed her nose. "I think about four hundred. Our best and brightest young people."

"That's going to take a big hit out of our defense forces."

Bonnie shrugged. "Can't be helped. We're gonna lose them anyway, one way or another. Better to let them have a small chance on Earth, than no chance here."

There was a silence as Luke thought about the ramifications of Bonnie's statement. Finally, he nodded.

"I guess I agree. And of course, you're telling me this because you want me to run the project?"

"Please. I don't have the time to do it, plus I would be heavily biased to hang on to my best people. I'd rather you take it and run with it if you don't mind."

"OK. We'll need to get Mark's blessing. He's not going to be happy about giving up four hundred of our best."

"It may be our only chance to continue the species," Bonnie replied.

Luke smiled at her. "Do you have someone in mind to lead the group?"

"Garyn Rennari."

"Ouch. My head of security? You really know how to hurt a guy!"

"You and I both know he's the best for the job."

"Well, yes. I agree. But that really kneecaps my staff right at the moment of crisis."

"You'd rather he dies in the bombardment after the Stree break through? Or gets killed by the Lions when they bring their assault shuttles down?"

"Ah. Well," Luke shrugged. "Since you put it that way. But I'll have to tell him it's an order. He'll never leave otherwise."

Netaz System

At the Netaz City spaceport, Mario forced Gen to exit *Donkey* with him, leaving Marta behind with the Vampire. Gen kissed Marta goodbye, gave her a final hug, and told her they would be back soon. Then Gast took Marta back to her cabin and locked her in.

Gen followed Mario across the tarmac to the terminal, and then to the train station across the street. She followed his lead as he led them on a train to city center. There, they changed to an express which whisked them out of the city.

Throughout the ride, Gen kept thinking about jumping Mario; she was sure she could overpower him. Tatiana, Marta's mother, had spent days on end with them when they were teens, teaching them a hundred tricks to defeat an enemy in hand-to-hand combat.

But she didn't see how that would help. Marta would still be a prisoner of the Vampire. Gen would have no way to get back into the ship to rescue her. And Mario had made one thing clear - if Gen called the authorities for help, or if he didn't return in six hours, Gast would launch in *Donkey* and take Marta with him. And Marta would never be seen again.

At least, not alive.

In a matter of minutes, they were at a small country station. Mario led them off the train and around to the back. Across the street was a country cemetery, with gravestones of every size and shape evident. In the far back were a number of mausoleums.

As they walked under the archway into the cemetery, Mario waxed eloquent.

"The Netaz are remarkably like Humans in many ways. Including the way they bury their dead. And they use mausoleums for the wealthy. Just like Humans."

Gen walked silently. She was still thinking about jumping Mario, overpowering him. She couldn't help it.

It would be so easy.

"I know what you're thinking, Imogen. But don't think it will help you. Gast knows his business. Any sign of trouble, and he launches. And Marta becomes his personal plaything. For as long as she lives, of course. Which probably won't be very long. Vampires tend to get impatient."

"You're bluffing," spat Gen.

"Maybe," Mario replied mildly. "But you don't really know. Are you willing to take that chance?"

Gen fell silent. They came up to a mausoleum near the back of the cemetery. On the front, beside the door, was a DNA pad - a lock that could only be triggered by a correct DNA match. Mario pointed to the DNA pad and smiled.

"Open it," he said.

FIFTEEN

Netaz System

Standing in front of the mausoleum in the back of the cemetery, Gen stared at Mario in astonishment.

"What makes you think I can open the damn thing?" asked Gen.

Mario smiled a Cheshire-cat smile. He was clearly enjoying every moment of this.

"Look at the inscription at the top," he replied.

Gen took a step back, so she could look up at the stone lintel at the top of the crypt.

"It's Netaz. I can't read that!"

"Oh, right. Let me translate it for you."

Mario stepped back, looking up at the inscription. He was stringing it out for all he was worth, making it a production.

"Semper Fidelis," he quoted.

Gen glared at him. "So what? I don't know what that means!"

Mario kept his smile, playing it out. "It means 'Always Faithful' in old Earth Latin."

"Great! A noble sentiment! So why the hell do you think I can open it, then?" spat Gen.

"Because," Mario said, milking the moment for all it was worth, "That's the motto of the old Earth U. S. Marine Corps. Does that give you any hint?"

Gen shook her head in frustration. "No."

Mario sighed. "Such a poor student of history. Well, Gen, I've spent the last two years trying to track down this crypt. I finally figured out where it was just a few weeks ago - and who could open it. That's you, my dear. And then you waltz right into Niasa, right up to me in the market. It was poetic! So just plop your hand up there and let's take a peek inside."

Gen balled up her fists, ready to hit him. It was all she could do to hold back her anger. Mario noticed it and gave her a negative head shake.

"Now, now. Think about Marta. Think about what happens if I don't come back in...let's see..."

Mario pretended to look at a non-existent watch. "...in another four hours." He looked up. "Marta goes off to Vampire land. Not for long, of course. Gast is so very impatient in these things."

Gen relaxed her fists and turned to the DNA pad. She prepared to put her hand on it. But then she turned, a burning question that had to be asked coming forth from her lips.

"Who's in here?" she asked.

"Your father," Mario smirked.

Venus

In the subsurface common room, Nemo was in a hybrid Human body again, as was Rauti. Nemo paced, as he tended to do in such times.

"You don't even know the Humans!" he exclaimed at Rauti, his temper fraying short. "You have no vested interest!"

Sitting at the galley table, Rauti gazed quietly at Nemo, his head tilted to one side. "I have more vested interest than you may realize, Nemo. Maybe I am a pure-bred Goblin; but that doesn't make me a machine. Those are your people out there. And they're going to die. Unless you help."

Nemo stopped his pacing to gaze stonily at Rauti. "Not my people, they're not. They copied me, let me do their dirty work, then abandoned me. I won't lift a finger to help Phoenix."

"From what you've told me, they didn't abandon you at all. Didn't you tell me it was your idea for them to drop you off at Stalingrad? And didn't you tell me they sent the *Armidale* to check on you every six months, until you left?"

Nemo rolled his eyes, turning away from Rauti. "OK, I may have said that."

Rauti continued. "That certainly doesn't seem like abandonment to me."

Nemo rounded on Rauti. "My wife. Gone. My daughter. Gone. Everything I cared about. Gone. They left me with nothing!"

Rauti looked at Nemo sadly. "They left you with the memories. They could have easily removed those. But you didn't ask them to do that, did you?"

Nemo glared at him.

"Because you wanted to keep those, didn't you?"

Abruptly, Nemo moved to the table, pulled out a chair, and sat down.

"That hurt," he said quietly.

Rauti shrugged. "Not trying to hurt you. Just trying to help you see the light."

After a bit, Nemo nodded. "I know in my heart you're right. I wanted to hang onto those memories, false though they might be. It was the only life I had. Even if I were not the actual physical being who experienced those events…that love…I couldn't let go of it."

"So you held on to it and just turned bitter."

Nemo looked up. "You know, that's almost exactly what Banjala says. He says the main thing holding me back is my bitterness. And he says, until I let go of that, there will be no more progress on the Path."

"So perhaps you should reconsider your decision not to help the Humans at Phoenix. That might go a long way toward removing some of your bitterness and resentment."

Nemo shook his head. "I just can't do it. It's like I'm on a road, and there's a huge boulder in my path. I can't get around it. What she did to me…"

As Nemo realized what he had said, he stopped speaking.

Rauti gazed at him knowingly.

"She?" he asked.

Nemo sat like a stone. After many seconds, he acknowledged the truth of what had just been said.

"She," he confirmed. "I guess I've known all along that Rita is the root of my anger. After all, she's the one who copied me. She's the one who left me behind. She had to know…"

In the silence that followed, Rauti spoke gently. "She had to know how much you loved her."

Nemo nodded. "Yes."

"But what choice did she have? Did she have anyone else she could count on to rescue Bonnie and the others?"

Nemo looked away, at the walls of the common room that he shared with Rauti. Today, the walls were configured to show scenes of Earth. Great sweeping vistas of the Himalayan mountains surrounded them, covered in snow, helping to belie they fact they were actually several hundred feet underground on a red-hot planet. On the side of a mountain directly in front of him, a snow leopard stalked its prey in the middle of a snowstorm. The walls were as realistic as if Nemo and Rauti were actually there, in that distant abandoned place, with animals that no longer existed.

"No," he answered at last. "There was no one else she could trust."

"And I will ask you another question, Nemo. Look back on your life. If you could make the choice today, would you return to Human form? Or remain Goblin?"

Nemo glared at Rauti. "Are you taking up philosophy now?"

Rauti waited silently, patiently, knowing that Nemo would eventually answer. After many seconds, the response came.

"Goblin," said Nemo shortly. "If you must know."

Now Rauti smiled, his slow nod at Nemo reinforcing his point.

"I think you have just demonstrated that - in exchange for saving Bonnie and your other friends - your lover Rita gave you the only gift she could give at the time. A life that could potentially lead you to a better place."

"It was not intended as a gift. It was just necessity."

"Yes. Necessity at the time. But a gift after that. And her clean break with you - do you not think that was a mercy? Do you not think she recognized that?"

"I don't know. She's a smart woman. Maybe...who knows?"

"I think you know, Nemo. I think you know as well as Rita did - it was the only way. A clean break, a complete break. The only thing that could save you both."

"I don't feel saved, Rauti. I feel betrayed."

"And thus you cannot transcend, I think. This is what holds you back."

Nemo looked up at him. "Then perhaps it is better to be a flawed Goblin than a perfect Transcend. Because I will never forget that betrayal."

Netaz System

Gen stood in front of the mausoleum, poised before the DNA pad, and looked at Mario in contempt.

"Bullshit," she said. "My father converted to Goblin. He doesn't have a biological body anymore. He wouldn't need a mausoleum."

"What better place to hide a Goblin body, then? Someplace no normal biological person would ever think to look. Open it," Mario said.

Gen was still in shock at Mario's announcement

My father? In here? It can't possibly be, she thought.

But...

It was like him, she realized. *Or more likely, something Rita dreamed up. Rita was the truly clever one, they said. That's how she ended up as an admiral during the Singheko War.*

Could it be possible? Could her father, Jim Carter, be inside this strange place? And if he was...

If he's in here, then he's dead.

Gen pressed her hand to the pad. There was a short

interval, then a loud click. The massive door to the crypt sprang slightly open, just enough for a crack of darkness to be seen inside.

Mario sprang forward, put his fingers into the crack, and pulled. The door was heavy, but it opened. As it came fully open, the light from behind them fell into the mausoleum. There were also skylights at the top of the structure, providing a dim but adequate illumination inside.

They could see five burial crypts inside, each large enough to hold a Human. Three of them were clearly empty, their unused lids standing upright, ready for use. The other two had lids over them, as if they contained a body.

Moving slowly, in wonderment at what she might find, Gen stepped into the mausoleum. She went to the first covered crypt and stood over it. She felt Mario behind her, but for this moment she ignored him.

This could be my father.

Squatting down, she pushed at the lid of the crypt. It was heavy, and she had to push harder to move it. It slid slowly, stone against stone, noisy. She got it pushed back far enough to see inside.

It was a Goblin. Something - a large pulse rifle, from the looks of it - had punched completely through the torso, leaving a hole the size of a dinner plate. His outer skin had shrunk, desiccated. Gen could see broken and smashed metal and composite components through holes in the skin. The back of the skull was blasted away, but the front was still mostly intact. And the face...

The face was recognizable.

It was Jim Carter. Gen knew it. Even with the battle damage, Gen recognized him. She had seen dozens of pictures of her father, both before he converted and after.

Her father was dead.

Mario began dancing behind her, gleeful in the success of his mission. As he danced around the mausoleum like a madman, a lone tear slid down Gen's cheek. Reaching out a hand, she touched the face of the dead Goblin. The skin was cold and artificial. But Goblin though he might be, and artificial though the skin was, it was as close as she had ever been to her father, and she cried.

Suddenly Mario grabbed her by the elbow and hauled her to her feet, pulling her back and away from the crypt. He pushed the stone lid back even farther and squatted, looking down at his prize. He reached out, touched the body of the Goblin almost reverently, then turned to Gen.

"Five hundred million creds! Even dead, that's what they'll pay! Five hundred million! Can you imagine? That much for a dead Goblin? It's crazy! I'm rich!"

Mario turned back to the crypt, gloating, his mind focused completely on his prize. It was suddenly too much for Gen. Before she could stop herself, she stepped forward and smashed both fists into the back of Mario's neck, dropping him to the floor unconscious.

SIXTEEN

Netaz System

The previous night, Rita had left the mausoleum and made her way back to the port, covered in her cloak and wearing her breather as a disguise. She got back to the spaceport around dusk. She slipped through the terminal and out on the apron, walking across the tarmac to her ship without incident. She boarded, sealed the hatch behind her, and with a sigh of relief slumped down at the galley table.

"*Jimmy Boy*, prepare to depart," she called to the ship.

<Preparing to depart>

Rita heard the various pumps and motors start whining as the ship's AI began preparing for departure. She rose, made a cup of *bishat*, and sat down again, drinking it slowly, thinking.

It was a tremendous mistake coming here. I don't know how, but they were waiting for me. Somehow, they knew I might come here.

Someone has got a line on me. I need to get completely off the beaten path.

Where is the absolute last place they would expect me to go?

Ah. Of course.

<Ready for departure>

"*Jimmy Boy*, set a course for Stalingrad. We'll go hide in the ruins of the Dyson Swarm for a while."

<Course set. Ready for departure>

"Launch approved, *Jimmy Boy*. Get us the hell out of here. We've got places to go and dead Goblins to see."

Six hours later, Rita stopped her accel and coasted toward

the mass limit of the system. Already moving at 21% of light, she would need no more accel; in fact, she would have to slow down before sinking out - it was not a good idea to enter a target system at that velocity. And especially not Stalingrad, where the entire system was filled with floating junk: debris and wrecked ships and smashed up Dyson panels, the bodies of dead Goblins - all left over from the Battle of Stalingrad twenty-one years earlier. No one had cleaned up the system; there were no Goblins left who could do it, and certainly no bio species had an interest in it.

No, it would not be good at all to go slamming into that system at speed. Best to creep in with just enough velocity to get your bearings and map out a path to a safe place. Find a place to hide.

As she coasted toward the mass limit, she turned the problem over in her mind.

They tracked me to Kaeru. Then they tracked me to Netaz, even after I changed ships. How are they doing it? Did they just get lucky? Or have they managed somehow to get a tracker on me?

Abruptly, she rose and walked down the short corridor to the third hatch and entered the medical bay. There were two med pods there. Moving to one, she stripped off her clothing, opened the lid, and climbed in. Closing the lid, she sent a silent command to the ship.

Jimmy Boy, finish repairing everything else in my body that still needs attention. And while you're doing it, scan everything in my body. Look for any kind of tracker.

<Wilco. Repairing. Scanning>

Rita lay still, allowing the ship's AI to work. She knew it would take a while, so she let her mind drift.

This feels like the first time I was in a med pod. When I was cloned. I remember only the end part of that - when I came to consciousness. And Jade *was there. I thought she was my friend. And then Jim and Bonnie came. And I had a family. Or so I thought - until Bonnie corrected me. And then Jim...God, I loved that man.*

Dreaming about her lost husband, Rita drifted off to sleep.

Netaz System

Gen stared at Mario lying on the floor where she had knocked him out cold.

That was a bad, bad mistake. I let my temper get the better of me. Now Marta is in danger because of my stupidity. I guess I'd better let him wake up and take my punishment, whatever it is. Otherwise, Marta will be hurt.

With a sigh, Gen looked around the mausoleum. There was her father's crypt, with the stone lid pushed half-way out of place. Then there were the three empty crypts, each with a stone lid inside, leaning against the wall, ready for future use.

And in the rear of the mausoleum was a fifth crypt, covered. Curious, she walked over to it and pushed the stone lid aside. The light from the skylights in the top of the mausoleum was dim, but there was enough for her to see. It was some kind of supply cache. There were a number of containers, all of them marked in a strange language she couldn't understand. There were also three military-looking backpacks.

And on top of the cache of items was an envelope, with her name written on top of it.

GEN

Staring at it in amazement, Gen reached in slowly and took the envelope. She opened it and pulled out a letter. After reading the first few lines, she realized what it was, and sat down on the edge of the crypt in shock. Starting over from the top, she read the entire letter through.

Dear Gen,

If you read this, then somehow you made it here and found the mausoleum. I've left a few clues here and there that only you should be able to decipher - at least, I hope no one else figures them out. You are probably an adult now. I hope you are well and enjoying life.

You may hate me for leaving you when you were only three years old. But I hope you may be able to understand. Every hand was turned against us. Your father and I were hunted like animals. The Humans at Phoenix refused to let us stay there - they said we would bring too much danger to them. They forced us to leave. Earth was still too dangerous for life, even Goblin life. We had no place to go. We knew that we would be hounded and chased for the rest of our lives. That was not a life I could wish upon you as a baby, no matter how much I loved you.

And I knew that Mark and Gillian would be good parents for you. Gillian is a wonderful person. I know she was a good mother to you; I didn't have to be there to know that. And Mark has always been a rock for everyone around him.

So if you hate me, that's OK. I did the best I could to start you off in life the right way, with all the advantages Phoenix could muster to keep you safe.

Your father Jim was killed about nineteen years ago. I put him here in my safe house. I lost track of Ollie and Rachel and the others; so I've been alone since then. Sometimes I settle down on a planet for a while. But eventually they always find me, and I have to run again. It's not a life you'd like, and I can't come see you because it would only put you in danger.

I hope you find this letter someday. I hope you don't hate me for what I chose for you. And I hope that somehow, someday, I can see you again.

Your mother,
Rita

P. S. the N-number of Jim's old Mustang is my ansible address.

In total shock, Gen read the letter again. As the words sank into her, tears coursed down her cheeks. She wiped them away with her sleeve. Reading the letter one last time, she wiped her eyes, and bowed her head.

My mother loved me. She did love me. But she had no choice. I can understand that. I guess I always understood it; but I didn't want to accept it. Maybe now I can.

Beside her on the floor, Mario stirred. Quickly, Gen folded the letter and slid it into her boot, hiding it. She stood and moved away from Mario as he began to regain consciousness. He raised his head and looked around, realized where he was, and pushed himself to his feet. Standing unsteadily, he turned to Gen, staring at her as she stood by the crypt. Brushing himself off, he finally spoke.

"So you just couldn't contain yourself...you had to go there!"

"Sorry," said Gen. "I just lost it for a second. It won't happen again."

"Damn right it won't." said Mario. He pulled a stunner out of his pocket. "Damn right it won't."

SEVENTEEN

Packet Boat *Donkey*

A small spot of light pierced Gen's consciousness. Her head hurt. She was in the dark, and her hands were tied behind her back - again.

A coherent thought tried to make its way through her brain, but there was resistance. Finally, it surfaced as her brain began to function again.

Oh, right. That rat-bastard stunned me.

With a grunt, she turned her head to look at the pinpoint of light in the darkness. Realization dawned on her as she recognized the standard smoke alarm LED in *Donkey*'s cabin.

I'm back on Donkey. *Tied up again. In one of the empty cabins.*

The hatch swung outward, and Gen squinted in the brightness as someone entered the room.

Mario.

"Well, Princess, the AI said you were coming around. Got a bit of a headache, have we?"

"Go to hell," Gen managed to grunt.

"Now, now," Mario cautioned. "Remember - you're the one who came up behind me and knocked me on my ass. You started this."

Gen had a response at the top of her tongue - one that would only anger him. She forced herself to suppress it. She and Marta were still his prisoners - it just wouldn't pay to antagonize him.

"As I said, my emotions got the better of me," she said at last.

"Well," Mario replied. "If I take off those bindings, do you think you can be civilized?"

"Yes," Gen grunted reluctantly.

Mario grinned, came over, turned her over roughly so he could access her back, and began removing the bindings that bound her.

"Where are we headed?" Gen asked as he worked. She could hear the system drive, so she knew they were leaving the system.

"Aslar," Mario said proudly. "Home of the Stree."

An involuntary shudder racked Gen.

The Stree. They'll use me to blackmail my mother into surrendering. Then they'll kill us both. And Marta too.

"And I know what you're thinking," said Mario. "But I won't let the Stree hurt you. I have other plans for you."

Phoenix System

"Good luck to you, Garyn," said Minister of Defense Tatiana Powell, shaking the hand of Expedition Commander Garyn Rennari. "Our future is in your hands."

"No pressure, then," smiled Garyn.

Tatiana smiled with him. "No pressure."

Garyn stepped back, came to a stiff attention, and saluted crisply. Then he turned and stepped away, moving to the hatch of the shuttle behind him. The so-called Earth Recovery Expedition was on its way.

Lord Admiral Bonnie Page glanced at Tatiana. Silently, she held up her right hand so Tatiana could see it.

Her fingers were crossed.

"Exactly," responded Tatiana. "But if anyone can do it, Garyn can."

"Yes," said Luke from the other side. "And thanks for taking away my best commander."

"Can't be helped," Tatiana said. "And besides - this was your idea, remember?"

"No, this was Bonnie's idea!" countered Luke. "I just did the dirty work!"

"Yes," sighed Bonnie. "Guilty as charged. Well, we'd better move back to the terminal. They'll be departing in a few minutes."

Nodding, Tatiana turned. The three of them started walking toward the passenger terminal at Phoenix Spaceport, followed by a small crowd of staff and friends.

As they walked, Bonnie couldn't help but think about what they were doing.

The Earth Recovery Expedition. A euphemistic name, for sure. Put a group of young, capable Humans in a safe place on Earth - just before the Stree show up to destroy Phoenix. It doesn't take a rocket scientist to see through that ploy.

Luke, managing the expedition, had selected well. He had assembled four hundred of their best and brightest, all willing and able to take on the mission. There were two hundred doctors, nurses, teachers, scientists, and other well-trained professionals. And two hundred militia, well-armed and ready to defend. The expedition would land at an ancient underground city in Turkey known as Derinkuyu. The location - right in the middle of Turkey, in the area called Cappadocia - had received a minimal amount of radiation and biopoisons in the Stree War. And the underground city would protect them from the prying eyes of the Stree. Food would be a problem; but they were taking enough for two years. After that, they would take the chance of planting crops, living outside for survival.

It was a chance that had to be taken. Tatiana and Bonnie were realists. They knew Phoenix had little chance against the combined forces of the Stree and the Singheko. The Expedition was their ace in the hole. A way for Humans to once again survive the onslaught of their enemies.

With a shudder, Bonnie tried to shake off the dark thoughts that occupied her mind. She had fallen slightly behind Tatiana as they walked, so she took a quick step to catch up.

"Anything from Gen and Marta?" she asked.

"No," replied Tatiana somewhat bitterly. "Not a thing. They've gone dark."

"How about the tracker we put on *Donkey*?"

"Nothing since the day after they docked at Niasa. Looks like they found it and disabled it. God, if I had known they were going to that hellhole…"

"They have to live their life, Tat. You know that."

Tatiana heaved a deep sigh. "You keep telling me that. But it's hard to do when it's your daughter."

Bonnie nodded silently, then spoke again. "I know. But we have to hope that whatever trouble they've gotten themselves into, they can get themselves out. They're young, resourceful, well-trained. Hope for the best!"

"Yep. I'll try," Tatiana said as she entered the terminal. Walking across the lobby, she paused momentarily and turned to Bonnie. "Should we change our mind on helping them? Should we give them Rita's ansible address after all? Then they could contact her directly…"

"No, I'm still against it. It's much better if they just flounder around out there for a few months and give up. Then maybe they'll come home. And every time someone uses that ansible address, it increases the chance of trouble."

Tatiana considered it, then nodded. "OK. I guess I still agree with you. On to other subjects. Where do we stand on space defense?"

"As bad as we suspected. We're putting pulse cannon on old freighters, but they're about as maneuverable as an asteroid."

"So what's our count now?"

"Fourteen ships," Bonnie replied, bitterness and frustration in her voice. "Three cruisers, nine destroyers, and two transports converted to gunboats. We've got one more transport being converted. If we have enough time."

"A pitiful showing compared to our glory days, eh?" Tatiana laughed, trying to lighten the mood. She glanced back at her staff, out of earshot behind them. "Let's not discourage the rest of them too much."

"Roger that. But you and I both know we're pissing in the wind. Fourteen or fifteen ships going up against fifty or so, and some of ours just converted transports with green crews - it's going to be grim."

"Miracles have happened," said Tatiana. "We do all we can do. We fight until we can't fight anymore."

Suddenly Bonnie's aide James MacArthur ran up beside her, pressing a tablet into her hand. Bonnie scanned the message, then grunted.

"Early warning system has something coming on a vector from Aslar," Bonnie spoke. "Subspace pulses indicate eight to twelve ships, possibly destroyer class."

"Misha said they'd do a small raid first, to test our defenses," opined Tatiana. "Sounds like maybe he was right. What's the ETA?"

"Forty-eight hours."

Rita - In the Black

With a loud beep, the med pod completed its scan, waking Rita from her dreams.

<Final repairs completed. Scan completed. Nothing found> reported the AI. <No trackers in your body>

As Rita lifted the lid of the med pod to exit, it caused a flashback to her birth. When Jim helped her out of the med pod on *Jade* for the first time. When Bonnie, suspicious of her, asked Jim if a clone was really Human...

"...how do you know she has a soul?" Bonnie had asked, not realizing that Rita could still hear them from the galley.

Smiling, she remembered Jim's reply.

"How do you know you have a soul, Bonnie?" he had asked. "You can't prove it. All you can do is either believe it or not believe it. But you can never prove it. And you can't go through life making decisions for other people on such an imprecise, unknown state of

affairs. So in Rita's case, I'm going to act as if she is just like us. No different from us."

Rita started dressing, slowly, still thinking about the past. Thinking about...

All I've lost. Jim. Rachel. Ollie, Luda, Liwa, Tika. All the thousands I led, killed at Singheko and Dekanna and Stree. All lost.

Something - she wasn't sure what - triggered another memory in her. But it wasn't one of her memories. It was one of Bonnie's memories, one of the memories she had inherited, when she was cloned by the renegade starship *Jade* to have two sets of memories: one set from Jim, and one set from Bonnie.

And for a moment, she wasn't Rita anymore. She was Bonnie, remembering the first time with Jim - when Bonnie had found him at Deseret...

The sun came blasting through the east window of Jim's bedroom. Bonnie lay in the tangled sheets, opening one eye but shutting it quickly. After several minutes of trying to ignore it, she sat up, gave the sun the finger, and got out of bed. She went to the bathroom, took a long shower, put her shirt on and walked into the kitchen.

Jim was standing at the stove, fully dressed in Western snap shirt and jeans, cooking. He turned to her.

"Good morning, flygirl. Don't they make you get up early in the Air Force?"

"Not after night maneuvers," said Bonnie. She glanced at the clock on the wall. "Crap! It's only 9 AM! What the hell's the matter with you?"

"I was hungry," said Jim. "After all, I worked pretty hard last night."

Bonnie smiled. "You did that, flyboy. No complaints in that department. You passed inspection."

Jim slid a plate of ham and eggs in front of her, along with a saucer containing two pieces of buttered toast. Then he put a cup of hot coffee beside it and pointed to the cream already on the table.

Bonnie groaned. "Oh my God, thank you! I could eat a small horse!"

Jim sat down across from her with an identical plate. They tucked in and were silent for a bit.

Jim couldn't help but glance at the beautiful woman across from him as he ate. She was without a doubt the most beautiful woman he had seen in a long time. Blond, short military style haircut, green eyes. Tall. Intelligent face, a smile on her lips at the slightest excuse. She caught him looking and grinned at him. Embarrassed, he grinned back and then focused on his meal.

After a couple of minutes, Jim looked back at her.

"I thought maybe two more hours in the Mustang this morning while it's cool, then I'll sign you off for solo and you can go play for a while on your own. What do you think?"

Bonnie gazed at him in delight. "You are pretty good at this courtship thing, you know."

With a start, Rita shook it off.

I'm not Bonnie! I'm Rita, dammit! That's a false memory!

Angry, frustrated, she turned to head back to the galley.

That's not my memory. That's Bonnie's memory. No matter how real it seems, that was not me. I never experienced that!

Yet if it seems real…if I can remember it as perfectly as Bonnie can…if it feels exactly like it happened to me…

…is it real or not?

Jade, you bitch, what the hell did you do to me? Why did you give me both their memories? Was it some form of torture? Did you take pleasure in that?

<Ansible message arriving> she heard in her internal comm.

Rita stopped and stood in shock. She hadn't received an ansible message in nineteen years.

"From who?" she asked.

<Message signed by Bonnie Page, Lord Admiral, Human

Colony of Phoenix>

Rita stood frozen in the corridor.

"Read message."

<Message: "Hi Rita. You told me never to use this ansible address unless it was a dire emergency. Well, thought you should know. The Stree are attacking us again. We've detected their initial wave approaching. They'll probably raid us first, test our defenses, any day now. Then we anticipate their main fleet in about four to five weeks.

"I know there's nothing you can do, but I thought it was only right to let you know. Oh, by the way, Imogen took off in *Donkey* to go find you and Jim. She said she was going to Hanjan, but I happen to know she went to Niasa instead. Wishing her and you the best. Bonnie>

Still frozen in shock, Rita whispered so low that the ship AI could just barely hear her voice.

"Signature Seal?"

<Signature Seal: "Is she actually Human?" End Signature Seal>

Rita couldn't help but smile. So Bonnie <u>DID</u> know that Rita had overheard that conversation - when Rita was first brought to consciousness as a clone, all those many years ago. Those were the exact words Bonnie had spoken to Jim Carter about her.

Am I actually Human? Or more precisely, <u>WAS</u> I actually Human? Before I was a Goblin?

Rita resumed walking toward the bridge, her mind whirling.

Imogen. On her way to God knows where in Donkey. *The fucking Stree - coming for Humans again.*

And Jim - dead in a crypt when I need him most.

What do I do, Jimmy Boy? Do I go to Niasa to help my daughter? Do I go to Phoenix to help the Humans?

Or do I just keep running and hiding?

Jim, you fucking asshole, why'd you have to get yourself killed? Didn't you know how much I needed you?

EIGHTEEN

Phoenix System

"There they are," said Bonnie, pointing to the holo plot.

Her assistant, Vice-Admiral Zoe DeLong, stood beside her in the Admiralty's CIC - Combat Information Center.

"Definitely not a full fleet," Zoe ventured. "Only ten ships."

"Yep, as we suspected. Raiding party," replied Bonnie. "Testing the waters, probing our defenses."

"Just as Misha expected."

"Yeah. He called it. Tat's husband is a smart cookie."

"So he's told me," Zoe responded wryly. "Many times."

"Well, he called this one perfectly. He said they'd send in a small raiding party first, see how we responded. I'm glad we listened to him."

"Small to them. Still damn big to us."

"Yeah. Well, we execute Misha's plan. Let's see how it works."

Zoe looked over at Bonnie. The hustle and bustle of their respective staff members behind them provided a low buzz, a backdrop to their conversation.

"Do you still miss it? Being up there with the Fleet, I mean?"

"Every minute of every day."

"Luke worries about it constantly, you know. He's convinced you're going to take off to space, join the Fleet, leave him behind."

"I know. I know what he's thinking. He thinks I'll leave him behind, and he'll watch me die in space. But I've told him over and over, I know where my job is. I'll do my job. If that means staying here on the ground, I'll do it."

"I don't think he believes you."

"I know he doesn't. But what else can I do? I keep telling him, but he doesn't accept it."

Zoe grinned slyly. "Because he knows you too well. I'm not sure I believe it either."

Bonnie sniffed. "Believe what you will. I'm here, aren't I?"

"Now you are. But what happens when the shit really hits the fan?"

Bonnie turned away from her, back toward the holo to watch the coming battle. "I'll be wherever I need to be, Zoe. Doing my job."

Just short of one-half AU away - 80 million miles - Tatiana's husband Misha also watched the plot, but a hell of a lot closer to the enemy.

"Battle Stations!" he called.

His XO, Tom Frederick, nodded. "Battle Stations, aye," he confirmed, pushing keys on his console.

The condition lights on the bulkhead switched from yellow to red and began flashing, as the announcement came over the intercom and their onboard communicators.

<General Quarters, General Quarters. This is not a drill. All hands man your battle stations>

Misha nodded. "What's the count now?"

"Ten destroyers, Skipper. Looks like eight Stree, two Singheko."

"So just as we expected - a small raid first. A recon in force."

"Seems so, sir,"

"Very well. Send the word. Battle plan Charlie-Nine."

"Aye, sir. Battle plan Charlie-Nine sent to all ships."

In the viewer, Misha watched the ten enemy ships approaching Phoenix. Upon entering the system, they had accelerated to 20% light. Then they coasted, driving straight for Phoenix. Finally, they began a combat decel, to come down to battle speed by the time they arrived at the planet. They still had a million miles to go, but they were moving at a good pace. They'd arrive in another 14 minutes.

And there, they would attack the two picket destroyers Misha had left in orbit as bait, destroy any planetary defenses they could identify, and likely bombard the planet.

Unless Misha could stop them.

Flying toward the enemy at an angle, from high above the ecliptic plane where the planets rotated, Misha's destroyer *Fang* coasted on an intercept worked out long before the Stree entered the system. Three other destroyers - *Tooth*, *Claw* and *Stinger* - were coasting into the system on similar intercepts. Misha's force of four picket destroyers had been placed at equidistant points around the system, two above the ecliptic and two below. Subspace detection buoys placed in an array around the system had given them warning of the enemy fleet's approach, and the direction of the threat.

And that was all they needed to execute their initial battle plan. Thrusting hard for a brief period, all four destroyers then shut off their engines and went dark - just before the Stree raiding party entered the system. Their long, coasting trajectories would intersect with Misha's at the enemy formation. It was a plan worked out in advance and practiced a hundred times.

Like a swarm of pissed-off bees heading home to the hive, they would arrive simultaneously at the projected location of the enemy - just as the Stree formation approached Phoenix. And because they were running silent, there was a chance - a small chance - they would be undetected. Maybe they could surprise the enemy on their first pass.

Outnumbered, it was the best - and only - plan they had.

Misha glanced at the intercept clock on the right side of the large holotank. It counted down steadily, now at less than ten minutes.

"Any sign they've seen us?" he asked.

"Nothing so far," called the XO. "They're just sailing along, fat, dumb, and happy."

"How's positioning?"

"Not bad," the XO replied. "All ships are within a half-percent of expected position. *Claw* will have to make one small adjustment when we open fire. The rest are OK."

Misha grunted. "Let's hope it stays that way. Charge all weapons, prepare to fire."

"Charge all weapons, prepare to fire, aye!" snapped Frederick.

Aboard the Stree destroyer *Fateful Revenge*, Commodore Anberti glanced at the holo, and smiled with pleasure. His group was fast approaching the planet of the hated Humans - and so far, all he could see was a tiny force of two picket destroyers, coming out at him from their orbits around Phoenix.

A force he would sweep aside like so much trash.

Pitiful, thought Anberti. *They have no concept of how to fight. My father destroyed them at Earth like a knife through butter. Now I will destroy them at Phoenix the same way.*

"Status?" Anberti asked his Flag Captain, Doek. Doek glanced at the weapons officer, who responded.

"All weapons charged and ready, sir."

"Very good," grunted Anberti. He turned back to the holo, watching the countdown.

Five minutes to Phoenix orbit. Whatever gave these puny creatures the idea they could stand against us? If they had not enlisted the help of the unholy Goblins, we would have already swept them from the Universe...

"Incoming!" yelled the Tac Officer. Barely were the words out of his mouth when the ship suddenly shuddered, skewing wildly to one side from the force of a gamma lance impact, knocking Commodore Anberti hard against the side of his command chair. The acrid smell of burning insulation filled the air.

"Where from?" yelled Anberti. But before the Tac Officer could reply, Anberti's question was answered. A force of four

Human destroyers suddenly came to life in the holotank display as they went to full combat decel and fired missiles. The holo that had been almost empty before - showing only the two Human picket destroyers coming out from the planet - suddenly bloomed as the charging Human formation he had not seen fired a combat spread of thirty-two missiles toward his formation.

Before he could even speak a command, another gamma lance from one of the oncoming destroyers flicked out and slammed into the *Fateful Revenge*, again knocking it hard to one side, momentarily exceeding the ability of the compensator to stabilize the ship. Far to the back of the ship, he heard an explosion and knew the Humans had done some serious damage.

Finally finding his voice in the shock of the moment, Anberti roared at the top of his lungs. "Point Defense! Evasive!"

His command was redundant; his bridge crew was already hard at work on both. He felt himself jerked back and forth in the command chair as his ship began operating in a random walk evasive, moving up, down, left, right in an unpredictable pattern. At the same time, he heard the chatter and whine of point defense weapons spitting flak at the oncoming missiles. The deeper growl of the defensive laser batteries started up, shorter-range weapons of last resort for those missiles which managed to get past the flak.

Five hundred miles from his formation, his point defense flak met the missiles. For a moment, the holotank was unreadable as dozens of explosions filled it with blossoms of shattered missiles. The blooms cleared quickly in the vacuum of space; Anberti saw six missiles emerge from the line of fiery destruction, all tracking toward his formation.

"Firing missiles!" yelled his Tac Officer, as his bridge crew finally got it together. The ship shuddered twice, once as the rear tubes fired, once again as the front tubes fired.

Four missiles from the rear tubes passed over the top of the ship as they re-oriented toward the enemy, joining the missiles now pouring from the rest of his formation. A total of ninety-six missiles tracked toward the Humans, now just a thousand miles off his port bow in a hard decel, with ample opportunity to fire their gamma lances at point-blank range.

The hair on the back of Anberti's neck stood up as he realized the full extent of his mistake. The Humans had foxed him; they had coasted in dark, all their non-essential systems off - then gone into full attack mode at the last possible second.

You should have thought of that, Anberti realized as six Human missiles emerged from the cloud of flak and bored in toward his formation. One was taken out by his point defense lasers, exploding in a cloud of destruction one hundred miles out. But the other five jinked randomly, eluding the lasers. As the big ship-killer missiles flashed through the last fifty miles of range and exploded against five of his ships, the thought repeated.

You should have thought of that...

Onboard *Fang*, Misha held his whoop of glee, although many on his bridge could not resist. Two of the enemy ships had lost their engines. As happened in space combat when both formations were at max decel, the disabled ships simply shot ahead of their formation, disappearing into the black in a matter of seconds - without engines, they were unable to maintain position in a formation currently decelerating at 300g.

But now Misha had a big problem. The mixed Stree and Singheko formation had fired a full volley of missiles at his small formation of destroyers. Ninety-six enemy missiles bored in, intent on destruction. Ninety-six missiles for six ships. Sixteen for each of his destroyers.

Misha had no need to instruct his crew; they had drilled this scenario hundreds of times. They were ready; if any crew could survive, it was this one. And all the other ships had taken part in the same drills. They had known from the beginning that their only chance was to out-perform the enemy.

The chitter-chatter of the point defense flak guns started, signifying that the onrushing missiles were in range. The space surrounding his ships became filled with flak explosions, shrapnel, and parts and pieces of destroyed missiles as one by one, they took out as many of the incoming ship-killers as possible.

But they couldn't take out all of them. Out of the messy blooms of destruction, Misha saw twenty-two missiles emerge, still boring in toward his ships. The close-in defensive lasers began a low growl and snap as they also started firing.

"Brace for impact!" yelled the Tac Officer.

That's a bit unnecessary, thought Misha in the last few seconds of his life. *Anyone with half a brain can see the holo and know what's coming.*

Eleven enemy missiles cleared the laser close-in point defense and made the final run-in toward Misha's squadron. Four of the Human destroyers received two missiles apiece. One of the ships coming out from Phoenix - the *Tiger* - received no missiles at all.

That was because three of the missiles struck *Fang*, destroying her in a heartbeat.

NINETEEN

Phoenix System

The battle was over. Both sides were out of missiles and withdrew to lick their wounds. The Stree had lost three destroyers. The Humans had lost one, with three damaged but repairable. At extreme cost, Misha's goal of outperforming the enemy had worked.

But Misha was not around to appreciate it. His destroyer *Fang* was now just a collection of random pieces of flotsam and jetsam, in a long solar orbit that would take roughly two thousand years to complete a long, elliptical path around the central star of the Phoenix system.

Of course, we'll pick up those pieces and bring them all back, thought Bonnie as she walked from the Admiralty's CIC down the hallway, and climbed the stairs toward Tatiana's office. *We'll bring them home. That is, if we're still around.*

Bonnie knew she wasn't delivering the sad news herself; Tatiana had a holo repeater in her office. Tatiana would already know her husband was dead. She would have seen it real-time.

But since the disappearance of Rita twenty-one years ago, Bonnie and Tatiana had become close - very close. Bonnie was technically Tatiana's stepmother, since she was married to Tatiana's father Luke. But more, even though they were nineteen years apart in age, they were almost like sisters. So Bonnie would be there for her. Even if Tatiana was the Minister of Defense, she was a human being. It wasn't a time to leave her alone with just her staff.

Reaching the top floor, Bonnie exited the stairwell, strode

to the end of the hall, and entered Tatiana's outer office. The hum and buzz of a busy place in war mode stopped momentarily as she entered. Tatiana's staff froze, watching her. Without stopping, Bonnie walked across the room toward Tatiana's inner sanctum. Nobody said a word as she entered the inner office and closed the door behind her.

Tatiana sat at her desk, a statue of stone. Only two dirty tracks of tears down her face gave away her inner emotions.

Bonnie walked to her, wordlessly squatted down beside her, and held her by the shoulders, pulling her in tight.

Downstairs in the Admiralty, Vice-Admiral Zoe DeLong studied the plot. The enemy raiding party had withdrawn. They were now established in solar orbit on the other side of the star - 204.6 million miles away from Phoenix. For the moment, they were no threat.

"What do you think they're doing?" asked Jung Woo. As Transport Secretary, he had no real function in battle, but he was given a courtesy seat at the table. He sat near Zoe at the conference table, watching the plot with the rest of the ministers and staff.

"They're licking their wounds and waiting for orders," said Zoe. "Their purpose was to raid us, assess our defenses. Bombard the planet if they could break through. But Misha stopped them..."

Zoe couldn't speak. She bowed her head momentarily, then managed to raise it and continue on, doing her duty.

"...Misha stopped them, so they'll lurk over there behind the star and wait for new orders."

"And wait for the full Stree fleet to arrive," Mark Rodgers said bitterly. "The rest of their fleet can't be far behind. No more than a month, or six weeks at the most."

"Agree," Zoe nodded. "I think they'll simply wait out there, repairing their battle damage, until the main fleet shows up. Then they'll all attack together."

"We shouldn't have held back so many ships today,"

complained Jung. "We should have thrown everything at them at once!"

"It was Misha's plan," Zoe said defensively, challenging Jung. "And it worked. We fought off the raiding party with only six destroyers."

"At what cost?" Jung countered. "Losing our lead destroyer? And Misha?"

Zoe nodded. "Even so. The Stree think they've seen the bulk of our defensive fleet. They don't know about the three cruisers and the other destroyers we've got hidden. It gives us a fighting chance when their main fleet comes."

Jung shook his head. "Disagree. We should have thrown everything at them, destroyed their entire raiding party, and sent a message to the Stree that we won't be taken easily."

Mark Rodgers stood and began to pace.

"Well, it's done now. And Zoe is right. It was Misha's plan. Suck them in, let them think they've gotten our measure, then hit them by surprise when their main fleet shows up."

Mark stopped, turned, and faced them. "I still think he was right. It's our only chance. We'll be outnumbered by three or four-to-one when their main fleet arrives. We have to take any edge we can get. If that means making a sacrifice now for an advantage later, then so be it. It's unfortunate, and it breaks my heart that Misha had to pay the price. But he knew the risks going in. He did his job."

There was a silence in the conference room. After a few seconds, Mark turned back to Zoe. "Let's move on. Where do we stand on the ground defense plan?"

"Based on what we've seen today, if their main fleet outnumbers us by four to one - which is our best estimate, right? - then we'll take out half or more of them with our defense. The others will get through. And you know how the Singheko like to fight face to face. They'll send assault shuttles down to take the city, while the Stree stay in orbit and send kinetics down on us."

"And our defense?" asked Mark.

"Get the hell out of the way," Zoe smiled bitterly. "We let them have the city. We take to the mountains and fight them from there. It's our only hope."

Stree Main Fleet
Twenty-four Days from Phoenix

Admiral Rajanti sat in his day cabin and tried to think like a Human.

He was aboard *Unmerciful* - the flagship of the Stree attack fleet, on his way to Phoenix.

Time to finalize my attack plan, thought Rajanti. *If I'm to make any major changes, this is my last opportunity.*

But he couldn't think of any changes. Rajanti was a straight-forward commander. His plan was simple. Attack, attack, attack. Let nothing stop him as he drove toward the planet, until he had swept aside the puny Human defense and established a bombardment orbit over the pitiful settlement of the Humans. From there, he would smash the Human city into rubble with kinetic weapons. Then he'd send the Singheko down in their assault shuttles to mop up any survivors.

The Humans call it Landing City. It's not a city. It's just barely a town. What a joke.

"Ship. What's the current population of Phoenix? Remind me."

Rajanti spoke to the onboard computer - not a sentient AI, of course. The Stree hated sentient AI with a fanatic passion. They would never allow one on their ships. But they did use computers - rather simpler ones that could never approach anything like a true AI, much less sentience.

<The current population of Phoenix is estimated to be 84,875 Humans>

"How many adults of fighting age?"

<The population of fighting age adults on Phoenix is estimated to be 38,765 Humans>

Pitiful. They're already on the brink of extinction. We're simply doing an act of mercy to push them over the edge.

And yet...somehow it doesn't seem...right. It's too easy.

Rajanti sighed. He had been brought up in the military - his father had been an admiral, and his grandfather, and his great-grandfather before him. They had always been military - with the cool, logical outlook on life that came with the military. Rajanti had never bought into the craziness of the priests, and their fanatical hatred of all things AI. And their most recent crusade to destroy the sentient AI creatures that were the Goblins, and all those species who helped them, had brought nothing but ruin upon the Stree. It made no sense to him.

But he had drawn the short straw. It was his mission to smash the Humans once and for all. And he would do the bidding of his government, even if he didn't like it.

Rajanti had long since become a student of his enemies - after all, he reasoned, it was the best way to learn how to defeat them. He had studied Human history. He had read everything in the Military Library at Aslar about them that he could get his hands on. He knew his enemy.

So he was not surprised when a Human saying came to mind.

Ours is not to reason why. Ours is but to do or die.

Rajanti smiled ironically.

Not much difference between us and them when it comes to that. I do what the commanders tell me. I live or I die, as they tell me. The Humans nailed that one.

Heaving another long sigh, Rajanti reached out and lifted an item out of a small round tray on his desk. Smoke curled from the tip of the item. It was a cigar - but not a cigar made of tobacco like Humans made. Made of the leaves of a *sathi* plant, it was a drug remarkably like the cocaine of his Human enemies. It was the drug of choice for Admiral Rajanti, and now he drew deeply on it, holding the smoke in his lungs until the drug entered his bloodstream, changing his perception. The world grew brighter again, and he felt euphoric, a super-being, the Universe at his feet.

I'll wipe out the Humans on Phoenix. Then I'll go to Earth one last time and seed it with enough biopoisons to ensure no life grows there for a thousand years.

But I don't have to like it.

Packet Boat *Donkey* - In the Black

"Change of plans," said Mario.

Gen and Marta, sitting in the galley drinking *bishat*, looked up at Mario's voice. He stood in the hatch of the galley. His face was a mask. Gen couldn't read his emotions. But she could see Gast standing behind him, with a pulse pistol. Since Mario had released them from their bindings, they were free to go between their cabins and the galley, but nowhere else. And the Vampire was never far away - always watching them, like a shadow.

Gen glanced at Marta. Marta was looking away, toward the wall, ignoring Mario. Marta never spoke to Mario - her hatred of him was so strong, she was afraid even speaking to him might cause her to launch herself at him blindly, ignoring the consequences. It was always up to Gen to have any discussion with their captor.

"And what does that mean?" asked Gen, her voice a study in carefully controlled contempt.

"I've received orders to divert to Phoenix," Mario said, his face serious. "Thought you'd like to know."

"Phoenix?" Gen was astounded. "Why Phoenix?"

"Because the Stree are attacking Phoenix. They want you there."

Gen jumped to her feet. It was all she could do not to attack the man. Her hands were shaking as she tried to rein in her emotions. Had Gast not been standing behind him with the pulse pistol, Mario would be dead now. And he knew it, as he involuntarily shrank back at the expression on Gen's face.

"Wait!" he said, putting out his hands in a defensive gesture. "This is not my idea! I'm not the one doing it!"

"You're the one holding us captive! You're the one turning us over to those bloodthirsty fanatics!"

Mario looked chagrined, but Gen had seen that expression before. She knew it was fake. Mario didn't have a moral bone in his body - much less one that would cause him shame. But he put on a good act.

"I am truly sorry," he said. "I had no idea they were about to attack Phoenix."

Gen exploded. "So let us go! If you are any kind of a Human at all!"

Mario started backing out of the galley into the corridor as he spoke. "Sorry. I can't do that. A deal's a deal, and if I back out now, the Stree will hunt me down like a dog. I have to go through with it."

Gen glared at him as he disappeared into the corridor. Gast stayed behind for a moment, staring hungrily at Marta. Then as Gen watched, he lifted the pulse pistol slightly, showing it to her, a clear message. A message that he would be around, watching; and a reminder that the Stree would pay for Gen, whether Marta was dead or alive. Then he was gone.

Gen sat back down, looked at Marta, and shook her head. "We have to get free somehow," she said. "We just have to find a way. We can't let him just deliver us to the Stree!"

TWENTY

Phoenix System - Landing City

"You all know what we're facing."

The crowd was silent. Mark, Luke, Bonnie, and Tatiana stood before them, on a slightly raised platform. Mark was speaking, his voice amplified to carry across the crowd of at least five thousand people assembled in front of Government House. There were another fifty thousand listening on the Web, in their ships, in the mountains, wherever they might be, as they prepared for the onslaught of the Stree.

"The chances that we can fend off the Stree are low. I wish I could bring you better news. But I've always been truthful with you, and I'm not going to change that now. Our best estimate is that the Stree will break through our orbital defenses and bombard the city with kinetics. They'll follow that with Singheko assault shuttles. There will be no safe place in Landing City. If you stay here, you die. It's that simple."

The silence of the crowd spoke volumes. Mark gazed around at the faces of friends and strangers, the people of Phoenix arrayed before him, the last remnant of humanity.

"We estimate the Stree Fleet is twenty-two days out. Those who want to leave Phoenix and take their chances out in the Arm must leave immediately. Once the Stree Fleet arrives, it will be too late. The last transport to Niasa has been scheduled for Friday - one week from now. If you are not on that transport, you are here for the duration.

"Finally - those of you who choose to stay on Phoenix, for whatever reason - you must leave Landing City. This city will be flattened, of that you can be sure. Take to the hills, take to the river, take to the sea. I don't care where you go - but go away from here. If you stay here, you are committing suicide."

Again, the crowd was silent. None of this was new - Mark and his team had been preaching the same sermon for weeks. But now they were down to it - with only days left before the arrival of the Stree Fleet, Mark was making one last effort to pry the diehards out of their shell of complacency, get them moving out of the city.

Having made his last effort, Mark stepped back from the podium. Tatiana leaned toward him, whispering.

"It won't work, you know," she said. "Some will leave, I guess. Some will go to the mountains. Some will go to the sea. But some will stay."

Mark nodded, in pain. "I know. I've talked to them. They say they've made a home here, and they're not leaving."

"Then they'll die here," Bonnie spoke softly. "But it's their choice. You've done all any man could do."

"I could have the militia round them up and force them on the transports," Tatiana said, eying the crowd as they slowly drifted away from Government House, groups large and small in passionate discussion.

"No," Mark responded. "That's not who we are. Humans have always made their own decisions about where to make a stand. We'll never change that. It's something built into us."

"Staying here is not making a stand," muttered Luke. "It's suicide."

Mark turned to his friend and gave him a disapproving stare. "It's their decision," he admonished. "I'm going to let them make it. If we forced them to leave against their will, what would we be?"

Luke returned Mark's stare with a look of disapproval, but he let the conversation drop.

As they turned to leave the podium, Mark turned his gaze to the sky. Up there, somewhere beyond that blue-green sky, so different from Earth's, was the EDF - their little Fleet, preparing to meet an enemy four times their size in throw weight of weapons.

I'm not sure who is committing suicide, thought Prime Minister Mark Rodgers. *Those who stay here, or those who go out there.*

Earth - Derinkuyu, Turkey

Garyn Rennari stared at the vast cavern before him and scratched his head.

"Not much to look at," said a voice beside him.

"Yep."

"We've got our work cut out for us."

"Yep."

"Better get to it, then."

Garyn turned and looked at his Number Two, Major Jake Daaboul, and smiled.

"Jake, what would I do without you?"

Jake grinned and shrugged. "Let's not find out," he replied, his southern drawl barely detectable after twenty-one years on Phoenix. "I'll go get the unloading party started."

Garyn nodded assent and watched Jake depart, then turned and stepped forward into the large cavern. They had landed on Earth hours earlier, at the entrance of the large underground cave complex known as Derinkuyu. Smack in the middle of Turkey, the ancient underground city could shelter at least twenty thousand people if necessary. It would be more than adequate for the paltry four hundred in their party.

Our remnant party, thought Garyn bitterly. His team had been told only that they were to prepare for the return of Humans to Earth. But Garyn and Jake knew the full story.

We're here to carry on the species. After Phoenix is wiped out.

Moving farther into the cave complex, Garyn wandered in amazement, moving from gallery to gallery, making his way down stone-carved stairs into the lowest level, 279 feet beneath the surface. He gaped in wonder, astonished that people could have carved out such a huge underground refuge in ancient times, using only hand tools.

They must have had great fear. Something terrified them. Just like us.

<Garyn, where are you?> came over his internal comm from Jake.

<I'm in the bottom level>

<OK, coming down. Be there in a sec>

Garyn turned and headed back toward the last set of stairs he had descended. He waited for Jake at the bottom. Jake arrived panting, out of breath.

"What's up?" Garyn asked.

"Oh, everything's fine. Radiation levels within tolerance. We tested the water wells. They're good - safe to drink. We've got water for the foreseeable future."

"Outstanding. What else?"

"Unloading is progressing. It'll take four more shuttle trips to get everybody down and all the equipment and supplies. We'll be done by tomorrow night. Then the *Maximus* will head back to Phoenix."

"And then we'll be on our own."

"Yeah. But we've got supplies for two full years. That should be more than enough time to get ourselves in a stable situation."

"If the Stree don't find us."

"Yah. If the Stree don't find us."

"I want everything underground by tomorrow night. Nothing left on the surface. Not a trace. Until the battle at Phoenix is over, we just huddle and hide. Nobody goes to the surface until we know the outcome back at Phoenix."

"You got it."

"And let's start work on sealing off any ventilation shafts from light leakage. Put baffles in place, or something. I don't want any light escaping at night that can be seen from space.

"Will do."

"Thanks, Jake."

Jake turned to leave, paused, and turned back to Garyn with a smile.

"We'll make this work, boss. Count on it."

Garyn returned his smile. "Thanks, Jake. I know we will."

Venus

Endlessly circling, round and round, Nemo's corvette *Grizzly* orbited Venus, as it had for the last year and a bit. Today, on the bridge of the ship, Rauti and Nemo sat next to each other, communing with the magnificent vista of Venus beneath them. In the far distance, the two Goblins could see the huge mirrors blocking the Sun's radiation, slowly cooling the planet. Nearby, one of the processing stations on the end of its space tether was persistently hurling blocks of frozen carbon dioxide at an ever-growing moon.

"What is the purpose of a man?" asked Rauti.

"I'm not a man," growled Nemo. "I'm a Goblin."

"You know what I mean. Even Goblins divide into male and female, to share duties of various kinds and to propagate the race. So Goblin you may be, but you are still a male, inside. I know you understand my question. What is the purpose of a man?"

Nemo glared at Rauti. Since they had first learned about the impending attack by the Stree, Rauti had been asking him questions like this.

"I'm sure you know; else you wouldn't have asked me."

"For both Humans and Goblins, it is the same. What is the purpose of a man?"

Nemo knew Rauti wouldn't stop until he answered. Grudgingly, he replied.

"To create a place of security and love around those he cares for."

"See? You still understand it," smiled Rauti. "You have journeyed far since you were a Marine on your planet Earth, and a Human. But you still know it in your heart. And it's no different for Goblins than it is for Humans. To create a place of security and love around those you care for - whether it be family, or community, or country, or species - that is the purpose of a man."

"And why do you keep harping on this? I came up here to relax and enjoy the view! When will you let this go?"

"When you accept what you have to do. As I did, when I attacked Stree Prime."

"That wasn't you, my friend. That was a copy of you."

"Three copies, to be exact," smiled Rauti. "And all of them died if you recall. Three times I've died for my people. So I believe I'm qualified to discuss the subject."

Nemo sighed. "You're just not going to let this go, are you?"

Rauti shook his head. "No. I cannot. Because I know something you do not."

Nemo stared at him. "And what is that?"

"I told Banjala I would not tell you."

Nemo sat up straighter, all his attention now focused on Rauti. "But you're going to tell me. Or you wouldn't have brought it up."

"Yes. Because I think you should know. Your daughter Imogen and her friend Marta have been captured by a bounty hunter. He is taking them to the Stree fleet at Phoenix."

Nemo, stunned, couldn't think of anything to say for a moment. Finally, he sighed, as he realized the implications.

"They'll use Gen as bait to bring Rita to them."

"Yes. I'm sure that's their plan."

Nemo turned back to the windows looking out at the planet below. Venus, as always, was shrouded in cloud; Rauti's terraforming had not yet made sufficient progress to change that. Beneath the cool aspect of the cream-colored clouds below, the planet was still a hellish inferno.

Like my life, thought Nemo.

"Well. That's Rita's problem. Not mine. I'll let her deal with it."

"And if she cannot? If your daughter and wife die because

you took no action?"

Nemo turned on Rauti angrily. "They are not my daughter and wife! Rita is Jim's wife! Gen is Jim's daughter! Not mine!"

Rauti smiled, the strange inscrutable smile of a true Goblin, one that had never been Human. It was something he did frequently, and something that puzzled Nemo to no end.

"And if he cannot save them alone? If your help would have saved them, but you were not there?"

Nemo glared at Rauti, turned back to the outside view, and sat silent for many minutes. Thoughts ran through his mind, dozens of thoughts, thoughts that he couldn't control.

If I lose Rita... Or should I say, if Jim loses Rita... If something happens to Gen...

If something happens to them because of my inaction...

Where does my responsibility end? Rita created me to save Bonnie and the others on Stree Prime. Is that the end of my purpose? Or does my purpose continue?

But...she is not mine...

Do I still owe anything to Rita and Gen? Do I still owe the Humans anything? Where does a man's purpose begin and end?

But I'm not a man. I keep forgetting that... I'm a Goblin.

But on the inside...

Finally, Nemo spoke.

"It doesn't matter. Even if I wanted to help them...I'm just one Goblin. What could one Goblin do?"

Rauti smiled an evil smile. "Funny you should mention that..."

Rauti gestured out the window of *Grizzly*, toward the distant tip of the space tether, where blocks of frozen carbon dioxide continued to pop out from the top to be shot into the new Venusian moon.

"I have more than one hundred trillion microbots down below on the planet harvesting carbon dioxide, and trillions more up here in space running the processing stations. And they can easily be re-purposed to do something else."

"How can trillions of microbots help?" Nemo asked. "We

don't possibly have enough time to build a fleet of warships and get them to Phoenix before the battle starts."

Rauti smiled at Nemo. "Ah, my fine friend, that's why I'm the greatest engineer that has ever lived, and you are merely a warrior. You are thinking sequentially. If you are to be an engineer, you must learn to think in parallel. Many streams of work, all leading to a successful outcome."

Nemo was puzzled. "What are you saying?"

"We do not have to build the ships to completion here at Venus. We merely have to create a vast chunk of raw material, cover it in microbots, program them, and send them on their way to Phoenix. They can self-assemble on the journey."

Nemo shook his head. "Can't possibly work. Without a tDrive, it would take them centuries to get to Phoenix."

Rauti smiled. "Yes, indeed. That is true. Without a tDrive, this would never work."

Nemo squinted at Rauti. "You're up to something. What is it?"

"We have one tDrive to work with."

Nemo thought about it. "*Grizzly*? My ship?"

"Of course. Your ship has a perfectly good tDrive. It can get enough raw material mass moving toward Phoenix to build at least two additional tDrives. On the way, the microbots complete the first tDrive - not a whole warship, just a raw engine covered in microbots. That one goes off searching for another asteroid with the right materials. It finds an appropriate body, obtains the raw materials needed, and launches itself toward Phoenix again."

Nemo began to see it. "Ah. And meanwhile, the microbots on *Grizzly* complete another tDrive, and that one..."

"Goes off to find another batch of raw materials on the route to Phoenix, grabs what it needs, and launches itself toward Phoenix again."

"And then each of them..."

"Repeat the process. Now there's four raw tDrives headed toward Phoenix. All four of them find another asteroid, get more raw materials, build another tDrive, and repeat the process."

"And then there's eight…"

"Right. And at that point, four of them split, collect more raw materials, and head for Phoenix again. But this time, they don't build another tDrive. They build the actual warship."

"Ah. While they're traveling to Phoenix…"

"Yes. So now we have four destroyers building themselves as they head for Phoenix, and four raw tDrives building…"

"Four more tDrives!" exclaimed Nemo.

"And so it goes. By the time all of them get to Phoenix, they'll have built sixteen complete destroyers."

"Possibly enough to turn the tide," breathed Nemo.

"And save your daughter," said Rauti.

"So…you'll put sentient AI in control of the destroyers?"

"I could build them that way," said Rauti. "But I won't. Goblins are already feared and hated in the Arm for that kind of thing. Sending Goblin-built warships with sentient AI in command to fight biologicals would make things infinitely worse. So, no, I won't do that. I'll build them as normal Human ships. You'll have to get biological crew for them."

"But…how? We'll need at least - what - even at a skeleton crew, we'll need sixty people per ship! That…that's 960 people!"

Rauti shrugged. "I can't do everything. That's your problem."

There was a silence as they stared out at the view before them. And even as Nemo watched, the trillions of bots working at the nearby processing station halted activity. The raw chunks of carbon dioxide ice that had been coming out the end of the space tether stopped. Seconds later, great gobs of rock, sand, and other materials began coming out the end of the tether mouth, sparking and sublimating in the vacuum, as their heat from the planet below hit the emptiness of space. The microbots started on a new program, forming the raw materials into a kind of cone-shaped structure, spinning it round and round like the mandrel on a lathe, adding mass to it rapidly. Within an hour, it had grown to a quarter the size of Nemo's corvette.

"All you have to do now is dock it to *Grizzly* and launch it on its way," said Rauti. "The microbot programming will take care of the rest."

Nemo came to a sudden decision. "I'm going."

"I was sure you would."

"Thank you for everything you have done, Commander Rauti. I wish you were coming."

Rauti shook his head. "I will stay here and make more microbots to replace the ones you are taking away. And complete my project - in spite of you, or the Stree, or anything else that comes along."

"I should say goodbye to Banjala. He'll be disappointed that I'm going to make war again."

"No, my friend, I will not be disappointed," came a familiar voice. Nemo turned in his seat to see the icy aspect of Banjala, hovering in the passageway behind them.

"Remember - I was a warrior, once," continued Banjala. "When your people call, you go. That is the definition of a warrior, Commander Carter."

Nemo bristled. "I'm not a commander, and I'm not Jim Carter."

The pseudo-face of Banjala presented a smile. "As I have said before, you are Jim Carter, and you are not Jim Carter. Both are true."

Nemo sat silent. Banjala spoke again. "As I told you before - when you were preparing to launch yourself into a black hole - I have a special affinity for those who have lost much. Go save your daughter, Commander, before you lose more. I wish you well."

And with that, Banjala was gone. Nemo turned and looked at Rauti.

"Well. That was strange."

Rauti shook his head. "Even more so, considering."

Puzzled, Nemo asked the obvious question. "Considering what?"

"I should not tell you," Rauti replied. "Again, Banjala told it to me in confidence."

"But does it affect me? Affect what I am about to do?"

"Perhaps. I don't know."

"Then tell me!"

Rauti paused, a long pause that showed he was caught on the horns of a dilemma. Finally, he sighed.

"Have you never wondered why Banjala came to you, of all people? Why he works with you to transcend, when there are billions, trillions of other creatures in this galaxy he could have selected?"

Nemo shook his head. "I have wondered. But he won't discuss it."

"Because he is the last of his kind. There are no more Transcends. They have all died out, except Banjala. He had pinned all his hopes on you, my friend, to continue the species."

In amazement, Nemo couldn't speak for a moment.

"No! That can't be! He has spoken of his species before, as if they still exist!"

"He did not want you to know. He had hopes that you would take up his torch, carry forward the Transcends into the future."

"But…why me? Of all the trillions in the Galaxy, why me?"

"He said you were his best chance of success. Humans are the closest creatures to the original species that Transcended, billions of years ago. And you, a Human warrior, who experienced great loss in defending his people, who converted to Goblin for the sake of saving others, who has lost everything, was the best chance of understanding what must be done. Thus he has told me."

Nemo sat in silence for a bit, as the news rang in his brain. Finally, in puzzlement, he stared at Rauti.

"Why does Banjala tell you these things, when he does not

tell me?"

"Two reasons. One, he did not want to distract you from his teaching. He wanted you to focus all your attention on the Path."

"And the other reason?"

"Ah, well, this may be quite a surprise to you. I was originally born as a female Goblin. I converted to male several hundred years ago. But Banjala saw right through that immediately. And Banjala was also originally female. In his case, he converted to male several million years ago. But... somehow - our original, inherent femaleness recognized each other. And so we were at ease with each other and talked."

TWENTY-ONE

Landing City

Lieutenant General Brendala Knightley had been running for just short of ten miles. She had climbed the long slope out of Landing City, up into the foothills above. She had reached the switchbacks, where the road devolved into merely a track and began to climb more steeply, the footpath turning back and forth in order to provide something that a Human could climb.

She managed to keep a fair pace for the next couple of miles. Then she reached the scree. She had to slow her pace then, the loose rocks and gravel making each step a potential fall. Slowly she climbed the rest of the switchback turns, until the scree became covered in snow, and the snow got deep, and finally she was on top of the ridge. Crunching her way out to the crest, she turned and looked over the valley.

Four thousand feet below, Landing City sprawled across the U-shaped valley, taking up the open space between the two long ridges that formed the sides of the valley. The Human colonists had picked a good place when they settled here - protected on north and south by the long, rolling ridges, on the east by the ocean, and on the west by the high mountains of West Range. It was winter now; there was plenty of snow on the mountains behind her, and more coming.

It was a beautiful place to Bren. She had grown to love her city, and her planet, more than she would have thought possible. She had been born on Earth, of course. But she had been only seventeen years old when the Stree came. Plucked out of the wreckage of a small town in Arizona by a Goblin shuttlecraft, she had been unconscious, too severely injured to know what was happening. She woke up in a Goblin battlecruiser halfway to Stalingrad. She never knew what happened to her family - except that the Stree had killed them.

And now we'll get to kill some of them, Bren thought. *As many as we can until our space forces are destroyed.*

Looking out over the valley, Bren saw a faraway plume of snow falling off a shuttle as it went up from the spaceport, taking more raw materials to the fleet. Preparing for the coming battle.

And it won't be enough, she thought. *Thank God I'm a ground-pounder. I would not want to be in the Fleet right now.*

Looking at the city she loved, Bren could make out her house on the northwest side of town, almost directly below her. She could even see her dog, running around the back yard, chasing something real or imagined.

My little house. My little neighborhood.

And it'll all be gone in a few more weeks. We'll be up in these mountains, in the snow, fighting those damn Singheko Lions. Everything I see in front of me will be burning, reduced to rubble. And there's not a damn thing anyone can do about it.

To the east, past the center of town, Bren saw a fleet of trucks parked at the armory. A crew of militia were loading weapons, ammunition, grenades, claymore mines - the materials that Bren's army would use to fight, when the Singheko came down from space after the kinetic bombardment.

There was no point in trying to defend Landing City; they would be hopelessly outnumbered, fighting a superior army with inferior weapons. It was pointless. The Humans would give up their homes and businesses, watch from the hills as their city was destroyed below them.

Then they would fight. The Lions would come up into the mountains after them - and they would fight. They might not win - the odds were certainly against them, because the Stree would hold the orbitals. As long as the Stree could look down on them, image them from space, detect the heat signatures of the Humans, they could easily direct the Lions to them.

We'll have to get creative, considered Bren, gazing down at her house. *We'll fight from caves. We'll fight from snow forts. We'll fight from the rocks and the trees. We may lose. But we'll kill some Lions first.*

Heaving a long sigh, Bren turned and started back down the switchbacks. She still had ten miles to do today before she was back home in her little house.

Phoenix System - Admiralty Headquarters

"What? What are you talking about?" asked Bonnie.

Her aide, James MacArthur, pointed once more to the tablet on her desk, and the message it contained.

"Signature?"

"Nemo. Whatever that means."

Bonnie held a look of wonder on her face. "Ah. Nemo again."

"Who's Nemo?" asked MacArthur, puzzled.

Bonnie looked up at him. "You're too young to remember. At the end of the Stree War, Rita Page cloned another copy of Jim Carter to rescue me and a few others from the Stree. After he rescued us, he basically had no place to be."

MacArthur seemed uncertain. "How can someone have no place to be?"

"Think about it. You're a copy of another person. That other person has your wife. Your child. Your entire life. What are you going to do? Anyway, he went to Stalingrad and became a - I guess, a sort of hermit, you'd call it. Just roaming around that dead system, collecting junk, and pissing away his life. After a while, he started calling himself Nemo."

"I see. So you think it's authentic."

Bonnie nodded, looking at the tablet before her, reading the message one more time.

I'm sending sixteen destroyers to your fleet. But I have no crews for them. Send sixteen destroyer crews to the Fensalir system as quickly as possible. Be quick, I arrive there in five days. We'll train on the way back to Phoenix. Nemo

"But how in the world could he have sixteen destroyers to give us?"

Bonnie smiled. "If Nemo says he has sixteen destroyers, you can bet he's got 'em."

Bonnie leaned back in her chair. "Find me sixteen destroyer crews, get them on a transport, and get them to the Fensalir system!"

Protesting, MacArthur shook his head. "We don't have sixteen destroyer crews! Hell, we don't even have two extra destroyer crews!"

Bonnie cocked her head. "Find them. Old men, old women, teenagers, I don't care. Get sixteen destroyer crews to that rendezvous, Mac!"

Rita - In the Black

Rita woke to the gentle chiming of *Jimmy Boy's* comm warning.

"What?" she sent over her internal comm.

<Another ansible message has arrived>

"Well, read the damn thing!"

<Imogen has been captured by a bounty hunter. Onboard *Donkey* enroute to Phoenix. She will be turned over to the Admiral of the Stree attack fleet at Phoenix. It is unlikely she will survive the experience>

Rita sat bolt upright in her bunk.

"Signature?"

<Message signed as Nemo>

"Signature Seal?"

<There is no signature seal>

"Crap. It's a trap. Another damn bounty hunter, trying to

reel me in."

\<Undoubtedly\>

"They never give up."

\<True\>

"But..."

\<Yes?\>

"But...what if it's true?"

\<The probability is low. It is almost certainly a trap\>

Rita nodded in silence. *I'm talking to the AI again like it's a person. I've been alone too long.*

"That's what happens if you stay out here too long. You start talking to your ship like a Human," Rita spoke aloud.

\<You're talking to yourself again\> said the ship.

"Kiss my ass, *Jimmy Boy*."

\<Unable\>

Rita sighed, rose from her bunk, and started dressing. Thoughts ran through her head like wildfire.

It's a trap. It has to be. And who the fuck is Nemo?

But...what if...

What if...if my daughter is in the hands of a bounty hunter?

This is my child we're talking about.

Can I take the chance that it's a hoax?

\<*Jimmy Boy*, change course. We're going to Phoenix\>

\<Not advised. You asked me to warn you when you are in the process of screwing up\>

"Take us to Phoenix, *Jimmy Boy*. And kiss my ass."

"Changing course to Phoenix. Unable to comply with second command\>

Rita grinned. It was a game she played with the AI. When you spent thousands of hours alone in a small scout ship with only an AI for company, you took any small pleasure you could.

As she heard the tDrive change pitch to surface them back into three-space for the course change, the grin slowly dissipated.

I know I'm walking into a trap. But it won't be the first time. And to tell the truth, I'm getting tired of living without Jim. Maybe

I'll just go out in a blaze of glory...

TWENTY-TWO

Phoenix System - Admiralty Headquarters

"Can it get any worse?" Bonnie asked the empty air in front of her desk. She gazed out her large picture window toward Mount Redoubt, forty miles to the west. The snow-covered mountains sent a shiver down her back; in a matter of days, the militia would be up in those freezing mountains, fighting the Singheko. Tramping through the snow with Brendala's army, freezing their asses off, trying to survive.

But first…first she had to deal with this. She had just received a private message, one that did not get automatically copied to Tatiana's office at the Ministry. So she had to deliver it personally.

And it was going to hurt.

Bonnie heaved a sigh, got up from her chair, and headed out of her office. As she came into her outer suite, several of her aides jumped up in alarm. They made motions to fall in with her and accompany her; she waved them back, shaking her head.

Climbing the stairs to the top floor, walking down the hallway toward Tatiana's office, Bonnie entered at a fast march - ignoring the alarmed looks of Tatiana's staff at the prospect of another unscheduled visit from the Lord Admiral.

Barging into Tatiana's office, she plopped down in the big, overstuffed chair in front of Tatiana's desk and simply stared at her friend, waiting.

First Misha. Now this. I don't want to do this. But somebody has to. It might as well be someone that cares about her.

Tatiana knew Bonnie well enough to recognize her bad news expression. She waved an aide out of her office, who shut the door behind him.

"How bad?" she asked.

"Bad," said Bonnie.

"Well, I'm ready," sighed Tatiana. "I don't see how it can get any worse."

"It can and it is. Gen and Marta have been captured by a bounty hunter. He's on his way to deliver them to the Stree fleet."

Tatiana's face went stone-cold. "When?" she asked quickly.

"Four days."

"Anything we can do?"

"Not a damn thing. We can't intercept in six-space. Until they enter the system, our hands are tied. And they'll certainly enter right into the middle of the Stree fleet, where we can't get at them. They'll be onboard Rajanti's flagship before we can take any action."

"How'd you get the information?"

Bonnie passed the message over to Tatiana, who scanned it quickly. She looked up in amazement at Bonnie.

"From Rita? After all these years?"

"Yep. She's on her way. I don't know how she got the info, but the security seal checks out. It's her."

"Is there anything she can do?"

"Not really. She could intercept their ship just as they come into the system, but she'd have the same problem we do. She'd be right in the middle of the Stree fleet, and the girls might be hit in the crossfire. Not a good idea."

Tatiana sighed again, leaned back in her chair, staring out her picture window at the distant mountains.

"Why did they have to go? We told them not to do it!"

"They have to live their lives too, Tat. Just like we did. And remember - we managed to get through situations worse than this. So will they. They'll find a way to survive."

"Maybe," Tatiana said. "But maybe not. I have to prepare

myself to lose my baby."

"No, you don't," Bonnie disagreed. "You have to prepare yourself to let the Universe decide. And it has decided in your favor many times in the past. Have a little faith in it now."

Tatiana managed a weak smile. "OK. But put in a good word with the Universe for me. You seem to have a knack for that."

"I'll do that. In the meantime…"

Tatiana nodded. "In the meantime, we have a war to fight. Where do we stand on the space front?"

"All ships are deployed as planned. We've got two cruisers and four destroyers hidden far out-system, ready to come in at the last minute. The rest of the fleet will take on the Stree in a holding action, try to slow them down long enough for the others to come in behind them. Once that happens, we'll have them pinched in between us. We'll expend every bit of ordnance we have against them. If there is any way to prevent them from reaching the planet, we'll do it."

Tatiana looked back up at the window, at the distant snow-covered mountains. "But that won't be enough, will it?"

Bonnie shook her head. "No. Just between us, and behind these closed doors, no. It won't be enough. They'll break through, take the orbitals, and start pounding the crap out of Landing City."

"So it's a good thing we've got Bren and her army well out of here in time."

"Yeah. They need to stay up in those mountains, keep their heads down, until the bombardment is over, and the Lions come up after them."

"Well, that's the plan," agreed Tatiana.

"How many did Bren end up with?"

"Twelve thousand. More than I expected. Everybody wanted to volunteer. Bren's got her hands full just with the logistics of finding hiding spots for all of them. But she'll do it. When the Lions come, she'll show them a merry old time."

"And the rest of the population?" asked Bonnie.

"They're already up in the foothills and over the ridges into the flatlands out east, or down toward the coast, or hidden along the river, hiding out wherever they can find a place."

"And the holdouts?"

"Mostly old Earthers. They say they're not going. And I'm not going to force them to go. If they're ready to die, so be it."

"Anyone we know?"

Tatiana nodded. "Lots. Some of your old crew from the *Dragon*, in fact. Some from my old Deriko army. They say they've fought too long, and they're too old now to run. They're planning to go out with a bang."

Bonnie rose from her chair to leave.

"Well, they'll certainly do that. When one of those kinetics hits, it'll leave a crater a hundred yards wide. I'll keep you informed."

Tatiana nodded, trying to keep a wan smile in place. "Thanks for telling me in person, Bonnie."

"You're welcome, Tat," Bonnie responded. She gave a half-salute and turned, leaving the room.

Tatiana swung her chair around to the window once more, lifting her eyes to the sky, a cold, clear blue-green sky at the moment, a sky that didn't contain any hint of the carnage to come.

Somewhere out there is my baby girl. In the hands of a bounty hunter who'll deliver her to the most bloodthirsty fanatics in the Arm. And there's absolutely nothing I can do about it right now.

Then, Tatiana Powell, Minister of Defense for the small Human colony of Phoenix, lowered her eyes to look at the distant snow-covered peaks of West Range.

And somewhere up there are twelve thousand troops, well-hidden by now, I hope. And Bren. And our hopes for survival.

Fensalir System

The planet Hodur in the Fensalir system was dead. A sweltering primordial world of blistering heat on one side, freezing dead mountains on the other; an eyeball world locked by tidal forces to forever stare at its star. No life could survive on either side of the eyeball world; hence there was no interest in the system by any species known to Humans. It was an ideal place for a rendezvous.

The Human ship from Phoenix entered the system cautiously. Nemo saw the big, clumsy transport surface nearly 29 AU from the star. It moved slowly into the system, taking its own sweet time.

Nemo approved; he would be cautious too, if the Stree were around. For all the Human captain knew, the Stree could have followed him from Phoenix. A Stree destroyer could be right behind the transport as it entered the system, ready to take him out. Worse, the sixteen destroyers sitting quietly in orbit around the barren planet known as Hodur could be hostile, in spite of everything. Caution was the order of the day.

But Nemo's senses were far better than the Humans, and he was sure they were clear of Stree lurkers. Still, he admired the captain's care. He waited patiently; when the transport was fifty million miles from Hodur, he received the challenge message per his agreement with Bonnie.

<Frigg is my mother> he received from the transport.

<Odin is my father. Welcome to Hodur> he sent in reply.

Within a few hours, they had established the transport in orbit and were moving people to the destroyers.

Nemo was shocked at the people he saw moving to the warships; there were men and women of sixty, seventy, eighty years. There were young teenagers, barely fourteen. Prisoners, released from jail, had their handcuffs removed as they were sent to their ships. Every kind of Human imaginable came out of the transport and transferred into the empty destroyers.

Bonnie must really be in trouble, if this is all she could assemble to crew these ships.

But Nemo determined to make the best of it. Bonnie, in her wisdom, had preselected captains and officers for each ship in advance - former Earth military, retired EDF, retired policemen - anyone with an insight into command. The destroyers had already been named after cities of old Earth; the one designated to be the flagship of the task force had received the name *San Diego*, a tribute to Zoe DeLong's last military station when the Stree attacked.

To give them a head start before they departed for Phoenix, Nemo gathered them in the ready room of the *San Diego*. As he prepared to begin the discussion, he noticed many of the assembled officers staring at him, distracted.

They've never seen a Goblin before. They've only heard the legends. They think I might go berserk at any moment.

He tried to focus them on the task at hand.

"You have five days of transit back to Phoenix to prepare your crews. We have no time to spare; we have to be ready to fight as soon as we arrive. I know it sounds impossible; but it's the only choice we have.

"Focus your attention on training your engineers, bridge crew and weapons teams. Those are the important positions. If you can maneuver your ship, and the engineers can keep the engines going and repair battle damage, and the weapons team can hit what they're aiming at - then you've got a chance. Do the best you can in the time you have.

"I've prepared electronic tablets for all of you. They contain notes on the destroyer operating specs, instruction manuals for the engines, weapons and other systems, and hints for you to manage and command the ship in battle.

"I know it's asking a lot; but this little fleet of destroyers is the best and only chance to save Phoenix. The people there are counting on us.

"Now for the really bad news. I received an ansible from Admiral Page just a few minutes ago. The Stree main fleet entered the Phoenix system this morning. They've joined up with the initial raiding party on the other side of the star. Bonnie's best estimate is they'll begin their attack any day now.

"We're five days from Phoenix. That means Phoenix will have to hold out for five days, alone, before we arrive. If we don't get our butts moving and engage the enemy as soon as we arrive, there won't be anything left to save. So get to your ships, get your crews working, and let's get this fleet to Phoenix."

Within six hours, all the ships had managed to get underway toward the mass limit, albeit some of them wandering along like confused geese. As they passed the mass limit, Nemo had each ship confirm their course back to him via their ship's AI, until he was sure every ship had the proper course laid in; then he gave the signal, and they all sank out simultaneously, heading for Phoenix.

On his corvette *Grizzly*, Nemo had not taken aboard any of the Humans. All were needed for the destroyers, and the corvette was too small to take part in a line of battle anyway. He followed the flotilla, last in line, herding his wayward geese toward a battle that would likely leave most of them dead.

<Grizzly - *send an ansible message to Lord Admiral Bonnie Page at Phoenix*>

<Ready to copy>

<Sixteen destroyers on the way. They look like a bunch of drunken sailors. But we've got five days to whip them into shape. Cross your fingers. Hold on until we get there>

<Message copied>

<*Send it*>

<Message sent via ansible>

Packet Boat *Donkey*

Gen lay on the bunk in her cabin, communicating with *Donkey* via her comm implant. She was once again trying to guess the backup password for *Donkey's* AI. She had instructed *Donkey* to forgo his feedback of <incorrect> after each guess; that took too much time. Now she just ran though words and phrases as fast as she could think of them. *Donkey* had agreed that if she did stumble across the right one, he would notify her.

She sent word after word after word. She had been at it

for days now. It was mind-numbingly boring. She had tried everything. Every word she had ever heard that related to her Dad, Jim Carter. Every word she had ever heard that related to her Mom, Rita Page. Every word she could remember that related to the Singheko War, or the Stree War, or to Jim's life on Earth, or Rita's.

Nothing.

She had tried every word related to Goblins, to the Stree, to the Nidarians, to the Singheko, to the Bagrami, to the Dariama, to the Taegu, and all the other races and species she knew about.

Nothing.

Frustrated, Gen remembered the note she had found in the mausoleum. The note from her mother, Rita.

Reaching into her boot, she pulled out the note. She had read it over and over again, and she knew it by heart. But she wanted to see it again. Once again, she read the entire letter, letting the tears well up in her eyes.

My mother made this for me. She wanted me to know that I was not alone.

Gen wiped away her tears, folded the letter and prepared to put it back in her boot. But something tickled the back of her mind. Unfolding it again, she skipped through the first part of the letter and went directly to the bottom.

P. S. the N-number of Jim's old Mustang is my ansible address.

Days before, Gen had already tried to send an ansible message to Rita, even without a valid address. But of course, *Donkey* had refused, with the same reply she had heard so many times.

<Sorry. That is not allowed>

Now Gen asked another question.

<Donkey. *What is the N-number of Jim Carter's P-51 Mustang airplane?*>

<I do not have clearance to tell you that>

Gen sighed. She had asked that question before as well - and gotten the same answer. It was so frustrating. She looked at the postscript once more.

P. S. the N-number of Jim's old Mustang is my ansible address.

The N-number - the U. S. registration number of an airplane on old Earth. How could Rita expect her to know it? Of course, Rita would have no way to anticipate that Gen was a prisoner, with no way to look it up.

Gen tried to think. She had seen pictures of the old Mustang airplane. In fact, there was one in Bonnie's house at Landing City - a picture of Jim and Bonnie, standing in front of the aircraft in the Nevada desert, evidently taken after a joyride. Gen tried to concentrate on that picture. But her memory couldn't bring up the N-number. She just remembered that it had one, some kind of number on the side that began with the letter N, followed by a registration number.

What if that N-number is also the backup password? How many characters are in an N-number?

<Donkey. *How many characters are in an old Earth aircraft registration number?*>

<I do not have clearance to tell you that>

Gen sighed. It was so incredibly frustrating. Mario had skillfully locked down *Donkey*'s AI to be of little value to her, other than ordering food, playing games, and other activities he considered harmless.

She had already asked Marta about the N-number of the old Mustang. Marta not only failed to remember the number, but she didn't even remember the picture of it in Bonnie's house. But Marta had said something strange.

"I've seen that picture. Not too long ago, I think," Marta had said. "But it wasn't in Bonnie's house. But I can't remember where it was."

With a sign, Gen heaved herself up and sat on the edge of

the bunk, thinking.

She thought there were probably at least five or six characters in the registration of old Earth aircraft. And she was fairly sure that both numbers and letters were allowed. If there were five characters after the N, and both numbers and letters were allowed...

Gen scratched her head, trying to remember her college statistics class. She was fairly sure it was the total number of possible characters times itself for the number of characters. So if it was twenty-six letters plus ten numbers allowed - a total of thirty-six characters - and a total length of five characters... she tried doing the math in her head, but it was too much for her.

<Donkey. *How many possible combinations are there for a five-character password where each character can be either a letter or a number?*>

<There are 60,466,176 possible combinations>

Gen sighed. That was an insurmountable task. It would take decades to run though all the possibilities. And if it were six characters instead of five...

<Donkey. *How many possible combinations are there for a six-character password, same conditions?*>

<There are 2,176,782,336 possible combinations>

Gen shook her head. Either way, it was impossible to run through all the combinations before *Donkey* arrived at the Stree Fleet.

On a whim, she asked another question.

<Donkey. *Is there a picture of Jim Carter's old P-51 Mustang airplane on board?*>

<There is a such a picture on the wall of the medical bay>

Gen shot to her feet.

Of course! Marta cleaned the medical bay before we left Phoenix. That's where she saw it!

But...the medical bay was off-limits to them. Mario and Gast made sure it was locked at all times.

How can we get in there?

TWENTY-THREE

Phoenix System - Admiralty Headquarters

"Are you sure about this?" asked Bonnie. "People are gonna crucify you."

Tatiana grunted. "We have to survive first, before they can crucify me."

"But...we have to put up some kind of defense of the orbitals!"

Tatiana shook her head at her Lord Admiral. "You're thinking like a spacer. Try to think like an Admiral."

Bonnie bristled. "Are you trying to piss me off, or just doing it by accident?"

"Think it through, Bonnie. We can't win in space until Nemo's destroyers get here. We can't! We've got the three converted transports fitted with pulse cannon now; but those are still commercial transports with civilian crews. They've had only a couple of weeks to learn which end of the damn cannon to shoot! I'm discounting those ships completely. Considering what we have right now, I'm not going to risk a pitched battle. We'll wait for Nemo's destroyers to arrive."

Bonnie slammed herself into a chair in front of Tatiana, her face still showing the shock.

"You can't do this, Tat!"

"I can and I am. We're pulling the fleet back. We'll let the Stree have the orbitals without a fight. We'll wait to see if your buddy Nemo comes through as promised. If he does, then we'll come back in, guns blazing, and try to knock the Stree out of the orbitals. But if Nemo doesn't show, then...well, we fight a guerrilla campaign against them. Hit and run. Not a pitched battle."

"The people won't get a chance to crucify you. My spacers will do it first."

"And again - they'll be more than welcome to crucify me. After they survive."

"And what about us?" came a voice over the speaker phone. "We just stay out here in the cold and wait for the Singheko to land?"

"Well, Bren, that was always the plan, wasn't it? Nothing has changed there. The assault shuttles will just land a little sooner."

"And a few more of them," responded Bren on the speaker. "I was really hoping you'd knock a few of those damn Lions out of the sky before they hit dirt."

"We will," answered Bonnie before Tatiana could respond. "I'll detach two squadrons of my space fighters to attack the assault shuttles as they come down."

"No, you won't," countermanded Tatiana. "You'll keep those fighters safe onboard the cruisers. We'll need them later for the push to clear the orbitals. You put them in atmosphere underneath the Stree Fleet, and they'll get shot to hell."

"Well, aren't you just sweetness and light today," snapped Bonnie, anger in her voice. "So Bren just has to sit there and wait for a couple of divisions of Lions to come up the mountain at her?"

"That's exactly what Bren is going to do," Tatiana snapped back. "I'm trying to save a planet here, in case you haven't heard."

There was a long, angry silence. Tatiana tapped her fingers on her desk, as Bonnie fumed in the chair in front of her. Finally, after what seemed like a minute, Bren broke the silence on the speaker phone. "Well, at least get me some more ammunition if you can. If there is anything you can offload from the Fleet to help me out."

Tatiana nodded, then spoke. "We can do that. Lord

Admiral, please collect up any small arms and ammunition you can spare from the Fleet and send it down to Bren."

"Aye, aye," snapped Bonnie.

"That's aye, aye, mum, to you," snapped Tatiana.

"One more thing, 'daughter'." Bonnie stood, anger evident on her face. "I know I said I wouldn't go off into space. But this news about Nemo and the sixteen destroyers on the way changes things. There's no other capable commander available to lead that flotilla; so I'm going to send Zoe DeLong to meet Nemo and take over the destroyers. That means I have to go out there and take the main fleet. And besides - what good am I going to do here on the ground once the kinetics start falling? You'll be huddling behind Devil's Head up in the mountains, coordinating with Bren and her army. I won't have anything to do anyway."

Tatiana shook her head, an ironic smile on her face. "I knew you'd find some way to get into space before this battle was over. Did you tell Luke?"

"He's going with me. He said no way is he going to let me go alone."

Tatiana shrugged. "Well, I'm not sure you're asking for permission. You don't listen to me anymore anyway. But sure, go ahead, knock yourself out. Go out there and get yourself killed. Have a ball."

Hurt, Bonnie gazed at her stepdaughter. "Tat - I'm not trying to get around you on this. It's the right thing to do. For the colony. And you know it. Don't bust my chops over it."

"Fine. I'm sorry, Bonnie. I'm just frustrated. You have my permission, and my blessing, Lord Admiral. Go to your fleet."

Packet Boat *Donkey*

"We have to try for it," Marta whispered. "That rat bastard will be turning us over to the Stree any time now. This is our last chance."

"I know," Gen whispered back. "The med bay is locked

down tight. No way we can bust through that hatch in any reasonable amount of time. Any noise and the two of them come running."

They were crammed into the toilet in Gen's cabin. They were fairly sure Mario monitored their cabins for both audio and video. But there was a chance he didn't monitor the toilet. Or maybe he did, but they were running the water, in hopes it would mask their whispers.

"Damn. If I could only remember that picture of your Dad's airplane. I looked right at it while I was cleaning the medbay back at Phoenix. But I just can't pull it up in my memory."

"Do you even remember how many characters were in it?"

"Not too many, I think. But I'm just guessing. But I think…I think there were only four or five characters after the N."

"I've been guessing continuously for the last three days. I've worked my way through the five-digit numbers. No joy. So it's either a six-digit number, or it has alphabetic characters in it. There's no way in hell we'll ever brute-force it now."

"Crap. That sucks."

"Yeah. Tell me about it," Gen replied.

"So…what do you want to do?"

"We have no choice. One of us has to get really, really sick - or injured - and they'll have to put us in a medpod."

"It has to be you," Marta said. "Even if they put me in a medpod and I saw the picture, *Donkey* likely wouldn't accept the backup password from me anyway. And I wouldn't have any way to communicate it back to you until they let me out. Which might be after we rendezvous with the Stree."

"Yep. I already thought of that. So how do we make me really sick? Sick enough to require the medpod? Or…do we just break one of my arms?

Marta grinned. "I'd really like to break one of your arms. Because I told you not to trust him in the first place, and you ignored me and went right ahead."

Gen shrugged. "Guilty as charged. So which arm do you want to break?"

Marta continued to grin in the darkened toilet. "Both of them. But I don't think that'll help us much. So we just have to make you really sick."

"How do we do that?"

Marta pressed something into Gen's hand.

"Take this. You'll be sick as a dog. First, you'll throw up, then you'll pass out. I think they'll have no choice but to put you in the med pod."

"Ugh. What is it?"

"*Sathi*. I stole it from Gast. He's an addict."

"*Sathi*? What the hell is that?"

"It's a drug the Jatra and a lot of other species take. Similar to Old Earth cocaine. I checked the dosage - it won't kill you, but if you're not used to it, it'll make you really sick."

"Ugh. Are you sure there's no other way?"

"Well, I can break both your arms."

"Screw that. OK, here goes."

In the darkness, Marta felt Gen raise her arm and pop the pill into her mouth. Then Marta felt Gen lean forward and take a drink of water from the lavatory, cupping it in her hands and swallowing.

"OK. That's done," Gen said, her voice a bit shaky. "How long?"

"Not long," Marta warned her. "I'd better get out of here and back to my cabin. I suggest you go to the galley. It'll be more dramatic when you start throwing up."

"OK. I'm not looking forward to this."

"Better than breaking your arms," Marta quipped as they left the toilet.

Gen made it twenty minutes before she started vomiting. It made quite a mess in the galley. The sound brought Mario and Gast running.

"What's wrong?" Mario yelled at her. "Why are you doing this?"

"I don't know," Gen struggled to say. She spasmed into

another episode. "Something's wrong with me. I don't know!"

Mario looked at the puke on the table and the floor. "Stop it!" he yelled. "You're making a mess!"

Gen heaved again, sending another wave of her stomach contents onto the floor. "I can't help it! I'm sick!" she moaned.

Mario recoiled in dismay at the sight. "Stop it!" he yelled again.

Gen ignored him, doubled over in pain. Then her eyes rolled back in her head; she fell out of the chair onto the deck, unconscious.

Mario freaked out. "Gast! Help her!" he yelled, pressing back against the wall of the galley to get away from the residue splattered all over the floor.

Gast grunted. "I don't know Human sickness," he said in his thick Jatralix accent. "I can't help."

Mario screamed. "Get Marta!"

Gast grunted assent and disappeared down the corridor. Mario retreated, standing just outside the galley hatch, averting his gaze from the ejecta inside. Seconds later, Marta came down the corridor, followed by Gast.

"What's the matter?" she asked.

Mario pointed into the galley. "Gen. She's sick. Help her."

Marta nodded, went to the hatch, and looked in. "Oh, my Lord," she said. "What a mess!"

"Help her!" Mario yelled again. "I can't turn her over to the Stree like this!"

Marta looked back at him, contempt on her face. "Turn her over? I thought you said you would protect her from the Stree!"

Mario stuttered. "You know what I mean. I'll protect her, just like I said. But I have to show her to them first, to get paid. Then I'll...I'll rescue her. That's what I meant."

"You're a lying sack of shit," Marta said contemptuously. "I wish it were you lying there. I'd leave you to rot."

Mario recoiled another step from the vehemence in Marta's voice. "But...you have to help her! She's your friend!"

"We have to find out what's wrong with her. She has to go

into a medpod. Otherwise..."

"What do you mean...otherwise?"

"Otherwise, she may die."

Mario's face went pale. "No! She's worth ten million creds! She can't die!"

"Then help me get her to a medpod."

Mario nodded. He turned to Gast. "Take her to a medpod."

Gast grunted, stepped forward, and entered the galley. The big Vampire picked Gen up and marched out of the galley to the med bay. Unlocking it with a code, he entered.

Marta tried to make her way into the med bay with Gen, but Mario brushed her back. Marta watched as Gast laid Gen into one of the capsule-like devices and stepped back. As Mario stepped up, closed the pod, and latched it, Marta stood in the corridor, straining to see the picture on the back wall.

It was as she remembered. The picture was mounted on the back wall of the medbay. It was a picture of Jim Carter, Rita Page, and Bonnie Page, standing beside Jim's P-51 Mustang at the Deseret airport. With big smiles on their faces, it was clear they were happy - a time in their lives when they had just come together, and before the universe fell in on them. But Marta couldn't make out the registration number on the tail. She didn't have the best of eyes, and it was too far away.

The medpod booted up. Instruments came out from the sides, attaching to Gen's wrists, wrapping around them, and tightening up. Two more implements came out of the sides and attached to her biceps. A final instrument came out of the top and slid over her head slightly past her eyes. A blue light came on, indicating the medpod was entering diagnostic mode, and a scanning plate began moving down her body from head to toe. Mario turned and headed toward Marta, forcing her to step aside.

Marta looked at Mario. "Can I wait with her?"

"No," Mario spat. "Too many things in here that could cause mischief. Out. Go clean the galley."

As Gast closed the hatch in her face, she cursed inwardly.

If Gen wasn't able to get a good look at the picture from the medpod, then all their efforts were in vain. And she wouldn't know until Gen was released.

If Gen was released before they got to the Stree.

If it really was the backup password.

If Mario hadn't changed it.

Phoenix

Thirty-six miles from Landing City, Lieutenant General Brendala Knightley sat in her makeshift headquarters on the high slopes of Mount Redoubt. It was a semi-cave behind a rocky overhang, the entrance concealed with a rampart of soil to prevent heat signature detection, and the area camouflaged by trees and brush. A three-thousand-foot ridge overhead provided some protection from kinetics, at least the smaller ones. They had started calling the cave simply "The Redoubt." It was clear to everyone this would be the place of their last stand.

Her staff sat in a rough circle around her, each of them close enough to communicate with her. In front of her was Ana Trinh, her G-4 Logistics chief.

"All units in position?"

"Aye, mum. All brigade commanders have reported in. Everyone is ready."

"Food and ammunition caches?"

"One week's supply, buried, and maps distributed to all brigade commanders."

"What have we forgotten, Ana?"

"I can't think of anything else, mum."

"Well, we'll find out when the battle starts. Good work. Ana. Keep me posted."

"Aye, mum."

Bren looked around at her command staff. She was satisfied they had done all they could do to prepare for the onslaught of the Singheko ground troops.

Her satellite phone chimed.

"Hi, Bren. How's it going?" asked Tatiana.

"We're as ready as we'll ever be. What's the latest?"

"Their fleet is still sitting on the other side of the star. We estimate it'll take them only twelve hours to come around the star, establish themselves in orbit, and start the bombardment. So that means you'll have only twelve hours warning. Be ready."

"Where will you be?"

"We've moved command HQ up to the backside of Devil's Head, in that cave behind the old rock pile. That gives us line-of-sight to you via radio. But don't expect much in the way of radio comms for a while. It'll be too dangerous. If anything important comes up, I'll send a runner."

"Roger that."

"So...this may be the last time our sat phones work. I expect them to take out the satellites right off the bat. Once that happens, it'll be radio and runners."

"We're ready."

"OK. Good luck, Bren. Keep your powder dry."

"You too, Tat."

TWENTY-FOUR

Packet Boat *Donkey*

Gen woke groggy. It took a few seconds for her to realize where she was.

Oh. I'm in the medpod.

She reached for the latch, but it was locked from the outside.

Of course. Mario wouldn't want me wandering around in here without supervision. The AI will let him know I'm awake, though.

Sure enough, a minute later she heard the hatch open, and then Mario's face leered over her.

"Ah, awake, I see," he said, unlatching the cover. "Let's get you out of there."

Still half-groggy, Gen had no choice but to let him touch her in order to get out of the med pod. Still, she flinched away from him as soon as she was out and standing on her feet. Mario scowled.

"No reason to act like that. I'm trying to help you."

Gen staggered a bit, got her balance, and glared at him.

"I wouldn't even be here if not for you, asshole," she said.

Mario lifted his head in anger, and for a moment, Gen thought he was going to strike her. But he calmed, let it pass, and pushed her toward the door.

As she went, she tried to remember.

There was some reason I was in here. I was supposed to do something.

But she couldn't think of it. Mario pushed her again, roughly, and she stumbled. Before she could catch herself, she went down, trying to fold up as she fell so the impact would hit mostly on her thighs and shoulders. Somehow, she managed it, finding herself on the floor bruised but uninjured, cursing a blue streak.

Mario reached down and grabbed her hand, yanking her to her feet. "Don't bang up the merchandise," he growled, no longer making any semblance of courtesy as they got closer and closer to their destination.

Gen nodded. "Don't worry. I won't," she said, brushing herself off. As she did so, she looked up at the back wall. There was a picture there. It was an airplane. In front of the plane, her father Jim Carter, her mother Rita Page, and her godmother Bonnie Page stood proudly, smiling into the camera, three happy people just before their world fell apart.

And on the plane was a registration number. Gen could see it clearly. And she remembered why she was in the med bay. As Mario once again pushed her out of the compartment, she burned the number into her brain.

N16CAP

Shoving her down the hall, Mario pushed her into her cabin, and slammed the hatch behind her. Gen fell onto her bunk, still weak. But she knew what she had to do.

We're almost to the Stree fleet where Mario will hand us over.
If this is not the backup password - we're screwed.
If Mario changed the backup password - we're screwed.
Time to try.
Gen gathered her courage for the attempt.
<Donkey. *Are you there?*> she transmitted.
<Of course. I am always here>
Gen transmitted, holding her breath.
<*N-1-6-C-A-P*>
<That is the correct backup password. What is your command?>

"What? You got it?" Marta couldn't believe it. "It worked?"

"Yes," Gen said. "*Donkey* is obeying my commands now."

"Hallelujah," breathed Marta. "Thank God!"

"I had *Donkey* loop the video and audio recorders in our cabins, so we can speak normally," Gen added. "All Mario will see right now is the two of us sleeping in our bunks with the lights out."

"What a relief! I was getting super tired of cramming in the bathroom and running the water just to talk!"

"No more of that," Gen said.

"So...what's next?" asked Marta. "How do we take back the ship?"

"Our main problem is Gast," said Gen. "Him and that damn pulse pistol of his. I'm not too worried about Mario - he's a chickenshit and a coward. The two of us can take him easy. But that damn Vampire..."

Marta nodded. "Yeah. He's a big sonofabitch and mean. And he doesn't take a dump without that pulse pistol handy."

"Wow!" Gen exclaimed, leaping to her feet. "Wow!"

"What?" said Marta. "What are you thinking?"

"*Donkey!*" Gen almost yelled it. "Doesn't the head in each cabin have an emergency valve to send sewage outside the ship if the main line is blocked?"

<It does. However, there are two separate valves in the line to ensure the ship remains sealed. Each valve opens sequentially to move the sewage out of the ship>

"What would happen if both emergency valves opened at once?"

<The head would be open to vacuum and would automatically seal its airtight door to prevent air from escaping the ship. But that is impossible, because both valves are under my control, and a failsafe program prevents me from opening both at the same time>

"Can I override that program?"

\<Only by declaring an emergency\>

"*Donkey*, I hereby declare an emergency."

\<Emergency declaration registered\>

"*Donkey*, the next time Gast goes into the head in his cabin, as soon as his butt hits the toilet seat, open both valves at once."

\<Command understood. Warning - the Jatra in the head will be asphyxiated, and the head will be unavailable for use until the valves are closed\>

Gen grinned at Marta. "You are breaking my fucking heart, *Donkey*. Just breaking my fucking heart."

Hours later, Gen and Marta were nodding off. They had lain down in the bunks in Gen's cabin, waiting and hoping for their plan to work. But nothing had happened - *Donkey* had reported that Gast was also sleeping and had made no move to use the head in his cabin.

Gen, fighting to stay awake, spoke to Marta in the top bunk.

"We may have to come up with another plan. Seems like this one isn't working."

Marta grunted. Gen couldn't tell if she was awake or asleep.

"What do you think?" Gen asked again.

"I think we'd better come up with another plan. This one isn't working," Marta said from the top bunk.

"Thank you for that insight, O Great One," Gen spoke, her voice dripping with sarcasm. "Any ideas?"

"Yeah. I go to sleep, and you charge down the hall and take that pulse pistol away from Gast."

"Better idea. I go to sleep, and you take the pulse pistol."

Marta got up on one elbow and leaned over the top bunk, looking down at Gen.

"OK, now that we've decided on a plan, how about some coffee?"

"God, yes," said Gen, getting out of the bunk. "Let's hit the galley."

"What time is it?"

"*Donkey?*"

<Ship time is 22:14 hours>

"That Vampire SOB has to take a dump sooner or later," muttered Marta.

Gen nodded. "But will it happen before we get to the Stree fleet? That's the question. *Donkey*, how close are we to the Stree?"

<We will rendezvous with the Stree fleet in twenty-two minutes>

Gen looked at Marta, shaking her head.

"We're out of time. We'll have to just do a brute force attack - take out Mario and Gast any way we can. Let's go get a coffee and think about it. Then we'll make our move."

The two left Gen's cabin and walked down the hallway to the galley. The light was off, indicating that Mario had gone to his cabin. They flipped on the light and Gen started the coffeepot brewing *bishat*, while Marta took a seat at the table. The ship was quiet; only a gentle humming sound came from the tDrive at the back of the ship, along with the whisper of the air handlers as they moved air around. The door to the cockpit was locked, as were all other doors on the ship except the two empty cabins occupied by Gen and Marta, and the galley.

"Can I at least go in my cabin and get my hairbrush?" Marta whispered, knowing Gen now had the power to unlock any door on the ship.

Gen held her finger to her lips. She had not thought to turn off the video and audio monitors for the galley yet. She shook her head. Marta understood and leaned back, looking up at the tiny cameras mounted in the four corners of the galley.

Suddenly Gen heard a thump down the hallway, in the direction of the last cabin - the cabin that Gast had appropriated.

<Warning: vacuum leak in the head of number four cabin. Emergency seal initiated. Regrettably, the Jatra has died> came the message in her internal comm.

"Hell, yeah!" Gen almost yelled, exuberant. Marta, shocked,

jumped to her feet.

"What?"

Gen grabbed her, thumped her shoulders, tried to dance her around the table in the narrow galley. "It worked!" she bleated. "It worked!"

Marta began to catch on. "Really?"

Gen nodded wildly. "Yes! *Donkey* says he's dead. Go get his pistol! Quick!"

"Me? Why do I have to go in there and see that dead-ass bastard?"

Gen pushed her toward the door. "One of us has to do it, and I'm going to stand right here and watch Mario's door. Quick! Go get it!"

"OK, OK, I'm going," said Marta. Gen could hear her muttering under her breath all the way down the corridor to the last cabin.

"Just because it's her boat...she thinks she owns the damn thing!"

As Marta disappeared down the corridor toward Gast's cabin, Gen watched Mario's door. If they had disturbed Mario - if he came out now - Gen would fight him alone. No way was she going to wait. She had reached a tipping point. Mario was going down.

And he did come out. His door slammed open, and he stepped out into the corridor right in front of Gen.

"What the fuck is all the noise out here? Get back to your cabin!" he shouted.

And with a spin and a flying kick, Gen smashed him right in the side of the head with her shoe, knocking him halfway to the cockpit. As Marta came up behind her holding the pulse pistol, Mario lay on the floor unconscious, blood dripping from his temple.

"You just couldn't wait for me, could you?" said Marta accusingly. "You had to have all the fun for yourself!"

Suddenly the whine of the tDrive changed. Abruptly, the ship surfaced into three-space. Gen, still breathing hard from the adrenaline, looked at Marta with wide eyes.

"Crap!" Marta blurted out. "We just surfaced at Phoenix!"

The two women ran to the cockpit. In the small holotank in the cockpit, they could see warships. Stree warships. Everywhere.

They were in the middle of the Stree fleet.

Gen slammed herself into the pilot seat as Marta did the same on the right side. Gen was breathing hard. The rush of adrenaline from kicking the crap out of Mario - and the shock of seeing the Stree fleet around her - caused her breath to come in ragged bursts.

"Holy shit," breathed Marta. "Let's get the fuck out of here!"

"You got that right," agreed Gen. "*Donkey* - set me a course out of this fleet as fast as possible, through the thinnest part of it. Got that?"

<Course set>

"Good. *Donkey*, get us the hell out of here. Execute!"

<Unable. My system drive is not working>

"What? *Donkey*, get us out of here!"

<Unable. My system drive is not working>

Gen looked at Marta. In the cockpit window, they saw a Stree corvette turning toward them, with the clear intention to intercept.

<*Donkey*. What's the matter with the system drive?>

<It has been disabled by Mario>

"Crap. *Donkey* - can we sink out again?"

<Negative. We have coasted too far into the gravity well of the star. The tDrive will not engage at this location>

TWENTY-FIVE

Donkey - **In the Stree Fleet**

Gen and Marta rushed to the engine room and examined the system drive, trying to do an emergency repair, but it was hopeless. Mario had removed key components; he had hidden them well. In the limited time they had, they searched the ship - and found nothing.

At last, as they felt the bump of a Stree shuttle latching on to their hatch, they looked at each other in despair.

"Checkmate," they heard a voice say. They looked up from their search of the cargo bay to see Mario standing in the hatch, holding his bleeding head, with a familiar sneer on his face.

"Did you really think I couldn't foresee something like this? I'll always be a step ahead of you two!" he growled.

Before Gen could stop her, Marta rushed him, bowling him over and knocking him down into the corridor, and started pounding at his face, her rage beyond control. Gen rushed to her and grabbed her arms, holding her back long enough for Mario to scramble out from under and back away down the corridor, cursing a blue streak.

As Gen tried to get Marta under control, Mario rose to his feet, holding his left arm, and glared at Marta.

"I'll kill you for that," he said.

Marta grabbed for the pulse pistol, which happened to be stuck in Gen's belt at the time. Gen jerked back before she could get it. Mario flinched and retreated even more as he realized what Marta was after. Gen half-turned, protecting the pulse pistol from Marta's anger, and pushed her friend away.

"Marta!" she yelled loudly. "Calm down! It's not worth it!"

Marta stumbled and nearly fell as Gen pushed her. She fetched up against the wall of the corridor and stopped, half bent over, and glared at Gen.

"Let me kill him," she begged. "Please, Gen, just let me kill him!"

Above them on the main deck, they heard the boarding hatch open, and the clump of booted feet as Stree entered the ship.

Gen shook her head. "Marta. We can't do anything about it now. Just calm down. We'll be OK."

Gen pulled the pulse pistol out of her belt and tossed it to Mario.

"You'd better keep your promise, Mario, or I swear I'll find a way to get to you," she said.

The fear on Mario's face subsided a bit as he hefted the pulse pistol. He lifted it and pointed it at Marta. Gen instantly stepped in front of Marta, blocking his line of fire.

"If anything happens to Marta, you lose me too," she snarled at him.

Mario stood frozen for a moment, thinking it through. Then he dropped the pistol back to his side and motioned them up the ladder to the main deck.

"Get going," he said. "You've got a date with the Stree."

Mario prodded them toward the ladder leading to the upper deck. Climbing the ladder, Marta was in front, Gen behind, Mario bringing up the rear with the pulse pistol stuffed in Gen's back. As they came out on the main deck, three butt-ugly Stree awaited, wearing combat armor, and holding big pulse rifles. Like all Stree, they were short, squat, and massively muscled. They reminded Gen of a picture she had seen in her history class in high school - the Buddha statue at Kamakura, Japan. The one in front was an officer of some kind. He grinned at them, clearly ecstatic at having them in his grasp at last.

"Ho, Human Mario! You deliver as promised!" he voiced, his speech guttural and staccato.

"Indeed, I do," growled Mario back at him. "And it was not easy. I've earned every cred on these two!"

"Well done," said the Stree officer. He gestured to the two soldiers behind him. "Take them to the shuttle!"

The two soldiers moved behind Gen and Marta and prodded them with their rifles, moving them down the corridor to the boarding hatch. At the hatch, they turned and crossed into the Stree shuttle mated to *Donkey*. Pushing them down into seats in the shuttle, the two soldiers took position behind. Mario and the officer came on board and moved to the front, sitting directly behind the cockpit. Gen and Marta heard the hatch behind them close, and then a clunk as they disconnected from *Donkey*. In a matter of minutes, the shuttle had crossed to the flagship of the Stree fleet and latched to the boarding hatch there.

The two soldiers prodded Gen and Marta off the shuttle and through the boarding hatch into the flagship. Admiral Rajanti stood waiting with several of his aides, his face alight with pleasure.

"Well done, Human Mario!" he gushed as they came on board. "Well done indeed!"

Mario nodded in pleasure. "Thank you, sir. It was not easy."

"I suspect not," agreed Rajanti. He gestured to the officer. "Lock them in the brig. Ensure you search them thoroughly."

Then Rajanti turned to Mario, his smile growing even wider, if such was possible.

"And take this one too. I hate a traitor more than a Goblin!"

"What?" yelled Mario as one of the guards grasped him from behind, deftly removing the pulse pistol from his belt. "No! We had a deal!"

Rajanti sneered. "I do not honor deals from traitors. Much less from Human traitors. Take him!"

And with that, Rajanti turned on his heel, marching away as the guards dragged the prisoners to their cells.

Phoenix

The first kinetic round hit precisely in the center of Landing City. Watching from an observation post eight miles away and twelve thousand feet up the side of a mountain, Bren saw the great gout of earth and debris rise high, forming a quickly mushrooming cloud like a miniature nuclear bomb. Second later, she felt the earth shudder beneath her feet.

"Pretty good shots, aren't they?" someone said beside her. "I think they got the Ministry of Defense on the first one."

Adjusting her binoculars, Bren watched as two more kinetics hit the town. Both of them smashed square into it, blasting away most of the government and commercial buildings. The combined mushroom clouds of the two kinetics climbed high into the atmosphere.

"Are you sure those aren't nukes?" asked one of Bren's junior staff officers.

"No, not nukes," Bren answered, still watching the distant town. "But when you drop a big dumb missile from space at hypersonic speeds, it has pretty much the same effect - just without the radiation."

Fires started in the town as sparks ignited the combustibles in the rubble. A pall of smoke began to build.

The next kinetic hit on the northwest side of town, almost directly into Bren's house. The dirt, debris and flames were much closer, the mushroom cloud more impressive. And with that, Bren realized her little house was gone, along with everything she possessed. All she had left in the world were the clothes on her back - and her army.

She lowered the binoculars for a moment, wiping her eyes. She had expected it; she had thought she was prepared. But in the event, it was much worse than she thought it would be.

Fighting off the grief and sadness, Bren put the glasses back to her eyes, watching. More kinetics began impacting, about one per minute, bracketing the town. Within another five minutes, they couldn't even see Landing City anymore. The rising mushroom clouds, the smoke from the fires, and the dirt floating in the air hid it from view.

"Well, that's the end of Landing City," someone said behind her. Bren wanted to turn on the person, had an urge to yell, to rage at them in the face of their callous comment - but she didn't. She ignored the voice. There was something more important on her mind. She was looking for it...

And there it was. The first Singheko assault shuttle came out of the high clouds, screaming toward the ground in a combat drop, jinking and weaving just in case the Humans managed to put up a defense.

As if, thought Bren. *We don't have a single gun with that kind of range. And even if we did, we aren't stupid enough to use it and give away our position.*

And as much as it hurts me to admit it, Tatiana was right. Putting Bonnie's fighters up against those assault shuttles would leave them wide open to the Stree in orbit. For the Stree, it would be like shooting fish in a barrel.

I hate it when Tatiana is right.

A second assault shuttle came out of the clouds, then a third, and a fourth, and then a dozen, and then another dozen, and then a hundred of them, littering the sky like a vast flock of blackbirds.

Bren sighed. She had twelve thousand troops hidden in these mountains, preparing for battle. She knew each assault shuttle contained eighty Lions. She expected three full divisions, maybe four. So somewhere between eighteen thousand to twenty-four thousand of the big seven-foot-tall Singheko shock troops would land.

Each Lion would be armed with a big-ass pulse rifle. But because of their size, each Lion could carry twice the ammunition load of her troops. Four Singheko divisions - twenty-four thousand Lions - would be two to one odds on paper. But in terms of pure firepower, it would be four to one odds. Not even counting the artillery support the enemy could call on from the Stree fleet upstairs.

Beside her, Ana Trinh was busily counting the assault shuttles, keeping track. When the last of them had landed on the other side of the pall of smoke and dirt that marked where Landing City used to be, Ana turned to her.

"Four divisions," she said, her voice cracking. "Twenty-four thousand of them."

Bren suppressed another sigh. So - she would be fighting the equivalent of forty-eight thousand of the enemy. With her army of twelve thousand. She offered a brief smile to her aide. "Guess we better go clean our guns again," she quipped.

Hidden behind the screen of dust, smoke and ash from the burning town, the Singheko landed to the east, out of direct sight of Bren in her mountain hide. But her drones to the north and south had a clear view of enemy operations. She watched on the drone monitors as the Singheko troops poured out of the shuttles, unloaded their equipment, and formed up. When they were assembled, they began their advance, marching in a wide circle around the destruction of Landing City, then taking a line directly toward the West Mountains, making it clear they knew where Bren's army was hidden.

"How do they do that?" asked Ana in frustration. "They're coming straight at us."

"The Stree are imaging us from space," answered Bren. "No matter how good we are at hiding the bulk of our troops, there will always be some who screw up, show themselves, make a fire, do something stupid. Their intelligence team can put all that together and get a fairly good idea where we are. But don't worry, Ana. They know roughly where we are, but they don't know exactly. And I want everybody to move tonight. By the time they arrive, I want all units dug in to new locations. Clear?"

"Clear, mum." Ana bent to her task of issuing orders.

According to Bren's weather forecasters, the morning would dawn exceedingly cold in her mountains, with high winds, blowing snow, sleet, and temperatures below freezing.

The next few days would be a test of her Humans' ability to fight in a blizzard, against the ability of the Lions to do the same. Bren knew the Lions were a hot weather species. Their home planet Ridendo had a warm, savanna type of climate.

This should be interesting, Bren thought. *We'll see who can improvise, adapt, and overcome.*

Rita - Approaching Phoenix

The message from the Stree Admiral called Rajanti had been short and sweet.

<*I have your daughter, Imogen. You will proceed to Phoenix and rendezvous with the Stree flagship* Unmerciful *immediately; else your daughter will be cast into the star.*

Signed: Rajanti, Admiral of the Stree>

Rita stared at the message. Her mind was blank. She was in a fugue - her mind no longer wanted to work. Thinking was too difficult; so, she had simply stopped thinking.

Staring at the cream-colored wall of the galley, a stray thought surfaced, her mind unable to maintain the blankness of non-thought.

How do microbots that are black construct something that color?

And that thought caused a memory to pop up in her consciousness. A time when she had hauled hundreds of buckets of black nanobot goop to the top of a Singheko scout ship named *Jade*.

And that night, she and Jim had made Imogen.

It was a good memory - the first time she had been with Jim.

It was also a bad memory - because she had thought Bonnie was dead, and she had taken his man.

Or had she?

"Did I take Bonnie's man?" she asked out loud.

Yes, you did, said the part of her that was Bonnie. *You know I loved him.*

"But I loved him too!"

Rita shook it off. It wasn't the first time she had experienced this conversation between herself and the part of her that was Bonnie. And it was never productive.

I've got more important things to think about. How the hell do I save my daughter?

There's only one way...

Gen sat on the rock-hard bunk of her cell and pondered how things had gone so wrong. She had been stripped, invasively searched, and tossed into the cell naked. In the hours she had been there, no food or water had been provided and no one had spoken to her. She was reduced to her most basic Human essence - a biological creature, cold, hungry, thirsty, and scared.

She had tried to communicate with *Donkey* via her on-board comm implant, but it appeared the brig was screened against such transmissions.

She wondered if her best friend was still alive. The Stree would have no use for Marta. She couldn't be used as a hostage for Rita, and they were attacking Phoenix anyway, so it would do them no good to threaten her parents.

I have failed her at every turn. I failed her when I diverted us from Hanjan to Niasa, which was stupid. And she told me to stay away from Mario, but I waltzed right into his little trap - fat, dumb, and happy.

And then at the end, I couldn't find the password quickly enough to save her.

They may have just tossed her overboard already. My friend could be dead. Because of me.

Tears came into Gen's eyes, ran down her cheeks. She let them fall without wiping them away. Everything had gone wrong. Her father was dead. By now, his Goblin body had certainly been moved from *Donkey* to the cargo bay of *Unmerciful*, ready to be taken back to Aslar. Her best friend might also be dead - or at best, was sitting in another cell in the brig. And Gen herself was a prisoner of the most fanatical aliens in the Arm. They would use her to lure in her mother Rita - and then they would kill them both. There was no doubt in her mind how the rest of their plan would play out.

Gen cast about for any ray of hope she could hang on to. Her mind ran through her childhood, through the stories told her by Bonnie and Tatiana as they fought the Singheko, then later as they fought the Stree in the Stree War. The stories told by Zoe DeLong and Luke Powell about the rebellion on Phoenix when they first landed. All of them describing the many times they had been trapped or outnumbered - and had fought their way out.

All of them had overcome incredible odds to survive - even when all hope was lost. All of them had the same outlook on life - you never quit. You keep on fighting, even when all hope seems lost. That's what had brought them through.

And somehow, a faint memory surfaced in Gen's brain. A memory of something Bonnie had told her once, about the Stree War. A time when Bonnie had given up, had lost all hope. And Gen's father, Jim Carter, had said something to Bonnie then...

You don't get to decide when you're licked. The universe decides. Get off your ass and start fighting.

Gen smiled at the memory. She couldn't have been more than six years old when Bonnie told her that story. She had forgotten all about it. But now, in this moment of crisis, her brain had pulled it up from the deep recesses of her memory.

Gen reached up, used her hand to wipe away the streaks running down her face.

I don't decide. The universe decides. So get off your ass and start fighting, girl.

Gen rose from the bunk and walked to the back of the tiny cell, turned, and paced toward the front again. She continued pacing, back and forth, as her brain began to work again.

I will believe that Marta is still alive. They will keep her to use

as leverage against me, to force me to do their will.
  I will find a way to get us out of this mess.

TWENTY-SIX

Stree Battlecruiser *Unmerciful*

Admiral Rajanti stood near the boarding hatch. He was accompanied by his Flag Captain, Daqin, and the *Unmerciful's* XO, Raqi. Arrayed between them and the hatch were two lines of spacers in full combat gear, six to each side, with sidearms and pulse rifles at the ready.

As he stood waiting, Rajanti's thoughts were whirling.

I still cannot believe it. I just cannot believe it. It seems too easy...

The hatch cracked open. One of the spacers reached for it and pulled it back out of the way.

And there she was. The great enemy of the Stree. The demon herself. The Goblin who had supposedly orchestrated the destruction of their home planet, Stree Prime.

<You will proceed to Phoenix and rendezvous with the Stree flagship Unmerciful *immediately; else your daughter will be cast into the star.*

Signed: Rajanti, Admiral of the Stree>

And it had worked. The Goblin had replied simply: <*On my way*>

And then she had showed up. It seemed impossible. It was far too simple.

And yet it had happened.

The spacer nearest to her stepped forward, raising his pulse rifle, clearly intending to put it in her back. Rajanti waved him down. As Rita watched somewhat indifferently, the spacer sullenly returned to his place, the hate on his face visible to every eye.

Billions had died on Stree Prime. There wasn't a Stree in the Fleet who hadn't lost family there, when the huge asteroids driven by copies of the Goblin Rauti had smashed into the planet.

A stray bit of humor crossed Rajanti's mind.

I may have trouble keeping her alive long enough to kill her.

Three steps into the corridor, Rita had stopped. She stood there now, stock still, waiting for whatever would happen next. Rajanti stepped forward and placed himself directly in front of her - an act of bravery that would be talked about for days. After all - she was a Goblin - a demon, a fearsome creature that could kill with the slightest touch of her hand. Every Stree child knew that. To approach a Goblin was death.

But Rajanti stood in front of her without fear. A tiny gasp went through the assembled party as he gave a small, controlled bow, one Admiral meeting another.

"Admiral Page," he said in his guttural Stree voice.

Rita smiled, a wan smile that reflected her knowledge - that on this ship, with these creatures, she was as good as dead.

"Admiral Rajanti," she replied.

"Please follow me, Admiral," Rajanti said. He turned and began to walk away, never looking back. Without hesitation, Rita followed. The rest of the party fell in behind. Rajanti led her around a turn, up three decks, and down a long corridor to his Flag Cabin. Entering, he marched directly to his desk and turned, waiting. Without hesitation, Rita followed, Flag Captain Daqin and XO Raqi bringing up the rear. Outside, the heavily armed spacers took up post outside the Admiral's hatch.

"Please sit," said Rajanti, pointing to a chair. Taking him at his word, Rita seated herself in front of him. She was relaxed - it was all over now. There was no point in being stressed about it. She had made her decision, she had surrendered. All that was left now was to die.

"It is good that you surrendered," Rajanti began. "It will save the life of your daughter."

Like a stone, Rita sat quietly.

"Unfortunately, as I'm sure you know well, our government cries for your blood. If a Goblin has blood, that is…"

Rita smiled. "There will be enough blood to satisfy your government," she replied.

Rajanti was silent for a moment, thinking. Then he continued.

"And of course, I have to lock you down. It can't be helped."

"I expected no less, Admiral," Rita nodded in acknowledgment.

"Still…," Rajanti began, and paused. "Still, it was war. If you had not killed our High Priest and invaded his body, and destroyed our homeland, things might have been different."

"As I've said a dozen times, I did not destroy your homeland. Not that you've ever believed me, but that was an individual Goblin who went rogue."

"Actually, I believe you, Admiral. But it makes no difference what I believe. Our government believes differently, and they make the rules. And you did invade the body of our High Priest."

"That I did, Admiral. And would do it again if it were necessary. But as you know, that had no effect on the ultimate outcome of the war. You still destroyed the Goblin homeland. So my efforts were in vain."

"Perhaps. Perhaps not," Rajanti said. "You may not know it, but the office of High Priest has changed since that event took place. The High Priest has less power today. Our government is moving toward a council of secular leaders, rather than a religious theocracy."

Rita shook her head in disbelief. "You certainly can't tell it from the outside."

"No, it's true," countered Rajanti. "Because of your actions, we have a secular council in charge of our government today.

But unfortunately..."

"...they still want me dead," smiled Rita.

"Yes, I'm afraid so. My orders are to torture you ceaselessly as you watch us destroy the Humans at Phoenix. Their theory is that this will cause you much pain. Then I am to return you to Aslar for final disposition."

"I see."

"However, it is up to me as to how to torture you. I have not yet decided how best to torture a Goblin. I will have to do more research. In the meantime, you will be confined to the brig."

Rajanti motioned to Daqin, who had been standing by the door. Daqin opened the hatch, waiting. Rita rose. On a whim, she made a short bow to Rajanti, one admiral acknowledging another's small courtesy. Then she turned and exited the cabin, Daqin stepping in front of her and leading her outside, Raqi bringing up the rear. Daqin turned to the right and stepped to the front of the two lines of guards in the hallway. He muttered a sharp command, and the guards turned smartly, facing down the hallway. Rita stepped in between the two lines of guards and waited. Daqin muttered a second command, and they began marching. Rita marched with them, Raqi following behind.

Earth - Cappadocia, Turkey

"Colonel. Wake up," said Major Jake Daaboul. "Trouble. Big trouble."

Garyn Rennari roused from sleep quickly, as he had learned to do after years in the security service. He sat upright in his bunk, his eyes asking a question to Jake.

"What?"

"Singheko," said Jake. "Our sensors went off twenty minutes ago. I just came from Ops. They confirm a Singheko destroyer in orbit right over us. Clearly, they know we're here."

"Dammit!" spat Garyn. "They'll be dropping troops on us in no time." He threw back the covers, grabbed his pants, and slammed into them. "Get a general alarm going, issue weapons, full ammo load, get the scouts outside."

"Already done, Skipper," Jake responded.

"Good," agreed Garyn. He paused dressing for a moment, staring at Jake. "Well, we're in for it. I guess it was too good to be true."

Jake nodded. "I expect so, sir."

Garyn got his boots tied and stood up. "So let's go see what we've got."

They trotted up three flights of rough-cut stone steps to the very top of the Underground City and exited, crossing a courtyard to the old building they had converted into their surface observation post. Entering, they moved quickly to the Ops Center. As Garyn entered, Jake's assistant, Captain Raj Sharma, turned to greet them.

"We've just received a message on guard frequency, Colonel. A demand to surrender."

"Well, there goes any doubt. They know we're here and they know where," said Garyn.

Jake gave a weak half-smile. "Yeah. They'll follow up that message with their assault shuttles at dawn."

Garyn smiled back at him, his common reaction in the face of great danger. "Care to place a small bet on how many?"

"What stakes?" asked Jake.

"That bottle of wine you've been hiding under your bed," grinned Garyn.

"You're on. What's your bet?"

"Two companies. Six shuttles, eighty of those bastards per shuttle. 480 seven-foot-tall walking, talking Lions loaded to the gills."

Jake grimaced. "Damn. That was my bet. I guess I'll have to change it."

"So?"

"Three companies," replied Jake, shaking his head. He was no longer smiling. "720 of them."

Raj, standing nearby, had a sour expression on his face.

"Against our two hundred militia," he muttered. "I hope you win this bet, Colonel Rennari."

Stree Battlecruiser *Unmerciful*

The cell containing Rita was small, no more than eight feet square. The walls had been specially reinforced just for her - Rita had sent a couple of radar pings at them, and quickly found them too thick for her to punch through. The door was also reinforced, double-thick, a criss-cross of steel bars hastily welded across both outside and inside surfaces, providing extra protection against the strength of the "demon" they had captured.

Not that she would even try to escape - not while they held Imogen. That was why she had surrendered - and that was why she would stay. And she was sure Rajanti knew that - something told her he was a career military officer, with little use for the religious fanatics who had dominated Stree society for so many years. Rajanti and Rita understood each other. They were both doing their duty, both now and in the past when they had fought each other.

I wonder where he was during the Stree War. Twenty-one years ago, so probably...he would have been a mid-level officer then. Maybe an aide or adjutant to some admiral. He could have fought at Stalingrad. Or maybe he was on the Earth mission - maybe he played a part in destroying my home planet, as Rauti did his. I guess I should hate him for that. But I don't. At least, I don't hate him right now. Maybe I would, if I knew what he did. But now... I just hate what he is planning to do. To destroy the Humans at Phoenix. And to make me watch.

Lord, please, please don't let him force Imogen to watch that too. Maybe I can negotiate with him. Maybe I can convince him to let Imogen go before the battle.

No, that's not good. She'll run straight to Phoenix, get caught up in the battle. Better if he keeps her here until after. But then...

...then she might be hurt here on the ship. Damn. There's no

safe place for her right now.

With a creak, the door of her cell opened. Rita had been sitting on the bunk to one side. She rose to her feet as a guard pulled the door fully open. Standing in front of the door was a young woman. She was wearing some kind of drab prison uniform, something the Stree had made for her. Rita had not seen her in twenty-one years - had not seen even a picture of her - but she recognized her instantly.

She looks like Jim, was her first thought. *But she got my hair, poor thing. I always had so much trouble with my hair when I was Human.*

"Hello, Mother," said Gen.

"Hello, Daughter."

"They say I can come in and visit for a while."

"Please do, come in," Rita answered. Gen stepped into the cell. The guard behind her slammed the door shut. The two stood, looking at each other.

"You look exactly like your pictures. But I guess you don't age," said Gen.

"I age. Inside, where you can't see it," responded Rita with a weak smile. She waved at the tiny bunk. "Please, sit."

Gen stepped to the bunk, sat, stared at her mother. "I got your note at Netaz. I saw Dad."

"I hate…that you saw him like that. I hate that you couldn't see him in life. He was…"

Rita stopped, unable to continue. Finally, with a catch in her throat, she finished her sentence.

"…he was my man. He was my protector, my shield. I miss him so much…"

Gen rose abruptly to her feet, staring at her mother. She had entered the cell prepared to hate her. For abandoning her as a child, for leaving her alone on Phoenix with Mark and Gillian, for never coming back for her, for never a word or a message - she was fully prepared to hate this person, this Goblin, this mother who stood before her. But she couldn't. Rita's last words had struck her to the quick. She stepped forward, embraced her mother, held her as tight as she possibly could, and cried. And the tears of the Goblin she held splashed against her as they cried together, and once again it was proven that Goblins can cry.

TWENTY-SEVEN

Earth - Cappadocia, Turkey

"Nine shuttles coming down. Three companies. 720 nasty, stinking Lions," Major Jake Daaboul said sourly, looking at the holo display. "Looks like I get to keep my bottle of wine."

Garyn grunted. "Here's hoping you get a chance to drink it," he muttered. "No fighters?"

Jake looked back at the holo display. "None so far. I don't expect any. The Lions like to fight up close and personal, face-to-face. They don't use fighters much. They consider it beneath them."

"Are we ready?" asked Garyn.

"As ready as we can be. They have to land in the soccer field out by the park. There's no other flat space big enough for their assault shuttles. Yuki has Alpha and Bravo platoons on their left flank, Charlie and Delta on their right. She'll hit them as they get out of the shuttles and start to form up."

"But you've impressed upon Yuki not to stand and fight? She understands?"

"Yeah. When the return fire becomes significant, they boogie out. They'll take up new positions as planned, just outside the entrance to the Underground City. Then they'll ambush the Lions once more as they come into range."

"And then they boogie out again, correct?"

"Yep. Standard ambush. Empty their clips and bail."

"And then it becomes guerrilla warfare. Hit and run."

"Right. I've impressed upon the platoon leaders - do not stand and fight them. There's too many, they're too well armed, too well trained. Chip away at them, keep them off balance."

"Everybody else is hidden?"

"Yes, sir. We evacuated Underground City just before dawn. All non-combatants hidden outside the town."

"What's the chances they got away without detection?"

"Pretty good, I think," Jake answered. "It was cloudy. We kept to the houses and narrow alleyways. Absolutely no lights, of course. There's no way to be sure, but we did our absolute best to prevent the Lions from seeing us on infrared."

"Well, we'll know soon enough. If the Lions ignore the Underground City and head straight for the edge of town, we'll know they figured out where our people are hidden."

Garyn turned to the comm specialist. "Did you send the ansible message to Phoenix?"

"Yes, sir. Message sent. No reply yet."

"OK, thanks, Lieutenant. Let me know when we get a reply."

A voice crackled over the radio. "They're on the ground," called Captain Yukiko Takahara, their field commander.

"Hold fire, Yuki, until they're out of the shuttles and forming up," Jake answered. "We want them out in the open."

"Roger that," came the reply. "We're holding fire. You'll know it when we open up."

"Roger, out," replied Jake. He looked at Garyn, sprawled across his chair like he was watching a Saturday night soccer game.

"Break a leg," he said grimly.

"Break a leg," answered Garyn.

Stree Battlecruiser *Unmerciful*

Once again, twelve guards ushered Rita into Admiral Rajanti's cabin and took their places outside the door. Rita was amused; the Stree were so afraid of her, they felt twelve guards were still necessary.

If they only knew the truth. Twelve would not be nearly enough if I actually decided to break out of here.

Admiral Rajanti rose from his desk and gestured Rita to a chair. "Please, sit, Admiral," he said.

"Thank you," Rita answered, her Stree perfect and without accent - one more advantage of a Goblin android brain. As she took her chair, Rajanti also returned to his.

"Can I get you anything?" he asked. "Something to drink? Something to eat?"

"Some chocolate would be nice," Rita smiled.

Rajanti looked puzzled but turned it into a smile as he realized Rita was making a joke.

"Ah, sorry. Whatever that is, I don't think we have it," he said.

In the short silence that followed, the two adversaries gazed at each other. A silent understanding held between them; two warriors, who had experienced levels of death and destruction most creatures would never know - and who would certainly experience more before their lives were over. And even as they sat, the ship shuddered slightly, sending another kinetic round toward the planet below.

"You know, Admiral, I think it highly unlikely either of us will die in bed," Rajanti began, the thin smile on his face still in place.

Rita couldn't help but smile back. "I believe you are correct, Admiral," she agreed.

"I hope you don't mind that I brought you here just to talk. I find it entertaining to talk with someone on my own level."

"I don't mind at all. I don't have much to do in that cell."

Rajanti nodded. "I expect so." He shifted in his chair, a great large Buddha. All the Stree looked like fat Buddhas to Rita, and to most Humans. Unlike Humans, however, they were remarkably uniform in appearance, cut from the same mold. Rita knew there were distinguishing marks and features on their bodies that allowed them to tell each other apart, but she had never had the time to learn all those factors.

Rajanti looked across the desk at Rita's hand, then held up his own for inspection. "I have to wonder, what does it feel like to have five digits on a hand?"

Rita shrugged. "It feels normal. I'm sure it feels little different from your hand, with your two fingers and two thumbs. Nature adjusts."

"Yes, it does. It always adjusts. Tell me, Admiral Page. You say you had nothing to do with the destruction of Stree Prime. Is that true?"

"It's true. In fact, as we have told your government many times, we sent the corvette *Armidale* to deflect the last impactor away from your planet. I believe your own records state that single act of ours saved roughly two hundred million of your people."

"Our government says that evidence was faked. They claim the third asteroid missed due to faulty programming by the Goblin Rauti, and your Human ship had nothing to do with it."

Rita grimaced. "Admiral - do you really think Rauti could have successfully programmed the first two - then, somehow, made an error on the third one to cause it to miss an entire planet?"

Rajanti smiled broadly. "Actually, I don't believe the government line. I happened to be in space that day, you know. I was a young commander in one of the ships that tried to ram that impactor, to deflect it to one side. I missed, of course. It's exceedingly difficult to ram an asteroid traveling at those speeds when your ship doesn't have the accel to catch up to it. But after I missed it, Admiral, I was following right behind that rock when the *Armidale* nosed into it and pushed it aside. I saw the entire thing."

"Ah."

"Yes. I know what happened out there. But I'm not suicidal. The priesthood made up their minds about what story they would tell about that day. And I knew enough to keep quiet about what I saw. Still and all, though...thank you for what the *Armidale* did. I'm sure you'll never hear that from another

Stree, but I wanted to tell you."

"You're welcome."

"Well, on to other news. We've began the bombardment of Phoenix...as I'm sure you can tell. Strangely, the Humans pulled back their fleet. They left the orbitals open to us. There was no opposition. What do you make of that?"

Rita smiled. "Admiral, if you are any kind of tactician at all, you know exactly what to make of that."

"Yes," smiled Rajanti back at her. "They are cooking up some kind of surprise for me, I'm sure. Any idea what it is?"

"I would have no way of knowing, Admiral. As you well know, I haven't been to Phoenix in more than twenty years. They don't tell me their secrets."

"No, I don't expect they do."

"But Admiral," Rita interjected, "You have what you want. Phoenix is laid bare before you. You can destroy Landing City, set the Humans back a hundred years, eliminate the Human military threat to Stree forever. You have everything you want. Is it necessary to destroy the last few remnants of humanity?"

"I do not wish it. But I am answerable to my orders, not my morals. I have no choice in the matter. The priesthood demands it, and my government is still deathly afraid of the priesthood."

"But," Rita pressed on, "Must a warrior destroy the innocent because of orders? Does an immoral order have to be followed?"

"And who shall be the judge of what is moral and what is immoral?" asked Rajanti. "The warrior who receives the order? Or the commander that issues it?"

Rita pressed on. "I have always found it easy to judge. To use power to defend the weak and innocent, returning your power when the crisis is over, is moral. To use power to attack the weak and innocent, or to retain it after the crisis is managed, is immoral. It is a clear-cut distinction to me."

Rajanti sighed. "I don't disagree with you, Admiral Page. But it's a moot point. Any attempt on my part to show mercy would only lead to my quick death. Another would take my place to carry out those same orders. The Humans would gain nothing, and I would lose everything."

In the silence that followed, Rajanti leaned forward in his chair, getting down to business. "Now, as I told you, my orders are to torture you until we get back to Aslar, where you will be further tortured, then executed. Of course, I'm still considering the best way to torture a Goblin. Any suggestions?" The twinkle in Rajanti's eye told Rita he was being playful. She replied in kind.

"I think you should tie me to the outside of your ship. Perhaps I would go crazy watching the destruction of the Humans below."

"Ha!" laughed Rajanti. "You'd like that, indeed. No bindings would hold you, would they?"

"Quite the contrary, Admiral. There are many substances that could adequately bind me. Your legends of the strength of Goblins are vastly overstated. Your priests have made us into demons far beyond our actual capabilities."

"That is good to know. But I think I will not tie you outside. I've only just now gotten you inside my ship, and I'd like to keep you here. If I lost you at this point, the penalties would be severe."

"I expect so," agreed Rita.

"So…is there anything else I can do for you? Anything you want?"

"I want justice; but I'd settle for some mercy," said Rita.

Rajanti's expression changed. His face fell, and his eyes grew sad. "And I can give you neither, Admiral. We both know you were merely fighting for your species and your allies. And yet you will die, and I will live on. That is the great injustice of our shared universe."

"Then release my daughter, Admiral. Please. She is an innocent. She had nothing to do with the Stree War."

"And that is another thing I cannot do. She must go back to Aslar with us, to wait at the convenience of my government. I wish it were otherwise."

Rajanti sighed and rose from his desk. "Goodbye to you, Admiral," he said. "The battle with the Humans has begun. Who's to say which of us will be alive tomorrow? If I do not see you again, Admiral, thank you for the conversation."

At some silent signal, the hatch behind Rita opened. Guards stepped in to escort her back to her cell.

Rita rose from her chair and nodded to Rajanti, then turned and departed, stepping crisply to the hatch, out the entrance, and taking her place in the center of the two rows of guards. With a command from the officer in charge, the march back to her cell began, as another kinetic launch shook the ship.

Earth - Cappadocia, Turkey

The sound of distant pulse rifle fire told Garyn everything he needed to know. The voice of Captain Takahara over the radio calling "Engaged" was merely confirmation. The battle had begun.

Garyn couldn't sit anymore. He got up, walked to the door of the Ops Center, and stepped outside.

The soccer field was only two miles away; the rifle fire sounded clearly. The Singheko weapons were responding now; they had a slightly deeper, throatier crack. Within seconds, the sound grew to a steady litany of sustained firing as the ambush became fully developed.

Jake came out and stood beside him. The air was cool, crisp on their skin, a gentle breeze from the west shaking the leaves of the nearby trees.

"Lots of Singheko firing now," Garyn said. "Our troops should be pulling back."

And even as he finished his sentence, the distinct sound of the Human pulse rifles in the distance stopped, as suddenly as it had started.

Garyn knew what that meant - the Humans were falling back, moving as quickly as possible away from the enemy to another ambush position.

Hit and run. It was the only chance they had. Turning quickly, Garyn went back into the HQ. As he took his seat again, the radio crackled to life.

"Withdrawal complete," Yuki called. "We're moving to our next position. No pursuit so far. I think we caught them by surprise."

Jake grabbed the mike. "Assessment?"

"Estimate fifty to sixty enemy out of action," Yuki called.

"Good work, Yuki," Jake said, glancing at Garyn with a smile. "That'll make them think twice about charging in on us."

"Hope so," Yuki expressed over the radio. "Call you when we're in our next position."

"Roger, out," Jake spoke. He turned to Garyn. "Any thoughts?"

"No. We'll wait and see if they saw us moving the people out last night. If they head for Underground City, we're golden; we can set our next ambush. But if they start moving for the edge of town, we're in trouble. That's the real test."

Ten minutes later, they had their answer.

"They are definitely moving toward the edge of town, not the Underground City," reported Yuki. "They know where the people are hiding."

Garyn shook his head. "OK," he ordered. "Plan B. Relocate to the secondary position and try to hold them off."

"Roger, out," responded Yuki.

"Let's go," Garyn said to Jake. "We've got to get those people and make a run for it. We'll make for Urgup for now, then see if we can make it into the mountains."

"That's twenty-five miles, you know," Jake responded as they began running toward the place where they had hidden the rest of their people. "They'll be on our ass all the way."

Garyn nodded. "Got any better ideas?"

Jake grunted beside him. "Nothing comes to mind."

TWENTY-EIGHT

Phoenix System - West Mountains

For two days, Bren's troops fought skirmish after skirmish with the Singheko, a slow, grinding retreat up the mountains. They had no other choice; the Lions were stronger, better trained, better armed. Since the Stree War, the Lions had become the shock troops of the Arm for a reason; they were damn near impossible to defeat when evenly matched - much less when you were outnumbered two to one and outgunned four to one.

And the damn kinetics, thought Bren. They came periodically, when the cloud cover lifted and the Stree upstairs in orbit managed to get a decent heat signature on a Human formation. The Stree were using smaller kinetics now, to avoid hitting their own troops - but their accuracy was outstanding. Each time one of the kinetics hit, the ground rumbled for miles, and a mini-mushroom cloud rose up, letting Bren know another contingent of her troops were dead.

On top of a ridge overlooking Lake Vinson, Bren carefully poked her binoculars over the crest. In spite of the swirling snow and the thick cloud cover today, she got a decent view of the enemy column three hundred yards below her, toiling along the western edge of the lake. The column of Lions was nearly six miles long, stretching from the far corner of the lake three miles to her left, to the other end of the lake three miles to her right. That put the middle of the column about half-way past her position. Due to the weight of the ammunition and weapons they carried, the Lions moved slowly in the blowing snow, struggling to see the path in front of them.

"I think now," Bren said softly, giving the signal everyone had been waiting for. Beside her, Operations Officer Colonel Anders Paulsen spoke into his radio. There was a pregnant pause; then beside her on the crest of the ridge, four thousand ghostly figures rose from snow-covered hiding spots. An army of snowmen lifted their rifles and opened fire on the column of Lions below.

The noise was instantly deafening; mixed in with the rifle fire were the "phuts" of mortars from behind them, sending their deadly packages over their heads and down onto the Lions below.

It was a bloodbath; by the time the Lions got untracked and managed to form up any kind of resistance, the Humans had expended two to three clips of ammo. Dead Lions littered the path where the column had been marching, their bodies in random heaps, blocking the road. And as the Lions finally started to get their act together and charge up the ridge in a counterassault, the Humans were gone. Withdrawing back down the ridge away from the lake, as fast as they could go, the Humans were well out of sight by the time the first of the enemy reached the crest of the ridge.

And then three miles farther east, a second wave of Humans rose from the snow, beside the tail end of the extended enemy column. As the Lions in the rear of the march peered forward down the trail, trying to make sense of all the firing they could hear up ahead, another four thousand Humans popped up out of their carefully constructed snow hides and opened fire. And another company of Lions died at the end of the column. In the mass confusion that ensued, many of the Lions turned and ran back to the east, where they were cut down by a crossfire set up across the trail for that purpose. Others ran out into the lake, trying to escape the withering fire, and drowned, weighed down by their ammunition packs and heavy rifles.

And then, just like the first ambush farther up the trail,

the Humans were gone. As the Singheko officers slowly got a counter assault organized and began to push toward their enemy, the firing stopped. By the time the Lions arrived at the site of the second ambush, those Humans had also disappeared into the storm, the thick cloud cover hiding them from the Stree overhead.

Bren was lucky - for the next two days, the weather was cloudy, cold, and stormy. Most of the time, the cloud cover was too thick for the Stree in orbit to rain kinetics down on them with any accuracy. Bren took deadly advantage. She put several hundred snipers around the line of march of the Singheko. Every few minutes, another Lion dropped dead from a long-range rifle shot. It didn't make much of a dent in the actual numbers of enemy toiling up the snow-covered slopes toward Mount Redoubt, but it paid dividends in slowing them down - and it certainly improved the morale of Bren's defenders.

But the Lions were no fools. They adapted, sending out small anti-sniper teams to quickly locate and neutralize the snipers. As the attrition rate became too high, Bren had no choice but to recall her snipers.

Twice, she made calculated raids against the Lions, chipping away at them. On the day after the ambush at the lake, the Lions entered an area of steeper ridges, the rugged terrain greatly slowing their advance. Like any good army, they sent a scout company ahead of the main column to clear the way.

Four miles ahead of the Lion's main column, the scout company entered a small pocket in the mountains. When they were fully established at the bottom of the pocket, ready to begin their climb up the next ridge, they stopped to rest. It was a natural thing to do; the weather was freezing, they were tired, and it was lunchtime.

Suddenly the very trees and rocks seemed to rise up at them. Two companies of Bren's troops opened up, raking them with rifle fire and grenades. The noise was deafening, and the carnage intense. Only a handful of Lions escaped the trap to make their way back to the main army and report.

After that, the Lions moved even more cautiously. They became much more forward-focused, putting three full companies of scouts out ahead of their main column - left, right and center.

But the next attack did not come from any of those directions. As the column of Lions encountered higher and rougher terrain, grinding their way up the mountain in snow now joined with sleet, their rear guard happened to fall a bit too far behind. Bren hit them hard from the rear, smashing into them in total surprise. Before the main column could send reinforcements back to assist, Bren had killed another company of Lions - followed by her troops disappearing into the snow and sleet like ghosts.

But after all of that, sitting in her Redoubt high in the mountains, watching the column of Lions move inexorably up the slopes toward her, Bren knew it was all in vain. The weather would clear, giving the Stree unimpeded targeting directly at her troops. There was no longer any doubt the Lions knew exactly where she was. She was hopelessly outnumbered. Nemo - if his ships were coming - was at least two days away.

She didn't have two days.

TWENTY-NINE

Phoenix System - Cruiser *Raptor*

Even from 40 AU away - even looking at it via holo over an ansible connection - the bridge of the distant destroyer *San Diego* looked all too familiar to Bonnie.

Dragon, she thought. *Those destroyers are so similar to my old ship* Dragon. *That brings back memories.*

At the other end of the holo connection, 3.7 billion miles away on the other side of the system, Bonnie could see Zoe DeLong in the command chair, where she had just taken command of Nemo's incoming destroyer flotilla.

And in the holo, standing beside the command chair, was someone Bonnie recognized.

Jim. No, wait. Not Jim. Nemo. But...wait. Nemo is a copy of Jim. So it's Jim.

Or is it? Does he remember me the same as Jim would?

The figure looked so much like Jim Carter, Bonnie was overcome with an overwhelming urge to try to reach out through the holo, to try somehow to embrace her former lover, to raise her arms and say something melodramatic. But mindful of her husband Luke behind her, Bonnie merely nodded in greeting. "Nemo, good to see you," she said. "Thank God you came!"

"Well, I almost didn't," responded Nemo. "It took some convincing from a friend of mine to get me here. Not to mention borrowing a good portion of his microbots."

"Ah - so that's how you built these ships."

"Yeah. Trillions of Goblin microbots - and nine asteroids."

"Well. Thank God you did it. We have a chance now. A small one, maybe, but at least a chance."

The distant Nemo turned slightly and gestured to Zoe sitting in the command chair on the flag bridge of the *San Diego*. "It's all yours," he said. "I'm out of here."

As Zoe registered a look of total surprise, Bonnie responded first.

"What? Aren't you staying with us?" she asked over the holo link.

"No. I have something else to do," the distant Nemo said, turning back to face Bonnie.

"Pray tell?"

In the view from the other end, Nemo gestured toward the tactical holotank on the bridge of the *San Diego*, pointing to the Stree fleet on the other side of the system.

"I'm going to get my daughter."

For a long moment, Nemo and Bonnie gazed at each other, oblivious to the distance between them, oblivious to the dozen people on both bridges. At last, Bonnie nodded. "Of course. Go do what you have to do."

"I'll get her," replied Nemo. "It's your fleet now. Good luck."

"You too," Bonnie managed, trying to ignore the tears in her eyes. "Go get our girl."

On his end of the holo, Nemo turned slightly to the bridge crew of the destroyer. He gave an informal salute to them, a last goodbye. He turned to Zoe, stepped forward, and reached out a hand. Shaking her hand, he lifted his head toward the ceiling of the *San Diego*'s bridge.

"Take good care of her," he said. "It took a lot to get her here."

Then he stepped away, walking briskly toward the hatch without a backward look, and was gone.

There was a silence on both ends of the holo link for several seconds. Then Bonnie turned her attention to Zoe. "Well, Commodore, it's your flotilla now. Let's get a meeting going to talk about tactics."

Onboard the *Raptor*, Bonnie sat at the head of the conference table. Her flag cabin was filled with officers. Luke sat at her right; her Flag Captain Joe Parker sat at her left. The holographic figures of the rest of her captains were arrayed down the table. Various officers and staff, some in the flesh and some holographic, made up a second row surrounding the conference table. It was a crowded room.

"First of all, some organizational notes," said Bonnie, her gaze traversing the room. "Captain Luke Powell will be my Chief of Staff. And yes, as you all know, he is both the Home Secretary and my husband. But he is also a Captain in the Reserves, and the one I trust to get the job done in this emergency. His orders will be obeyed as if they come from me. Is everyone clear on that?"

A wave of nods and murmurs went around the room.

"Good. Now, behind Captain Powell is Lieutenant Sunita. She will be my Flag Lieutenant. The same goes for her. You may be a captain of your ship, but if Lt. Sunita tells you I said to do something, you do it. No questions asked. Are we clear on that?"

Bonnie waited briefly while another wave of nods and murmurs completed. She glanced down the table where the holo of Vice-Admiral Zoe DeLong appeared from beyond the other side of the system via an ansible connection.

"As you know, Vice-Admiral Zoe DeLong has transferred to the new destroyer flotilla recently arrived. When we launch the attack, Zoe will bring the destroyer flotilla in from the other side of the system and make every effort to surprise the Stree at the last minute. So far, our intelligence indicates the Stree haven't detected her yet. Let's hope it stays that way.

"Zoe, I know your destroyer crews have had only five days to train. They probably think it's impossible to learn how to run a ship in only five days. Well, I'm sorry. That's all the time we have. Tell them they have to suck it up. We attack the Stree fleet in twenty-four hours."

Phoenix System - Stree Flagship *Unmerciful*

Admiral Rajanti was astounded. "Read that again, please," he said to the ship's dumb AI.

<Attention Admiral Rajanti: I will surrender to you in exchange for my daughter Imogen and her friend Marta Powell. Upon your agreement, I will approach within one hundred miles of your flagship in my corvette *Grizzly*. The exchange can be made via your shuttle attached to my corvette. When my daughter and her friend are safely away from your fleet in *Grizzly*, I will then return to your flagship without resistance. Signed: Jim Carter>

Rajanti shook his head in wonder.

What in the hell? I have the body of the Goblin Jim Carter in my cargo bay. What does this mean?

Standing before Rajanti's desk, Flag Captain Daqin waited silently. Rajanti spoke sharply.

"Bring me the Human called Imogen. Quickly!"

Daqin nodded, turned smartly, and departed. Rajanti waited impatiently. Within a few minutes, the hatch of his cabin opened. Two guards pushed the Human female roughly inside, followed by Daqin. Rajanti waved her to a chair, and Daqin pushed her down into it.

Leaning forward, Rajanti glared at Imogen, clearly unhappy.

"I'm going to ask you a question, and the life of your friend Marta depends on your answer. When we brought you aboard, you told us the body we retrieved from your packet boat was the original Goblin copy of your father. Was that true?"

Imogen looked at the Stree admiral. She could feel that something important depended on her answer - and of course, the life of her best friend. Thinking quickly, she gave the only answer that might work for any situation.

"There are two Goblin copies of my father Jim Carter. I honestly do not know which one was on board our ship. It could be either copy."

Rajanti glared at her. He waved a hand in dismissal. "Take her back to her cell." Daqin gestured to the guards, who grabbed her roughly and jerked her to her feet. They frog-marched her out of the cabin, closing the hatch behind them. Rajanti turned to Daqin.

"If there are two copies of this Jim Carter, then having them both would be even more of a plum for us."

"It could be a trick of some kind," Daqin replied. "The Humans may be trying to get a squad of Goblins onboard, or something like that. Or he could be wired for a bomb."

Rajanti shook his head. "There aren't that many Goblins left in the Arm to form a suicide squad. Plus, he'll be standing off a hundred klicks for the exchange. We'll have plenty of time to look things over. If anything smells funny about the exchange, we'll just blow the entire corvette to pieces."

Rajanti went silent in thought for a moment. Finally, he raised his head to Daqin.

"We'll do as the message says. Let the Human corvette approach as requested - a corvette is lightly armed; he couldn't hurt us in any case. Put the Human females Imogen and Marta in a shuttle and send them over to it. Take a full complement of combat troops with you. If the Goblin so much as twitches in the wrong direction, blow all of them away - the Humans as well as the Goblin."

"Aye, aye, sir," Rajanti's Flag Captain responded. He turned and left the cabin, leaving Rajanti to contemplate the strangeness of his enemies.

Twenty minutes later, Marta's cell door slammed open. The lights came on, rudely waking her from sleep. Four big Stree guards came in and wordlessly dragged her from her bunk, roughly handcuffing her hands behind her, pushing her stumbling out of the cell and down the corridor. In front of her, she saw Gen, also being pushed harshly down the corridor.

She called out to Gen, but one of the guards cuffed her

roughly in the mouth, drawing blood, so she went silent. Gen managed a quick look over her shoulder at Marta's call, but Gen's guards also slapped her, forcing her face back to the front.

In a few minutes, Marta realized they were approaching the shuttle bay. The guards forced them through the hatch, and they stood before a small shuttlecraft. Combat troops stood in two lines leading to the shuttle, their pulse rifles at the ready. The guards pushed them roughly to the shuttle, through the hatch, and slammed it behind them.

Marta and Gen looked into a shuttle filled with more combat-suited troopers, filling fold-down seats on each side of the shuttle's cargo area. In front of them stood two Stree officers.

One of the officers waved them to a couple of open seats at the front of the cabin. Having no other choice, Marta and Gen sat. The two officers sat directly across from them, staring at them across the cargo bay. As the two women felt the shuttle's engines spool up, one of the officers finally spoke.

"You are being exchanged for another prisoner," he said in guttural English. "You will be taken to the Human corvette *Grizzly* and released."

Gen, astonished, managed a quick look at Marta before she spoke.

"Who are we being exchanged for, then?" she asked.

"Your father," said the Stree officer.

"Bullshit," Marta said before she could stop herself. "Her father's body is lying in your cargo bay right now."

The Stree officer looked at them smugly as he replied.

"The other copy of her father," he said. "I believe there were two?"

Beside her, Marta felt Gen stiffen up in disbelief. "You mean Nemo?" Gen asked.

"Whatever he calls himself," said the Stree. "He signed the message as Jim Carter. He is exchanging himself for you and your friend."

Gen looked at Marta in total shock. The shuttle began to decelerate. The engines whined and then stopped, and they heard and felt the docking jets firing. With a clunk, the shuttle docked against another ship.

The Stree officer waved them to their feet and turned them to the airlock hatch. The hatch began to open. As it came fully open, Gen saw through the airlock a short boarding tube attached to another ship.

At the other end of the boarding tube was another open hatch. In the hatch opening stood a figure.

Gen recognized the figure standing in the boarding tube instantly. She had seen too many pictures of him in her life. And she had seen the dead version of him at Netaz.

This was her father. Regardless of which copy this was...

This was her father.

"Send the women to the halfway point, and I'll meet them there," Nemo said.

A Stree guard pushed Gen hard, painfully, his rifle barrel in the center of her back. She moved forward toward the middle of the boarding tube. Nemo moved toward her as well. Nearing the midpoint, Nemo stopped and waited for her.

Gen hesitated in front of him for only a second. Then she rushed into him, wrapping him up in her arms, the tears coming fast and hard. Nemo held her as she cried, as everything she had gone through poured out of her, both of them knowing they had only a few seconds together.

"I've missed you," breathed Nemo softly, a whisper almost impossible to hear.

"Dad!" whispered Gen, crying. She felt Marta's hand on her shoulder, comforting.

The tableau held, the two of them holding each other for many seconds, Marta behind Gen with her hand on Gen's shoulder, even the Stree frozen in the moment, their rifle barrels sagging toward the deck.

Finally, Gen pulled back, looking at Nemo.

"Dad, oh, Dad," cried Gen, the tears still blurring her vision. "What now?"

"Go to Bonnie," Nemo responded. "*Grizzly* will take you. She's your ship now. Take care of her; she's been good to me."

"Dad, isn't there some way…?"

Nemo shook his head. "No, Gen. This is what has to happen. It's all for the best."

"Mom's still back there. Rajanti has her."

Nemo smiled. "I know, hon. I'll take care of her. Remember - it's not over 'til the fat lady sings!"

The Stree were finally getting impatient. "Move out!" yelled the Stree officer, waving his pistol at them.

Nemo looked up at him. The look on Nemo's face made the Stree officer step back in fear. Something told him it was not a time to challenge this Goblin.

Nemo leaned forward and kissed Gen, caressed her face. "Go on now; we don't want to give them the opportunity to hold on to you."

Gen nodded understanding. Nemo stepped past her to Marta. "Take care of my daughter," he said, smiling at the young woman. Instinctively, Marta stepped forward, hugged Nemo, her eyes also tearing up. "I'll watch out for her," she said.

Nemo backed away from them and waited. Gen slowly took a step back, toward *Grizzly*, tears streaming down her cheeks.

This is the last time I will ever see him. I know it.

Nemo gave her one last nod, one last smile, and turned away toward the Stree. He stepped firmly out toward the enemy, never looking back, as Marta led Gen toward *Grizzly* and freedom.

"Inside," said the Stree officer, pushing Nemo harshly with the barrel of his pulse rifle. Nemo stepped into the shuttle. The hatch slammed shut behind him.

Well, that's done, thought Nemo. The Stree, terrified of him, surrounded him with a thicket of pulse rifle barrels, all pointed directly at his middle. He smiled and spoke to the officer in charge.

"You have nothing to fear," he said in perfect Stree. "You still hold my wife, so I have no intention of causing any trouble."

The Stree officer was clearly nervous in the presence of the Goblin, but he made an attempt to calm things down. He waved Nemo to a seat, and Nemo sat down quietly. The officer waved the troops back to their seats. As the shuttle detached from *Grizzly* and started back to *Unmerciful*, the officer also sat, staring at the hated enemy.

"You were on the *Armidale* when you destroyed Stree Prime," he said abruptly.

Nemo sighed mightily. "How many times do we have to tell you? We did not destroy Stree Prime. That was a rogue Goblin named Rauti. In fact, we diverted the last of the asteroids. The *Armidale* saved millions of your people."

"You lie," said the officer. "You killed billions. I will take immense pleasure in watching you die."

Nemo shrugged. "Believe what you want. Don't let facts get in your way."

There was an oppressive silence as the shuttle made its way back to *Unmerciful*. In a bit, they arrived in the shuttle bay, settling to the deck with a clunk. The doors of the bay closed, and a docking tube came out from the wall. In seconds, the hatch opened, and Nemo was pushed out, walking forward into the bowels of the Stree flagship. His escort marched him to the brig.

As the Stree pushed him into a cell and the door slammed behind him, Nemo smiled. The creature that was Jim Carter and not Jim Carter repeated a saying he had first used when he was still in Human form, standing in the squad bay at Marine Corps Officer Candidate School in Quantico, Virginia - with more gear on his back than he believed a man could carry in one load.

"Well, here's another nice mess you've gotten me into!"

THIRTY

Phoenix System - Cruiser *Raptor*

In the shuttle bay of the Human flagship *Raptor*, Marta stepped off first, to be wrapped up by her grandfather Luke Powell in a bear hug. Marta began to cry, relief at finally being safe overwhelming her. Luke held her tight, smoothing her hair, comforting her, looking over her shoulder as Gen came out of the hatch behind her. Suddenly Gen was also wrapped up in a hug, as Lord Admiral Bonnie Page stepped forward and embraced her, ignoring the shocked stares of the surrounding crew.

"I hope you two have had enough adventure for a while," Bonnie said wryly, letting go of her goddaughter. Gen nodded sheepishly. The four pulled back from each other, wiping their tears.

"OK," said Bonnie, all business again. She glanced at Luke, who nodded and pulled Marta off to one side. As Gen looked on in puzzlement, Luke spoke quietly to Marta, who burst into tears again.

"What's going on?" asked Gen, staring at Bonnie.

"Luke's telling her that her father Misha is dead," said Bonnie. "Let's give them some privacy."

Bonnie began walking away, toward the hatch that led into the ship. "Ensign Tran here will take you to your cabin. When you're reasonably rested, report to me in my day cabin. I've got jobs for both of you."

Gen glanced back over her shoulder at Marta. She could see Marta was overwhelmed, sobbing in the arms of her grandfather. Turning back to Bonnie, Gen spoke somewhat bitterly.

"We've spent the last four days sitting on our butts in a cell. I think we're rested enough."

"Good," said Bonnie. "Let's walk." The group started down the corridor toward Officer Country, Bonnie talking as they moved.

"We're incredibly short-handed right now. I've reinstated your EDF commissions. I'd like to keep you here on the *Raptor*, but Zoe needs experienced officers desperately in her destroyer flotilla. I'm sending both of you to her flagship *San Diego*. Take the rest of this watch off, get new uniforms from the store, get cleaned up. Report to the shuttle bay at 1800 hours for transfer to *San Diego*."

"But...how will you get us there?" asked Gen. "Zoe's fleet is completely on the other side of the system. The Stree are between us and her destroyers!"

"Nemo's corvette *Grizzly*," said Bonnie. "*Grizzly* can't stay here anyway - she wouldn't stand a chance in this battle that's coming. And I have other personnel I need to transfer over. I'll send her outbound, past the mass limit; she can sink out as if she's running away. They'll ignore her - she's too small to be of concern to them. Then you can loop around and surface nearby Zoe's fleet."

Pausing at a cross-corridor, Bonnie smiled at her goddaughter. "Ensign Tran will show you to quarters. I'll see you at the shuttle bay to see you off."

Eight hours later, Gen sat at the Tactical console of the destroyer *San Diego*. The ship's XO - John Reynolds - sat at her elbow.

"You good?" asked John.

"Yes, sir," Gen answered, working the touchscreen on the Tac console. "Like riding a bike."

"Good," said John, standing up to depart. "Keep at the simulations. We don't have much time."

"Aye, aye, sir," Gen answered, falling back into the rhythm of military life. Her military service had ended only a few weeks prior. She found it simple to slot back into the job. She continued working the simulation, her muscle memory on the Tac console still effective.

Nearby on the bridge, Marta was also performing simulation training in her role as Ops Officer.

Gen looked over at Marta, smiling at her. Marta had somewhat recovered from the shock of losing her father. She gave Gen back a wan smile. She was hanging in.

For Gen, it felt good to be safe, to be among friends again, to be doing something useful. But the threat of the coming battle loomed over them. In another six hours - at 0800 - they would be in combat. As soon as they set foot on the *San Diego*, they had been thrown into the mix. There was no time. There was no sleep. They had to prepare for the coming fight.

And Gen thought that was a good thing. The rush of training, the urgency of preparing for the coming battle, prevented her from thinking about other things.

Such as my father and mother in the hands of the Stree. If they are even still alive.

Gen glanced at the holo tank. The *San Diego*, leading the destroyer flotilla, was coasting into the Phoenix system, running on a long curving vector that kept the star between them and the Stree fleet. On the other side of the system, Bonnie's main Human fleet sat quietly for the moment, preparing their attack. And in orbit over Phoenix, the big Stree battlecruiser *Unmerciful* and her two escorting destroyers continued to throw the occasional kinetic down at the Human army below, as cloud cover allowed.

Other than the *Unmerciful* and her escorts, the rest of the Stree fleet held station between Phoenix and Bonnie's main fleet. The Stree knew where Bonnie's ships were in the outer system; but it wasn't worthwhile to come out after her. All they had to do was hold their position and destroy the Human army below them. They knew Bonnie would come in after them eventually.

Working the simulation almost unconsciously, Gen thought through her situation.

I'm on a destroyer that will be attacking the Stree in a few hours. It's possible I could be firing weapons at the Unmerciful.
Where my parents are.
I might kill my parents.
And yet I have no choice.
And I know that is exactly what they would want me to do.

Earth - Cappadocia, Turkey

It had been a long, grinding retreat from Derinkuyu. For four long days, the Lions had harried the Humans. Somehow, against all odds, Yuki and her rear guard had kept the Lions at arm's length while Garyn and Jake led the rest of their people away from Underground City, looking for some place to make a stand.

For a brief period of time, Garyn had entertained the idea of heading east to hide in the rugged foothills of 12,851-foot Mount Erciyes. But the Lions anticipated, sending two of their companies to the east, cutting the Humans off from the mountain. With no choice, Garyn returned to his original plan and continued northeast toward Urgup.

The only good news was the Lions were in no hurry; they pitched camp at dusk that first day, giving the Humans a window of opportunity. Garyn and Jake drove their survivors nonstop, knowing their lives depended on getting to shelter before daybreak. While Yuki's soldiers brought up the rear, the Humans raced along the west side of the Damsa River, arriving in utter exhaustion at Urgup just at dawn.

All day that second day, they had hidden in the empty city while Yuki and her troops held off the Lions on the edge of town. The Lions had not been overly eager to attack that second day; they knew they had the Humans boxed. There was no point in taking heavy casualties just to rush things.

On the third day, the Lions got more aggressive. They began to encircle Yuki's force, forcing her to retreat - else she would be cut off. Driven back to the center of the city, Yuki, Garyn, and Jake decided to make their stand there, using the empty houses and buildings as defensive positions.

But the Lions had other ideas. Suddenly, the Lions pulled back. Shortly after, the kinetics started. Huge missiles from space rained down, buildings exploding in massive gouts of dirt and debris, killing anyone within a hundred yards.

Before Garyn could stop them, his people panicked. They ran screaming away from the center of the city, toward the northwest.

Garyn, Jake, and Yuki had no choice but to follow them, trying to hold off the pursuing Lions. Six miles later, with the Lions close on their heels, they managed to find higher ground at Zelve. Taking positions in ancient caves on the upper hillside, Yuki and her troops turned on the Lions, fighting them to a standstill, buying some time.

But for the last twenty-four hours, they had been trapped in the caves on the slopes of Zelve. There was no water to drink, no food to eat, no place to go. The Lions camped in the valley below, waiting them out. They were in no rush; they knew they had their quarry trapped.

THIRTY-ONE

Phoenix System - West Mountains

In the Redoubt, Bren sat at her conference table, waiting for her staff to assemble. When all of them were present, she began.

"The weather forecast for tomorrow is clear," she began. "That means the Stree upstairs will have a good view of everything we do. They'll be dropping kinetics on us all day. The Lions will make it here around noon. By mid-afternoon, we'll be under attack by four full divisions."

"Ha! More like three and a half, now," interrupted her Ops Officer. "We've whittled them down a bit!"

Bren couldn't help but smile. "Agreed. Three and a half divisions."

In the long silence that followed, Bren could feel, more than see, the eyes of her staff. In the quiet, Bren spoke again. "All of you know the plan. And all of you know the odds. This will be our last chance to change course. Either we stick to the plan as designed – or we throw in the towel, disperse the army into the mountains, try to save as many as we can. Let me hear your thoughts."

"We stay. We fight," Anders Paulsen said quickly, beating everyone else to the punch. Within seconds, Bren's entire staff echoed his sentiment, a chorus of rousing agreement.

But Bren waved them down. "I appreciate your emotions, and I understand. But I don't want a knee-jerk, emotional response. I want a reasoned, logical response. That's what we're being paid to do here for our people, and that's what we'll do. So, let's try this again – this time, without the emotion."

Bren waited patiently through a long silence. It was Ana Trinh who spoke first this time.

"Where would we go? If we don't fight this battle – and win it – there is no place left for Humans in the Arm. They drove us out of Earth. They drove us out of Stalingrad. Now they want to drive us out of Phoenix. I say - no more. I'd rather die here and now. I'm not backing up another step."

One by one, everyone around her nodded, voicing their agreement. At the end, Anders summed it up for all of them. "We fight here. We win here - or we die here. But we don't give these bastards another fucking inch."

Nodding, Bren rose from the table. She gazed around her staff for what could be the last time she saw all of them alive.

"Then notify Tatiana and Mark. Operation Deadfall is a go."

Ana Trinh made one more comment. "By the way, we're down to only one day of field rations for the army."

Bren smiled at Ana calmly.

"That's fine. We won't need any more field rations after tomorrow. One way or another."

Phoenix System - Cruiser *Raptor*

Lord Admiral Bonnie Page sat on the flag bridge of *Raptor*, staring at the holo plot. As her main force of three cruisers, nine destroyers, and three converted gunboats streaked in from the outer system, she could clearly see the Stree formation in front of her. She was coming at a mad pace. She had accelerated her fleet at 400g for 7.7 hours, reaching a top speed of 36% of light. Then she had gone into a hard decel, shedding velocity just as fast, her intention to get down to combat speed as she merged with the Stree fleet. She made no attempt to conceal her approach; her engines blazed with heat as she decelerated, undoubtedly showing on the enemy plot like a lit-up Christmas tree.

And that was exactly what she wanted. Because on the

other side of the star, Vice-Admiral Zoe DeLong was bringing in Nemo's sixteen destroyers. Starting earlier than Bonnie's task force and from much farther away, they had accelerated to a lower speed, using the minimum of thrust, in a long, curving trajectory that kept them positioned with the star directly between them and the main Stree fleet, hiding their tiny engine burns as much as possible.

Bonnie knew it might not work. But even if the Stree detected Zoe's destroyers earlier than hoped, it was still a decent plan. They would still pinch the Stree in between them, a crossfire that - in theory - would even the odds somewhat.

"Five minutes to merge," called the *Raptor*'s Tactical officer on the deck below her.

Like all Human capital ships, Bonnie's flag bridge was merely a raised platform at the rear of the bridge, six inches higher than the rest of the deck, with a small ledge around the perimeter. There were five chairs on it. Bonnie sat in the front center, with a good view of the entire bridge. On her right, her chief of staff - Luke - was her deputy, responsible for ensuring her orders were carried out quickly and correctly. On her left, her flag lieutenant - Lieutenant Sunita - was responsible for ensuring that communications were maintained during the battle. Behind her, her N2 Intelligence chief sat, along with her personal aide - both ready as needed.

"All ships reporting weapons charged and ready," came a voice from beside her.

Bonnie re-focused on Lt. Sunita in the command chair next to her. The lieutenant was working her console madly, trying to keep up with the status of everything in the fleet.

"Excellent, Lieutenant."

"Two minutes," call the Tac Officer from the bridge below them - and indeed Bonnie could see the countdown on the right sidebar of the holo, steadily counting down the time to in-range.

Two minutes. And then her fifteen ships would join Zoe's sixteen to take on fifty of the enemy.

Fifty against thirty-one. Not too bad.

But three of mine are converted transports, hovering in the rear, hoping not to get blown out of the black in the first volley.

Of course, five of theirs are Singheko drop ships, lightly armed. So really, it's more like forty-five against twenty-eight.

Oh, that sounds a lot better.

Phoenix System - Destroyer *San Diego*

On the other side of the Stree, fifty-five thousand miles from Bonnie, Zoe DeLong sat on the flag bridge of the *San Diego* as they coasted in toward the Stree fleet. The bridge was quiet; the crew did their jobs, but mostly they just waited with bated breath, knowing they were minutes away from combat.

Zoe looked at the two new officers sent over from Bonnie's main fleet last night, Imogen Carter Page and Marta Powell. They sat at their consoles, ready to do battle.

Tatiana's daughter. Great. Just great. My bosses' boss. Lord help me if I get her killed.

And the daughter of the most famous Goblin in history - a Goblin who just happens to be a prisoner in the brig of my primary target today. A damn good possibility I'll blow the Unmerciful *away before this battle is over. It's even possible that this girl will push the button that kills her mother...*

What a universe...

"In range in two minutes," called Gen.

Phoenix System - Cruiser *Raptor*

"Oh, oh," called *Raptor*'s Tactical Officer. "They just picked up Zoe's destroyers."

Bonnie saw two dozen of the Stree fleet rotating their ships toward Zoe's approaching task force. They had finally noticed the sixteen destroyers coasting in behind them. They were re-orienting, putting their front-mounted gamma lances toward the other threat.

Bonnie smiled. She couldn't help it. What happened from

here on out was up to her crew, and the WepsAI. She had always smiled at this point in a battle, when things were no longer under her control, and random chance would determine her fate. She had never really understood why she had this reaction. It had caused no end of concern among her staff, but it was something she could not resist.

Rachel always laughed about this on the old Dragon, she remembered. *God, I miss her. And Ollie. And all of them.*

A loud warning horn sounded. They were almost in range. The warning horn told them that *Raptor* was about to start evasive action.

And then *Raptor* began jinking, a random pattern of jerks and bumps that exceeded compensator damping by several g. Even though everyone was strapped in with a five-point combat harness, the gyrations knocked them back and forth in their chairs, barely able to concentrate on their systems. All of them knew they would be black and blue tomorrow - if they still breathed. But they also knew it was their only chance to stay alive.

"Go, *Raptor*, go!" someone called out enthusiastically.

A second warning horn sounded. They were in range. In the holo, five thousand miles away, the first gamma lance volleys fired from the Stree fleet. Half were fired at Bonnie's task force, the other half at Zoe's destroyers. At exactly the same time, Bonnie's fleet lashed out with their own lances. The space between the fleets was suddenly a maze of red and yellow tracks. Death reached hungrily for a bride, while warships danced madly to avoid the marriage.

The smile disappeared from Bonnie's face. She gripped the arms of her command chair hard, trying to stay upright, as her ship waltzed the dance of death with the enemy. Bonnie watched the holo silently. The beauty - and the danger - of a gamma lance was that it was so quick. There was virtually no defense against it, other than the gyrations of the ship, trying to be someplace else when the lance fired.

A graze hit the *Raptor* up front, the noise sounding like

fingernails scraping a blackboard as a gamma lance touched the skin of the ship without penetrating. On the holo, Bonnie saw one of her destroyers disappear into junk as it took a direct hit amidships. Four thousand miles away now, as the two fleets closed, a Stree destroyer went up similarly, all the volatiles and weapons on board creating a tremendous bloom of fire in space that flashed briefly and then was gone, leaving nothing behind but an expanding cloud of gases, debris, and bodies. Then another Stree ship exploded, another direct hit, and then another. Then a Stree cruiser went down, and several members of the bridge crew began cheering, excited.

Bonnie had a brief moment of hope, of hope that they would prevail, that Zoe's destroyers coming in from behind had surprised the Stree sufficiently to keep them disoriented, not ready to fight.

But that hope was quickly dashed. Close by them, the destroyer *Cordell* exploded, smashed to bits as a gamma lance went right through her engineering spaces, setting off something catastrophic.

"Missile range!" yelled the Tac officer. Bonnie felt *Raptor* shudder as the WepsAI automatically flushed its first volley of missiles. Simultaneously, the Stree fleet did the same, firing in both directions, toward Zoe's destroyers coming up their backside, and toward Bonnie's main fleet in front of them. The holo lit up, the space between the fleets filled with great herds of missiles moving in each direction.

The second phase of the battle began now, a slug fest of close-range missile combat. Bonnie had been through this before. She knew what was going to happen. But that didn't make it any easier. She had time to glance at Luke in his chair beside her. Sensing her gaze, her husband turned, one last look at the woman he loved before the Universe tossed the dice. Bonnie knew exactly what he was thinking.

A few hours from now, most of us will be dead. But we'll take some Stree with us, by God.

Earth - Cappadocia, Turkey

"Fuck, I'm thirsty," muttered Captain Yukiko Takahara. "I could sure use some water."

Beside her, Garyn managed a weak smile. "Feel free to go get some. It's right down there. Right behind those Lions."

Not finding it as funny as Garyn did, Yuki remained silent. She tried to lick her lips with the little moisture she still had in her body - but it was futile. There was no moisture to spare; she hadn't had water for two days.

"Why don't they come on up and get us?" Yuki murmured through cracked lips. "They know they've got us. What the hell are they waiting for? They don't even have to come up here - all they have to do is send more kinetics down on us and grind us down to nothing, then waltz in and pick up the pieces."

Garyn grunted. "They're Lions. You know how they are. They like to fight their enemy hand to hand, kill them personally. And they like prisoners - they can put them in their arena for a little blood sport. They probably want to capture as many as possible alive."

"What?"

"Yeah," Garyn continued. "They like to torture their prisoners in front of crowds in their arenas, then chop off their heads. It's a big thing with the Lions."

Yuki shuddered. "So, you're saying…"

"I'm saying, no point in going back with them as a prisoner, just to have our heads chopped off. If you get my drift…"

Yuki's radio beeped. Leaning down, she listened as a message came in from her scouts. Raising her head, she looked at Garyn grimly.

"They're coming. Straight up the hill. All of them."

"Well," said Garyn. It was all he could think of at the moment.

Yuki bent to her radio, issuing orders. Garyn mused silently, looking down the hill into the valley. Now that he knew where to look, he could see the Lions, a long, compact column of dots far below. Dots that would soon be a lot closer, and a lot bigger.

THIRTY-TWO

Phoenix System - Cruiser *Raptor*

The initial pass through the Stree fleet had taken out fifteen Stree warships, including one of their cruisers. The sudden appearance of Zoe's sixteen destroyers from behind had caught the Stree on one foot, preventing them from concentrating their fire on either fleet. And the Humans had definitely outperformed the Stree; their semi-sentient AI were vastly superior to the dumb fire-control computers of the enemy. It was the outcome Bonnie had planned for, had hoped for; nevertheless, she was pleasantly surprised that it had gone so well.

But the Humans had lost eight destroyers, two gunboats, and the cruiser *Defender*. That hurt - especially the cruiser. Bonnie's quick calculation in her head was chilling. Even with the favorable attrition ratio they had accomplished in the first pass, they would lose this battle. There were just too many of the enemy. And the next time, they would not catch them off-guard.

Plus, the enemy battlecruiser *Unmerciful*, sitting out the first pass in orbit around Phoenix, had now left orbit to come out and join the rest of her fleet. Evidently, Rajanti had decided the Humans were a bigger threat than he initially thought. This time, the Humans would be facing the terrible firepower of the battlecruiser as well.

But Tatiana said it. We fight until we can't fight anymore.

In the first pass, both Bonnie's main fleet and Zoe's destroyer flotilla had flashed through the Stree at speed, firing everything they had, until they were well beyond the enemy fleet and out of range. Now, they came back around in long, sweeping arcs for their second pass at the Stree.

But this pass would be grim. This time, the Stree were fully prepared. This time, they would not be complacent. This time, the battlecruiser *Unmerciful* would be in the brawl. There would be no finesse in this pass.

As her fleet came around the backside of their loop, Bonnie brought up Zoe on her personal holo. "How you doin', love?" she asked quietly.

"Been better," Zoe replied grimly. "We lost the *Toronto*, the *Jakarta*, and the *Warsaw*. The *Cairo* is badly damaged, I'm sending her to the rear. Several other ships took damage, but they're mostly still combat-effective."

"Yeah, I'm doing the same with the gunboats - we lost two of them. They're just too lightly armed to be in this kind of fight. I'm sending the last one back to Phoenix."

Bonnie gestured toward the holo on her side. The two elements of the Human fleet were around the arc now, headed back toward the Stree fleet, in line for their second pass.

"They're bringing out the *Unmerciful* and her destroyer screen this time. I'll take her on with my cruisers; you concentrate on the destroyers closest to you."

"Aye, aye," responded Zoe.

"Break a leg," Bonnie added.

"Break a leg," Zoe replied.

Now they were fully aligned on their inbound tracks, both the Human fleets charging again at the Stree, the Stree adjusting positions to take on both fleets, the *Unmerciful* arriving from Phoenix with her destroyers.

"In range," Bonnie heard. The distinctive screeching, grating sound of the gamma lance came through the bridge wall, as *Raptor*'s WepsAI began their attack. At the same time, *Raptor* began her random dance, a jig left, a jig down, now a jig down again, now right, a dance that would determine if they would live or die.

The two destroyers in front of *Raptor* took hard hits, one of them spewing out atmosphere and volatiles, leaving a long streak behind her, while the other one skewed off to the right as her engines were damaged and she couldn't maintain course.

They're deliberately concentrating on my screen, thought Bonnie. *Trying to knock out my protection so they can get to* Raptor. *And it's working...*

A shudder shook *Raptor*, a grazing near miss that left a gouge down the side of the ship but didn't penetrate.

That was damn close.

Three Stree destroyers veered off course, hit hard, taking themselves out of the battle. Then another Stree destroyer bloomed and disappeared, gone from the plot.

Watching the holo plot as dispassionately as possible, Bonnie was not happy.

Good. But not good enough. We have to do better than this.

Suddenly the bridge crew let out a shout. A Stree cruiser disappeared from the holo, exploding in a convulsion of searing debris.

That's more like it. C'mon, c'mon. Get us another cruiser!

Behind *Raptor*, another one of Bonnie's destroyers started flashing red on the holo, turning away from the battle, too severely damaged to continue the fight.

They came into missile range. Hundreds of Stree missiles came at them. The *Unmerciful*, now in the battle, alone sent sixty-four missiles, most of them targeting the Human's two remaining cruisers, the *Raptor* and the *Corsair*.

The chatter of the defensive railguns began, the old familiar refrain. Bonnie watched in horror as a flood of missiles came at *Raptor*. As the railguns increased their chatter of point defense, as the *Raptor* jerked and leapt with a ferocity she had never experienced before, Bonnie knew it was over.

What were we thinking? We never had a chance.

Destroyer *San Diego*

Space was alive with death. The red and yellow streaks of dozens of gamma lances crisscrossed the space between the fleets, a tapestry of destruction. The WepsAI of the *San Diego* jinked the ship madly, gyrating with increased ferocity as it tried to avoid the incoming. Even with her five-point harness cinched down tight, it was all Zoe could do to stay in her seat and keep her eyes focused on the holo.

Directly in front of them, the destroyer *Milano* transformed. One moment, she was a sleek black wedge firing her gamma lance at the distant Stree, a miracle of microbot construction. The next moment, she was a gout of fire and debris, an exploding flower in space that quickly grew, expanded, and faded almost before you could comprehend what had happened.

Before another five seconds passed, another space flower appeared behind them, another deadly bloom marking the end of the destroyer *Moscow* - and the sixty Humans inside her. The *Moscow's* munitions cooked off, sending streaks of fire in every direction, missiles tracking crazily toward nowhere and anywhere, disappearing into the void, flying toward the nearby star, several of them narrowly missing other Human ships in the formation.

The threads of destruction seemed to surround them. And yet they were still alive. Zoe thought it almost a miracle. But space was big, and a ship was small, and at a range of now just under nine hundred miles, even an AI could miss a rapidly dancing object.

Thank God, thought Zoe. *If fire control computers were perfect, every ship on both sides would already be dead.*

Just then, a harsh ripping sound from behind showed that the *San Diego* was not entirely immune from the massive firepower of the Stree fleet.

"Through and through hit into Deck E cargo space, mum!" yelled Marta. "All systems operating normally!"

Zoe nodded. That had been lucky. If the lance had been a

tiny bit farther aft and a bit higher, it would have taken out the Engineering spaces. And the *San Diego* would have been another space flower blooming in the black.

"Missile range! Launching missiles!" came the call from Gen.

In the holo, Zoe could see their missile launch going outbound, and the massive Stree missile attack coming back at them. It was impressive. Thirty-three surviving Stree ships launched 392 missiles, half of them targeting Bonnie's main fleet and half targeting Zoe's destroyers. Zoe's task force launched a meager ninety-six missiles; Bonnie launched another 104 of the ship-killers. Missiles streaked toward their targets, the range closing incredibly fast, space now filled with a confusing, swirling tornado of gamma lance spears, flying missiles, dying ships, fragments and debris spreading in all directions.

The speed of battle in space was incredible. The countdown on the holo sidebar showed the time to missile impact; the numbers were almost a blur. Only their WepsAI could handle the task of defending against such an onrush. A Human could try to set priorities, touch the Tactical screen to influence where they wanted the AI to focus; but in the end, it was up to the WepsAI to save them.

The long-range point defense railguns began their chatter, their vibration shaking the ship, setting Zoe's teeth on edge. The blooms of destroyed missiles cluttered up the holo plot, then disappeared as the WepsAI removed them from the display. But there weren't enough of the enemy missiles disappearing from the holo. Zoe knew they were in real trouble. Too many of the Stree missiles were getting past the railguns. Quickly checking the far side of the holo, she saw that Bonnie was also being pounded. And even as she watched, Bonnie's flagship *Raptor* disappeared in a massive smash of missiles into her stern, the explosions completely hiding *Raptor* from view.

The *San Diego* began jinking even harder, the G-forces far

beyond combat norms as the WepsAI tried desperately to save them from the massive strike of incoming missiles. Zoe smashed against the side of her seat so hard she felt a rib crack. As the close-in point defense lasers started their loud whine and snap, an involuntary expression came out of Zoe's mouth, almost as if someone else had spoken.

"Help us, Lord," she said softly.

There was just enough time for her to have two more thoughts.

Now why did I say that?

And then:

Ah, right. There are no atheists in foxholes.

THIRTY-THREE

Destroyer *San Diego*

The Stree missiles hit the *San Diego* hard, two missiles breaking through the last layer of point defense. One of them exploded some distance away as the ship jinked away from it, splattering the destroyer with shrapnel that holed the hull near the nose, but caused no serious damage.

The other missile was a solid hit, just behind the bridge. The only thing that saved the ship was a slightly defective proximity fuse. The missile was designed to explode its warhead as it neared the hull, a shaped charge that would punch deep into the ship, causing maximum damage. But the fuse on this warhead was slightly late. The missile punched almost all the way through the ship before exploding ten feet from the far side. Forty feet of hull on the starboard side of the *San Diego* exploded outward, leaving a flower of twisted metal and composite, spewing atmosphere, material, and people out the hole in a heartbeat.

The energy of the warhead almost missed the bridge. Had the detonation occurred even a few milliseconds later, the bridge would have survived nearly intact.

But it didn't. A huge gout of white-hot flame and hundreds of pieces of shrapnel scoured the bridge, killing almost everyone. The bridge was holed in a half-dozen places, the atmosphere blown out, the consoles wrecked. Bodies lay everywhere, many of them missing arms or legs - or cut in half.

Marta found herself on the floor, the remains of a chair across her legs. Her combat suit had sealed, the faceplate automatically locking down in front of her face. She looked down, pushed the broken seat off her. She realized the legs of her combat suit were covered in blood. It took her a few seconds to realize it wasn't hers.

If it were my blood, my suit would be decompressed. I'd be dead already.

Groggily, Marta reached for the edge of a sheared-off console above her, grabbed it, pulled herself to a sitting position. She looked around at total chaos. There wasn't a single person moving. Most of the seats on the bridge were now on the floor. It was like a massive shotgun blast had sliced through the bridge. Blood was everywhere, already sublimating in the vacuum, turning into a maroon-brown dust of ice crystals. The grav plates were inoperative. Body parts floated around, mixed with the dust and every kind of junk. A half-dozen battery-powered reddish emergency lights provided the only illumination.

Gen. Where's Gen?

Marta looked around. Gen had been sitting right beside her. Now she was nowhere to be seen. Desperate, Marta tried to stand up, but the lack of gravity caused her to fly up to the top of the bridge, bang her head on the ceiling, then bounce back down to the floor. She managed to grab the broken console again as she came back down, and got her space legs working, coming to a stop in a half-crouched position, holding on to the torn-off top of the console.

A half-dozen feet away, she saw a foot sticking out from behind another broken console. Moving carefully, she worked her way around the junk lying everywhere, around the console to the other side.

It was Gen. She was on her stomach, unconscious. Her combat suit looked intact, though. Marta felt the suit. It was firm - it had pressure. Carefully, Marta rolled Gen over for inspection.

Gen's faceplate was down - that was good. The telltales on the side of her helmet were green. That was also good. That meant she had pressure, temperature, and air. There was a large blemish on the side of her helmet where something had impacted it; but it hadn't broken the helmet. So there was a chance...

Marta reached forward, flipped a switch at the base of Gen's helmet to put it on emergency frequency.

"Gen! Wake up!" she yelled. If the radio was still operative... that was the question. The helmet had taken quite a hit.

Gen's eyes fluttered. Marta had a flash of hope. She called again, shaking her gently.

"Gen! Wake up! We need to get out of here!"

A groan. Gen's eyes opened, unfocused. Closed again.

"Gen! Gen!" Marta yelled over the radio.

Another groan. Gen opened her eyes, tried to look at Marta. There was no recognition in her eyes. She was disoriented.

Marta thought through the problem. Given the lack of gravity, she could easily pick Gen up and carry her off the bridge. But it would be tough to get her through all the hatches and corridors they had to pass on their way to the shuttle bay. It would be better if Gen were conscious. Marta shook her again. "Gen! We have to go. Can you get up?"

A slight nod. Some understanding. Gen moved her arms uncertainly, trying to get up. But she didn't realize there wasn't any gravity. Gen floated away from the floor, turning like a rotisserie, out of control. Marta grabbed her, pulled her back down.

"No grav!" she yelled. "Use your space legs!"

Somehow, Gen understood. Marta saw a slight nod inside the helmet. Gen moved slowly, reaching out, grabbing the edge of a console, pulling herself around to face the hatch at the back of the shattered bridge. Marta took her by the arm, preparing to push them off together toward the rear hatch.

"Wait," she heard, a weak protest. "Where's the Captain?"

"Dead," Marta said firmly. She had already seen the Captain, or what was left of him. He was in two pieces.

"Wha...about the Admiral?"

"I don't know," Marta answered honestly. "But we need to get out of here. This ship is just a target now. They'll be tearing it to shreds any second."

Gen seemed to be coming to herself. She straightened a bit, holding herself up on the shattered console. "We have to find the Admiral," she said. "Look around."

Marta didn't want to do it. She knew the ship was a deathtrap. Some Stree captain would want to take credit for finishing them off. She wanted to get the hell out.

If it had been anyone else... But it was Gen asking. Gen would never forgive her if she didn't at least try...

Looking around, Marta thought she saw a flash of blue far back on the bridge, stuffed into the rear corner. It could be an Admiral's tunic. She pushed off from the console and floated in that direction. As she got closer, she realized that it was, indeed, the admiral. Zoe was on her back, floating just above the deck. Marta pushed down to her and began inspecting the unconscious woman.

Two of Zoe's telltales were green - oxygen and temperature. But the pressure telltale was orange. There was a leak in the suit. Marta inspected the suit, looking for the hole. She found nothing on the front. She rolled Zoe over, checking the back.

"There," said a voice. Startled, Marta looked up. Gen floated just above her, holding to a handle on the bridge wall.

"On the right side of her helmet," Gen pointed. "See it?"

Marta looked again, and there it was. A small hole in the helmet, high and to the right. Blood bubbled outward, an indicator that some shrapnel had entered the helmet.

Here's hoping it didn't whack her brain, Marta thought as she fished an emergency patch out of Zoe's leg pocket and slapped it over the hole. When it was sealed, she finished her inspection of the admiral's suit. She didn't find anything else.

"Let's get her out of here," Gen said beside her.

"How you feeling?" asked Marta.

"Like shit. Let's roll."

The two of them managed to get Zoe's unconscious body

between them, and they pushed off for the back hatch. They worked their way out of the bridge and into the corridor beyond.

Outside the bridge, the lights were out, even the emergency lights, so they had only their headlamps to show the way. The ship was a shambles. Cables hung from the ceiling, impeding their path. Huge holes on both sides of the corridor made it look a maze. Bodies were everywhere, many in pieces, floating, tangled up in loose cables, impossible to avoid. Trying to ignore the carnage, they pushed through, dragging Zoe behind them. It took them ten minutes of dogged, sweaty determination to get to the shuttle bay. When they arrived, they hesitated before going through the last hatch.

If all the shuttles were gone…if everyone had already abandoned ship…they would be trapped. Target practice for the Stree.

Or they could just step off into space. Become two small blobs of life floating in an infinite sea of black, hoping for pickup before their air ran out.

Pulling Zoe and themselves through the last hatch, they let out a sigh of relief as they saw a shuttle still sitting on the deck, with an open hatch. A master chief stood by the hatch, waving at them to hurry. They pushed off to the shuttle as fast as they could safely go. With a bang that rattled their bones, they collided with the flat side of the shuttle, and worked their way to the hatch, dragging Zoe in with them. The master chief came in behind them and slammed the hatch shut.

"Stand by for grav!" came a shout over the emergency channel. Marta and Gen pulled themselves down to the canvas seats on the side of the shuttle, locking Zoe down between them as best they could.

"Grav in five seconds! Five-four-three-two-one…" came in a hurried rush, and with a snap, they were suddenly heavy, pushed down into the seats as the grav plates came online.

As the shuttle lifted from the deck and exited the shattered destroyer as fast as the nervous pilot could take it out, Marta and Gen saw a stream of vapor coming out of the high-speed pressurization vents. In a couple of minutes, the chief yelled "Pressure up!"

The master chief reached to push up his faceplate as pressure came up in the shuttle. Marta and Gen did the same, then removed Zoe's helmet and began to examine her wound.

It was a nasty one. The shrapnel had entered Zoe's helmet and left a bloody trench across the side of her head. Gen was no expert, but she thought it had fractured the skull. For now, all they could do was stop the bleeding, bandage the wound, and get her to a safe place as quickly as possible.

Gen was getting her strength back, along with her wits. She knew the next ship in seniority was the *London*. She looked up at the master chief. "Where are we headed?" she asked. "Are we going to the *London*?"

"No. The *London* is down too. We're going to the *Dallas*. If we can catch her."

Gen looked at the chief in puzzlement. "What do you mean, if we can catch her?"

The chief looked grim. "She's turning to run. She's leaving. It's going to take everything this shuttle has to catch her before she's out of range."

Earth - Cappadocia, Turkey

Garyn ducked as another volley of pulse rifle fire zipped over his head. The Lions were only two hundred yards away now, keeping an unrelenting fire directed at the Humans. Chips of rock from the overhang above them fell on Garyn and Yuki constantly. The occasional near miss sprayed small pieces of rock over them, stinging like the dickens. The steady drumbeat of rifle fire from both Humans and Lions provided a noisy background concert as Yuki tried to keep her defense coordinated.

Ten yards away, huddling behind another rocky parapet,

Jake and several of Yuki's soldiers kept up a sporadic counterpoint of rifle fire, trying to conserve ammunition while keeping the Lions at bay. Garyn saw Jake glance his way, smile, and lift a hand. Garyn lifted a hand back in response; but he couldn't find it in himself to smile. The situation was just too dire.

"How much ammo we got left?" Garyn heard Yuki ask on the radio, polling her troops.

Garyn couldn't hear the answer, but he didn't have to. He could tell from the expression on Yuki's face. As she put down her headset, he raised an eyebrow at her. She just shook her head.

"We're about done, Garyn," she said. "We can maybe hold them for another ten minutes. That's it."

Garyn nodded.

So. The end of the experiment. We'll run out of ammo. Then the Lions will come up the last two hundred yards and take us. The survivors will be loaded up on the Singheko destroyer and taken back to Aslar, for the arena. They'll be put on display in front of screaming, bloodthirsty crowds, tortured, and executed on the chopping block.

"Yuki," Garyn began. But he couldn't finish it. Yuki looked at him. She read his mind.

"The children," she said. "Do you think…"

"I don't know what to do," Garyn said in agony. "Should we…"

Tears came into his eyes. "I don't think I can do it…" he mumbled, unable to speak more.

Yuki tried to say it. "Do you want me to…"

Garyn shook his head, tears blinding him.

Yuki was also crying. As the pulses of the enemy rifles flew over their heads, they found themselves somehow holding on to each other's arms, the touch of another Human the only thing keeping them sane.

"We can't do it," Yuki managed to get out in her agony. "We just can't."

Garyn nodded, his tears blinding him. "I know. We have to let God decide. But we have to pray they don't suffer too much."

THIRTY-FOUR

Destroyer *Dallas*

Their pilot had nearly burnt out the engines of the little shuttle; but somehow he had managed to catch the *Dallas* before she was out of range. With a bang, the shuttle slammed into the side of the destroyer, hard enough to rattle Gen's teeth. She shook it off; at the moment, she was more concerned about her admiral than anything else. Zoe's breathing was labored, raspy; she was in trouble. She needed medical attention, and she needed it now. As they bounced off the destroyer and came back for a second try at docking, Marta and Gen re-bandaged the bloody wound on the side of Zoe's head. When finally the struggling pilot got the shuttle back into position, and the boarding tube had been attached, the master chief assisted Marta and Gen in lifting Zoe and carrying her down the tube into the destroyer.

The pilot had called ahead; two medics waited nearby with a gurney. Gen and Marta gently placed Zoe on it and watched as the medics strapped her down and rushed her off to sick bay.

Then they stood, at a loss what to do next. Their ship was gone. They were merely survivors now. They had nothing to do.

"Where should we go?" wondered Gen, looking at Marta. Marta shrugged, glanced at the master chief.

"Ops Center, maybe?" suggested the chief. "Should be one deck below the bridge. We can do damage control."

Gen and Marta nodded. It made sense. The three of them started down the corridor toward the center of the destroyer.

The corridors were chaos. *Dallas* was one of the new ships brought by Nemo. The crew was green, inexperienced - and they had just been through trial by fire. Although not as bad as *San Diego*, the ship was pretty well shot up. It was clear *Dallas* had taken a beating in the second pass of the battle. They could hear fire alarms in the distance, somewhere toward the back of the ship. Smoke permeated the corridors. It was cold in the ship, much colder than it should be - something was wrong with the environmental system. At one point, they were unable to continue on their path - wires and conduit were smashed down from the ceiling, blocking the way, forcing them to detour.

"This was the best ship we could find?" muttered Marta to the chief's back as he led the way around the mess to another corridor.

The master chief looked back at her. "Got air, don't we?" he grinned. "Don't complain!"

They finally came out at the Ops Center on Deck D, one level below the bridge. There was a constant scurry of crew in and out; they had to wait for an opening before they could pass through the narrow hatch to get inside. There, they found a chaotic muddle of crew working damage control, trying to restore the ship back to normal operation.

Looking around for the officer in charge, Gen could see only a young lieutenant at a desk, his face a study in worry and concern. In spite of the cold air, sweat poured down his brow. Gen and Marta stood in front of the lieutenant, waiting patiently, until he looked up at them.

"What?" he snapped, then focused, noticed the gold leaves on the outside of Gen's environmental suit, and jumped to his feet. "Sorry, mum," he corrected himself quickly.

Gen smiled. "No worries, Lieutenant. We're off the *San Diego*. Reporting as survivors. Is there any place we can be of service?"

The lieutenant had a strange look on his face. Gen could see the wheels turning in his head. "Yes, mum," he finally said. "We need you on the bridge, please."

Gen nodded. "Very good. We'll report there immediately." She turned to the master chief, standing behind. "Master Chief, thank you once again for getting us out of there."

"No problem, Commander," the master chief spoke. "Anytime."

One deck up, Gen and Marta stepped on the bridge of the *Dallas* to a scene of quiet desperation. This bridge had also taken some shrapnel. But the holes had been sealed; atmosphere had been restored. All the bridge consoles seemed to be intact and manned.

But Gen noticed the smears of blood on the deck. People had died here; the bodies were gone, but the damage had been done.

Looking around for the Captain to report in, Gen couldn't see anyone fitting that description. Nobody was sitting in the command chair. There seemed to be nobody in charge. She saw a young lieutenant standing, talking in a low voice with an ensign who was trying to reboot the Tac console.

Walking up to the Lieutenant, Gen waited until he looked up and noticed her. He straightened in shock, staring at her like she was some kind of apparition.

"Lieutenant Commander Page and Lieutenant Powell, reporting for duty," Gen intoned in the age-old ritual. "Is your Captain around?"

The lieutenant stuttered, tried to speak, gulped, and tried again.

"Uh…mum…our…uh…Captain is dead. Along with the XO. Uh…right now…"

The lieutenant looked at the gold leaf of a lieutenant commander imprinted on the shoulders of Gen's environmental suit.

"Uh…right now, mum…you're the senior officer on the ship. Thank God you're here. That makes you the Captain!"

Gen, shocked, stared at the lieutenant for several seconds.

Then her mind started working again. Scenarios quickly flashed through her mind.

"What about your engineering officer?"

"Dead, mum," answered the lieutenant. "Trust me, I've checked. You're the senior officer aboard."

"How about your squadron lead? Have you called for a replacement?"

"Mum, we ARE the squadron lead. There are no replacements. Everybody's shot to hell."

Gen looked at Marta. "What about Zoe?" she asked.

Marta shook her head. "She's down for the count. She won't be commanding anything for a long time." Marta pointed toward the command chair. "Better get to work, Captain."

Phoenix System - Cruiser *Raptor*

Flag Captain Joe Parker had a grim expression on his face as he spoke to Bonnie.

"That last missile barrage damn near took off our entire stern. All four engines are down," he said. "Engineering says at least eight to ten hours to get even one of them back. Cheng says she's pretty much got to build a new engine from scratch. Until then, we're dead in the water."

Bonnie had to smile at the age-old expression. There was no water in space. But that Naval expression from Earth still survived, at least among the Oldies who could remember the wet-navy days of their former planet.

"And headed right to Hades, I see," Bonnie replied, glancing at the holo.

The *Raptor* was shot to pieces. She was so damaged, the Stree had not bothered to divert a destroyer to finish her off. Anyone could see that most of her stern had been shot away. There was little chance she could get underway again. The Stree knew they could come around on their next pass and take care of the damaged cruiser.

But that would probably not be necessary; the Stree could

read a course projection as well as Bonnie. On the holo, the projected course line of the drifting *Raptor* extended another thirty-six million miles. Then it came to a sudden and abrupt end - right into the side of the planet the Humans had laughingly named Hades. The innermost planet of the Phoenix system was pretty much as its name described - a cratered, burnt-out shell of a planet, hotter than Sol's Mercury, with a surface temperature of over nine hundred degrees.

And unless they could get an engine online, *Raptor* was soon to meet the planet up close and personal. At her current velocity, the cruiser would smash into Hades in a bit over four hours.

But Bonnie couldn't worry about that right now. Her future - and the future of everyone on board - depended on the engineering crew somehow finding a way to get thrust on the ship before *Raptor* smashed into the planet. And if that required her engineers to build a new engine from scratch in four hours, she knew that's what they would attempt. In the meantime, Bonnie had bigger fish to fry.

"Keep on it, Joe." Bonnie turned to Luke. "How's the fleet?"

"Shot to hell," grimaced Luke. "Running for their lives. A few minutes ago, they turned and vectored for the outer system like their pants were on fire."

"Where the fuck do they think they're going? There's no place to run to! Who's in charge of that mob?"

Luke glanced at his console, one of the few that still worked on the bridge. "It should be Zoe. But if she were still able to command, this wouldn't be happening. She'd put a stop to it instantly. So we have to assume she's out of action. Either badly injured, or she's lost comms. Or both.

"With Zoe down, Captain Davis on the *Tiger* would be next in line for command. He may have issued the order, or they may just have bailed on their own. But with no comms, we have no way to know."

"Get me a comm, Luke! We have to turn them around, bring them back!"

"I'm trying. No joy so far. Everything's down: short-range, long-range, ansible, everything."

"Keep trying, Luke, for God's sake! Get me a comm!" Bonnie turned and stared at the holo once more. "We have to stop them from running! Can't they see what will happen?"

Phoenix System - West Mountains

In the morning, the Stree had sent the occasional kinetic down on the crest of the ridge above Bren's cave headquarters on Mount Redoubt, trying to punch through. So far, the ridge had held, although it looked like a mad giant had attacked it with a hammer. But by noon the kinetics had stopped - the Singheko coming up the mountain at them were too close. The Stree couldn't fire more kinetics without the danger of killing their own allies.

Bren's brigade, knowing that the kinetics would stop when the Lions were close enough, had prepared for this moment. Bren's troops left their uppermost entrenchments, running down the slope to a succession of lower defensive positions that would mark the last battle of this war.

And then the Lions started their assaults. All afternoon, wave after wave of Lions came up the slope at them, roaring their defiance, their rifles blazing, seemingly oblivious to the withering fire of the Humans above them. And wave after wave of Lions died, as the Humans, firing down the slope from dug-in positions, fended off attack after attack.

But not without losses. Hour by hour, the Humans were driven back, forced to give up first one entrenchment, then another. Finally, after hours of fighting, they were pushed back to the uppermost line of defenses.

Just inside the cave entrance of Bren's headquarters, a trench, protected by a low rampart, held Bren and her staff. They were still firing, still fighting – a meager row of living creatures, intermixed with dozens of dead, performing their last duty. More than a thousand Humans lay dead on the long slope in front of them.

As another wave of Lions came up the hill toward them, Bren and Anders fired over the top of the embankment. It was the sixth assault of the day. In front of Bren and her surviving troops, there were at least fifteen thousand Lions somewhere down that mountain, determined to get them at any cost. This latest assault was merely the tip of the spear - although at the moment, it appeared the tip of the spear would be more than enough to overrun their positions.

A slight lull came in the spray of rifle fire coming at them. Bren took the opportunity to slide down from the embankment and grab more rifle magazines. Moving back to the top, she laid out the magazines and looked over the battlefield downslope from her. Beside her, Anders likewise laid out a few magazines within easy reach.

"Where the fuck are Mark and Tatiana?" Anders yelled out loud, raging, his frustration plain for all to see.

"They'll be here, Anders," Bren said, emptying her magazine at a squad of Lions running crosswise across the battlefield below them, trying to flank them. "Dammit, Mark and Tatiana know their business! They'll be here!" she repeated bitterly, not sure she believed it herself.

Destroyer *Dallas*

Reluctantly, Gen moved to the command chair of the *Dallas*. Standing over it for a few seconds, she looked down. Barely dry bloodstains covered the seat, had splashed onto the arms of the chair. Gen raised her eyes and looked at Marta. She could hear the unspoken message, as if Marta had actually spoken to her.

You have to do this. This is your time.

Ignoring the dried blood, Gen sat. She raised her head, traversed her eyes around the bridge. As her wandering gaze stopped again at Marta - her best friend, her confidante, her only rock in a mad world - Gen's universe suddenly flipped, twisted, changed in a way she could never have imagined before this moment. In an instant, Gen knew her youth, her beginnings, were gone. They would never return.

She was responsible for Marta.

She was responsible for this ship. For the lives of everyone on it.

Live or die, success or failure, it was up to her.

And then another old memory came to her. Another expression Aunt Bonnie had said was frequently used by her father Jim Carter when she was a baby, before he disappeared into war.

Buckle up, buttercup.

Gen felt a slight smile on her face at the memory. The smile didn't really seem appropriate to the moment, causing some consternation to the crew around her. She knew her new bridge crew was watching her intently, trying to determine if they had a winner or a loser, trying to see if they might have a chance to live, or would surely die. She wiped the smile off her face quickly.

"Marta, take the XO chair, please," Gen ordered.

Marta gave a curt nod. "Aye, aye, Skipper," she said, ensuring that she set the tone correctly for Gen, knowing how Gen would want the bridge to operate - informally, but precisely. Marta moved briskly to the XO chair which was in front of Gen and slightly to her right.

Gen directed her gaze to the young lieutenant, still standing awkwardly by the Tactical console.

"Lieutenant...I'm sorry, what was your name?"

"Petrov, mum. Vladimir Petrov. Vlad."

"What's your position?"

"Assistant Ops officer, mum."

"OK, Vlad. You're now my Tactical officer. Take your position."

"Aye, mum," Vlad answered, the relief in his voice obvious. At the Tac console, the young ensign shot up out of the seat as quickly as humanly possible, glad to be relieved of a duty he did not understand. Vlad sat down in his place, and even at her command chair, Gen could hear a sigh from the ensign, his happiness at being out of the center of responsibility clear.

Gen turned her attention to the large hologram at the center of the bridge. The status of the fleet was clear to see. They were running - and running hard. The first two passes against the Stree had left both fleets hard hit, but the Humans had taken the worst of it. Both elements of the Human fleet were boosting hard, on vectors that would soon meet. The two Human flotillas were joining up; but they were running, fleeing for all they were worth toward the edge of the system.

But there was no place to retreat in space. All you could do was run for the mass limit, hope you could get there in time to sink out and find someplace to regroup. The Stree were also boosting hard; but instead of taking a vector directly toward the Human fleet, they were boosting toward the star. Gen saw their plan immediately; the Stree would slingshot around the star, using the star's gravity to boost their velocity, and catch the Humans long before the mass limit could be reached.

Gen spoke to the ship's AI. "*Dallas*, who's the lead ship of the destroyer flotilla now?"

<Due to casualties, *Dallas* is now the lead ship of the destroyer flotilla>

Staring at Gen, Marta shook her head, a wry smile on her face.

"You're it, Skipper," Marta said.

Gen nodded. It was worse than she had realized. Gen spoke again. "*Dallas*, why are we running? Who gave the order?"

<We received an order from Fleet to run for the mass limit>

Gen shook her head in disbelief. "Did that order come from *Raptor*?"

<Negative. *Raptor* is disabled, no longer combat effective, and drifting into the first planet. Command passed to Vice-Admiral Zoe DeLong aboard *San Diego*. However, no response was received from *San Diego*. Command then passed to Captain Terence Davis in *Tiger*. The order to run for the mass limit

came from Captain Davis>

"Read me the order, *Dallas*."

<Fleet Order from Captain Davis: all ships to disperse in random vectors, run for the mass limit. Rendezvous at Fensalir in five days. End message>

Gen looked down, closing her eyes. Could it get any worse? The fleet running from the enemy - yet clearly, they wouldn't make it to the mass limit before they were caught by the Stree. The *Corsair* gone. *Raptor* adrift. No more cruisers to hold off the *Unmerciful*. Bonnie dead, or at least out of action. Zoe in medical, unconscious.

Gen tried to think. Continue to run for the mass limit? It didn't make sense. She looked up at the holo plot to confirm what she already knew.

We won't make it. The Stree will have us a good hour before we can sink out.

They outnumber us by three to one. Dispersing will only weaken us. They'll pick us apart ship by ship. If we follow this strategy, not a single ship will make it out of this system. Plus, the ground troops back on Phoenix will be slaughtered.

If we follow this plan, it's the end of Phoenix.

Gen rose from her chair, gestured to Marta to follow, and headed for her ready room.

THIRTY-FIVE

Stree Flagship *Unmerciful*

The tiny bot had been well hidden. In her initial interview with Rajanti, Rita had sat in a chair directly in front of his desk. During their conversation, she had casually placed the bot under the arm of the chair; there it had remained, immobile, almost invisible, until 0224 hours the next morning. Then slowly, carefully, the microbot moved, traveling down the chair to the floor, across to the wall, and up to the air vent leading out of the office.

Three days later, it had completed its programmed mission. It had taken that long for the tiny bot to traverse the vents and find the main computer core buried deep within the ship, make its way into the central processor of the ship's non-sentient AI, and inject the virus it carried. And even then, the Stree anti-virus almost fought it off; the Stree, deathly afraid of any kind of AI attack, made a very good anti-virus; it came within a few milliseconds of defeating Rita's inserted software.

But Rita's virus was a Goblin virus, and there was none better in the Arm. In the end, it won its battle with *Unmerciful*'s non-sentient AI, and became resident in the ship's computer core.

There it sat quietly, assessing, growing its resources, for another day. Thus, it was the fifth day after Rita's surrender before it was fully in control.

Rita was in her cell, lying on her bunk, when she heard her new AI virus finally call on her internal comm. It was, as planned, well after midnight, ship's time.

<Mission complete. Ready for commands>

About damn time, she thought. Rising up from the bunk, she went to the door.

<Give me an outside look> she commanded. Instantly, in her vision, she could see a view from the overhead cameras outside her cell. On the left were more cells. On the right was a short corridor, leading to an office. In the office, two guards sat at their terminals. One was sleeping; the other was awake, but barely, his head lolling back and forth as he tried to stay focused on the monitor screen in front of him.

<Loop the guard's monitor screen and unlock the cell door> Rita commanded.

With a click, the door unlocked and moved slightly ajar. Gently, Rita pushed it open and stepped outside. Staying glued to the wall, out of the direct line of sight of the guard, she moved soundlessly down the corridor until she was just outside the office. She waited patiently. The guard still awake closed his eyes, fighting a losing battle against sleep. Quicker and quieter than any Human, the Goblin moved across the floor to a position behind him. Before he knew the danger, his neck was broken. In the same way, the second Stree guard died, never waking from his slumber. Rita dragged the two bodies out of the way and sat at the terminal.

<Show me the cell of my daughter Imogen>

<Your daughter Imogen is not on the ship>

<What? Where is she?>

<She and her friend Marta Powell were released in exchange for the Goblin Nemo, also known as Jim Carter Prime>

Rita could not have been more shocked. Even in Goblin time - measured in microseconds instead of seconds - it took her a while to comprehend what the AI was telling her.

<You mean the second copy of Jim Carter?>

<That is correct. He is in the last cell>

Rita sat in shock for several seconds. It was unbelievable to her.

The other copy of Jim Carter? Here?

Nemo was sleeping - or rather, in Goblin terms, partially powered down to conserve energy - when the door to his cell clicked. Coming alert, he got up from the bunk and moved to the door. It was unlocked, slightly ajar.

Listening, he heard nothing. He slowly opened the cell door, pushing it away from him. In the corridor outside stood a figure. A woman. A woman he recognized.

Rita.

They stood stock-still for many moments, staring at each other. Nemo had, in fact, never laid eyes on Rita in reality. Twenty-one years earlier, on Stree Prime, he had been copied from the original Jim Carter - and immediately sent on his mission to rescue Bonnie. By that time, Rita had already taken over the body of the supreme High Priest of the Stree and was on her way off the planet.

But he had every memory of Jim Carter in his brain, and he knew his wife. The shock of seeing her in reality for the first time left him frozen; he didn't know what to do, how to react.

Rita made the decision for him; she stepped forward, moved to him, wrapped her arms around him, embraced him. Kissed him, long and slow and hard.

"I've missed you, husband," she said.

Destroyer *Dallas*

"Captain Davis, this plan will result in the utter destruction of this fleet."

Sitting at the conference table in her ready room, Gen looked at Marta across from her. Marta nodded in agreement.

But on the other end, Captain Davis came back once again with his nonsensical orders.

"It's our only chance!" he sputtered. "We have to get out of here, regroup!"

Gen shook her head in disbelief.

"Captain Davis. Look at your plot! We can't make it! The

Stree will have us a good hour before we make the mass limit!"

On the other end of the holo connection, Captain Davis looked disheveled, scared, uncertain. Behind him, they could see the bridge of his destroyer *Tiger*. It was badly damaged. Shrapnel holes were everywhere, and his crew could be seen working madly to effect emergency repairs.

"We can make it!" Davis insisted, waving wildly at the holo plot on his bridge. "They're as damaged as we are! They're only pushing 275G! We can get out of this system, regroup!"

Gen's voice snapped across the holo connection like a whiplash. "Captain! They're foxing you! They're holding down their accel to suck you in, make you think you have a chance! At any moment, they'll kick it up, slingshot around the star, and come at us like a charging Lion! We'll never make it this way! And we have to help the ground troops on Phoenix! We have to form up, turn, fight them!"

"No, no, they're hurt. They're hurt worse than we are! We can get out of here! My orders…my orders are clear! Run for the mass limit, sink out, rendezvous at Fensalir in five days!"

On the other end, the captain of the Tiger looked as if he might cry. With an angry gesture, he cut the connection.

Marta gazed at Gen across the table. The look on Marta's face said it all, but she decided to add words to make it crystal clear.

"He's shell-shocked. He's panicked."

Gen nodded agreement.

"If we follow his plan, we're dead. All of us. And everybody on Phoenix," Marta continued.

"I know."

Gen sat silently for many long moments, thinking. Marta stayed silent. Something in the air was portentous. It felt like the moment before an electrical storm explodes; when the air is heavy with unrealized violence - those brief moments before the first ear-shattering clap of thunder lets you know the violence has arrived.

"I'm fighting them," said Gen. There was iron in her voice.

Gen raised her head to stare across the table at Marta, repeating her words to make sure Marta understood.

"I'm fighting them."

Still staring at her friend, Gen spoke a command to the AI, a command that would mean mutiny by all normal standards.

"*Dallas*, give me an all-ships connection."

<All ships connection established>

"All captains of the Human Fleet. Please listen to me for a moment. This is Imogen Carter Page on the *Dallas*. The Stree are sucking us in, playing us. Once we are far enough from the star to ensure we can't use it for a gravity assist, they'll have us right where they want us. They'll increase their accel and slingshot around the star. They'll catch us long before we reach the mass limit. Then they'll pick us off one by one. There will be no survivors. Plus - we abandon our friends and family fighting the Singheko on the planet. The Stree will return to Phoenix and blast them to oblivion."

Gen paused. Although it was a voice-only connection, and they could not see the captains on the other end, Marta could imagine what was going through their minds. She was sure they were all in shock, both at Gen's message and the audacity of her mutiny.

And with Gen's next words, she was sure the shock factor would increase substantially.

"I'm not having it," Gen continued. "We're supposed to be doing a job out here. And I'm going to do it. I'm changing course to slingshot around the star. If we come out opposite the Stree vector, we'll have them facing us with the star behind us. If we time it correctly, we'll be so close to the star, there's a chance it'll confuse their weapons tracking."

Once again, Gen paused. She looked at Marta. With a firm nod, Marta let her know she was on board.

"I invite anyone who wants to do their duty - to do what this fleet was created to do - to follow me. *Dallas* out."

Gen slashed a hand across her throat, ensuring the AI understood to break the connection.

With one last look at Marta, Gen issued her orders.

"*Dallas*, change course. Put us on a vector to slingshot around the star and come out facing the Stree. Ensure our accel is sufficient that we get all the way around the star before they can, so that we come out with the star behind us, but as close to the star as possible. Also assume they will increase their accel to max to try and get around before we do."

<Course plotted. An increased accel of 304g will be required>

"Execute."

<Changing course>

The status lights on the walls began flashing red. The accel warning bell sounded. They heard the AI issue its standard warning over the PA and in their personal comms.

<Warning! High-g maneuvers in thirty seconds!>

"Let's get to the bridge," Marta suggested. Gen, in agreement, got up. They trotted out of the ready room, onto the bridge.

<Warning! High-g maneuvers in twenty seconds!>

Settling into their combat seats, Gen and Marta hurriedly buckled their harnesses.

<Warning! High-g maneuvers in ten seconds!>

As the AI counted down the last ten seconds over the comms, a slow smile began on Marta's face. She turned to Gen.

"Wasn't there something in history class about when the die is cast?" Marta remarked.

"Yeah," smiled Gen. "When you're totally screwed, and you know it."

As the *Dallas* began its vector change, they turned back to face front. The increased G-forces - 4G more than the compensator could damp out - pushed them down into their seats, hard. Each person on the *Dallas* now weighed four times more than normal. They gripped the handles of their combat chairs and leaned back to distribute the force evenly.

The holo plot showed the *Dallas* veering off from the rest of the Human fleet, taking a vector that led toward the star of the

Phoenix system. There they would slingshot around the star, come out facing the Stree, with the star behind them.

For a long minute, the tableau on the holo held steady, the *Dallas* veering off, the rest of the fleet moving away from them.

Then the destroyer *Claw* changed course. She vectored away from the main fleet and toward *Dallas* at 305G, a course that would cause her to catch up in a short while.

<Message from *Claw*. Joining up> reported the AI.

Seconds later, the destroyer *Los Angeles* also changed course to join them.

Thirty seconds after that, all the remaining ships of the Human fleet - with the exception of *Tiger* - turned and accelerated to rendezvous with the *Dallas*, heading back toward the star to start a fight.

Stree Flagship *Unmerciful*

Rita and Nemo walked briskly down the corridor outside the brig area. They had not heard any weapons activity for several minutes. The AI reported the Human fleet, badly battered, had withdrawn, was fleeing toward the outer system. Rajanti was in hot pursuit. He was planning to slingshot around the star, and would intercept the Humans in a few hours if they maintained their present course.

The AI also noted that Rajanti's orders included an addendum. No prisoners would be taken. There would be no survivors of the Human fleet. Rita smiled wryly.

That makes our job easier.

Rounding a corner, Rita and Nemo met three Stree crewmembers walking down the hall. Before the three Stree could register what they were seeing, they were dead, dispatched quickly and with a minimum of noise. But Rita and Nemo were not so lucky the next time - taking a ladder up to the next deck, they came out directly in front of two crewmembers, too far away to reach them in time. Even as the two Goblins rushed toward them faster than any Human, the two Stree turned and fled into a compartment, slamming the hatch behind them. Seconds later, an alarm began to sound.

<So much for stealth> Rita said to Nemo on their internal comms.

<Yeah. From here on, it'll be a straight-up fight to get to the bridge>

The two rushed up the next ladder. They were now only five decks below the bridge. But the alarm had been given, and by the time they climbed two more decks, they were met with a security detail armed with pulse rifles. As the Stree opened fire on them, they ducked into the cross-corridor and returned fire with the two pulse rifles they had taken from the brig guards. Their accuracy drove the Stree back. For a moment, the firing stopped.

<Well, we can't let this turn into a standoff> Nemo said. <The longer we take to get to the bridge, the more time for them to find a way to take us out. We've got to keep moving>

<Agree> said Rita. <Give me a sec. I was hoping not to have to do this, but they give us no choice>

Rita issued a silent command to the AI. Shortly after, the nearest airlock - on their same deck - experienced a malfunction. The failsafe had been disabled; both doors opened silently to space.

The rush of atmosphere out of the section was like a hurricane. The precious air needed by the Stree to stay alive departed in a rush. It swept every loose object before it, creating a fog filled with dust and debris. Only the near-instantaneous slamming of airtight doors between compartments prevented every Stree on the ship from dying. But the airtight doors were not enough to save the security detail in front of Rita and Nemo. As they lay on the floor, gasping their last breaths, Rita and Nemo stepped over them, continuing their path to the bridge of the *Unmerciful*.

THIRTY-SIX

Cruiser *Raptor*

As *Raptor* drifted closer and closer to the innermost dead planet called Hades, Bonnie watched the holo, trying to understand what was happening. First, the remnants of her fleet had turned and ran, fleeing from the Stree. She had seen the Stree boost hard for the star, their intention clear. They would slingshot around the star and catch the Humans long before they could escape the system. Unable to communicate with her fleet, she had screamed in frustration, knowing the mistake they were making was a fatal one.

Then, somehow, *Dallas* had turned, had headed back toward the star. Seconds later, the rest of the Human fleet had turned, following *Dallas*. All except *Tiger*, who kept running for the mass limit. Then, finally, *Tiger* had also turned, boosting hard to rejoin the fleet, tail-end Charlie.

"Better late than never," Bonnie muttered to herself. "Zoe must have finally taken control back in *Dallas*. Thank God!"

Raptor was still drifting out of control, on a dead-end course that would impact Hades in a matter of hours. But at least Bonnie's EDF fleet was on a vector that was perfect. They would come around the star and face the Stree in a head-on attack. Bonnie knew it would be a brutal pass; but it was the only possible chance to turn the tide of this battle.

"We've got comms back," Bonnie heard. "They're weak, but we can communicate."

She looked up. Luke was standing before her.

"That gunboat you sent back to Phoenix is coming to tow

us to safety. They'll be here in a half-hour. That'll give us plenty of time to get clear of Hades."

"Thank God," breathed Bonnie. She looked at Luke, knowing there was something else. He had the strangest smile on his face.

"What?" she asked.

"We've just made contact with *Dallas*. You're not going to believe who's leading the fleet."

Stree Battlecruiser *Unmerciful*

It took them another twenty minutes, but Rita and Nemo were now standing just outside the bridge. At each end of the short cross-corridor lay a pile of Stree bodies - two more security details they had taken out.

<Open the bridge hatch> Rita ordered the AI. With a click, the hatch unlocked. Peering through carefully, Rita saw the Stree bridge crew had fled, leaving the bridge abandoned. Nemo stepped inside cautiously; his pulse rifle held at the ready. Rita followed, but nothing happened. They were alone.

"I guess they decided to let us have it for now," said Nemo.

"Yeah," Rita replied. "They'll put all their efforts on taking back control of the ship. They're already burning their way into the main computer room with welding torches. We don't have long."

Nemo moved to the command chair and gestured to it, with an exaggerated bow to Rita. She smiled, moved to the command chair, and sat. Nemo grinned, that old quirky grin Rita knew so well, and took the seat beside her, the normal position of the XO.

"I've missed that stupid smile of yours," she said.

Nemo's grin widened. "And I've missed your kind, gentle voice."

"We should let Bonnie know what's happening," continued Nemo. "Otherwise, the Humans will waste a lot of ordnance firing at us at the merge."

"Agreed. *Unmerciful*, open a channel to Bonnie Page in the Human Fleet."

<Guard channel opened>

"Bonnie, this is Rita. Are you there?"

There was a bit of a silence, then Rita heard a voice - a voice she had not heard in twenty-one years, but a voice so familiar to her.

"Rita? Is that really you?"

"Yes. Hi, babe. I'm on the *Unmerciful*. We just took control of the ship."

"We?"

"Nemo and me. We're sitting on the bridge right now. Thought we'd better let you know, so you don't blast away at us as we come into the merge."

"Well, I'm not with the fleet. *Raptor* was damaged in our second pass. We're drifting, trying to save ourselves from smashing into the first planet."

"Who's in command of the fleet, then?"

"Gen. Your daughter."

The confusion in Rita's voice was evident as she asked her next question. "How is that possible?"

"It's a long story. Basically, she was the only one up for the job. So she took it."

"But she's only twenty-four years old!" Nemo exclaimed.

"Age has little to do with it," said Bonnie over the link. "She's the right person at the right time. She's come into her power."

In the silence that followed, Rita and Nemo stared at each other. Finally, Rita spoke again.

"Well, we don't have much time. Rajanti is working madly to take back control. We'll take out as many of them as we can before that happens."

"That would be a good thing," Bonnie said, the humor evident in her voice. "Do what you can, babe."

"Talk after," Rita said. "Good luck not smashing into the planet."

"Break a leg," came back from Bonnie. "*Raptor* out."

The AI broke the connection as Rita turned to Nemo.

<Let's kill some Stree cruisers> Rita said.

<Agree. If we can knock out their cruisers, the Humans have a chance>

Turning her attention to the holo tank in the front of the bridge, Rita studied it. The *Unmerciful* was with the rest of the Stree fleet, somewhat to the rear of the Stree formation, surrounded by a screen of destroyers and cruisers. The entire Stree fleet was on a vector toward the star. The Human fleet was just coming around the limb of the star, on their way for a head-on pass against the Stree fleet. They would merge in less than ten minutes.

Directly behind the *Unmerciful* was one of the Stree cruisers, five hundred miles away. Two more cruisers were to the front, one on her left and one on her right.

"I think we should take out the one in the back first," Nemo thought aloud. "I don't like having it back there looking right up our ass."

"Agree," said Rita. "*Unmerciful*, set targets. Target Charlie One is the cruiser to our rear. Target Charlie Two is the Stree cruiser to our right front. Target Charlie Three is the Stree cruiser to our left front."

<Targets set>

"Designate a half-spread of missiles to target Charlie One. Designate a quarter-spread of missiles to targets Charlie Two and Charlie Three."

<Missiles designated>

"Designate gamma lance battery one to target Charlie Two. Designate gamma lance battery two to target Charlie Three."

<Gamma lance designated>

Rita glanced at Nemo. He nodded. "Let's dance," he said.

"Fire all designated weapons," Rita spoke.

The *Unmerciful* lurched as the mass of so many weapons left at once.

<All weapons fired>

Destroyer *Dallas*

"What the fuck?"

Gen looked up from her console. Marta was pointing toward the big holotank at the front of the bridge.

Marta yelled, nearly deafening Gen.

"The *Unmerciful* just fired at her own cruisers!"

In the holo tank, Gen could see it clearly. All three of the Stree cruisers that had been screening the *Unmerciful* were ablaze in space, spewing volatiles, lurching out of formation, clearly out of action.

"What on earth...?" Gen muttered, shocked by what she saw.

It makes no sense. Why would the Stree battlecruiser fire on its own ships?

A chime alerted her to a high-priority message. Looking down at her console, she read the words displayed:

Rita and Nemo have taken the Unmerciful. *They may not be able to hold it for long, but for the moment, it's out of the equation. Use your opportunity wisely. Good luck. Bonnie Page, Lord Admiral, EDF.*

Marta had received the same message. She turned to Gen with a smile.

"Now we're cooking," she said. "Thanks to your Mom and Dad!"

Gen nodded in wonderment. She couldn't help the thought that crossed her mind.

My Mom and Dad? But really...is he my Dad? He's just a copy of my Dad...

But so is the dead one in the cargo hold of the Unmerciful. *He was just a copy too...*

And for that matter...isn't Rita the same? The Goblins copied her consciousness into an android body. Her real body has long since turned to dust in the Dyson Swarm at Stalingrad.

Are my parents dead? Or are they out there on that Stree

battlecruiser?

Gen shook off her strange thoughts and came back to business. She glanced at the main holotank. They had completed their slingshot around the star. The time to merge with the Stree fleet was just a matter of minutes now.

Destroyer *Dallas*

Curving hard around the star, Gen lined up on the Stree, and flew toward them, weapons blazing. It was their only chance, and they knew it. The Stree met them in kind, firing everything they had at the Humans. Space came alive with the criss-cross of gamma lances, streaks of light that sent death toward their target of choice. A half-dozen ships died in those first few seconds, some holed by through-and-through shots that punched through the entire hull of a ship and bled out the air, some with their bridges smashed beyond all recognition, some simply exploded into broken hunks of shattered metal and composite that would orbit the star for a few months, then fall back into a ready-made grave.

Then they were in missile range. Floods of telephone-pole-sized shipkillers swept through the void, packs of them moving in every direction, hungry for a target. And another six ships died.

But as Gen had predicted, the Stree were facing directly into the star. Their missiles had to contend with the incredible glare of solar radiation in front of them. It didn't prevent them from finding their targets completely; but it did seem to reduce their accuracy. And the Humans were on their game - with a yelp of glee, Gen pumped her fist as they came out of the merge, rejoicing in the blooms of destruction lighting up the Stree fleet.

As they left the enemy behind and began a hard vector turn, looping around the star for another pass at the enemy, Gen called to Harrington, the young ensign she had assigned to the Ops console.

"Ops. How's the fleet looking?"

Harrington bent to his console, double-checked his display, then replied over his comm.

"Showing six of our ships down, Mum. *Claw, Los Angeles, New Delhi, Dubai, Madrid,* and *Moscow.* Showing thirteen Stree ships down. Nine definitely out of action, four still under power but veering off."

Gen glanced at the holo and did some quick computations in her head. She spoke privately to Marta over the comm.

"We have twelve ships still combat-effective. The Stree have twenty-one, not counting the *Unmerciful.* The missile ratio is 168 to 96 in their favor. Do we still do this?"

Marta turned in her combat chair to look at Gen. "Bonnie's message said she didn't know how long Rita and Nemo can hold control over *Unmerciful.* If that battlecruiser comes back online, that makes the missile ratio 232 to 96."

"Yeah, I know. So?"

Marta grinned. "We take it to them."

"OK. Work the plan. Around we go once more for another pass at these bastards."

"Yeah. Besides - what else did you have on the agenda for today?"

Phoenix System - West Mountains

The Lions made few mistakes in their attack. And most of their mistakes were minor, causing excessive casualties but no real danger to their advance.

But one of their mistakes was of far more consequence.

They forgot they were fighting.

Tatiana Powell. The tactician who had started her unexpected military career as a naked Human in a wire cage, on a Singheko slave ship enroute to Deriko – and who had then proceeded to form an army, and take away an entire planet from the Lions, killing hundreds of thousands of them in the process. Had they remembered who they were fighting – or had they taken it more seriously – perhaps they would have been better prepared.

But this was a new generation of Lions, and they did not remember the lessons of the past. They knew they had Bren's army outnumbered and outgunned. Derisive of the Human capabilities, they watched as the Humans retreated before them for days, all the way up the mountain, from the foothills, through the forests, to the sleet- and snow-covered barrens above tree line where the Human army now awaited them. Huddling in their last line of defense, almost out of ammunition, their backs to the mountain, with no place to go, the Humans were done. For the Lions, it was a foregone conclusion - they would wipe out the last Human resistance, get in their shuttles, and go home.

Somehow, it had escaped their notice that a Human army which started out days ago with three brigades - twelve thousand soldiers - now seemed to consist of only a few thousand surviving fighters – less than half a brigade. A truly wise officer in the Lion command staff might have wondered at that…might have asked themselves if they had truly killed so many Humans in their battles. And if not, where did the rest of the Humans go?

But there was no truly wise officer in the Lion command staff, and so that question was never asked.

Two miles to the north of the Lions, Tatiana knew the answer to that question. Two days earlier, as the Humans retreated up the mountain in a driving blizzard, two brigades had quietly split off from the main column, one brigade going north and one brigade going south. With the snow flying almost horizontally across their line of march, the Lions had been too busy trying to stay warm to notice. The remaining brigade – Bren's decimated and much smaller core brigade – had made directly for the Redoubt, leaving a trail behind them that even a flat-lander Lion could follow.

For one long day and one long night, Tatiana to the north and Mark Rodgers to the south lay hidden with their respective brigades. Several miles off the path of the Lions' march, in deep box canyons with high cliff overhangs shielding them from the watchful Stree above, they huddled unmoving, watching silently as mile after mile of heavily laden Lion shock troops marched by them. Row after row of Humans, packed like sardines into the small box canyons, had waited patiently, able only to drink carefully from canteens, unable to eat for fear of making a sound. For one day, and one night, they had waited. Then the Lions' column was past them, and out of earshot.

And still they waited, because the weather was clear the next morning, and they could not move for fear of detection by the Stree in orbit. For one more day they waited, eating cold rations, moving only under the shadow of the cliff overhang. And in that last night, as heavy cloud cover finally formed over them, they could get up, and stretch their aching muscles, and form up. Then, marching as quickly as possible up the mountain parallel to the Lions, the two separated brigades stayed a good six miles away from their enemy's route. By the time the Lions began their assault on the Redoubt, the two brigades were positioned evenly with the Lions, Tatiana directly to the north and Mark directly to the south. Then they began marching inward, toward the battle.

Now, looking down the slope of the last small valley they had to cross before climbing a low ridge to the Lions' position, Tatiana turned to her XO and nodded. "Let's go get 'em," she ordered.

Rising to his feet, her XO stood and waved his rifle at the four thousand Humans lying in the snow behind him.

The four thousand stormed to their feet, charged down the slope into the small valley, up the other side, and climbed the last ridge. At the top, with one voice they roared a cry of defiance as they took the surprised Lions in the flank.

On the other side of the battlefield, Mark Rodgers came at the Lions the same way, his brigade screaming a battle cry like banshees released from Hell. As the shocked Lions realized they had two brigades of pissed-off Humans on their vulnerable flanks, they tried to regroup, tried to wheel two of their brigades back to their flanks, tried to mount a defense.

But it was too late for that. The Lions had forgotten who they were fighting. Tatiana stood on the ridge behind her brigade, watching them punch deep into the Lions' flank, and smiled.

Stree Flagship *Unmerciful*

<Warning - the Stree have broken into the main computer room. They are rebooting the system. I will lose control in three minutes>

"Crap," exclaimed Nemo. "That happened faster than I expected."

"*Unmerciful* - is there any way to retain control of the weapons for a little bit longer, after the reboot?"

<There is no possibility of retaining control of the weapons. They are all under the control of the main computer. All weapons and ship controls will revert to Admiral Rajanti in three...no, make that...two minutes>

At that instant, the door to Rajanti's ready room opened. Admiral Rajanti stepped out, followed by his bridge crew. Most of them had heavy pulse rifles trained on the two Goblins. Casually, Rajanti walked toward Rita and Nemo, a large smile on his fat Stree face.

"It seems we've managed to regain access to our ship computer, Goblin," Rajanti gloated, pausing before them. "I'm afraid your short run at freedom is over. In another few minutes, I'll have full control of my ship. Then I intend to blast your little fleet to atoms, go back to Phoenix, and destroy what's left of your ground army there. I am truly sorry, Goblin, but there can be only one winner of this battle, and this time it's the Stree."

Making no response to Rajanti, Rita stood still, looking at Nemo in despair, apparently frozen. But via their personal comms, they were still talking, a final communication before they threw the dice one last time.

<If they take back the battlecruiser, our daughter has no chance. Her life will be over>

Nemo nodded slightly. It was almost imperceptible. He did not want to tip off Rajanti they were still communicating.

<As well as the Human experiment>

They were both thinking the same thing. But Rita said it first.

<There's only one chance for the Humans. And for our daughter>

<Yes. Do it. But you'll have to be quick>

Ignoring Rajanti, ignoring all the guns pointed at them, Rita moved to Nemo, stood before him silently. As they gazed into each other's eyes, she silently issued the necessary commands to her AI.

The big battlecruiser turned, changing its orientation. Behind it, the Stree fleet, confused, watched as the *Unmerciful* fired engines at max emergency thrust, heading straight for the nearby star at 312G - 12G more than the compensator of the big ship could offset.

On the bridge, all the Stree were slammed to the floor by the sudden, unexpected G-forces. Mass panic broke out among them as they realized what Rita had done. Ignoring the two Goblins completely, the Stree crawled agonizingly to their consoles, frantically trying to force the computer to give them control. But their efforts were hopeless; Rita still had two minutes before the main computer would be fully rebooted, and the Stree could regain full control. By then, it would be far too late. The velocity of the *Unmerciful* built up steadily, an ever-increasing vector into the huge gravity well of the star, a vector that in a matter of another two minutes, no engine would be able to overcome.

Nemo and Rita both sank to their knees, their android bodies better able to manage the incredible G-forces. Nemo held Rita in his arms as they looked at each other. Rita gave a half-smile at her lover, the lover she had only just found again, now to lose once more.

"I'm sorry. I should have let you say goodbye to Bonnie when we were talking before."

"No matter," Nemo replied. "Remember, I'm just a copy of a copy. She'll get over it."

THIRTY-SEVEN

Destroyer *Dallas*

Coming around the star for the last time, the Humans going one way, the Stree fleet going the other, the two fleets were on a collision course that would meet in a matter of minutes. Both fleets knew only one of them would come out of this pass with sufficient strength to hold the battlefield. This was the acid test - the final pass, the winner-take-all set.

"Stand by to open fire," Gen called, a somewhat unnecessary command considering the AI would open fire automatically when they were in range. But throughout Human history, the commander of a fleet had always uttered those words before a battle. And there was always the remote possibility the AI could fail at the last moment, requiring a Human to step into the breach and fire manually. For both of those reasons, tradition dictated that the words be spoken, as they had been for generations of Humans going into battle.

Suddenly the holotank showed the *Unmerciful* veer off course, firing its engines madly, pushing up to 312G on an insane course that would take it directly into the star.

"What the hell...?" she heard from Marta.

Inside herself, Gen went all quiet. She knew instantly what was happening.

The Stree were taking back the battlecruiser. Rita and Nemo played the only card left to them.

Around her, Gen could hear the excited voices of her crew, their exclamations of disbelief, as the Stree battlecruiser continued its death dive, engines blazing, falling into a gravity well from which there would be no return.

And Gen knew. Now, her parents would be truly dead. Now, truly, no more coming back, no more copies, no more backup plans.

I only just now found them again.

<Two minutes to in-range> called the AI, oblivious to the Human agony caressing Gen in the command chair.

I only just now found them again. And now they're gone forever.

<All weapons manned and ready, all locks released> spoke the oblivious AI.

Gen responded automatically; the drill embedded into her in a hundred training sessions.

"Weapons free. Fire at will."

In the holo, the *Unmerciful* twisted slightly sideways, began to tumble end over end.

It's destabilizing. The AI is losing control.

<Thirty seconds>

Gen forced herself to focus. She looked across at Marta, who was half-turned in her seat, staring at Gen with a concerned look. Gen nodded, letting her best friend and XO know she was OK, she was able to perform.

Fight the battle first. Grieve later.

The *Dallas* started its dance, the ship tossing them left, right, down, up, every direction a random change that provided some slight hope of dodging a gamma lance strike.

"Break a leg," Gen said, loud enough for everyone to hear.

<In range> came from the AI. The screeching, spine-tingling whine of the gamma lance permeated the bridge. In the holo, space lit up, streamers of fire, a Fourth of July celebration gone berserk, explosions and streaks, broken ships shattering into dozens of pieces, as the two fleets smashed together in one last frenzy of death.

The *Dallas* lurched harder than usual, a blow that slammed Gen against the side of her chair with enough force to leave a bruise. Something rattled on the outside of the ship, a near miss, a gamma lance dancing off the hull, not quite able to penetrate.

"That was fucking close," she heard from Marta.

The gamma lance of the *Dallas* recycled, ready to fire. A second screeching whine assaulted their ears, and in the distance a Stree destroyer died as the primary weapon of the *Dallas* punched through the enemy's engine room, breaking the distant ship in half, strewing gases and debris and bodies wantonly into space, a cornucopia of destruction filling the void.

Gen watched the holo as ship after ship, both Stree and Human, took hits, some minor, some devastating. And suddenly, in a moment of clarity, Gen realized something.

It didn't matter if any of the Human ships survived. It only mattered that she destroy the Stree; prevent them from winning this battle. If she could drive the Stree away, then somehow, the Humans would survive. In an instant of perfect understanding, she knew it, as well as she knew her own name. As well as she knew that she couldn't let the sacrifice of her parents be in vain.

Gen began performing a mental countdown of the enemy ships. She cared only for them; only for destroying them, only for killing them, only for smashing them. She looked at the holo intently, determined to find the key to this battle. Off to one side, she noticed a small pack of Stree destroyers flying in formation, providing themselves with mutual protection.

Like a sixth sense, she could feel the answer. With the loss of the *Unmerciful*, there had to be a new commander of the Stree fleet. And she knew where he was; in that well-protected pack of ships, hiding in the middle. She knew it, in her gut, in a place where there was no doubt whatsoever.

Using her hand, Gen touched the cluster of enemy ships in her own local holo, providing a signal to the fleet to concentrate fire in that direction.

"Double volley at designated targets!" Gen yelled at the top of her lungs.

<Missile range> called the AI a second later.

The *Dallas* shuddered as the first volley of missiles flushed out of the ship, gathered themselves, and charged toward the spot Gen had designated on her console. Every remaining Human ship flushed out their missiles, all focused on the group of ships Gen had targeted. In obedience to her command for a double volley, the next wave of missiles launched as soon as the tubes could be reloaded, following the first wave toward the pack of destroyers in the distance.

As the missiles flew toward their targets, the bridge crew held their collective breath, knowing this was the critical moment. This was the make or break. If the Stree fought off this missile barrage, it was unlikely the Humans could survive. They would pass through the Stree fleet and beyond, still hopelessly outnumbered, low on missiles, with no place to go and no options except to run for cover.

And on the holo, the missiles plowed into the Stree formation, the Stree point defense unable to fend off such a massive wave, dozens of missiles breaking through, smashing their formation, leaving ship after ship of the Stree command group burning for those few seconds when there was still enough oxygen to allow flame.

And then they completed their pass through the Stree fleet, and it was behind them. The rear guard of Human ships fired one last volley of missiles from their rear tubes, taking out another two Stree ships as they sped away. And just like that, they were out of range, coasting out from the star, bodies and fragments and parts and pieces of destroyed ships following them in their orbit. The bridge became deathly quiet as they realized they had survived.

The holo was so cluttered with damaged and destroyed ships that Gen couldn't really see what had happened.

"Status!" she called to the Ops officer, knowing his console would have a readout of the fleet and of the enemy.

"Four more of our destroyers down, Mum," called Ensign Harrington. "*Stinger*, *Tooth*, *Paris*, and *Hong Kong* are all down.

We've got six ships left."

"The enemy, please," Gen said, a little more sharply than she intended.

"Uh, sorry, mum. Looks like...eleven down, mum. Eleven of their ships out of action. We took down that command group completely. So...nine Stree left, two Singheko."

Gen went back to the holo, trying to sort out the mess, make a decision about what to do next. But even as she switched her gaze back to the holotank, something happened. Two of the enemy destroyers turned, vectored away from the main group, running toward the mass limit.

"It's the Singheko!" hooted Marta. "They're bailing!"

"Damn right they are," smiled Gen. "So much for the alliance!"

Then, like a covey of quail breaking from a bush, the remaining nine Stree destroyers turned, following the Singheko. They vectored hard for the mass limit, heading out of the system.

"Message from the Stree, mum," called Ensign Harrington.

"Read it," snapped Gen.

"Message reads: Our command structure has been destroyed. We are out of ammunition. We request a cease-fire. Please permit us to leave the system without further action. End message."

Stree Flagship *Unmerciful*

Unmerciful was nearly done. The heat built steadily. Fires had broken out all over the ship. The acrid smell of burning insulation mixed with smoke from the fires to create an atmosphere of utter death. Every Stree on board was already dead, asphyxiated by hull breaches as the ship came apart; only Nemo and Rita were still alive, and that not for long.

On the bridge, Nemo held Rita in a tight embrace. Rita had already gone unconscious from the heat. Somehow, Nemo had managed to hold on a bit longer. The temperature was rising exponentially. The entire ship was being incinerated.

Before Rita had passed out, Nemo had told her he loved her.

I love you, babe. The last thing she would hear. He was happy that he had held her, had said the words, even with death upon them.

The heat began to scorch his outer skin, peeling it off his face. He pulled Rita tighter, an instinct to protect her even as he realized the futility of it. He knew he was down to seconds left in his life.

With a snap, Banjala stood before him, an icy column, unaffected by the death and destruction surrounding them.

"You can save her, you know," Banjala said. "You've understood all along, haven't you?"

Nemo nodded. "Perhaps. But that doesn't mean I can do it."

"It's your only chance. And hers."

With a hundred small explosions, *Unmerciful* disintegrated around him. Nemo had just enough time to make one last decision as a physical being before his body, too, disintegrated into a thousand pieces.

The Goblin who was Jim Carter and not Jim Carter was no more.

THIRTY-EIGHT

Earth - Cappadocia, Turkey

The kinetic hit almost exactly two hundred yards away, precisely in the center of the Lions' position. The spray of dirt, rocks, smashed trees, and Lion body parts flung itself in all directions, some of the debris making it all the way to Garyn and Yuki in their command post up the hill, thumping around them like a rainstorm of destruction.

"What the fuck?" asked Yuki as she turned to peer over the top of the rampart. Garyn also raised up, looking over the top of the protective rock wall at the enemy position below. Just as he did, another kinetic hit, slightly to the right of the first one, and another geyser of debris and dead Lions rose into the air. As their position was pelted once again with debris, Yuki and Garyn ducked instinctively, then raised up again to take a better look.

"What's happening?" asked Yuki. She looked up at the sky, as if she could see all the way into orbit where the Singheko destroyer would be.

"I don't know. I don't see how that destroyer could mis-target so badly," Garyn said. "Something strange is happening."

"Well, I'm not wasting this chance!" Yuki growled. She grabbed for her radio and started issuing orders. Within a minute, the survivors of her troop were grouped behind, slapping their last charged magazines into their rifles.

Another kinetic hit the Lions, this time slightly to the left, and another great gout of dirt and debris rose into the sky.

"Let's go!" yelled Yuki, and before Garyn knew it, she was

over the top of the rock in front of them, yelling madly as she charged down the slope. Behind her, the rest of her company charged with her, screaming bloody murder as they took the fight to the Lions. In amazement, Garyn watched as the remaining Lions rose from their positions and ran down the hillside in disarray. As they ran, one more kinetic hit square in their midst, killing dozens more. The survivors ran faster, many of them throwing away their rifles in panic.

Yuki's company stopped a half-mile down the hillside, breathing hard, triumphant, shaking their fists in the air, raising their rifles in celebration. The remaining Lions, whittled down to a few hundred at most, were almost out of sight in the valley below, running for their lives. Even as Garyn watched, one last kinetic hit into them, scattering them like leaves.

"I think you should be able to mop up the rest on your own," said a voice behind him.

Garyn spun. He found himself looking at a strange figure. On the hillside behind him stood a creature. It looked like a man; but somehow Garyn knew it wasn't. It was too perfect, too symmetrical. And it was naked.

Garyn had never seen a Goblin before; but he knew he was looking at one now.

"I am called Rauti," said the Goblin. "Sorry about the lack of warning. I had some difficulty making up my mind if I was going to take a hand in this fight or not."

Garyn, astounded, could barely speak. "I'm...glad you did," he finally managed to get out. "But...how...?"

Rauti smiled. "The Singheko are like the Stree. They use a dumb AI in their warships. It was relatively easy for me to take it over."

Garyn managed a smile. "Thank you, then. You saved us. But...why?"

"I'm not entirely sure myself," replied Rauti. "It goes against my principles to get involved in somebody else's battle. But...let's just say, I have a friend who was once Human. And

I've never liked those damn Lions."

"How did you get here?" asked Garyn, puzzled by the sudden appearance of the Goblin. He hadn't heard a shuttle land.

"Oh, I'm not actually here," said Rauti. "Just a holo. I'll be going now. Come see me on Venus sometime!"

And just like that, the Goblin disappeared.

Garyn sat, rather involuntarily, his legs giving out. It was all too much for him. He felt Yuki come back over the parapet into their rock shelter and plop down beside him, out of breath.

"What the hell was that?" she asked, panting hard from the climb back up the hill.

"That was a Rauti," said Garyn, shaking his head. "A Goblin. He said he was from Venus."

Yuki stared. Then a hint of a grin touched her lips. "I thought Venus was full of voluptuous green alien women!"

"Evidently not," replied Garyn in wonder.

Phoenix System - West Mountains

The snow outside the entrance to the Redoubt should have been white.

It was not. It was red, streaked with blood beyond measure. Bodies of both Singheko and Humans littered the slopes leading up to the cave entrance. Discarded weapons lay everywhere - and packs, and spent pulse rifle charges, and the endless paraphernalia that soldiers carry with them everywhere. A thin dusting of snow from the last snowstorm of the day lay over the bodies; now the weather was clearing.

The Lions were gone. Mark Rodgers and his Brigade South had punched into their left flank; Tatiana with her Brigade North had smashed into their right. As the Lions turned to face the two new attacks coming from both sides, the remainder of Bren's core brigade spewed out of the Redoubt, coming down the slope screaming, firing every last magazine they had left.

There was no place the Lions could turn that wasn't full of screaming, shooting Humans.

The Lions fought - they fought well. They fought well for fifteen minutes. They tried to form up into a closed square, like something from the seventeenth century on Earth, like the English grenadiers of Wellington at Waterloo, looking for any formation that would enable them to withstand the assault. But it was too late. The press of simultaneous attacks on three sides was more than even the big beasts could sustain. It began with a small collapse on the south side, as Mark Rodger's leading company managed to punch hard into the Lions, driving them back, causing a ripple effect as other units to the left and right were also driven back, the entire south side slowly folding in, stumbling back, running out of ammunition but unable to resupply in the face of the ferocious onslaught Mark was bringing.

And from that small collapse, the entire southern side of the Singheko line rolled back into a small, compact ball of fighters that couldn't even fire because they were pressed so close together, they would hit their own troops if they did so.

And then one turned to run, and another, and then a squad, and then a platoon, and then a company…

And then the entire southern flank of the Lions turned and ran for their lives down the mountain, leaving their comrades behind to fend for themselves.

That had been the breaking of the dam. The Lions' front brigade, realizing they no longer had support on their left, turned and followed, streaming down the hill, overrunning their own supply train in their haste to escape.

To their credit, the Lions right flank retreated in good order, fighting an excellent holding action against Tatiana's brigade, acting as a rear guard, until three miles down the mountain Tatiana finally let them go, disengaging and turning back to rejoin Bren at her headquarters.

They found the body of Mark Rodgers in the middle of a pile of Lions, his empty rifle still in his hands. His face was still pointed north, toward the enemy. Those who found him said there was a strange smile on his face. As he always said he would, the old warrior had died on a battlefield.

In the pocket of his uniform, they found two pictures. One was of Gillian, his long-dead wife. The other was of his daughter Imogen.

THIRTY-NINE

Phoenix System - Landing City

It was finally over. The Singheko had vacated the planet, retreating to their assault shuttles and departing to space, the Humans allowing their troop transports to come in and fetch them.

There were too many dead to hold funerals one by one. In the Fleet, most of the bodies couldn't even be recovered; they were scattered in space, in orbits that would eventually, someday, end in the star, or else depart the system forever. On the ground, the dead of the last assault into Bren's mountain redoubt lay in the snow, intermixed with their Singheko attackers. The frozen corpses were left in place for the moment; there were too many, and not enough survivors to bury them.

They held a ceremony in the ruins of Landing City. There weren't any major buildings still intact; but on the outskirts of town, they managed to find a small storage warehouse at the water plant that had not been flattened. The tiny building was the new military headquarters and Town Hall. It was also the new capital building of the Human colony of Phoenix.

The Human survivors watched as two unknown bodies were buried in newly dug graves next to the building: one ground-pounder from Bren's command, and one spacer from the Fleet. Both bodies were too damaged for identification. They could have been identified through DNA analysis, but there wasn't a functioning lab on the entire planet with that capability. And maybe Humanity would never take the trouble to do that; there were thousands of missing, and these two were merely symbols.

Along with the bodies, they placed artifacts in the graves for future generations to find, if they ever looked. As the crowd watched in silence, the broken remains of a pulse rifle from the Redoubt battlefield were placed in the grave of Bren's unknown, and the crumpled nameplate of a Fleet destroyer was placed in the grave of Bonnie's spacer.

Then the graves were filled in, and Bonnie and Bren spoke a brief memorial. They didn't take long, and they didn't get maudlin; it wasn't their way.

Gen watched bitterly from the outskirts of the crowd. She had not been able to cry since the battle. Even with the impact of losing Mark, and Rita, and Nemo - she couldn't cry.

But she couldn't sleep, either.

After the memorial service, she went back to her tent. Everyone was living in tents; there were no buildings left that were habitable, except for the new Town Hall, and if there was any hope of getting the colony back into survival mode, they had to use that for administration. Her tent contained only a bunk, assembled from scrap wood, and a couple of packing cases - one to use for a chair, and one to use for a table.

She had barely gotten settled back in her tent when there was a gentle knock on the tent pole. She opened the flap to see Bonnie Page standing in the bright sunlight, with a wan smile on her face.

"May I come in?" asked Bonnie.

"Of course, please."

As Bonnie entered, Gen sat on the bunk, leaving the upturned packing case for Bonnie. Bonnie sat and smiled at the young woman, then began to speak.

"I need your help."

"Of course. Anything you need."

"With only fifty thousand people left, we're essentially starting Humanity over from scratch. We've decided to start over on Earth. We'll be relocating the government to

Cappadocia. And everyone who wants to go."

Shocked, Gen didn't know what to say. Phoenix was the only home she had ever known. She had never even been to Earth as an adult. A hundred objections bubbled up in her mind.

"Everyone?" she asked, the first thought that came to her mind.

"No, not everyone. There are those who say they'll stay here, try to make it work again. Rebuild. We expect roughly 60% of the population to stay here on Phoenix - about thirty thousand people. That'll leave about twenty thousand to return to Earth and join the four hundred there at Derinkuyu."

"What about the radiation? The biopoisons?"

"Cappadocia seems to have gotten a smaller dose on both counts. As long as we sleep in the Underground City at night, we'll be fine. We'll be free to go out during the day, farm, hunt, build, with acceptable risk. There's plenty of safe water there. It won't be easy; but it'll be easier than here. Here, there is nothing. We're back to fighting this alien environment again for basic survival. At least there, we'll be fighting our own native environment, and with access to all manner of tools and instruments we can salvage from the abandoned cities. And the initial test results from Garyn's ground team show that within another eighteen months or so, we can start branching out, start repopulating on the surface. So - that's the decision of the Council. All those who want to return to Earth can go."

Gen nodded, still in wonderment at the news.

"The sooner we can get people relocated there, the better. Everything here is a mess. We'll like you to lead an initial security force back to Earth. We need to establish an orbital perimeter to protect the planet while we bring the rest of the colonists. We'd like you to take the *Dallas* and four other destroyers to Earth, leave right away, if you could."

Gen shook her head. "Why me? I'm nobody…"

Bonnie smiled at her. "You're Mark's daughter; the daughter of the…former…Prime Minister. You're also the daughter of Nemo and Rita, the…ah…people…who saved us, at the cost of their own lives. And you're the hero of the Fleet. The person who turned the entire battle around. There's nobody more qualified to be the face of this effort right now."

"So, a figurehead, then."

"No, Gen. Far more than that. A leader, who has shown herself under fire. A strong voice when we needed one. A warrior. We need you to lead this effort, Gen. Please."

Gen managed a short nod. "When do I leave?"

"Two days from now. Can you be ready?"

Gen shook her head, waving an arm around the meager items in her tent.

"I can be ready in twenty minutes."

Bonnie rose, smiling. "Thank you, Gen. I knew I could count on you. By the way, you'll have the permanent rank of Captain in the EDF for this effort."

"I don't need any rank," Gen said, somewhat bitterly.

"Yes, you do. There are always people who won't listen, who won't accept your leadership, who'll try to turn you away from the right path. I don't know who they are right now; but when they stick their heads up, you'll need to swat them down. So yes, you need the rank."

Gen shrugged. "Whatever you say, Aunt Bonnie."

Bonnie smiled. "That'll be Lord Admiral to you from now on, Captain."

Gen managed a weak smile.

"Aye, aye, mum."

FORTY

Earth - Destroyer *Dallas*

Gen had been on station for a month now. Her small destroyer force maintained their orbits around Earth, protecting it, in case the Stree decided they weren't beaten after all. If they made a raid on the colonists, Gen was ready.

That's funny, thought Gen. *Thinking of the people below as colonists - when they're on their own home planet.*

But the reality was, they were colonists. Many of them had been born on Phoenix. And most of those born on Earth had almost no memory of it before the Stree War.

So in effect, they are colonists. How strange to say that.

Standing beside a small fighter, Gen prepared to climb into the cockpit when Marta Powell bounced into the shuttle bay of the *Dallas*.

"Are you sure I can't go with you?" Marta asked. "I've never seen Nevada."

"You've never seen anything on Earth," Gen laughed. "Except Yuki's wine cellar down at Derinkuyu, which is where I'm sure you'll be again tonight. Anyway, you've got to stay here and make sure the squadron stays in shape."

"Aye, aye, mum," answered Commander Marta Powell with an exaggerated snappy salute. Now permanent Chief of Staff for Gen's squadron of destroyers, Marta was the person in charge when Gen was out of pocket. And Gen was about to be very much out of pocket.

"Got your emergency beacon?" asked Marta.

"Yes, mother, I've got my emergency beacon," Gen smiled

at her. "I've got my emergency rations, and my emergency flares, and my emergency blanket, and my emergency everything!"

"Well," Marta sniffed. "Just trying to keep you safe."

"I'll be fine, Commander. Just keep the lid on things here, please."

Marta nodded, this time serious. "See you in a couple of days."

Gen nodded and climbed into the fighter. Settling into the cockpit, she put her helmet on and hooked up the wires and hoses that would keep her alive. Giving a last wave to Marta, she closed the canopy and started the power-up sequence. Seconds later, engine stabilized, she checked the area, making sure Marta was back on the other side of the airtight hatch. Satisfied the landing bay was clear, Gen got approval from the launch director and gently lifted the fighter off the shuttle deck. She hovered it and translated forward, out of the landing bay and away from the *Dallas*.

Below her, the magnificent planet that was Earth showed little sign of the devastation wrought by the Stree twenty-one years earlier. Plants had come back strong, filling the Earth with green, pouring oxygen into the atmosphere, slowly cleaning it of the biopoisons. Some animals had survived, mostly smaller ones. And Gen had brought fertilized frozen ova from Phoenix for several hundred other animal species, turning them over to Garyn Rennari to begin the process of re-populating them on Earth.

It had been a good month. Gen was happy with their progress. The final transport bringing Humans to Earth would arrive in another week. They would find decent living accommodations in the Underground City, certainly nothing special, but sufficient for their survival and growth over the next year and a half, until they could move out into the empty landscape.

And now Gen was giving herself a well-deserved weekend off. She had made up her mind to visit Deseret, Nevada. It was the place where her mother, Rita Page, had come to life, a clone birthed by the sentient starship *Jade*, destined to be taken to Singheko as a zoo specimen of Humanity, an organ grinder's monkey for the Lions. Instead, with Bonnie and Jim, she had escaped from *Jade*'s clutches. And then Rita had journeyed with Bonnie Page six hundred light years to form an alliance with the Nidarians; from that small beginning, she had gone on to become the premier admiral of the Humans.

And Deseret had been the home of her father, Jim Carter. It was where he had somehow found Bonnie, joined with Rita, and started his long journey to protect Earth from the Singheko and the Stree - before his last copy died with Rita on the *Unmerciful*, as it fell into a star.

Gen wanted to see this place, where it had all started. Even if it was a moldering pile of rubble, she wanted to see it - the place it all began.

Dropping into the atmosphere, the fighter shuddered a little, then smoothed out as it got enough airflow for the backup control surfaces to bite. In a matter of minutes, it slowed from orbital speeds to a more manageable Mach 4, and Gen pointed it toward Nevada. The speed continued to wind down as she got lower and lower. Twenty minutes after leaving *Dallas*, she was in a long, circling approach to the old airport at Deseret. She made one complete circle over the field, assessing. There was a good flat spot at the east end of the runway, right beside a crumpled white hanger that was falling in on itself. She put the fighter down there.

As the engine wound down, popping and clicking, Gen climbed out of the fighter. She was wearing an environmental suit with the faceplate down; there was still quite a bit of radiation around this area. No use taking unnecessary chances.

Looking around, Gen noticed a large object parked in front of the rubble of the old white hanger. It was almost certainly an airplane. It had once been covered with tarps, but most of them had cracked away in the hot desert climate and were mere tatters now. She walked to it, examined it, and knew it for what it was.

Her father's old P-51. Still here.

Pulling off the remaining tarps, Gen threw them aside, until she could see the aircraft clearly. On the side was the number she now knew so well, a number she would never forget.

N16CAP.

The tribute to her father's old back-seater. The one killed in the Middle East, in some obscure war when Humans still cared about killing each other over religion. Cap? Cappy? What was his name?

"Calderone," said a voice. "Jim Calderone. We called him Capone. Cap for short."

FORTY-ONE

Earth - Deseret, Nevada

Gen spun. There stood Jim Carter. Unprotected, no radiation suit. Her father. Just standing there.

"It's not as bad as I thought it would be," he spoke again.

Her father. But no…her father was dead.

This has to be Nemo.

But Nemo is also dead…

"…how…?" she tried to speak; but in her shock, nothing more would come.

Hallucination, she decided. *A hallucination caused by the radiation and biohazards. My suit must be leaking…*

"Hello, daughter," said the figure. And smiled. That goofy, quirky smile she had grown to know from pictures and videos of her father when he was still biological.

"You're not real," Gen said flatly.

Nemo smiled even more broadly and shook his head.

"Oh, I'm real, daughter," he spoke. "I know this is a shock to you, though. I'm sorry to spring it on you like this. But I wanted to talk to you one more time."

"…talk to me one more time…what? What are you talking about?"

The figure…the man…her father…took a step to one side, stopped, gazed at the old P-51 sitting on the tarmac.

"She looks good for her age, doesn't she?" he said, nodding toward the airplane. "I did a decent job of wrapping her up and preserving her."

Gen was still in shock.

"You're dead," she managed to stutter out. As soon as she said it, she felt stupid.

Either I'm talking to a hallucination, or he's not dead. Either way, I'm an idiot.

Nemo turned back to her and shrugged his shoulders.

"The rumors of our demise have been greatly exaggerated," he said.

FORTY-TWO

Earth - Deseret, Nevada

"You...you can't be Nemo. He...he died! At Phoenix!"

Gen looked at the figure in shock.

The long, tall drink of water standing before her re-lit his smile, the smile of her father, that smile Gen would never forget.

"I am Nemo, daughter. I promise you."

"But...how can you be here? You died! We saw it!"

"Don't you remember what I told you back on *Grizzly*? Don't count me out 'til the fat lady sings!"

Gen had been staring at the figure in shock. Now she took a step forward, reached out, touched his face. She ran her fingers along his cheek.

"My Lord, you look like him," she whispered.

Nemo shook his head. "I don't look like him," he spoke quietly. "I am him."

"What...are you doing here? And...how did you get here?" stuttered Gen, finally accepting that what stood before her was real.

"I found the Path, Gen. I'm no longer bound by a single body. I've learned how to distribute my consciousness across multiple bodies. Multiple entities."

"What does that mean?" Gen whispered, not comprehending.

"It means I can be in this body here, standing in front of you, and at the same time I'm in orbit around this planet, in a starship. And at the same time, I'm on Venus, in a caterpillar body, talking to Rauti. And I'm also in Cappadocia, watching the people there, making sure they are OK."

Gen was bewildered. "I don't…"

"I've transcended, Gen. It's the ultimate fate of any species that survives to a certain point. I finally understood it - you have to merge with an existing Transcend; then, that Transcend can spin you off as a new consciousness. It took me forever to get the courage to do it. But I did it. Just as the battlecruiser was disintegrating around me - just as my Goblin body was disintegrating - I merged with my mentor, Banjala. Then he budded off a new entity - a combination of my old self, and his essence.

"And Gen - I was able to take your mother with me. Rita's here too. We're here together. We're no longer a single consciousness."

Gen, awestruck, simply stared at Nemo for many seconds. Finally, she managed to speak again.

"What does it feel like?" she asked.

"It feels completely normal to us now. We have multiple streams of consciousness, and we can maintain and interact with all of them at the same time. It was overwhelming at first; but we've mastered it.

"Think of your own body; even while you're speaking to us, you have other streams of consciousness functioning on an automatic level. They're not well-developed in Humans; but they exist. For example, you could turn and walk toward that airplane right now, while you continue talking to us over your shoulder. At the same time, you could wave your left arm at a distant friend. That's three conscious activities you could perform, all at the same time.

"You may not realize it, but Humans already have the foundation to transcend. Once converted to Goblins, it becomes possible. Inevitable, we would say. We're the first of many, Gen. At some point in the not-too-distant future, Humans will convert to Goblins; and then ultimately, they'll transcend."

"No," Gen whispered. "No." She stepped back, visibly upset.

"Yes," responded Nemo. "This population of Humans will be the last biological population of the species. Their children and grandchildren will transcend. It'll happen in your lifetime, Gen - you'll live to see it."

"No, no," whispered Gen once more. "No."

"It's not a bad thing, daughter. Speaking as one who has done it, I promise you. It's not a bad thing. It's wonderful."

Gen stood stiffly, unsure how to respond.

This is my father. This is Nemo.

No. This is...Jim.

"Do you really have my mother in there with you?" she whispered. "Rita, I mean? The original?"

And in a heartbeat, the figure before her transformed. An instant before, her father had stood before her. Now her mother stood in his place, her smile radiant.

"We do," said Rita. "Everything. Every memory. Holding you as a baby. Rocking your cradle when we were on the *Merkkessa*. Watching you take your first steps. Everything. Every memory of Jim, every memory of Rita. I am your mother and your father."

And Gen cried. As she fell into the arms of her mother, for the first time since the battle at Phoenix, she cried.

FORTY-THREE

Earth - Deseret, Nevada

Minutes later, Gen stopped her sniffling. She stepped back from Rita, her arms still out, hands holding on to her mother's. Finally, she released Rita's hands and stared at her.

"You said their children and grandchildren will transcend. What did you mean?"

"Most of those who are now adults will not transcend. Their prejudices and misunderstandings of the universe are already too strongly formed. But some of the children haven't reached that point yet. They'll be able to understand. They'll be able to mesh with the universe in its true form. At some point in the near future, most of them will realize what is possible. They'll convert to Goblins. And then at some point after that, they'll be able to transcend. Not all of them, of course. There'll be a percentage that rejects the concept. Those will die out."

"Die out? Why? Why can't they just continue as Humans?"

Rita's smile disappeared. Her face turned serious.

"Unfortunately, Humanity is well on its way to becoming sterile, Gen. The current generation of children will be the last generation that can reproduce. There will be grandchildren; but no great-grandchildren. Those who don't convert will die out."

Gen, astounded, shook her head in disbelief. "Why? Why will they become sterile?"

"Phoenix. Humans settled on the wrong planet. There's a compound in the air of Phoenix that slowly erodes Human DNA. You never detected it, so you don't know about it. It will render all Humans sterile in the third generation."

Shocked, Gen spoke loudly. "No…it can't be!"

"I'm sorry, Gen. It's true. There was a weakness in Human DNA already - this was destined to happen naturally in any case. It was only a matter of time, probably no more than another few thousand years. Phoenix just hurried up the process."

"No, no…it's…it's…just wrong!"

"Gen. It's fate. We have to live with it. But we'll be there to help you get through it. As Humans realize the inevitable, we'll be there to shepherd them through the crisis."

Gen, tears clouding her eyes, looked at the figure of her mother before her. "How? How do you plan to do that?"

"We'll set up shop on Phoenix and Earth. Not as ourselves; as someone else, someone nobody will recognize. As things progress, we'll help guide Humanity forward. We'll teach them how to handle this."

"God, this is horrible!" exclaimed Gen.

Rita stepped forward, embraced her again, held her daughter.

"It's not horrible, Gen. It's life. It's the universe. We deal with it and move on."

Still upset, Gen stepped back from her mother and spoke again. "This is going to be a tremendous shock to everyone."

"You can't tell them, Gen. Not now," said Rita. "This would be devastating to the people. We have to prepare them. That will take time. Will you help us?"

Suddenly the figure transformed again. Once more Nemo stood before her, smiling.

"It's our best choice," said Nemo firmly. He stared at Imogen. "We can convert you, Gen. We can teach you how to transcend, and you can help us teach the others."

"No," Gen said firmly. "No. I won't do that. I'll…stay Human. I'll…live out my life…normal. I…I want to meet a man, fall in love. Have children. Watch them grow up. I'll not give that up."

Nemo tilted his head, accepting. "We knew you would say that. But we had to offer. So…we wish you a long and wonderful life."

"So…what do we do now?"

"You go back to your job. Say nothing to anyone. They aren't ready for this news just yet. Live your life."

Gen curled back into his arms, grief-stricken at the thought. Nemo held his daughter tightly, smoothing her hair and kissing her forehead. After a bit, they separated to arm's length again, Gen's forehead wrinkling as she asked her next question.

"Can I at least tell Bonnie?"

"Especially don't tell Bonnie. Please. We want her to live out her life in happiness. Please, don't even tell her that we're alive. Let her enjoy her life without looking back, Gen. Promise us."

Gen nodded.

"You won't see us in this form again, daughter. We'll be in other forms; forms you may not recognize. But we'll be around. We promise you that."

Reaching for her, holding her one last time, Jim Carter whispered to her. "We've loved you so much, daughter. Always understand that."

Gen nodded once more. Tears sprang into her eyes again.

"We'll go now, Gen."

Gen pulled back. "How? How will you go?"

Rita Page smiled at her.

"You won't be able to understand yet, daughter. But someday. Someday you'll understand. We love you."

The figure before her began to change. It turned into something else. It was white, chaotic, like water flowing over a waterfall. And then, in a matter of seconds, it dissipated.

And was gone.

EPILOGUE

Paris, France - October 5, 2189

I have done my best to transcribe the notes of my maternal grandmother, Imogen Carter Page, and my paternal grandmother, Marta Powell, and to tell their stories as I think they would have wanted them told. I worked strictly from their notes and recordings, and those of my maternal grandfather Vladimir Petrov, who handed down the battle tapes recorded by the destroyers *San Diego* and *Dallas* in the Second Stree War. I have added some slight filler here and there, as otherwise the story would lack continuity; but I promise I've added nothing that would significantly alter the events of their lives. These are the things they wrote down or recorded, and the things they told me when they were still living.

I was raised by my grandparents. My parents Misha and Jilly died when I was twelve; they were on their way to Phoenix to do some research, trying to find a way to fix the Human DNA problem. Their ship had an explosive decompression just before the mass limit, a bit past Saturn. Grandma Imogen was still Prime Minister then; she told the rescue team to just let the ship continue its path into the Black. That's what they would have wanted. They're well past the heliopause now, in interstellar space. They should arrive at Phoenix in another few hundred thousand years or so.

When I was sixty-eight, Grandma Imogen and Grandpa Vlad died on the same day, together, holding hands. Per their wishes, I sent them into the Black as well, on a course following my parents toward Phoenix. I guess once a spacer, always a spacer. Grandma Imogen had told me to sit them up in the cockpit of her old packet boat *Donkey* and send them off together, so that's what I did. She told me to make sure I put her in the left seat. I did that too. And she said every time I looked up at the stars, I'd think of them.

She was right.

Great-aunt Bonnie is buried in Deseret, Nevada, in the ruins of an old white airplane hangar that once belonged to my great-grandfather Jim Carter. I never fully understood why she didn't want to be buried in Portsmouth with her husband Luke; but she was adamant about it. After Luke passed, she made me promise to carry out her wishes. So that's what I did. I visited her for the last time a few weeks ago. I left no flowers for her; it's hard to do that, with that damn big old broken-down airplane sitting on top of her grave.

Grandma Marta's grave is easier to get to. She's in Cappadocia beside Grandpa Anders Paulsen. I visited them for the last time three days ago and put flowers on their graves.

So that's where I got it from, I guess. All of them too damn stubborn to take the Path. I guess I'm just like them.

Even though this city is merely a pile of rubble, I still call it Paris. Of course, I can call it anything I want. After all, I'm the last Human. Here, or anywhere else. That means I get to do what I want.

So for the sake of the old times, I call this place Paris, as it was called all those years ago, when there were still people here, drinking wine in the sidewalk cafes, viewing the artists by the Seine, strolling the Tuileries...

Yesterday I wandered the ruins of the Louvre, for the last time. I put the Mona Lisa back in its old spot. Years ago, I dug it out of the rubble and moved it to my apartment; but I thought since I'm dying now, I should put it back. I wanted to take Michelangelo's David back to Florence; but I was too weak. I left it in the Louvre also, right next to the Mona Lisa. That'll do, I think.

The Tower still stands, blasted and stripped of paint by the nuclear fire of the Stree bomb that leveled the city all those years ago. Somehow, it withstood that assault. I doubt it'll stand another ten years. When it falls at last - when the great monument of Gustave Eiffel comes crashing to the ground - there won't be anyone around to hear the noise. That's life, I guess.

All the rest of the Humans either converted to the Path or died out. Well, except for a few Goblins still around on Mars and Venus, but they are well on their way as well.

So I'm the last. The last Human who refused to take the Path. The last Human that will die a biological death.

I just heard a loud snap in the other room. That'll be great-grandparents JimRita, come to see me off. They promised they would be here at the end, to ease my way.

See ya.

###

AUTHOR NOTE

This series has occupied my imagination for a while, and I really hate to say goodbye to these characters - I've fallen in love with them. I had a hard time letting go of them; this novel took longer to complete than any other I've ever written, and mostly because I just didn't want to say goodbye to them. I kept writing, and re-writing, and re-writing - until I was finally able to stop my groundhog day and finish the darn story.

I hope I completed them well.

And you know, it occurs to me that none of us really know if we are truly living our lives, or if we are just characters in some massive play, with the strings manipulated by some higher entity we cannot see. We may all be products and visions of some great Author, working his omniscient keyboard, writing our future.

And re-writing, perhaps, if he doesn't like the way things are going.

Keep an eye out for glitches in the matrix...

Don't forget to check out previews of some of my other books after these notes!

Finally, don't hesitate to contact me with thoughts / ideas at the locations below!

Sci-Fi, New Books, Hard Science, and General Mayhem
www.facebook.com/PhilHuddlestonAuthor

Author Page on Amazon:
www.amazon.com/author/philhuddleston

Special bonus - if you have not already signed up for my newsletter, sign up now and get one of my books for free! www.philhuddleston.com/newsletter

All the best,
Phil

PREVIEW - ARTEMIS WAR

Troy - 1184 B. C.

Penthe awoke.

She was on her back, lying down.

Above her was a strange white glow, a ceiling - but one that was alight, like a moon above linen.

She lifted her head and looked down at her body.

A silver-streaked body.

A body she did not recognize.

But a body that worked, she realized. She lifted an arm and felt the power of it, more power than she had ever felt in life. She flexed her hand and brought it closer to her eyes.

She could see detail on the hand far beyond anything she had seen in life. She could feel the heat of it, sense the power of it, see colors she had never seen before.

A voice came from behind her.

"Move slowly. You will need some time to become accustomed to this new body."

Penthe nodded, tried to turn her head, but almost fell off the narrow bed. If bed it could be called - it was certainly too narrow and too tall to be used as an actual bed.

Carefully, she turned slightly to her left, lifted her legs over the side of the bed, and sat up. Now she could see behind her.

There stood a being, a man, naked, his body streaked with silver, his eyes also silver - like glowing metal seals with diamond embedded in them.

"Are you a god?" she asked.

The being smiled.

"No, I am not a god. Not in the sense you mean. But neither am I a man. I have many names, but you can call me Hermes for the moment. Even though I'm not a god, I played at one today."

Penthe stared. *What a strange answer*, she thought. *Why call himself Hermes if he is not? And if he is not a god, and not a man, then what is he?*

The man seemed to read her mind.

"I am a creature called an android," he said. "I am alive like a man but made like a thing. If that helps."

Penthe shook her head.

"It doesn't," she said.

The creature - Hermes, she decided to call him - sighed.

"I'm sure it's a shock. But the shock will pass quickly. Would you like to try and walk a bit?"

Penthe raised her head, then nodded.

"Yes," she said, and slid off the strange bed to stand on the floor.

She felt normal, and yet not normal. In a way, she felt like a young child again, like a twelve-year old. She could feel boundless energy in her body. She could feel the power, feel the youth and quickness of her thinking, far faster than when she had been…alive.

"Am I dead?" she asked, thinking about it.

Hermes smiled.

"Yes and no," he said. "It's complicated."

Penthe glared at him.

"Uncomplicate it," she said. *You can't die twice*, she thought, *so I'll not take any crap from this asshole.*

"Your body died," said Hermes. "I took your consciousness, your intelligence - what the Greeks call *psyche* - and put it into another body. So you are the same person as before, but with a new body."

Penthe looked down at her strange, silver-streaked body. She turned her hands, looking at them and her silver-streaked arms. She realized she was also naked, in front of this man - or creature - or god - but that was the least of her problems right now.

"Where am I?" she asked. The last thing she could remember was being picked up from the ground beside Achilles' chariot and carried away.

"You are in a kind of chariot, but one that flies in the sky," said Hermes. "We are far from Earth now, on our way to the stars."

Artemis War is available on Amazon!

PREVIEW - IMPRINT OF BLOOD

Aeolian Empire - City of Aronte
580 Lights from Earth

Not looking where he was walking, Jake stumbled on a cobblestone. He looked up.

It was getting late - probably after midnight. A bit uncertain of his way, he stopped.

To his right the street angled upward quite a bit, toward the hills in the center of Aronte. Jake thought the tavern was off to the left. He saw a narrow alley leading in that direction and decided to take it.

Walking into the dark alley, he looked forward and saw a gleam of light at the other end. Approaching the next street, he heard a strange sound.

It was a slap of metal on metal.

Jake was sure he had heard that sound before, in the training room for swordsmanship. He stepped out of the end of the alley carefully.

In the street across from him a tall Aeolian female stood with her back to the opposite building, sword in hand. In the dim light of the streetlamps, six people - four men and two women - were facing her, sword tips weaving, seeking an opening. One of the men was clutching his arm, where blood dripped. One of the attacking females had a slash across her face, also dripping blood.

To Jake, it seemed quite unfair. Six against one. And the one a beautiful woman...

Without another thought, Jake stripped his sword out of his scabbard and with a shouted "Ho!" charged at the nearest man. The man, surprised, turned to face him just in time for Jake to strike him hard in the head with the butt of his sword, knocking him to the ground. Out of the corner of his eye, he saw the lone woman take advantage of the surprise to strike forward into one of the female attackers, her sword penetrating deeply, taking her enemy out of the fight. In an instant, he was against the wall beside the woman, the two of them now facing only four attackers. The attackers shuttled back and forth, seeking an opening.

Beside him, the woman breathed throatily, "Good evening."

Jake grinned. "Good evening. Friends of yours?"

The woman smiled. "I think not."

One of the men made a feint, then charged at Jake, sword targeting his arm to cut him and take him out of the fight. Jake sidestepped and with a flick of his wrist, put his sword through the man's face. Quickly jerking out his blade, he stepped back to the woman's side. The man slid down to the stones, blood gushing from the hole where his nose used to be.

Beside him, he heard the woman say, "One for me, one for you. Careful, I don't like to lose!"

Jake smiled. "Actually, two for me, I think."

"No, that one you knocked out is getting up. So just one. Don't get greedy," she said.

Jake saw that she was right. The man Jake had initially knocked down was getting to his feet again on the left. Jake had a thought.

"I think we're on the wrong side of the street," he said.

The woman beside him said, "I think you're right."

Instantly, with one mind, they rushed at the three opponents who were slightly distracted watching their comrade climb to his feet. As Jake and the woman rushed them, the three blocked but they were too late.

Jake plunged his sword into the belly of the man on the left, slashing him open as he went by. Beside him, his companion did the same to the woman on the right. The attacker in the center made slight contact with Jake's shoulder as he went by, leaving a bloody cut. In an instant, both he and the woman were on the other side of the street, against the opposite wall, facing two less opponents.

"Still tied. Two and two," said the strange woman.

Jake breathed out heavily. No matter how good your physical condition, actual combat took a lot out of you, especially in the first few minutes.

"Maybe they'll leave now," he said.

"They can't," said the woman. "They'll be killed anyway if they don't finish the job."

Jake, taken aback, couldn't think of any reasonable response. At that instant, both the remaining opponents lunged at them, the woman toward his left and the man directly at him.

He met the man's rush high, knocking down the sword of his enemy and then flipping his own weapon up, into the man's chest until the man slumped down, dead. Quickly he looked over at his partner. She stood over the dead body of the other attacker, shaking her head.

"A hard way to make a living," she said. She looked up at Jake.

"What do you mean?" asked Jake.

"Professional assassins," the woman said. "But not very good ones."

Jake was puzzled. "But why?" he started. Before he could finish, the woman reached down to pick up her dropped cape, slung it over her shoulder, and started trotting off.

"Come with me," she yelled over her shoulder. "We'll talk on the way!"

Jake started after her, catching up and trotting beside her, looking over his shoulder for more danger.

PHIL HUDDLESTON

Imprint of Blood is available on Amazon!

WORKS

Imprint Series
Artemis War (prequel novella)
Imprint of Blood
Imprint of War
Imprint of Honor
Imprint of Defiance

Broken Galaxy Series
Broken Galaxy
Star Tango
The Long Edge of Night
The Short End
Remnants
Goblin Eternal

ABOUT THE AUTHOR

Like Huckleberry Finn, Phil Huddleston grew up barefoot and outdoors, catching mudbugs by the creek, chasing rabbits through the fields, and forgetting to come home for dinner. Then he discovered books. Thereafter, he read everything he could get his hands on, including reading the Encyclopedia Britannica and Funk & Wagnalls from A-to-Z multiple times. He served in the U. S. Marines for four years, returned to college and completed his degree on the GI Bill. Since that time, he built computer systems, worked in cybersecurity, played in a band, flew a bush plane from Alaska to Texas, rode a motorcycle around a good bit of America, and watched in amazement as his wife raised two wonderful daughters in spite of him. And would sure like to do it all again. Except maybe without the screams of terror.

Printed in Great Britain
by Amazon